ASK ME TOMORROW

Ask Me Tomorrow.

JAMES GOULD COZZENS

HARCOURT, BRACE AND COMPANY *hb* NEW YORK

LC #40-11104

Typography by Robert Josephy
PRINTED IN THE UNITED STATES OF AMERICA
BY QUINN & BODEN COMPANY, INC., RAHWAY, N. J.

AJAX: Why should a man be proud? How doth pride grow? I know not what pride is.

AGAMEMNON: Your mind is the clearer, Ajax, and your virtues the fairer. . . .

—*Troilus and Cressida*

ASK ME TOMORROW

One

EVEN at its occasional best Florence is a forlorn city. It is not sad in any beautiful, comfortable way. It is really sad. It depresses you. The famous, decrepit churches; the heavy, meanly-placed palaces; the long galleries with pictures and other treasures (too numerous to mention) may seem all there is of Florence to the newly arrived tourist; but to one who is at melancholy home in the streets these objects of interest seem incidental. You turn a corner and come on them like ruins of some former civilization in a built-up wilderness. When you look across the storied river, half sludge, half stagnant water, you see the beautiful cupola of Santo Spirito troublingly out of place, as though the church under it were sinking in a swamp of factories and tenements. The Ponte Vecchio, which, indeed, deserves no better fate, is jammed like an alley in an amusement park with the trinket-mongers' shops. Trams swing grinding around the Baptistry with those bronze doors. Viewed from the street beside it the dirty old Duomo is not worth anyone's second glance. In a taste that we may be glad is not ours, the lines of Giotto's tower are ingeniously defaced by the appalling inlay of colored marbles.

This was ten or more years ago, but it seems unlikely that any of the things mentioned have changed. In those days you tried to get to Doney's at noon and drink vermouth with the cheese cakes brought out hot in pans. The several rooms overflowed into each other and were quite cheerful. You were bound to find people you knew. Americans more or less owned the place, though there were Italians there. Clasping their scabborded swords, doffing their capes and those top-heavy caps that make even the most amiable face look peeked and furtive, Italian officers came in (perhaps with the wistful idea that they were going to meet and then easily marry a girl with a hundred thousand dollars) and sat and husbanded their drinks. You could count on them for a sort of free show.

After an hour at Doney's most foreigners went home to their damp hotels or pensions to eat their cheap or expensive but never—nowhere in the whole city—good luncheons. After a while it would be time to have tea. At eight o'clock you were generally glad to go out, if anyone, no matter who, had been kind enough to ask you, and dine in a somber shadowed loft with a sparse assortment of monstrous renaissance furniture and a glimpse of the desolate lights on the Arno between the velvet curtains; or in a grand drafty marble apartment at one of the hill villas then rented for a song. You ended by playing bridge, usually in French out of consideration for the large grinning Russian, or the shabby scatterbrained Papal countess who was present. Shivering, your stomach soured by the Florentine food and the amount of wine necessary to make it taste better, at last you took your departure and began to search for a cab in the midnight streets and vacant piazzas. Climbing into whatever musty wreck you found, at a snail's pace you would clop-clop, as though through an endless ill-lit cemetery, to wherever you were living.

4

I

THE HOTEL of the second class on the Via Solferino had been made over from a couple of large private houses so most of the rooms were big. In the room they had given Francis Ellery, his mother sat in an armchair beyond the unmade bed looking at him. The window was behind her. Through it Francis could see the thin sunlight falling on the bare trees and the wet red tiles of the houses across the street rising against a chilly pale blue sky. Francis closed his last bag. He set it with the others by the door and pressed the bell button three times. He looked at his watch and said, "I'd better keep moving."

His mother said, "It only takes a few minutes to the station. Victor knows you're going. He'll have a cab."

Francis sat on the edge of the bed and fished out a package of cigarettes. "Let me have one of those," his mother said. He brought it to her, standing by her chair while he struck and held a wax match for it. When the cigarette was lighted she took it from her mouth in her left hand, laid her right hand on Francis's arm and said, "Well, tonight you'll be in Milan. And tomorrow night in Montreux."

Francis said, "I don't know that I ought to go. You'll be all right, of course. But—" She had been very ill in Paris earlier in the fall and Francis was obliged to see that, sitting there under the window, she looked ill now. The cigarette had not been what she wanted and she let it burn between her fingers. "I'm much stronger," she

5

said. "I shan't mind it." She released his arm. "You might write me from Milan. Or, no. That's silly. Write me from Montreux Wednesday. You'll do that."

"Of course," Francis answered.

"Yes, I know you will. You've always been very good about letters. You know how I'll be depending on them."

There was a rap on the door and Francis yelled, "Avanti!" not sorry to interrupt, for the subject made him uncomfortable. He would have preferred to think that she hardly gave him a thought. Knowing the vain wish to be a real and deep one, he had to accuse himself of selfishness.

When the bags were out his mother said, "I suppose you'd better go. I won't come down. I wish you'd look out a little for Faith Robertson. She'll be on that train, and she's all alone. I told her mother you would."

"Well, I won't," Francis said. "She's perfectly capable of looking out for herself."

"I wish you could be pleasanter to people, darling. I think she was rather taken with you the other day."

"I wasn't much taken with her," Francis said, which was indeed the case, for she was a plain girl of a brisk and sensible type. Whatever his mother fancied about it, Francis had been well aware, on the few occasions of meeting Miss Robertson, that she thought, for reasons best known to herself, either not at all, or very little of him. He said: "These musicians! They're all simply insufferable. Like actresses. There's always something wrong with a person who performs in public. If you have any sense you can't want to do it." He knew that dislike of the Robertson girl made him overpositive; yet he had seen enough of music and the stage to know that, as a matter of course, the people connected with them reached heights of conceit and pretentiousness that painters and writers, for instance, hardly dared dream of. He said, "She's perfectly able to get to Milan without any supervision from me."

"Well, darling, never mind. It doesn't matter. But some day you'll see that it's just easier to be pleasant." His mother stood up and came and kissed Francis. "Tell Mrs. Cunningham that I'm really very glad to have you with her." She let him go. "God bless you," she said.

"Fine," said Francis. "Take care of yourself, and for God's sake see that they keep you warm."

He went quickly downstairs, through the lower hall and out onto the pavement in the thin noon sunlight. He gave the porter a filthy five-lire note and was slammed into the cab. The wretched horse struggled and clashed his hoofs, the wheels ground sideways, scraping the thin muddy slime that covered the paving stones. They got around and went off with lively jolts. Not until the cab had gone a few blocks and was cutting through the Via Bernardo Rucellai did Francis remember that his mother had probably been watching from the window upstairs for him to wave.

✦

The made-up train was moving in along the platform sheds when Francis went through the barrier. Though there was some sun on the edge of the paving, a bleak wind smelling of oil and steam and the lavatory traps blew hard down the moving cars. Tottering with his strapful of luggage over his back, the porter swung on a passing step while he held the door handle of a second-class compartment. Walking below to keep up with him, Francis turned to see how much of a crowd there was going to be. Not looking where he was going, he very nearly bumped into Faith Robertson.

She had on a spotted fur coat of what is called leopard skin. Skirts were short that year so the coat did not come much lower than her knees and out from under it issued directly her big silk-covered legs. A green felt hat was pulled down on her blonde hair. Since she looked straight at Francis, he felt compelled to take his hat off, for he never had the courage of his distastes, nor the simple composure to be frankly and openly rude. He stood embarrassed and bare-headed while Miss Robertson said, "Oh, hello. Where are you going?"

"Montreux," said Francis, "unless I get killed in the rush."

"There's never much of anyone on this train. I've taken it dozens of times. You'll have to change at Milan."

"So I've been told," Francis said, somewhat distantly, for if he were unwilling to look out a little for her, he was even more unwilling to have her look out for him. Although his tone, suggesting that she mind her own business, had no visible effect on Miss Robertson, the sound of it embarrassed Francis himself. He attempted to modify it by adding, "I'll have to stay over at Milan. I can't get a connection. It's very boring."

Her full, freckled face was turned toward him and she gave him a composed, critical look. "Why?" she asked.

"I think Milan's one of the most boring cities in the world," Francis answered. He realized at once that Miss Robertson, who spent most of her time there, might not, and in fact did not, like the disdainful reference to her

8

city. She said sharply, "I always think it's one's own fault if one's bored. I wouldn't think you'd be. I mean, a writer—" Though this was an oblique acknowledgment that something about him was known to her and remembered, the tinge of chiding disapproval in her voice hinted that she found him not half the person someone had led her to suppose he was.

"Nevertheless I think Milan boring," he said in tones intended to be dry. She paid no attention. Instead she jerked her green hat at the porter with Francis's luggage, who, as the brakes went on, snapped open the door and shouldered himself into the compartment. "Come on," she said. "We can make sure of the corner seats at any rate." From behind her she caught up a small suitcase and gave his arm a push.

"Let me have that," said Francis.

"I'm not a cripple," she said tolerantly. "There's nothing in it but a bathrobe and a pair of pajamas." She looked up at the porter who was heaving Francis's bags onto the rack. "Sooner or later," she said, "you'll learn to travel with less luggage." She glanced at him. "I'll bet you couldn't change trains by yourself."

"Yes, I could," Francis said, a good deal nettled. "My mother pins my name and address on me and I go and show it to the chef de gare." She gave him a stare and then she reluctantly laughed. "Well, I couldn't," she said. Francis had taken out some money. He folded over a five-lire note. "Don't give him all that," she said. "It's silly. He doesn't expect it."

"Then I'll surprise him," said Francis, who habitually overtipped, feeling that money spent in averting the possibility of a row was well spent, even when he was very

9

little able to afford it. Miss Robertson shrugged her leopard skin shoulders. "Vi prego!" she said with an excellent accent to the porter whose broad back blocked the door while he stood wiping his forehead elaborately. She stepped up with a strong clumsy movement, giving Francis a glimpse of her thick bare leg above the top of the rolled stocking. She elbowed the porter aside, swung her suitcase, which clearly held not more than she said it did, with one hand onto the rack and dropped into the corner by the window. Francis handed over the five-lire note, got a gratified look, and followed her. "Close the door," she said. "We'll probably have this to ourselves." She passed her eyes over Francis's luggage on the rack above. "What's that?" she asked. "A typewriter?"

"Yes," said Francis.

"Do you write right on a typewriter, or do you have to write it out first?"

"I write right on a typewriter," Francis said.

"I should think the noise would drive you crazy."

"Well, maybe it does," Francis said. "I've often wondered."

Outside there were mournful cries passing down the platform. The carriage shook and began to move. This seemed to put a period to the conversation. At least, Miss Robertson automatically looked out the window and Francis was able to take a book from his overcoat pocket and open it. When, a few minutes later, the conductor slid back the corridor door, Francis, looking up, saw that Miss Robertson had been reclining with her eyes closed, as though trying to get some sleep. She produced her ticket from a small alligator pocketbook. When it was returned to her she settled her head and shut her eyes again. Francis handed over his own tickets in an American Express cover and waited while the conductor examined them all with interest. From his pocket he pulled a booklet, consulted it, and addressed Francis in Italian too fast for him to understand. "Cosa dite?" Francis said doubtfully.

Without opening her eyes, Miss Robertson said, "He says you won't be able to get a connection for Brigue tonight."

"Io lo conosco, grazie," Francis said to the conductor, flushing. "Much obliged," he said to Miss Robertson. She nodded, still not opening her eyes, and Francis began to read again. The book, a volume of Baudelaire, did not interest him much and soon he had begun to think about the half-completed manuscript of the book he was writing. In this way almost an hour passed. He glanced out the window and saw, surprised, the jumbled buildings of Pistoia surmounted disproportionately by the cathedral's great ruddy dome. The train passed into the shadows, jarred, and there was a sudden silence as it stood still.

Though he did not think Miss Robertson was really asleep, Francis got out as though trying not to waken her. He walked over to the buffet and drank a glass of vermouth, standing at the counter. This cheered him a little. When he got back, Miss Robertson was eating a huge roll with a slice of some sort of sausage that looked like soiled red leather in it. She had another lying on a bit of waxed paper in her lap. Her mouth was too full to talk, but sliding her hand under the waxed paper she held it out to Francis.

The gesture, cordial and casual, took him by surprise. He shook his head, smiling. "No, thanks," he said; both because he was not hungry, and because he could see, not far off, the vender from whose basket she had bought them, and he was very dirty. "I couldn't possibly."

She managed to say, "You don't know what's good." And after a moment, "I really got it for you. You don't eat enough. You're thin as a rail."

"I eat all I can stand," Francis said. "Eating in Italy isn't any pleasure. Even drinking is pretty bad," he added, still tasting the vermouth.

"It's pretty bad for you," Miss Robertson said authoritatively. She seemed displeased because he had not taken the roll. "I suppose in Paris you sat around drinking all day."

"And most of the night," said Francis, nettled again.

Miss Robertson wiped her mouth with the waxed paper and began on the second roll. "Didn't you?" she asked.

"No," said Francis. "Not that I wouldn't have liked to, but it's too expensive." The train had begun to move and they came out of the shed into the sunshine. He opened his book again. Miss Robertson said with what appeared to be contempt, "You're awfully touchy, aren't you?"

"Yes," said Francis.

"Well, it's silly of you. I always say what I think, and I expect other people to say what they think. It's the only way to get on."

"Not with touchy people," Francis said. "With them, you have to sit and say how wonderful they are. They like that."

"I should think you'd have got enough of it in Paris."

"I never get enough of it," said Francis. "And what is this business about Paris, anyway? I was only there a few months. My mother was ill at the American Hospital and I was living most of the time in a pension in Neuilly."

"Well, I was in Paris last week. It didn't sound as though you'd had too bad a time. I happened to meet someone who saw quite a little of you."

"Did you?" said Francis as casually as he could. Miss Robertson looked at him intently. She must have decided that his indifference was assumed. "Yes, I did," she said. "Lorna Higham told me all about you."

Francis looked out the window. Moving slowly and laboriously, the train was beginning the climb to Corbezzi and the cold clear Tuscan plain was already spreading out behind. The tones of black and purple and olive in the thinly sunlit distance seemed sadder than anything in the world. "I didn't know you knew her," Francis said.

"She was one of my best friends at school."

"At Vassar?"

"I didn't go to college. If you sing, you haven't time for any of that."

"I expect not," said Francis. He let his eye fall on his open book, reading at random: *Quelle est cette île triste et noire? C'est Cythère* . . . Then he looked up again. Miss Robertson was still studying him and he felt foolish to have shown so naïvely that he was not at ease. Miss Robertson said, "I don't know anything about writing, but I don't believe you'd have much time for anything else either, if it seemed important to you. I haven't read any of your books. How many have you published? Two?"

"Yes," said Francis. "And it does seem important to me. You see, I have to eat. I don't know any other way to go about providing for that."

Miss Robertson smiled coldly. "Why can't you be natural?" she asked. "Why do you bother to try to cut a figure?"

"I wasn't conscious of bothering," Francis said. He detested Miss Robertson.

Concluding that he had no better answer, Miss Robertson said, "What are you writing now? If you want to tell me, that is."

Even if he had liked her, Francis would not have wanted to tell her. It gave him no pleasure to talk about his writing and he was never able to say what he meant about it in reasonable compass. Confused, fragmentary things he could say served only to reduce whatever idea he had in mind to its essential banality, and the more he explained what he was planning to write, the sillier it seemed to bother to write it. "I'm not sure I'll get very far with it this year," he said. "You see, I had to take a job. It ought to give me some time, but I don't know how much."

"Lorna told me," Miss Robertson said. "I think you're making a mistake."

"Maybe I am," said Francis. Under the relentless, inquisitive fire of Miss Robertson's fault-finding he was too harried to make a stand, though surely no one had asked her for her opinion. Moreover, he did not want to talk about Lorna with her, so he said, "I don't like the idea a great deal. It wasn't any choice of mine. But I was lucky to find it."

The train, getting up into the hills, passed with a long anticipatory roar into a tunnel. Out of the total darkness Miss Robertson, raising her voice, said with derision, "It sounded like a pretty soft job to me." Through the windows, wreathed with smoke and steam, daylight appeared again.

"It isn't my idea of a soft job," Francis said. "They're

nice people, and the kid's all right; but I don't fancy it."
The roaring darkness enveloped them once more, continuing second after second. This, he found, was not a subject he wanted to discuss with her either. "As a matter of fact," he said, "the book I'm trying to write is about an incident in the war between Chili and Peru in 1879. Do you know anything about it?"

"I never heard of it," said Miss Robertson.

"Well, it didn't amount to much as a war, and that's part of the point. The causes and so on don't matter a great deal. On October 8th, 1879, the Peruvian turret ship *Huascar*—it was the only ship they had that was any good —commanded by a Rear-Admiral Grau who had previously had several small successes, was caught off Angamos —I want to call the book, 'Action off Angamos.' It was hopeless, but they put up such a fight as you wouldn't believe. Of course that's just the setting. On board the *Huascar* from three A.M. when they sighted the Chilian ironclads, until eleven, when there was no one left to fight her any longer—"

Light was at last coming down the sides of the car, the shadow sweeping back. Clouds of smoke rolled and rose by the dirty glass. Francis could see a little stone hut close on the hillside and some sloping patches of tiny cultivated fields. The glass cleared, the hillside swung away, opening an enormous windy vista of purple receding hills. Sunlight fell on his lap. "It's hard to explain what I mean," he said. "The situation is ironic, but also heroic. I don't think I can explain. But at any rate, that's what the new book will be about—if I ever get it done."

Miss Robertson's plain freckled face was composed. "It sounds very exciting," she said.

15

Francis winced, for he had more in mind, even if he had not been able to say it, than that. "Well, we'll see," he said, wishing, as always, that he hadn't spoken of it. He lit a cigarette. After a short silence, Miss Robertson, leaning her head back, shut her eyes again.

✦

At four o'clock the change in the afternoon, apparent as soon as they were across the high divide in new pallor of sky and sicklier sunlight, had become complete. Over Bologna more of the endless rain was imminent. While they drew out of the railroad yards the first slanting drops began to strike the dirty windows. It became immediately a downpour as, moving much faster now, they headed up the great plain to Modena.

Near the end of the corridor, balanced to the rapid shake of the car, Francis stood depressed watching the driving rain. It hid the mountains in successive heavier veils. The autumn afternoon was turned to an early twilight, somber on the wet countryside—the ditches full of spattered water; the drenched field and puddled lanes; the occasional rows of leafless dripping poplars. "The Æmilian Way," Francis said to himself. "The Via Æmilia. The great military road. M. Æmilius Lepidus (and who else?) being consuls—" He saw an old bust; a solid, square stone face with blank stone eyes, the stone toga folds thrown across the powerful shoulder. "Et facere et pati fortia Romanum est—" he said aloud. "I wouldn't have lasted a minute. They'd have given me

16

one look—" Who knew what Marcus Lepidus or any Roman republican like him would think seeing Francis twenty-one centuries after that consulship standing there looking out at the plain through a pane of rainy glass while he was moved along the line of the Æmilian Way, two days' forced march every hour? "God!" said Francis, "I wish I had a hundred thousand dollars."

But he could easily believe that he never would have. He would just go on to the end of his days never knowing where money for his next extravagance was coming from; yet never, probably, being quite destitute enough to have to give up thinking of extravagances. How many times at college would an extra fifty dollars have made all the difference between—between what? Between the peace of mind in which one could properly lose ten dollars at bridge, buy a few quarts of gin, and send a girl gardenias enough to cover her shoulder for the Hale House Ball; and that unquiet in which one lost the money anyway, accepted a little too often somebody else's gin (he could feel the hard shape of the silver flasks, taste, as he tipped them, the scald of the reclaimed alcohol and water, see the crooked ties and bulged stiff shirt fronts in the crowded subterranean glare of the men's room), and did a tailor out of what the dance cost.

His mind recoiled, humiliated; but at once Francis heard music . . . *one little kiss, and then we will whis—* (a dying fall. Oh, it came o'er my ear like—indeed, yes!)— *per good night.* . . . The wheel of movement shifted, serenely turning in the variegated dusk below the ballroom balconies. Up through the music . . . *stay at home, play at home, eight o'clock sleepy time* . . . rose the murmur of hundreds of voices, the shift and scrape of in-

17

numerable feet. Francis breathed the sweet hot air; he smelt the dampened powder. Skirts, down that season far enough to cover the shins, switched and swayed; the bare round arms lifted, the innocently rouged faces kept turning up to talk. They bent their bodies back, balanced in a lithe way from the hips. "Ah, you damned fool!" Francis said.

Yet it was hateful, he had sense enough to see, not because of its folly or triviality. He hated it for the small wounds to pride, the private chagrins, the anxieties of living, because you felt that you had to, willfully beyond your means, that distempered a pleasure, to everyone else he knew apparently so pure. Of what he had left from all that now, Francis would rather forget everything—just forget it, however; not change it to something more estimable, like solid work or the fruits of scholarship. The drafty cold of the corridor was making itself felt, for he had learned at school that it was indecent to wear woolen underwear and this truth still seemed to him self-evident. He might as well go back to Miss Robertson.

Miss Robertson met him half way. She was coming down from the lavatory at the other end of the car. "Oh, don't look so downhearted," she said with partly humorous impatience. "What have you got to worry about?"

Francis made an effort. "Life," he said. "I worry about life. And money. And love. I'm freezing to death." He slid the compartment door back and she went in. "I don't know how you stand it in Italy."

"You get used to it," she said. She put her skirt straight with a jerk and sat down. "Where are you going to stay tonight?"

"The Palace, I guess."

"It'll cost you fifty lire. I was going to suggest you come to my place. I guess you don't worry about money much; just about life and love."

Whatever happened, Francis knew, he was not going to her place. He said, "I never know where one begins and the other leaves off. What do you pay?"

"Eighteen, pension. And it's plenty good enough. The wife of the man I study with runs it. Of course, it's out by the Porta Vittoria, and I don't say it would be fancy enough for you."

"I thought you studied at the conservatory," Francis said, feeling that he had heard enough about himself.

She smiled. "The conservatory's just nonsense," she said. "You have to be on the rolls, but studying there's just a way of getting a hearing. If you're good, the director can do a lot for you—not musically. He's a second-rate composer and the way you handle him is with an aria from an awful opera he wrote. But he can get you on at La Scala if anyone can. And I'll say this for him. You don't have to trade him anything. Of course, if you're pretty, too, there are people who can save you time."

"Really?" said Francis, little interested, for he did not believe her. "I thought that was just something in a book."

"Well, it's not. God knows I'm not pretty, but I wear a skirt, so every now and then somebody in a position to help makes me a proposition."

"And what do you do?" asked Francis, tempted to see what she would say.

Miss Robertson shrugged. "A girl from England I got to know quite well last year had to sleep with five different men before she'd finished. She had a fairly good voice; but she wouldn't even have had a chance otherwise."

Involuntarily Francis's eyes rested on Miss Robertson's body. He snapped them away, relieved to see, at the same time, that Miss Robertson had been looking out the window. "Well," he said, "they tell me it's really more fun than work." A disagreeable vision of Miss Robertson, in a state of beefy nature, grimly advancing her art on a bed with some wop whose amorous taste was catholic enough to include anything he could get, interrupted his pleasantry. "That would certainly be more work than fun," he said to himself.

"You think it's funny," Miss Robertson said. "You wouldn't if you were a woman. You're as likely as not to end up with syphilis. That's not so romantic."

"On the contrary," Francis said. "Syphilis is extremely romantic. It's in the grand tradition. All the great men had it. What it's not, is practical, or sensible, or good for you." He had been taken unprepared, for in talking to people like Miss Robertson he was accustomed to be the one who made harsh observations at the expense of romance and sentiment.

"What silly rot!" cried Miss Robertson. She was quite angry, Francis supposed, because her mood was solemn as she considered the hard life of the artist and the woes of women. She did not relish levity on sacred subjects. Francis would just as soon have annoyed her more by developing the theme; but he could not very logically, he saw, be ironic in so many different ways at once. The alternative was to declare in earnest for wholesomeness, virtue, and common sense. Those were things certain to be dear to Miss Robertson. Wholesomeness and common sense were what made her so hard to stand; and, as for virtue, if there were any truth at all in her implication, and if she actually had been obliged to sacrifice her virginity on the altar of her career, it wouldn't count in her own mind. She would retain her natural impatience with lapses occasioned by mere concupiscence, or by curiosity, or even by that muddle of indecision that at some unplanned and pleasureless moment made girls of less sound sense than Miss Robertson distraught accessories-before-the-fact to the loss of their virtue.

"Yes, it is rot," Francis admitted, meaning to extricate himself. "I don't recommend it." But, perversely, he had to add, "Just the same, I wouldn't take your English friend's sufferings too seriously. This reluctant maiden business is all right once maybe. But the fifth time—it's like the song, 'Once again she lost 'er nyme. . . .'"

"You men!" said Miss Robertson. "Because you can only think of just one thing—"

The remark, with its air of knowing prudishness and affected propriety, stung Francis. It sounded like those amateur Central Square tarts who took their pay for wrestling with drunken sophomores in the form of automobile rides and tickets to burlesque shows. "And why not?" he said flatly. "What in God's name else is a woman supposed to make you think of? What else is she for anyway?"

"You would say that!" said Miss Robertson. "You would! Because you happen to be good-looking, or think you are, I suppose you imagine every girl you see is just crazy to have you make a pass at her. You don't know a thing about women."

The startling news that Miss Robertson considered him

good-looking, even if quickly qualified, brought Francis up. The instant's halt, in effect like counting ten before you say it, enabled him to speak good-naturedly. "I may not know as much about women as some men," he said, "but at least I know more about them than any woman does. A woman can't see herself any better than a man can see himself; but, in addition, she's psychologically incapable of seeing another woman objectively—with enough detachment to realize what a woman actually acts, looks, and sounds like—" Francis spoke fluently, for the statement, once he had stumbled into it, was one he had composed long ago in mental answer to a critic, a woman, who had printed, commenting on a piece of action in his last book, a similar accusation. Not yet insensible either to the pleasures or the pains of his trade, Francis could spend a good deal of time enjoying praise and taking blame to heart this way. "I don't expect you to believe me," Francis continued, feeling that the statement was getting too literary, that it too clearly answered the critic according to her folly, "because, of course, if you were able to believe me it wouldn't be true. What women don't credit themselves with and don't see in each other is the principal thing about them—a sort of vital, sustaining bitchiness. Did you ever keep a dog? Mrs. Cunningham has an old bull terrier called Rose with her—older than God and hardly able to walk. I was admiring it in Paris. I don't think I'd ever noticed an old bitch before. They're still just like women. You wouldn't believe how much like an old woman that dog is—and, of course, vice versa—" He broke off, for Miss Robertson, standing up, turned and took her suitcase out of the rack.

"What on earth are you doing?" Francis asked.

22

"I'm going to sit somewhere else."

Francis began to laugh, the burden of disadvantage that Miss Robertson had managed to keep him at all afternoon dissolving. "What did I do? Insult you?"

"You don't insult me. You bore me."

"Don't be such an ass!" he said. "Put that back and sit down. You act like a two-year-old." He stood up himself, twisted the suitcase out of her hand and replaced it.

Miss Robertson cried, "Let me alone, please!" Apparently abandoning the bag, she gave him an angry, ineffective shove with her elbow, trying to get to the door.

Still laughing, Francis stepped that way, too, blocking her, so she drew back. "Don't be such an ass!" Francis repeated. He caught her by the forearms—through the supple layer of spotted fur her arms were firmly rounded, with big biceps, and it occurred to him that if she resisted in earnest he would have his hands full. "I said, sit down!" he told her.

She was facing forward so the motion of the train was against her. Easily enough, he controlled the rebellious indignant squirm by which she tried to get free and sat her down just where she had been before. Her attempt to rise again needed no more than a hand put hard on her shoulder to stop it. "Now, that will do," Francis said, taking his hand away. "I'm sorry if you thought I called you a bitch. It's at least two-thirds a compliment. Besides, it's nothing to what you've been calling me." He sat down in his own corner and looked at her amiably.

Regarded with the indulgent eye of a victor, breathlessness and higher color had much improved Miss Robertson's appearance. It did not make her pretty, but her physical presence lost that forbidding quality that you associated with brisk, competent school teachers and strong, dictatorial trained nurses. The warmth of her cheeks and her flustered manner gave her the absurd yet engaging air of a disgruntled school boy who had just, to his own surprise, got the worst of a tussle to which he had committed himself not quite so seriously as to leave him altogether humiliated, and yet seriously enough to make him wonder what the spectators were thinking and to feel that he ought to do something to show that he had been only fooling around.

"I didn't know you were so athletic," she said sarcastically, but the sarcasm itself was flustered, and sounded half hearted—a last hitting-out of that alert disagreeableness, meant to show that, though defeated, she would scorn to court anyone's favorable opinion by losing with good grace; and that if she acquiesced, she didn't do it humbly, and no one need suspect her of complaisance.

Since Francis could not help liking people who amused him, he now felt well-disposed toward her. "What kind of music do they give you in Milan?" he asked.

✦

Music was not one of Francis's natural interests or pleasures, for he was practically tone-deaf; but the love of it is a mark of superior culture, and so he had heard a great deal of music while he was at college and supported with disciplined patience many concerts and evenings of opera rather than have his friends suppose he was in any respect their esthetic inferior. Those days, no more than two years back, seemed long ago to Francis. He had begun to draw off. He was more and more ready to leave music to people who liked it; partly because, becoming a published writer, he felt that he had established his claim to intellectual distinction in a modest but sufficient way, and no longer needed to give examples of it in every field; and partly because he had come to observe that instead of making himself impressive, a person putting it on may make himself ridiculous. Francis had a sense of narrow escape. Two years ago he would have been as likely as not to try to impress Miss Robertson. He did not think she would be slow to grasp so glorious a chance to make a fool of him.

Since he took care to tell her right away that he knew nothing about music, Miss Robertson was, to start, grudging and reluctant. She spoke of the role she was getting up—it was the one Mary Garden had sung in *L'Amore dei Tre Re*. Soon she found that Francis had been too modest. His comment, though brief and diffident, showed her that he had heard—and after all he had; he had required himself to hear—practically everyone and everything and that he was capable of appreciating music's paramount place in human endeavor. Miss Robertson became more voluble and informative, making it unnecessary for Francis to comment at all. She took the trouble to tell him about ideas and feelings of her own which might make what she meant clearer. She repeated, deprecatingly, yet with the candid tone of one musician to another, some interesting compliments that had been paid her.

Smoking, Francis listened in much the same way that he used to listen at concerts, paying outward attention. Inconspicuously he sought the frequent relief of thinking of something else. He thought of the blind king strangling Mary Garden, who had worn a remarkable wig. He thought of this or that person at college with whom he had often attended the opera. As Miss Robertson talked more and more about herself and her prospects, he tried to decide whether or not he did believe that she was going to be a great singer. To do this, he had to project himself into the future and to imagine, as a sort of test, that she had come to be acclaimed universally as the greatest singer of her age; and how well he would remember that curious rainy afternoon on the Milan train; and would he or would he not be surprised, now that he thought it all over? He looked at her in a careful detached manner and thought that maybe he would not be surprised. After all, she had the physical vitality that plays so large a part in any sort of success, and she had it abundantly—at a tangent, Francis saw that this was something he had neglected to consider when in his mind he had marveled at the anonymous, if not imaginary, wop who had felt enough of a fancy for her to make a proposition. Though Miss Robertson's face and manner did not offer much of an invitation to love, that vital fleshiness might stir an experienced lecher who had long ago sated himself with delicate or pretty girls. In fact, though stocky and thick set, her figure was balanced and symmetrical. It might be thought good by someone who didn't find an harmonious heaviness distasteful.

As well as physical vitality, Miss Robertson showed an aggressive firm purpose. Supposing she had any voice at all, it would surely carry her further than she could ever get with the same voice, or even a better one, seconded less ably. Supposing she really did have, actually or potentially, a voice of the first rank, why shouldn't her triumph be inevitable—far more inevitable, Francis thought, than any notable success in writing would be for him? Whatever his natural talent (and he did not think too poorly of it) his purpose, though not changing, did not drive him so hard; and, as Miss Robertson pointed out in her disagreeable earlier mood, he was not ready to make wholesale sacrifices of his comfort and convenience. This reflection filled him with a foreboding, or uneasy dismay, lest he be throwing away, through supineness of will and undisciplined habit of mind and life, certain opportunities for greatness that might have been his, but, every day, perhaps every minute now, slipped by his own fault through his hands.

Several agitated resolves were hazily taking form in his mind when he realized that it had been a long while since he had let himself hear what Miss Robertson was saying. Returning with a start, he found that he was in the nick of time, for she had interrupted herself to say: "It's freezing in here. They've let that heat go off."

This was true, Francis realized, though he might have been a long while in noticing it. In Europe he was used to being always more or less cold. He said promptly: "Well, suppose I find the conductor and raise hell."

"It won't do you any good." Miss Robertson huddled her coat about her and shifting sideways brought her feet up on the seat, clasping her hands over the top of her instep. She peered out the dripping window. "This is Parma," she said. "Maybe we'll get some heat when they put the lights on." Francis could see the sidetracks and switches, the crowded dull-colored backs of buildings in the rain-hazed dusk beyond. They were in practical darkness when the station shadows fell, and at once the lights did come on. Francis stood up and opened the door. "I'll see if I can get you some coffee or something," he said.

"You can't."

"I can try." He stepped down on the gritty paving and slammed the door behind him.

When he came back he carried a stack of paper cups, a bottle of mineral water with the cork drawn, and a flask of brandy. "It's probably poison," he said, drawing the door closed and setting these things on the window ledge, "but it's bound to be warm." He separated two cups, poured an inch of brandy into one and filled the other with mineral water. "Just take a deep breath and swallow that," he said, holding them out to her. "You'll think it's summer."

"That's much too much," Miss Robertson said. Her fingers touched his as she took the cups. "You're the one who needs it," she said. "Your hands are like ice."

Shivering, Francis said, "And how!" He poured brandy in another cup and tasted it. "It's dreadful," he said truthfully, and swallowed it.

Miss Robertson, holding both cups, tilted the brandy and took a little gingerly. She drew her face up and gulped the water. "I don't see how you do it," she gasped. She put the cups on the ledge, pulled a handkerchief from her sleeve and wiped her mouth hard.

Francis said, laughing, "Better drink the rest of it and get it over. It works. I can tell you that." He reached and took the paper cup and poured more mineral water in it.

"I will in a moment," she said. "If I take it all at once, it goes to my head."

Francis held up his own cup and looked at it carefully. "You have to watch it," he said. "Probably it will eat a hole through paper. I've seen so-called *fine* eat a hole through leather. Lorna Higham and Gwen Davis and a chap named Bancroft—do you know him?—and I went up to Amiens to look at the cathedral one day last fall. It was raining, of course, and we got soaked, so we tried some brandy in a disgusting little grog shop. Lorna spilt a drop on her bag and before she could wipe it off it had definitely begun to eat through."

Miss Robertson raised the cup. Shuddering, she emptied it and seized the water. "It does help," she said when she could. She wiped her mouth again. "I never saw much in the cathedrals," she said. "I hear you know all about architecture."

"I don't know anything about architecture," Francis said, "but some of them are pretty good—just as things to look at."

"I always thought the cathedral in Milan was hideous."

"And so it is," Francis said. "Next time you're in France, go and see Bourges."

"I went to Chârtres," she said. "I thought the glass was beautiful."

"Yes," said Francis, dismissing it, for after all Chârtres was pretty well done to death, and you could hardly admire it without sounding like a Paris-in-seven-days tripper. "There's rather a curious cathedral at Angers," he said. "I happened to be driving back from Brittany up the Loire valley last August and we stopped overnight there—"

"You certainly know a lot of France," Miss Robertson said. She spoke admiringly, without the least malice; but the way in which she had reduced to its simplest terms the idea conveyed by what he said, made Francis pull up. The only "rather curious"—a phrase from the college jargon of critical understatement meaning "extremely interesting"—thing about the cathedral at Angers was that few people Francis talked to would ever have seen it. Ashamed of himself, he said: "I don't know France at all. The truth is, I hate these people who always know something perfectly wonderful somewhere out of the way where only a few rare spirits like themselves have ever been. I suppose that's what I sounded like."

"No, you didn't," Miss Robertson said. She raised a hand, grasped the edge of her hat and pulled it off. "Warm is right," she said. "I shouldn't have drunk that so fast."

Francis, about to make some inconsequential answer, stopped, almost staring, for he had never seen her bareheaded before. From the blonde bits of it showing around her hat brim he had formed an idea of what her hair would be like. As he had expected, there were great quantities of it, and it was slipshodly bundled up; but the released loose coils shone with metallic luster. You felt that, weighed in your hand, a braid of it would be as heavy as gold. It was so clearly operatic, fit for a Wagnerian heroine in stage armor, that, in itself, it seemed to show that her future was assured, already stamped on her.

Into his cup, shaking with the train's motion on the window ledge, Francis thoughtfully poured brandy. Examples of appearance as a form of destiny occurred to him and without waiting for the many, perhaps more, exceptions to present themselves, Francis began to apply it, wondering whether he already showed that he was bound to become a distinguished writer, or whether what he showed was that he never would be one. Since he had the

matter at heart, he tried to dismiss such disquieting specu-
lations; for where would he get the courage to hear the
answer if someone in a position to see offered to tell him?

Miss Robertson said: "Lorna's pretty, isn't she?"

Brought sharply out of his preoccupation, Francis said,
"She's charming." The word pretty was not a word he
liked or used in that connection and he corrected it; but
he did not know what to make of the sudden remark, or
of the fervor with which Miss Robertson spoke. He could
not see that she and Lorna had anything in common, and
he had put down the acquaintanceship to one of those
formed at school, and then accidentally maintained
through the years in disregard of the fact that both the
onetime friends have long been dead and gone, leaving
only two in all but name strangers to share an unreal,
embarrassing intimacy.

Miss Robertson said: "I hope you're going to be nice
to her."

"You hope I'm going to be nice to her?" Francis repeated. He spoke blankly; but before he had said the last
word, he got it. Limply, affecting continued incomprehen-
sion, he said, "Why shouldn't I be nice to her?"

His confusion—the implications of Miss Robertson's
remark seemed to rise one after another and burst like
rockets in his mind—let him do no more than go on gazing with a controlled blank expression at her. It occurred
to him then that the stiff shot of brandy had made Miss
Robertson, not used to drinking, drunk. His relief was
enormous. He had met the shock of the idea that Lorna
would talk to someone like Miss Robertson about him and
been ready to accept it—as he had learned to accept and
even expect all those rank offenses to dignity or reticence

that a woman thinks nothing of, and must actually enjoy, since so many of them are able calmly and cold sober to make confidences to the first acquaintances they meet of things that a man, blurting them out drunk or beside himself, could not for years afterward remember saying without a convulsion of mind; but Francis passionately preferred to think that Lorna had said nothing to Miss Robertson. General conversation, or some chance comment of Gwen's, had given material for a romantic conclusion, the least little bit tipsy, of Miss Robertson's own.

Francis guessed that protests would only make her rally him the more intolerably. He smiled, and since it would let her have her sly idea, and yet might get her away from the present or immediate past, said with what seemed to him adroitness: "Tell me what she was like at school." He saw in imagination a thin, large-eyed adolescent girl, the same flush of color near her cheekbones, standing breathless in a middy blouse, bloomers, and hockey pads, on the playing field. She had the air of finding this game a silly one, yet she was jubilant with excitement and interest, even so. He could think of her in the morning, slight-breasted, in a sweater; her narrow legs crossed under a short serge skirt, biting the end of a pencil over an algebra paper to which, frowning, whispering figures, shaking back her fluffy hair, she added neatly and accurately fresh equations.

Recognizing fancy at mawkish work on these pictures, Francis discounted them. He forced himself to guess that, more likely, Lorna had been skinny and anemic with a poor sallow complexion. Far from being youthfully engaging, or showing any resemblance to what she was today, her manner and ordinary temper had probably been sullen and moody. Good spirits and amiability—he told himself—were very much a physical thing. Physically, Lorna never could have been robust. If she were not robust there was a good chance that the menstrual function, establishing itself, had made her wretched and so for several years more or less hysterical. At fourteen or fifteen (a left-handed tenderness lay in thinking this way, that it was not really her fault, poor kid. Francis saw it; but perhaps because of her present charm for him, he did not reject it, once he had put it in realistic terms) he was prepared to believe that she might have been as disagreeable and unattractive a girl as any fair-sized school could show.

Miss Robertson said, "Oh, she was frightfully clever. She was very quiet. In the lower school they used to call her the Dago." Miss Robertson's voice was gently bemused. While the brandy was no doubt having a genial effect on her memory it was possible that Miss Robertson had been—in fact, at the time; not in later sentimental retrospect—happier during those years at school, before her ambition got a grip on her, and before she felt the full melancholy effects of having so few of the qualities that would attract boys, than she had ever been since. "They took me out to study voice before I graduated," she said. "I used to see her during vacations. While she was at college I went to Europe. I just happened to meet her in Paris. We hadn't seen each other for years."

There was a long pause, either because Miss Robertson was feeling what she had drunk enough to be afraid that it would show in her voice; or because she felt pleasantly numb and talking seemed unnecessary. She sat gazing owlishly at the window pane and after a while Francis

33

helped himself to a little more brandy. He remembered coming back from the excursion to Amiens, rain running down the black glass like this, the cold arc-lighted caverns of the Gare de l'Est late at night. Although, actually, it could have been no more than six or seven weeks ago, it seemed hopelessly past and regret consumed him. He could have wished the autumn to go on that way forever; and, from regret, his spirit sank to a mute and helpless resentment that refused comfort and despised hope.

After a long while the train began again to slow down. Miss Robertson said in a normal-sounding voice, "This is Piacenza. I think we're late." She opened her bag and looked at a cheap watch she had in it. "Half an hour," she said.

Francis roused himself. "Does it matter?" he asked.

"No, except I won't get any supper."

"Eat with me," he said, taking himself by surprise. "It would be a great kindness," he added, recovering; for even the company of Miss Robertson seemed, now he thought of it, a little to be preferred to this wet and dreary evening alone. "After all, it's my last day of freedom and I feel very low."

"I don't think I'd better. Signora will give me a couple of sandwiches."

"Doesn't she approve of your dining out with men?"

"She doesn't care what I do as long as I pay her every month. But why should you take me to dinner? I thought you were taking a job because you were broke."

"Not as broke as that," Francis said, "and beginning tomorrow night I have no more worries. I'm being kept."

"Well, we could get something in the station."

34

"Yes, but we're not going to. I feel bad enough anyway. We'll go across to the Palace and get a decent dinner,
if they have one."

2

RAIN drove against the high windows of the elegant,
though old-fashioned and somewhat hearse-like bus. Rain
beat loudly on the roof while Francis and Miss Robertson,
the only passengers, were carried in a sedate circle around
the piazzale. Perhaps the driver had been told to make
the most of this trifling trip from the Central Station steps
to the doors of the hotel. Noticing the maneuver, Francis's
impulse was to comment; to say that the conscience of the
management could not be wholly dead since in exchange
for the "omnibus incl. luggage, 10 fr." sure to appear on
the bill, they were supplying as much travel as they possibly, short of approaching the hotel by way of Venice or
Genoa, could.

He did not say it. His glumness or grumpiness following the bright feeling of the brandy as he regretted Paris
and deplored his fortunes had been aggravated by difficulty in getting a porter; then, by the slowness of the hotel
runner to appear; and, particularly, by the moving crowd.
The Milan station was full of people who seemed to
imagine that if they waited a moment the rain might stop.
They crowded all the doors. When any mouth opened,
out came a jabber of Italian, that, for Francis, rarely contained an intelligible word. Those who crossed brusquely
in front of him, or loitered senselessly so that he could not
get by, in speaking Italian sounded as well as looked like

even greater imbeciles—asses, apes, and dogs!—than the people who normally compose all crowds of strangers. Sunk in the shadows of the lumbering bus, cold and disgusted, Francis despaired of humanity. He could not see the use of saying anything.

Miss Robertson did not say anything either. Indeed, it was too late to expect her to say just once more that she thought she'd better get home. She sat quiet on the narrow seat, her leopard skin coat held close about her, her green hat and impassive face lit up now and then as light passed on the glittering windows. Francis wondered if he might say: "Look here, I know you're bored to death by this. I'll just leave my bags and get a taxi and run you home—" But he hesitated, not sure enough that he could say it with the right tone, and unwilling to risk the embarrassment of behaving—or, by a wrong tone, of letting Miss Robertson see that he was behaving—in a mannerless way. The bus at a crawl came around between the dark clumps of dripping shrubs and the flowerbeds full of withered stalks and dead plants. The runner snapped up a great umbrella and opened the door.

In the shelter of the glass roof of the portico Francis drew a breath. His eyes met the many slabs of marble affixed to the vestibule walls, each commemorating in gold letters an occasion on which some person of royal blood had been the hotel's guest. Francis's poor spirits involuntarily lifted. "How marvelous!" he thought. "How marvelous! The gracious monarch! The well-conducted hotel proprietor!"

It was like a sudden glimpse of that other sunny basking world before the war. Francis seemed to hear in solemn obbligato faint strains that proved to be the music of *Pomp and Circumstance.* Up the cleared steps, with a measured affable inclination of the head toward twenty or more frock coats bent by simultaneous constantly repeated bows, clad maybe in the duster and goggles of an early motoring costume, came King Edward VII. Innumerable gray and white hairs spoiled his beard. Majestic dissipations had puffed and thickened his face to the tight, fat remoteness of a graven image. The dignity of his swollen abdomen acknowledged his long hard life of pleasure. Yet no ignoble consciousness of self showed in the matter-of-fact acceptance of respect due his exalted station. The King did not give the least sign—held at a distance, an idle friendly rabble cried, "Viva il Re! Viva l'Inghilterra!"—that he understood the preposterousness, surely taught him by age and illness, of being a person whose stop at a hotel was event enough for bows, crowds, and cheers; and advertisement enough to be subsequently celebrated on a marble tablet.

The doors closed out the rainy night behind. Francis and Miss Robertson advanced into a warm silence, sparingly but snugly lighted. It smelt of old plush, of furniture polish, of pomade. The concierge in his decorated, gold-laced coat bowed. The man behind the desk inclined his gleaming head. Miss Robertson said, "Look, Francis. I really think I'd better go home. I'll just pick up a taxi—"

"Now, do we have to go through all that again?" Francis asked benevolently.

✦

37

The waiter turned about and went.

"Wine is good for you," Francis said. "Drink it. Drink it. You're more trouble than any ten girls I ever met."

Miss Robertson said, "I'll be tight. I'll bet you'll be tight—" The first sound of her voice had been critical or reproving; but it wavered unexpectedly loud to something like a giggle.

"Nonsense," said Francis, but he looked at her attentively. Miss Robertson's forehead as well as her cheeks were suffused with a pleasing animated pink; but at the same time a relaxing of muscles subtly broadened her already too-broad face. She sat heavily in her chair. Her big square shoulders were a little bit stooped and she rested her elbows hard on the table, as though propping herself up. Francis said, "Don't drink it if you don't want it."

"It's that cocktail," Miss Robertson said. "Don't you feel it?"

Francis smiled, but he let his glance go off in a quick turn around the dining room. At a table thirty feet away a party of Germans or Swiss seemed engrossed in their food. No other people remained. "You underestimate me," he said; though in fact he had acquired a wonderful renewed sense of vivacity and well-being. Miss Robertson, going to wash her hands, had taken some time. Francis registered. He handed over his passport for the police. He spoke to the concierge about the luggage. He did his own washing. Miss Robertson still did not come, so he drank a martini at the bar, had in a waiter from the dining room, and ordered dinner. He had drunk another martini before Miss Robertson reappeared. Then he took one with her. Three cocktails were more than he needed; but, cursorily examining his present feeling, it seemed to him that he could truthfully say he did not feel it in the sense Miss Robertson meant. "You underestimate me," he repeated.

"Oh, no, I don't," Miss Robertson said. She set down her glass and made a little, to Francis somewhat alarming, motion with the fork she had been raising to her mouth. "I don't underestimate you at all," she said. "Don't think that. I wouldn't be here if I did."

"Could you make it a little clear?" said Francis, grinning. "That has a sinister sound."

"I just mean I wouldn't waste my time with somebody who hadn't anything to him. I don't underestimate you at all. There are things about you that ought to be changed; but—how old are you? About twenty-three?"

"Yes," said Francis, "but I think I look older."

"I'm serious," she said. "You'll grow out of them." She gave a wise nod. Suddenly she laid her right hand on the table, palm up. "Do you see that?" she said, indicating a perpendicular line near the edge below the little finger. "You don't often see that. It's intuition. I can tell what's going to happen."

Francis looked at his own palm. There was certainly no such line to be seen on it; but he laughed. "Chiromancy!" he said, "but if you really want to know what's going to happen you ought to try alectryomancy. Now, that really is something. You describe a circle on the ground and mark around it the letters of the alphabet. On each letter you drop a grain of corn. Then you tether a cock in the center and every time he eats a grain you write down the letter he took it off. I never make a major decision without—"

39

"You can laugh," said Miss Robertson. "Laughing's one of the things you'll get over when you get older."

"Don't I know it!" said Francis. " 'The last stages of an infirm life are filthy roads. I find the further one goes from the capital, the more tedious the miles grow, and the more rough and disagreeable the way.' Lord Hervey wrote that in 1743 to Lady Mary Wortley Montagu. It's still true. I don't expect to find anything funny about it."

"That's another thing you do," said Miss Robertson portentously. "You're pretty fond of showing how much you know and how much you've read."

Francis had no trouble in laughing. "Drink some wine," he said. "I'll have to get your critical faculties dulled. All I did was try to amuse you with small talk. It's unkind to start again on my failings. People won't like you if you do things like that."

Miss Robertson said nothing for a moment. She stared fixedly at her plate. She put her fingers around the stem of her wine glass, started to raise it, and then decidedly put it down. "Forget it," she said. She made a short little angry gesture. "I have a mean disposition, I guess." Her words were laborious. "I say things—I don't know why. I wish I didn't."

"Ah, how we all wish we didn't!" said Francis.

The painful, harshly forced out answer disconcerted him, but expressions of regret always filled him with the tenderest compunction. Even when he had been injured or was righteously angry, a word of this kind was enough. He was placated not so much because his heart was charitable, or because he loved concord, as because he felt, knowing himself, a moral vulnerability that the saints are not alone in feeling. Self-indulgent people may lack the temperament to sink under the awful conviction of sin, and they may not know the daily need to get right with God; but many of them sink daily under the awful conviction of unwisdom or short sightedness. To Miss Robertson Francis said, "It was entirely my fault. I—" But before he could bring himself, even in his new state of grace, to make a gracious or respectful reference to the science of palmistry, Miss Robertson, having suffered all she could stand of whatever she did suffer when she apologized, interrupted him. Roughly she changed the subject. "Tell me about this boy, this Cunningham boy," she said. "Isn't there something wrong with him?"

"No," said Francis. "Well, he had infantile paralysis. One foot isn't so good. He has to wear a brace. But he gets around much better than you'd expect. He plays tennis. You have to feed your shots to him, but you'd have to, anyway—it's what you're paid for, after all." That was not fair, he reflected at once. Walter, skipping, dragging his foot agilely, could move along the base line as fast as he needed to. He could even get up to the net for a return not cut hard. Walter never complained—or, never had to Francis on the one occasion Francis had played with him on an indoor court in Paris—either of balls he could not reach, or of balls placed where he couldn't help reaching them. Francis said, "I think he also gets asthma. Maybe it's the same thing. I can only say he puts up with it all a damned sight better than I would."

"Well, what's he doing over here?"

"Oh, that's a sister of his, I think. She's having a year at one of those schools in Paris where they teach you est-ce-que French and cultivate you with performances of Phèdre and visits to the Louvre."

"Lorna knows her, doesn't she?"

"Yes, but Lorna's friend was an older sister. There are two older ones. I think, both married. They're quite nice people."

"So you said."

The words, with their effect of detached, gently sardonic comment on the incoherent or repetitious ramblings of a person amusingly unable to say what he means, surprised Francis; but he saw that Miss Robertson could not have meant them that way for she appeared hardly aware that she had said anything.

"So I did," Francis said. "I'm afraid I can't be very bright about it." He drank some wine. "It's a shocking thing to be rich," he said. "You hire somebody like me, which is very nice of you really; but do I like it? I do not; and so when your back is turned or you're out of earshot beyond the Alps—" He shook his head. "I didn't order anything else," he said. "I thought you might like to—"

"Oh, I couldn't eat another thing." Miss Robertson's voice was faint and far-off. Worried, Francis saw that her expression was very much like that indecisive stare, fixed inward, often appearing on the face of an unpracticed drinker who has, perhaps, topped off his whiskey with a little gin and is beginning to wonder. "Look here," he said, "do you feel all right?"

Miss Robertson stirred in her chair. The expression that disquieted him was gone and almost absent-mindedly, but warmly, she smiled. "I feel marvelous," she said. "I didn't, for a while. But all the time you were talking I could sort of feel it—I must be really tight. I never felt like this before. It's very nice."

"Men beat their wives and starve their children for it,"

Francis said. "It ought to be good—" He broke off. A moment before he had been feeling what might fairly be called marvelous himself; but now all this changed for he was thinking about the things he had said about the Cunninghams. He not only did not like these things, but discussing the Cunninghams at all seemed in questionable taste. Inspecting himself, he did not think that he was drunk; yet he knew from experience that this reaction, deferred numbly until it had to emerge slow and irrelevant through a succeeding and different line of thought, this plummeting to distaste, this exaggerated intensity in scrutinizing himself, proved that he was not sober. "You've had about enough," he thought. "All another drink will get you is a head in the morning. You know that." Aloud, he said, "Shall we get out of here, then? We'll have some coffee outside."

In the hall, following Miss Robertson into the empty lounge, he was still intent on repairing his lapse. "Walter's really a very engaging kid," he said, "and his mother was as sweet as possible to me—over there," he said to the waiter. They sat down beyond a large palm in a pot. "Have some brandy?" he asked. Nothing seemed to him less likely than that Miss Robertson, after her afternoon's experience, would want brandy, so it was a question perfectly fair to his intention of not having any himself.

Plumping down under the palm Miss Robertson said: "Oh, I don't know. Do you think I'd better?"

"Well, you're the best judge of that," Francis said, smiling. To the irritated remonstrance of his own mind, he pointed out that he could not very well say, "No, I think you'd better not." On the other hand, he very carefully hadn't said, "Yes, you'd better." In acknowledgment he got only a knowing sneer. Vexed by the justice of it, he said aloud, "It ought to be fit to drink here."

"No, I know what I'll have," Miss Robertson said. "I'll have some crème de menthe. Don't you like that?"

"No," said Francis. "I'll have some brandy."

He sat silent and defiant while the waiter was out. Tomorrow morning, when this triumph over the plaints of his better judgment would sicken him with exasperation, was somehow receding. Tonight, though diminishing hour by hour, magically expanded. The barrier of time that it set between now and the oppressive forlornness, the whole hateful matter of getting to Montreux loomed paradoxically larger. Tomorrow, on the other side of it, could take care of itself.

The waiter had set out the cups and glasses. Miss Robertson said, looking at the green gleam of the crème de menthe, which had been brought frapéed, "I like this. That English girl I was telling you about used to like it. She used to keep a bottle up in her room, and days it rained we'd go up after lunch and have some. She called it our cold medicine. She was lots of fun." Miss Robertson bent forward and sucked at the small straw.

She did not, Francis reflected, sound any too funny. His brandy had come in a balloon glass and he raised it to his face, sniffing the acrid fumes, wondering who on earth this English girl was. "Oh," he said, "you mean the one who—"

"I guess I shouldn't have told you that," Miss Robertson said. "I don't know why I did."

"You gave it as an example," Francis said, abstracted. He thought how true it was that you ought to be careful what you told a person you did not know. You might get

44

to know him better. But he was more interested by the discovery of obvious mistakes he had made in summing up Miss Robertson. Mixed with, even accounting for, the pity and indignation that she had expressed in giving him an example of the sacrifice, so many times repeated, for art, Francis had credited Miss Robertson with a native distaste, a severe censoriousness. If this English girl had been intimate with her, perhaps her best friend, Miss Robertson might have felt many things, but not that.

Francis let himself picture those rainy days—the monotonous studies and exercises through the raw morning: the unappetizing rapidly served food and empty polyglot gabble of a cheap pension luncheon table; Miss Robertson and the girl from England going upstairs to a constricted, uncomfortable bedroom where the mouthful of crème de menthe gave them who-knew-what illusion of zest or good spirits or even of gay sophistication, while they turned over magazines or musical scores that they had seen before, gossiped about their work, or gazed out on the hazed, wet street—Francis's thought went off the track, for the picture of the ghastly day crowded out, by its universality, its part in everyone's experience, Miss Robertson and her friend. Francis himself sat at the gloomy luncheon table, he climbed the stairs, he saw the room and the wet street and faced the afternoon.

He said: "You didn't tell me her name. I'm not ever likely to meet her. I wouldn't be likely to hold it against her. The truth is, I thought maybe you did hold it against her."

"Against her?"

"You can sometimes see that a thing is not a person's

45

fault; but it does not always make you like it or him any better."

"I'd be a fine one to do that," said Miss Robertson. With the straw she poked at the mush of green ice in her glass. "Why should I? I don't blame anyone for anything. Don't imagine I haven't any feelings." She took up a package of American cigarettes which Francis had laid on the low table before them.

"Sorry," Francis said, "I didn't know you smoked."

"I don't often." She felt in the package. "Never mind," she said, "there aren't any."

Francis looked around. The lounge was empty. The waiter had withdrawn. "They ought to have a bell," he said. "I have a carton upstairs. We may as well use those. I doubt if I get them by the Swiss frontier."

"I don't really want one."

"Well, I do." He swallowed his brandy. "I'll only be a moment. Look, don't you want another of those?"

"No, I mustn't. It must be awfully late."

"It's barely half past ten," Francis said. He went out into the hall. The waiter who had served them put his head past the door jamb up by the bar. "Two more of those," Francis said to him. He looked at the number of his key and went up in the elevator.

A light had been left on in the large heavily furnished room. The red curtains were drawn and it was very warm, perhaps because it took European systems of central heating all day to get up steam and they began to function only when you no longer wanted heat. Putting the curtains aside, Francis jerked up the windows a little, looking down at the piazzale and the station façade through the steadily falling rain. His luggage had been arranged against the wall by the door. Coming from the window, he stood a moment staring at the row of bags, for the heat, after the chilly breath of air, set his head swimming, though not unpleasantly. The cigarettes, he remembered, were in his small bag, and, moving toward it, he saw suddenly that the concierge had simply sent up all the luggage, Miss Robertson's black suitcase, too.

"Hell!" Francis said, picking it up to take down with him. Halfway to the door, he remembered the cigarettes. He went back and unlocked his bag. Taking out a couple of packages, he straightened up, the movement making his head swim again; and he waited a moment, breathing deep, steadying his vision on the big bed with the covers turned back. "Ellery," he said aloud, "you're pretty drunk—"

But it was impossible to put much reproach in the admonition. The immediate sense of pleasure, of being invulnerably committed to the principles of pleasure without fatigue or disgust, made reproach absurd. It would be absurd, having stumbled into this rich state of enjoyment to want it changed, or to find fault with it, or to leave it any sooner than he had to. It occurred to him that going to Montreux tomorrow was not strictly necessary—at least, not until tomorrow night. Nothing was more easily missed than a train connection. The evening would simply extend itself through the next day; and suddenly he heard Miss Robertson's moody voice saying, "Don't imagine I haven't any feeling. I don't blame anyone—"

Francis stood still another moment. "Ah, what the hell? Why not?" he said.

He went out and closed the door. In a careful, controlled way he walked straight and quiet along the shad-

47

owed hall, and, not ringing for the elevator, down the two flights of stairs. In the lounge Miss Robertson sat where he had left her. He saw that the waiter had brought another glass of brandy and more of the crème de menthe. "There you are," said Francis, sitting down. He opened a package of cigarettes and offered them to her.

She took one. "I've really got to go," she said.

"I don't think that follows," said Francis.

"I really do. Signora won't know what became of me."

"I have it on good authority that as long as she gets her money she doesn't care what becomes of you."

This chit-chat, Francis saw, sobered out of some of his warm immoderate confidence by the imminence of definite steps, of decisive things to say, was hesitancy on his part, a postponing. For an instant he contemplated, moved to take it, the ready relief he could get if, instead of going on with it, he abandoned the still desirable but somehow risky project. As though aware that his mind was no longer entirely made up, and that raised expectations might in another moment find themselves cheated, physical urgency flooded his body in a vast impatience, recommending to his mind the idea or image of Miss Robertson's female body. Its effort was intense enough to make Francis tremble a little; and blowing out the match he had lit for her, he tried to get himself in hand by being quick. "I'll tell you something," he said. "It's going to pain and surprise the management if you leave. What have they put upstairs with my luggage but your suitcase?"

"My suitcase?"

"Your suitcase. I wish I could—" Francis found his voice not entirely steady. The distress of jeopardy or riskiness was stronger than ever, and this was ridiculous,

48

the infirmity of a schoolboy. He put himself in mind of a remark, thrown out once by a college friend who had seldom much to say about love but whose almost satyr-like successes spoke for him, that had frequently helped at such moments: *What are you fooling around for? You know what you want. Ask for it, for Christ's sake! You'd be surprised* . . . Francis repeated, trying for a lightness of tone, "I wish I could say it was by my subtle design—" It was not light enough. Whether through desire or nervousness, it did not ring quite true; but he could not quit now. "On the other hand, it seems to be fate. We can't struggle against fate, can we? It would be ungrateful and impious. The wise man always takes care to be on destiny's side—"

Francis stopped. By letting himself talk on, even in a way meant to be fluent and confident, for talking's sake, he did not show the right confidence. "So," he said, "with credit and good conscience, I think we ought to go to bed." He picked up her hand and raised it to his lips—his movements, he was pleased to see, were precise and easy. He took the cigarette from her mouth and dropped it on the floor. With a convenient movement, he put his arm around her. "As Doctor Donne so well wrote," he said, " 'Come, Madame, come, all rest my powers defy—' "

His success appeared to be complete. Miss Robertson drew a curious long breath and seemed to let herself slump against his arm. Francis lifted his hand, took her hat by its short brim and twitched it off. "Oh, don't!" said Miss Robertson. She started to raise her own hand to her hair but Francis put a finger on the wrist and she let it fall back. "Never mind that," he said. "It's wonderful

49

the way it is. You can fix it tomorrow, if you feel you must. Now, we're going upstairs."

"No," she said.

"It would be much better. Think how the waiter would feel if he came wandering in. Come. This is a very pressing matter."

"Oh, no," said Miss Robertson.

"Oh, yes," said Francis. "You'll see."

"No," she said again, straining away against his arm. "No. You don't give a damn about me. You know you don't. You—"

Francis knew. Hopeful, he must have been going on the hopeful assumption that Miss Robertson's experiences in Milan and the world of music had prepared her to do without all that—the jockeying for emotional position, the protestations of devotion, the tedious running of the unsmooth course of true love to the pale, musty O Promise Me flowering, associated by Francis with late June afternoon weddings, one or two of which he had assisted at as an usher for some college friend, among the well-to-do simple society of small upstate cities. He saw the marquee on the lawn joined by a canvas tunnel to the big old-fashioned house, the five hundred guests who had to be asked and the men who kept an eye on them as they filed through the improvised museum of wedding presents, the quick shots of rye in a bathroom or secluded library, the evening clothes in the still bright sunlight making you feel like a waiter—all the tiresome (something borrowed, something blue) elaboration of naïve or sentimental custom that went into a lovely wedding.

This is joy's bonfire, then—Francis thought; derisively, for the epithalamium ought to include some mention of those humorists of the college party slipping downstairs again into the bedlam (after the orange blossoms and the Baptist or Methodist organ music it was hard to blame them; perhaps they were the true Elizabethans). They had cunningly eluded the best man and made themselves a laughter-shaken opportunity to get at the groom's luggage and scissor out the front of all his pajama trousers. There was the jocular kissing of the bride; the caterer's expensive, hard-to-swallow food; the bouquet falling from the stairhead; the rice, the shoes—the sweetest story ever told.

The succession of quick, untoward pictures brought Francis within a jot of stopping to set Miss Robertson right on what was decent and what wasn't. He recovered himself in time. "Why should I ask you if I didn't give a damn?" he inquired. "I find you urgently attractive. Don't tempt me to demonstrate it here."

"You wouldn't say that if you weren't drunk," Miss Robertson said. Her tone of nervous accusation seemed to imply that he had protested undying devotion, and that was all very well, and she didn't find the possibility of its being genuine as fantastic as the possibility of genuine undying devotion to Miss Robertson appeared to Francis; but he owed it to her to make so important a declaration soberly.

"Possibly I wouldn't," Francis said. "Now, are you satisfied? Probably I'd be too depressed to say anything. That's one of the nice things about drink. It eases constraint. Come. You'll enjoy it."

Miss Robertson turned her head down and away. "I have to go," she said.

51

"Of course you don't have to go. You don't even want to go."

"Yes. Yes. You mustn't ask me. You mustn't—"

"Now, why do you want to go? It's raining hard. It's a nasty night. Consider it carefully."

"Please," said Miss Robertson, "please." She shook her head back and forth. "I wish you wouldn't. Why do you want to do this to me?"

"What on earth do you mean by 'this'?" said Francis. In the warmth of his mind a coldness toward Miss Robertson must, at some point, have begun a gradual unnoticed growth. He noticed it now. Looking at her with his face still set in an expression intended to present amiable amusement, he found that he really disliked her a good deal.

"I mean," said Miss Robertson, at last looking him in the eye, "why do you want to sleep with me?"

The effect of her solemn, rather lumpish gaze was to repell him further. Francis viewed this reaction with curiosity. To his senses she made no more actual appeal than a cow, but he heard himself saying: "Well, you see, it's part of nature's great plan. One of the few good parts. That explains everything, doesn't it? Now, come upstairs."

"No, no," said Miss Robertson. "Francis, it would be so silly. Tomorrow we'd both be sorry. It isn't worth it. You know it isn't."

She was right. It wasn't worth it. Francis had the ineluctable evidence of his own eyes. He had, too, the easily examined evidence of his imagination, which foretasted, half-appalled, remonstrative, the crude, not-very-exciting stripping in the bedroom, the heavy sweaty mechanical exercise of the bed. He said, "Ah, but I know it is."

Miss Robertson moved her body desperately. Her big knee, shifting, hit the edge of the table. The crème de menthe glass rocked on its stem, went over and rolled, fell from the edge, and broke on the floor. "Oh!" said Miss Robertson. The waiter appeared, hovering at the door.

"Very neat!" said Francis. Again he was surprised to hear himself, for he spoke savagely, in cold anger, as though some low trick had been played on him. One moment, he was conscious of his surprise at himself and at his unreasonableness—the interruption was obviously not fatal, nor even serious; the next, this surprising anger, like an incoming tide, reached his mind and poured into it. Immediately he was enraged by the very consciousness that rage was unreasonable, that he was letting it serve as a stupid and unfair excuse for the failure of a stupid and unfair attempt. His anger grew with his inability to control it, or to prevent senseless fresh angers from joining it. He was angry at Miss Robertson for being so unattractive, and yet having the damned impudence to resist. He was angry at himself for the crazy effort to get what was patently repulsive and not worth having. He was angry at his ineptitude for failing to get it, worth having or not. He snapped at the waiter, "Get out of here! See that somebody finds a cab for the signorina. Subito!" He broke off, checked, for he had been taught that he had no business to speak to a person in the waiter's position that way. He swallowed the brandy in his glass, got hold of himself, and stood up. "I'll have the elevator man bring down that bag of yours," he said with enforced calm. "I won't offer to see you home. I expect you've had enough of my company."

"I didn't do that on purpose," Miss Robertson said.

In the door the concierge had now appeared. Francis said to him, "That small black bag shouldn't have gone up. It belongs to the signorina. Please have someone bring it right down." To Miss Robertson he said, "As you say."

"You think I did, don't you?"

"Perhaps we'd better go out in the hall."

"Well, I didn't."

"Ah, hell!" said Francis, smiling, not able any longer to keep the plain fact that his lofty manner was ludicrous hidden from himself. "Of course you did. Don't you know that the reflexes have reasons that the heart knows not of? You do what you have to do. I do what I have to do. I'm sure we should all be as happy as kings—" He searched about in his mind for some concluding phrase; something telling, philosophic, genially cynical, and likely to make her feel a little foolish.

It was a large order, and his mind's contents seemed inaccessible. Fumbling with it, Francis grew conscious of a faint nauseated feeling, a starting-out of sweat in the palms of his hands and on his forehead. "If you'll excuse me, I'll say good night," he pronounced with some difficulty, for that sensation, he very well knew, ended in only one way.

Two

WALTER CUNNINGHAM said, "Well, I didn't get it all. I didn't get—"

"Let me hear what you did get," Francis said patiently. "I'll find out about what you didn't get soon enough."

"Don't I know it!" murmured Walter. He twisted himself in his chair and drew a deep breath. "It snowed at Caux last night," he said.

"I doubt if it snowed much," Francis said.

One of the narrow casement windows that allowed you to step out on the little balcony stood ajar. The mild damp air was not warm, but neither was it cold. The pall of clouds, low above the lake, was brightened by approaching noon, and while Francis looked, across a mile or two of quiet gray water one thin steeply slanting golden shaft broke through. Sunlight swept a narrow course along the precipitate dark lower slopes of the Savoyard mountains and went off toward Evian. "The sun's out up at Caux," Francis said, "any snow they had last night is probably melted."

"The concierge said it snowed a lot. There was snow before that. He said there'd be lugeing."

"Now, when did you see the concierge?" asked Francis. "You haven't been downstairs this morning."

"He came up. Mother wanted to find a vet to take

55

Rose to. He told her somewhere, and she and Maggie went. I'd better see if they're back yet. It must be pretty near half past twelve."

"No, it isn't," Francis said. "It just seems that way."

"Let me see," said Walter, seizing Francis's hand to look at his wrist watch. It was five minutes of twelve. "It must have stopped," Walter said, bending his ear down toward it.

"Sit up!" said Francis. "Line twenty. Get going."

"*His Caesar*," said Walter with a burst of energy, "*ita respondit . . .*"

Wheeling in-shore, the gulls floated and fell against the low gray clouds. Footsteps crushed the pebbles on the promenade under the bare lakeside willows. Somewhere a door opened downstairs, letting out the sharp voices of women, kitchen workers. Francis heard each word, distinct, known to him, yet in the quick ellipsis of the slang they spoke, hard to follow.

"C'est un as!" The voice had a blank, surprised sound. (An ace of what?)

"—l'ai pesé en moins de deux—" A door slammed, cutting off the scornful answer. Perhaps it meant, "I sized him up—it didn't take me two minutes to get his number." What matter it concerned, what circumstance of money or love, or politics; of tips; of triumph over the management; of contempt for some guest, or some fellow worker; of the man who wanted to marry the bitter speaker, or was married to her, or hadn't the faintest intention of marrying her, Francis would never know. Without preparation or warning he found himself saying silently: "Think and die! Think and die!"; for that inward eye, that bliss of solitude, had presented Francis with a lively and scarifying re-enactment—no appalling detail, no horrible trifle obliterated by the weeks between—of Miss Robertson and himself under the palm in the hotel at Milan. Stringently revolted, his stomach folded up. His frantic mind backed away; but Francis could not stop seeing it. "Christ Jesus!" he said, soundless.

Walter's voice, which had been growing more and more uncertain, ceased. Walter's straight hair was that light, dusty-blond color that darkens later. Blankly, while his mind stirred in its numb and bruised obtundity as though wondering where it was, Francis considered this nearby head of hair. His silence probably alarmed Walter. Walter turned furtively, looking sidelong up through his lashes. He had his mother's eyes, which were close to the esteemed shade called violet by her generation.

"That child has the prettiest eyes—" Lorna had remarked. Francis could remember her saying it as they walked in the foggy dusk along the iron fence of the Tuileries garden. They had been having tea at the Cunninghams' hotel. "It's not fair," she said. "He ought to have been a girl." Francis could hear her heels on the pavement. Her arm was through his, her gloved hand laid on his wrist. Across her shoulders the fur of a silver fox trembled with a fine beading of moisture. White under the hazed glow of a lamp standard her face lifted as she spoke and shadows fell from the depressions at the temples past the evident high cheek bones. Light filled the delicate hollows under them and for an instant you could see that her eyes were blue. Francis took off his hat. Not stopping, he bent his head down and kissed her mouth. Taken by surprise, her breath caught, gasping.

She got it again and laughed. "Why, my dear!" she said. "In public! I'm surprised at you—"

"Well," Walter said defensively, "I told you I didn't get one part."

Francis dropped his eyes and compelled them to focus on the printed lines. "Try thinking of it in direct discourse," he said.

While Walter affected this trail, Francis managed to read the passage himself, and then read it again. He went on: "Think what Divico would say if he were speaking. He'd say: *Helvetii instituti sunt*, wouldn't he? That gives you your tense. This is it, literally: 'Divico replied, thus the Helvetians by their forefathers to have been trained.' "

An expression of exaggerated anguish crossed Walter's face. "Now, pay attention!" Francis said. "Don't look at me. Look at the text. It's simple. Here is what their ancestors trained them to do—" He had to pause, for the words refused to make sense. He saw the shop windows glowing out of the fog through the arches of the arcade, the radiance in gilded columns shining up the wet asphalt. A gloved hand squeezed his wrist briefly.

"It's a result clause after *uti*," Francis said; and saw, relieved, that so it was. "The Romans thought differently, remember. *Ita uti*—'in such a way that as a result'—of the way they had been trained—hostages, *accipere*. What is it?"

Walter writhed in his chair. "Well, it means to suffer, doesn't it?"

"In a different use. You don't suffer hostages."

"Hostages," repeated Walter, bending his head down almost to the page and screwing his eyes closed, "*accipere* —uh, they killed them."

"Oh, God!" Francis said to himself. "Would you mind sitting up?" he asked.

Walter sat up. "Hostages," he began again, *"accipere—"*

"Yes, *accipere!* What does it look like? To accept, to take, receive. *Accipere non dare consuerint.* 'They were accustomed to take, not give, hostages.' "

"Oh. Well, what's it mean?"

"It means that Divico is trying to get tough with Caesar. He goes on: *eius rei populum Romanum esse testem.* Literally—look at it!—'of the thing the Roman people to be a witness.' It's a wisecrack. He's saying: 'Listen, the Helvetians weren't brought up to give anybody hostages. They take them. You ought to know that.' He means that, in earlier times, the Romans of the province had to give the Helvetians hostages."

Since it was the end of the passage, Walter had allowed himself to relax again. He thrust out his left foot. There was a felt slipper on it, and in the mornings he did not wear his brace so the trouser leg of the dark gray flannels gave no sign of anything wrong. He cocked his head and eyed the slipper. "Wasn't Caesar sore?" he asked idly. He moved a hand with caution, pretending he thought Francis might not notice it, and touched back Francis's sleeve to see the wrist watch. Francis removed the hand and looked at the watch himself. "All right," he said. "We'll find out tomorrow."

"I can hardly wait," Walter murmured. Francis said to him, "What did you say?"

Walter giggled. "Nothing. I didn't say anything."

"One more like that, and we'll find out right now," Francis said, obliged to laugh himself. He closed his text. "Do what you can tonight with the next section," he said, reaching over and putting a pencil check beside it in Walter's copy. He piled his books together.

"O.K.," said Walter. "I guess I'll go and ask the concierge where we can get some skis. Shall I get your mail?" He put a hand to his knee, stood up, and with a quick skip reached the connecting door. There was no answer to his knock and he opened it. "They're probably still down with Rose," he said.

"If Rose is sick," Francis said, "your mother may want to stay here this afternoon."

"Maggie can stay. Anyway, mother doesn't have to go. If we're skiing she'd just be standing around. I'll tell her we're going up to Caux."

"We'll see what she thinks."

"She said to see what you thought."

"Well, I'll talk to her about it."

"Oh, it's all right," Walter said tolerantly. "The doctor said it was all right. I can do it."

"I wasn't thinking of that," Francis told him, disconcerted. He had no prepared explanation of what, if not that, he was thinking of. He said, frowning, "I don't know anything about skiing over here. It may be pretty dangerous. It certainly would be around Caux."

"Fellows from the English school at Glion ski there."

"We'll see," repeated Francis. "Are you going to get that mail, or aren't you?"

"Sorry," said Walter. "Can we have lunch right away?"

"We can't have lunch until your mother's ready to have lunch."

Francis went into the hall and down to his bedroom at the other end, still constrained—when simply to ignore Walter's disability? When to acknowledge it as the most

natural thing in the world? The occasion that brought up
the matter of skiing he remembered very well. They had
bicycled to Aigle one damp gray afternoon. Sitting on the
bridge end, their bicycles leaning against the wall, they
rested while Walter tossed pebbles into the rapid cold
stream. An open truck heaped with skis and luges, probably going to some resort hotel, passed them. Francis
could just as well, and not very untruthfully, have said
that he didn't know how to ski; but that was during the
first week with Walter, and Francis supposed that his
impulse had been to make the most of any accomplishments he had with the idea of fostering a useful admiration. Walter asked at once if they could try it.

Francis might have answered simply and directly, "I
don't think you'd be able to manage skis." He did not.
He felt an irrational embarrassment, as though he owed
Walter an apology for the callous and cruel way in which
he, Francis, walked around on two good legs; and to
cover up this unfair difference, his impulse was to talk
down or make little of the advantage he enjoyed, to imply
that Walter could do anything he could—certainly not to
imply, let alone directly say, that Walter mustn't hope,
being partly crippled, to attempt the activities of happier,
normal people. "There won't be enough snow," Francis
had said to both Walter and himself, "for a long time
yet. We'd better start back. I told your mother we'd be
at Zürcher's before five. She was going to have tea with
us."

Francis dumped the books on his bed. From a brief-case
on the floor near the small writing table he took the file
folders that held the manuscript of his book. Earlier in
the morning he had thought of something that he meant

to change, or see to. Though he could not now remember what it was—perhaps a word in Walter's spelling lesson that he recognized as the one he wanted in some particular passage—it had impressed him as an important improvement. He was still searching, hoping, if he hit on the part to be changed, it would recur to him, when he heard the uneven quick sound of Walter's footfalls coming up the hall from the lift. "Yes!" he said.

Walter slid into the room, laid the envelopes he held on the table. The bed squeaked as he dropped bouncing on it. Francis closed the folder. Deliberately, he lighted a cigarette and took up the envelopes. "Well, what about Caux?" he asked. He turned the first envelope over. It was from his mother in Florence.

"Look," said Walter, "could we go to Les Avants instead? They've been skiing there for a week. It's good there. The proprietor told me. He said he'd tell mother. They have a funicular up to a place. Do you know where it is?"

"I expect we could find out," Francis said casually. He looked at the last envelope, shrugged, tapped them together and stood up.

"What's the matter?" Walter said.

"Nothing at all," Francis said, looking down at him. "Why?"

"Oh, you sounded kind of funny. Don't you want to go to Les Avants? The proprietor says it's swell. He says his regiment practices up there. On skis. Did you know that? They have soldiers who have skis."

"Yes, I knew it," Francis said. "They're very good troops, the Swiss. What's *accipere* mean?"

"Means to accept, receive, take—and to suffer in another use. Fooled you."

"So you did," Francis said.

2

TEN MINUTES out of the Montreux station the Oberland-Bernois train, in an unhurried electric glide, climbing silent, hardly vibrating, reached the clouds. Mist closed in like a white tunnel. The long rising folds of land, the leafless stone-walled vineyards, the evenly planted, bare-branched orchards, all disappeared. Walter, his nose against the oblong of plate glass, said, "Look at the snow! Look at the snow!"

Through the white mist snow could be seen in a low pile along the bend of the track. A tall dark shape arose in the obscurity, became suddenly a clump of pines, the branches lightly whitened with snow. "My, my," said Maggie, "isn't that pretty!" At once she added, "Oh, dear! Mrs. Cunningham, I've gone and—" Her lean face lengthened. Through her horn-rimmed spectacles she stared with dismay at the knitting she held. "I lost my count. I believe I should have begun narrowing." She unfolded the knitted strip and blinked at it. The ball of wool rolled from her lap and Francis bent forward and picked it up. "Oh, dear—" Maggie said again. "I thank you very much, Mr. Ellery."

Mrs. Cunningham said, "Let me see it, Maggie. I don't think you ought to be narrowing." She drew the gloves from her small, prettily formed hands—quickly from the right hand, from the left with caution of habit, for she wore on it, next to her wide gold wedding ring, what had been her engagement ring; an inconveniently large diamond made more inconvenient by the old-fashioned mounting. She smoothed the gloves and laid them neatly in her lap. In the capacious embroidered bag beside her she had all sorts of things—a Tauchnitz novel, knitting of her own, smelling salts, a little round box of local chocolates, some cubeb cigarettes in case Walter had a touch of asthma, a gold fountain pen, a writing tablet whose sheets could be folded on themselves to make their own envelope. She felt these things over. Then she investigated the pockets of her Persian lamb coat; and then the pockets in the suit of violet tweed that she wore under it. From one of them she produced her glasses' case, giving Francis a fleeting sympathetic smile, as though she felt that her stupidity in not knowing where she had put the case must be painful to anyone watching her. She lifted her face a little, closed her eyes, and pushed the ear pieces into the waved almost white hair covering her ears. Tapping the bridge into place on her nose, she opened her eyes and took the knitting from Maggie.

Francis looked at her with liking. Not too directly, he continued to watch her while she examined the knitted rows. Mrs. Cunningham looked no less than her fifty-two or -three years. As the underlying tissue lost its tone, her cheeks had filled out and her skin showed loss of freshness and the signs of sagging. Though her ankles, crossed one on the other in thin wool stockings, were shapely, her figure was the necessary figure of fifty. The remarkable thing, Francis thought, was that though time had made so many changes and she looked no longer as she had looked when she was twenty, you could still see what, at twenty, Mrs. Cunningham had looked like. The girl's face remained close behind the relaxed cheeks and the wholesome but aging skin. The shape was strangely unaffected; just as her wide, well-placed eyes and candid brow were not themselves affected by the glasses, horn-rimmed like Maggie's, that she had imposed on them. Undoubtedly she had been beautiful.

Francis acknowledged it. He saw, too, that his acknowledgment might be an understatement. She had really been more than that—what, at the turn of the century, they probably called a raving beauty; and her husband had very likely considered himself the luckiest man in the world—without, Francis guessed, finding later that he was very much in the wrong, either. A photograph of the late Mr. Cunningham stood among the numerous photographs—of all three of the girls, of the husband of one of them, of Mrs. Cunningham's sister—that crowded in their folding leather frames Mrs. Cunningham's bureau top. The placid, intelligent face suggested sound principles and a financial acumen of the prudent sort fit not to make a fortune, but, more decently, to conserve one already made. Indeed, in the picture itself was proof enough of Mr. Cunningham's importance. That flowing mustache, that two-inch collar closed in front over a retiring ribbon of necktie, could only have been worn, when the comparatively recent photograph was taken, by an officer so high in a bank so old, rich, and powerful that direct contacts with the public and its changing fashions were for him unnecessary.

The ridiculous mustache, the ridiculous collar were obviously those worn by the bridegroom or the young

65

father of the late nineties, so they helped Francis to form a picture; yet the picture, being obscured by the gentle absurdities of a day too remote to be real, yet not remote enough to have accumulated the dignity of history, left unanswered most of the questions in Francis's mind. When young Mr. Cunningham, with his high collar and softly curved mustache, beheld in yon window-niche his statue-like Psyche, fresh from regions which are holy land, what reverent agitation swelled his breast? For that matter, what of the other agitations, the visions somewhat less chastely classic, that, though not in those days mention-able, might be assumed to have received private considera-tion, and to have played some part in Mr. Cunningham's hope that she would consent to be his? And when this decorous young man with his sound principles and flowing mustache came to make her his, what scenes of frightened embarrassment, what palpitations of horrified innocence, surrounded the nuptial couch where, surely not helped much by the hyacinth hair, the classic face, the Naiad airs, a prompt impregnation was nonetheless achieved?

Tugging sharply, Walter took hold of Francis's arm. "The sun's coming out!" he said.

Beyond the windows the dense whiteness had bright-ened to a yellow shimmering haze. A curved white slope dimly marked with pines and a black mass of rock showed through. Then abruptly sunlight itself poured on the snow. The interior of the carriage lit up. The mist-dewed glass shone like gold.

"How perfectly glorious!" Mrs. Cunningham said. She was folding up Maggie's knitting. Giving it back, she said, "It's the next row you begin to narrow in." She re-moved her spectacles, gazing with pleasure at the light

66

and the golden window. She turned to Francis a smile of great sweetness, as though she were crediting him with being responsible for the blue sky, clear now behind the last shimmering whisps of cloud to the high horizon, the immaculate snow fields marked in the hollows with deep clean shadows and gilded on the sunny rises. Not far off, Francis could see the village roofs, the tiers of hotel windows, which, no doubt, was Les Avants.

✦

Fretting at all delays, fidgeting even in the midst of the pleasures of picking out skis (as though he were so hemmed in that he did not know where to turn, and grudged time spent at any given enjoyment since it was just so much time taken from other enjoyments to come), Walter got off toward the funicular ahead of everyone else.

"Now, darling!" Mrs. Cunningham said.

"What?" said Walter passionately. "What, mother?"

"You know," Mrs. Cunningham said. She slipped an arm around him, slowing him down firmly to walk with her. Walter made an excited motion to wriggle free, but she did not let him go and the strong pressure must have been significant to him. He submitted to it with an effort, his face pink, his eyes still sparkling, his rapid breath visible on the frigid mountain air.

Getting the skis together had delayed Francis a moment. He stood supporting them against his hip while he pulled on his gloves, gazing after Walter and his mother who were already across the road approaching the ticket window. He had heard their voices. Mrs. Cunningham's arm about Walter, and Walter's self-imposed obedience touched him and Francis did not like to find himself touched. Working his fingers with care and exactness into the gloves, he stood unseeing, his face blank, for that particular sensation, described so well as a tug at the heart-strings, put Francis unpleasantly in mind of the things as a rule tugged up, the treasures of sensibility ancient and modern. Old fools remembered, they remembered the house where they were born; horrible little boys asked where mamma had gone away to; in more than fair ex-change, a tear was wiped at sight of the little toy dog covered with dust.

Francis wanted no part of it; but, want it or not, there it was. The mingling of pity—like parting, such sweet sorrow; of pain, you could hardly say what pain; of the sense of things gone, of the unfairness of fate, of disap-pointment, of disillusion; perhaps, of the hour of death and the day of judgment, all thrust toward the bowels of his compassion. They were bowels not particularly easy to get at; but, on close inspection, were they any different or any decenter than the man of sensibility's bellyful? Eviscerated, gushing freely out, all bowels looked alike, and Francis in revulsion, snapped himself up. Ill at ease, he had to remember that a painful moment of the same affecting sort might be coming if Walter, putting on his skis full of hope, discovered that his brace wouldn't sup-port him under such novel and peculiar strains. Francis did not think Walter would make a fuss, which was all you could ask of anyone, and more than you would get from most people. You could not ask Walter to decide at once, if he found skiing impossible, that he had never wanted to ski anyway, and, in the interests of sparing a spectator, not merely to act, but to feel accordingly.

Skis on his shoulder, Francis had caught up with Maggie. Maggie was still on this side of the road. She picked her distrustful way over the packed soiled snow, which had been softened earlier when the sun was on it, and now, in the shadow, was freezing again. A procession of sleds carrying milk cans approached and Francis stood still beside her. "Dear, dear," Maggie said cautiously, "Walter's all flushed up. Mr. Ellery, it's a thing I dread. For what it might lead to." Her lined face, wary and apprehensive, twitched as she noticed, apparently for the first time, the passing horses. She went back a step in case one of them should reach out and try to bite her.

Francis knew nothing about asthma, but he said judiciously, "We'll stop this pretty quick if he seems to be having trouble."

"Oh, Mr. Ellery," she said, "that's the worst of it. You can't tell until afterward. With poor Rose being so sick and all, I wasn't watching him this morning. He begins being excited, you know. As soon as he gets up. About nothing, that is."

"He seemed all right this morning."

"Did he now? Well, I'm glad of that. Oh, the times we've been through! That he's alive at all seems a miracle. It's from the paralysis, you know. As a baby he was never sick a day, not one. He was delicate looking, not so fleshy as the girls when they were little, but never sick—"

Francis had heard most of this recital before. No matter where she began Maggie would presently arrive at it, turning it over and over in sad, incredulous tones for as long as she had a listener. In Francis she had a good if unwilling one. Not knowing that Maggie expected, as a matter of course, that he would interrupt or cut her off without ceremony whenever he had the notion, Francis thought that he ought to wait for a conversational pause in order not to hurt her feelings by boredom or indifference. In Maggie's recount there never were any pauses, either for breath or for lack of material. With money so little object, Walter's medical history had been extensive. A dozen specialists were known to Maggie by name and she remembered where and when each saw Walter, and in a general way she could sum up what each said or did. By their works she knew them, too; and she showed it in minute changes of tones. Some had helped Walter. Others might get themselves a reputation all over the country; they might put on airs and talk very wisely— you could imagine Maggie, inconspicuous in the background, probably not even noticed by the great man, seeing everything, hearing everything, thinking her own thoughts—but their knavish duplicity was proved by the event. They had pretended to know about poliomyelitis and then had not done a thing for Walter. Maggie would never in this world forgive them.

More than loyalty, you had to realize, this was love. A wish to please, even an attachment to duty, could be hired; and money would buy a convincing affection and a very good show of interest; but not that brooding concern that retained every trifle, relevant or irrelevant, that absorption, tragic yet tiresome, that could not stop thinking or talking about the awful thing.

"Then this other doctor," Maggie said, "came from somewhere in the west. Perhaps you'd know of him, Mr.

Ellery. He was very well known—" The sleds and their savage or dangerous horses had gone by, and Maggie, word following word in the hypnosis of her theme, perceived that the road was clear. She stepped out. Her overshoe descended on snow polished by the sled runners and she almost fell. She staggered sideways against Francis, who was close enough to catch her elbow, and had to break her narrative to apologize, gasping with embarrassment, for it took a moment to get her balance and she naturally seized hold of him. "Oh, thank you, Mr. Ellery!" she said. "I'm so terrified of falling! There's this sister of mine, she's in a convent, who fell two years ago and fractured her hip. She isn't off her bed yet."

That Maggie had a sister who was a nun was news to Francis, but not surprising. Half hidden in mufflers, sweaters, and the collar of some unnameable gray fur on Maggie's black cloth coat, she wore on her bony breast a small gold cross entwined with gold thorns and roses. Under the black cloth dress Francis knew that she wore in addition, a number of medals, for Walter had described them to him with interest. Presumably Maggie was able to believe that a look at Saint Christopher would keep her safe all day; and if it didn't, the valuable periapt of Saint Benedict must, by its formidable initials, give the devil pause; and if the worst came to worst, there was the scapular of some confraternity, probably associated with whatever order this unfortunate sister of hers was professed in, to cut a little shorter Maggie's detention under the pains of longing and of material fire in purgatory. "That's too bad," Francis said sympathetically.

"Oh, it's terrible," said Maggie. "They may have to

take her up to a shrine in Canada, Saint Anne's, it's called, to be cured."

Francis nodded, sober and sympathetic still; but the marvelous, matter-of-fact statement filled him with delight. Why not? Why not? What could be better—parmaceti for an inward bruise—than thaumaturgics for a fractured pelvis? Why not take a train to Quebec and get some? The heart swelled with glee. It shook with the silent peals, cruel but refreshing, of that genuine Homeric laughter—the mirth of the younger world. By all means, the train to Quebec; and, borne by pious friends, in haste to the half-rebuilt basilica! Saint Anne, seeing a sufferer earnestly venerating pieces of her precious bones, could not but be touched. God, listening indulgently to His Grandmother, formed the awful thought: *I will: be thou clean*, and there you were.

Francis was sure that he had not smiled; but he saw Maggie blinking doubtfully at him. Recovering from the distraction of her alarm and embarrassment, Maggie deplored her incaution in mentioning to Francis things that were not for him. Guiltily she pressed her lips together, as though reminding them of the virtue of silence. Francis did not think his sober air had deceived her. Just how good a joke he found her faith she might not know, but she knew enough to be sure that it was a faith he could not share nor take seriously. She was not offended. In this case, silence was a privilege, not an imposition, and though she made most of her life the property of the Cunninghams, there had to be things—her religion one of them—that she kept for herself. She would have done anything for Walter, but Francis doubted if the idea of inducing Saint Anne to take a hand in Walter's cure had ever so much as crossed her mind. In the Episcopal church they did not have miracles or interceding saints—an arresting example of the Divine Economy, perhaps; since relatively speaking, the need was less acute. Maggie would not be likely either to wish or pray for anything so surely contrary to reason and what Mrs. Cunningham would like as Walter's conversion. In the end, on the last day, it would probably be all right. Anyone could see that committing a lady like Mrs. Cunningham to hell was out of the question.

Francis supported Maggie's elbow. He got her across the road. They went through the gate to the waiting funicular and he found a place to stack the skis. Walter, though sitting down with his mother, could not sit still. He had kept his ski poles and he balanced his hands on them. He jabbed the worn floor with their metal points. Supported this way, he swayed from side to side. His cheeks were still flushed and his eyes darted here and there, delighted with everything. He nudged Francis with his elbow. "Gosh," he breathed, swinging himself over close. "Pipe the motormen's hats."

"Don't shout," Francis said. "They're English."

He had already observed the two young men Walter nodded at. Though he was seeing them worn for the first time, it had been apparent to Francis at once that those were the skiing costumes he and Walter ought to be wearing. The baggy trousered suits of blue-black flannel, the straight visored caps of the same material heavily stitched, contrasting with his own sweater and golf trousers made Francis uncomfortable. If he were going to ski often he saw that he would have to do something about that.

Unabashed, Walter rolled his head around, taking in

through his lowered lashes the other passengers. These were French, or possibly the gayer or more Gallic sort of Swiss from Geneva or Lucerne—two men with big pointed noses, long loose lips, and no color; and two young women. All four, like Walter, bubbled over with pleasure and excitement. They never stopped talking and laughing. One girl, whose curls were colored the unnatural yellow of egg yolk, constantly touched, patted, and held onto her escort. She looked at Francis and smiled. She looked at Walter and became suddenly grave, for she must have noticed his brace. Francis could not hear her, yet from the motion of her lips as she squeezed her companion's arm he was surprised to see how simply and surely the words *pauvre* and *petit* could be read. He looked indirectly at Walter; but Walter's whole attention was given to the other girl who had a sleek bang of jet black hair coming from under her beret down her forehead almost to her eyebrows. She kept her eyes on her young man's face. She held a lighted cigarette and with surprising skill was blowing smoke rings towards him. In the disturbed air most of them never arrived, but when one did, they both cried out with delight. "What's she trying to do?" Walter whispered.

"Convey her affectionate regards, I expect," Francis said. Forgetting a moment to whom he was talking, he went on, "It's like a picture in *Le Rire*—" He had in mind one of those gayer, less anatomical jokes that light-heartedly demonstrated the conventional French proposition that, in life, the really important (but not serious) thing was love. Love was so amusing, so delightful, and fortunately to be found everywhere and all the time—in the black-haired girl's swelling breasts and blown smoke

74

rings; in the yellow-haired girl's limber amiable mouth and kittenish hand strokings. Just in time, Francis saw Walter's interested expression and checked the comment he had nearly made on the gay relationship. "We ought to start," he said.

This was enough to distract Walter. He twitched about, looking out at the man in uniform who stood holding what seemed to be an old-fashioned automobile horn. "Hey!" Walter said, "Nous voulons partir!"

"Walter!" Mrs. Cunningham said. Walter put his hand over his mouth. "Excuse it," he said. "Frank thought we were going."

The horn honked. Humming on the overhead wires they moved. They swung slowly out above the long slope of the snowy fields. "See!" said Walter. "See!"

The yellow-haired girl smiled again at Francis and then tenderly at Walter, but Francis looked away. Checking the remark that he had almost made had served to check, too, that love said to be felt by all the world for lovers. Francis considered coldly the ridiculous yellow dyed hair. He sized up the dark girl's stupid thick features under the coarse bang. Something from *Le Rire* was right! *Le Rire's* advertisers spoke to you of love. What about the pied-à-terre grand luxe always open and the articles d'hygiène en caoutchouc? What about something for les soins intimes (que des larmes évités!); and if that did not work, the Sage-Femme 1ᵉʳ classe discrétion absolue? What about the disorders of the voies urinaires, the pilules and pastilles good for impuissance, acte bref, and frigidité féminine? You couldn't say they hadn't told you!

"Ah!" said Francis, shaking his head. Below, the long road on the hill bent from left to right and back to left again in easy gradients. Directly underneath them moved the horse-drawn sleds with the milk cans, the same ones that had held him and Maggie up. The moment's audible jingle of metal made him think suddenly of the story about the sleigh ride. *Then I put my hand up all the way*, boasted the lewd little boy. *Well, what was that like? I don't know*, the simpleton confessed, *I had mittens on.* . . .

Francis suppressed indignantly the mind's idiotic quiver of laughter; but laughter startlingly filled his ears. The French party was convulsed. Francis dared say it was a joke of the same sort, for the blonde girl was blushing. She bit her lip, shaking her head in vehement protest, trying not to laugh; but with triumphant pleasure her companion pressed his advantage. Bending forward he dropped an emphatic hand on her leg, through her wool skirt frankly palming the inside of her thigh, and said something more. Everybody cried out again with laughter, the speaker himself loudest of all. In the transport of mirth his foot shifted and hit the end of the ski that the nearer of the two English youths had been sighting along critically to see whether it needed more wax.

The Frenchman turned his still-smiling face and instantly apologized. He got for it a short nod, a chilly withering glance. Drawing up his kicked ski, the English youth waited a bare moment, then moved six inches farther away. From his mouth he took an unlighted pipe, lifted his eyebrows, and said, perfectly audible to Francis, "Shan't be sorry when we get to Grindelwald."

"Quite," said his friend, removing for a moment a pipe of his own. Although naturally round and ingenuous, his plump boyish face stiffened in a demeanor much too old for it, a diverting expression of weary dignity. He passed

76

his eye over Francis, not unobserving, but not interested, and looked away.

"Simple ass!" thought Francis, partly amused, since the two were several years younger than he was; yet partly annoyed. "These Britishers!" he said to himself. "It's really time they were put a stop to—" He shook his head, ruminating the joke of England in case the round-faced youth happened to look back. But the round-faced youth, looking back, if he happened to, would never dream of what was so amusing.

Francis's mind took itself disconsolately away, wishing not for any single thing, but for vague new states of things which would—comfort and relieve him according to his several necessities! He brightened a little, unable to see his so-called necessities without irony. He was comforted and relieved already by the ludicrous ending of solemn obsecration in the wish to be more appropriately dressed for the occasion, so that, exchanging cool stares with Britishers, he need rest at no disadvantage.

That took care of that; but he had deeper discontents, and even they were not exactly necessities within the Prayer Book's meaning. Francis did not know why he got no letters from Lorna in Paris, and the worried mind could not expect much comfort or relief there. He did not dwell on it because he could not endure to; but what about that detestable misbehavior of his in Milan? Rationally or irrationally, the inexpungable suspicion of the anxious heart is that the gods may be just; that you reap what you sow; that the nature of things operates by an awful law, a sort of *lex talionis*, which, whether you revere or deride any given moral code, will take an eye for an eye and a tooth for a tooth, and complaining will not help you.

Formulation was, however, a defense; for the gloomy notion was most effective when half-felt, when pushed away where the sharp eye of the mind saw its terrific shape in the dark, but not its cumbersome construction of who-knew-what remnants of taboo or blood-guilt, or tribal magic. Put in words, it sank to more or less imposing rodomontade. "Accuse not nature," Francis found himself declaiming—what a priceless old imbecile Milton was!—"she hath done her part—"

He stopped dead.

With a jolt Francis lost interest in old imbeciles. The head-filling recitation broke. "Lord God!" he said to himself, "she hasn't been in there, of course—"

Francis started to get up. He was indefinitely impelled to do something—stop the funicular, get out, rush off to—well, perhaps to telegraph. Hung on a cable halfway up a hill this was not practicable so Francis did not complete the movement. He sat staring, at once frenzied and perfectly still; stabbed to the heart, yet thinking clearly; as, detail by obvious detail, the stupid, the ruinous reason why he had not heard from Lorna after that first letter, demonstrated itself.

It might be weeks before she happened to go into Morgan Harjes. Any fool could see that, for what would she expect to find? By now, there couldn't be anyone who ever wrote to her who didn't know where she was staying. Had he thought she might be in for money? How could he think it? How could he? Had he lost his mind? He had been with her the day she cashed all the rest of her letter of credit—it was on George Bancroft's tip, got straight from someone on his paper, who got it straight from someone who must not be named in the Agence Havas, who got it straight from M. Poincairé's secret memorandum to the Governor of the Bank of France, that the franc was to be supported. Gwen Davis kept her travelers' checks on the off-chance that, despite George, the Agence Havas, and the secret memorandum, what the franc was really going to do was collapse entirely; but the tip had been good. They would not need money from the bank. They had it already in ten-thousand franc notes deposited in the hotel office safe. You might ask what Francis could have been thinking of.

Francis could answer, though in despair, that he had been thinking of the mail brought up in the morning, with Gwen wandering in, drinking her chocolate, ripping open her own letters, probably reading aloud and commenting on what she read. In Florence two days after he got down, replying to Lorna's first—her only—letter, Francis had thought of it. Not that Gwen could possibly be in doubt about him and Lorna, nor that she had ever showed anything but friendliness; but, even so, when he came to address the envelope, he wrote *14 Place Vendome*. There it went; and three or four others after it; and there, presumably, it stayed.

"Lord God!" Francis said again.

When Lorna had remained silent he had found reasons. Understanding her, it seemed to him, so well, he could understand it. With the letter gone, she regretted, too late, too late, the impulse that had made her write out her heart, an hour's painful pleasure, saying what would soon seem to her so much more than she was obliged to say, so much more than Francis needed to hear or know. *My dearest,* she wrote, *you can see that I'm not the same person who came to Paris in August so blissfully uncertain of what Fate had in store for her.* . . . . In contrast to the careless rush of the wording was the fine, finished, vaguely runic script; the backhand "P" of Paris driven like a little flag, the "my" of my dearest one level line decisively ended by the struck down tail, as like her in its controlled nervous grace as the ready-made phrases about blissful uncertainty and Fate were unlike her. To have their real meaning they must be read by someone moved as much as she was; and Francis could imagine her recalling them the day after and wishing she were dead. No matter how much his reply reassured her, she might normally wish so still; until enough of his letters had come to make it sure that he was the one who waited and wondered, not she.

"But as it happened," Francis said ponderously to himself, "she didn't get any answer. None at all."

Francis supposed that he could, as his first impulse had been, telegraph her that there were plenty of answers in a pigeonhole at Morgan Harjes; but even he could see that after so many weeks, his answers could be in hell for all the good they would ever do her or him. "And that's that," he said aloud.

"What?" demanded Walter, swaying over against him.

"Nothing," Francis said. "I was just thinking."

✦

The stubborn thick leather of the strap resisted his cold fingers. Francis said, "Hold still!"

"I'm sorry, Frank," said Walter. "Maybe it's busted."

"It's all right," Francis answered. He managed to force the buckle pin through the next hole, pressed it flat, and snapped over the metal catch that locked the harness around Walter's heel. "I'm just not very bright. I should have done that before you put your foot in." He heard his voice full of pettish exaggerated blame.

"Well, gosh, thanks very much," Walter said, plainly supposing that in some way not clear to him he had offended Francis.

Francis arose from the packed snow. "It's not your fault," he said. He smiled, the grimace stiff and arbitrary on his cold face. "How does it feel?"

"O.K.," said Walter. Francis had been warmed by his exertion with the straps but he saw that Walter, forced to stand still, was shaking with cold. "Move out into the sun, there," he said. "Don't try to pick your feet up. Just slide them." Walter shuffled cautiously a yard or so out of the shadow. He turned then, looked up and waved a stick to the glass-enclosed porch of the little hotel, hardly more than a small chalet, at the head of the funicular. Mrs. Cunningham waved back. Maggie, in eloquent pantomime, went through gestures meaning, tuck your muffler in.

Francis repeated his unreal smile. Kneeling again, he slid up one of his own skis and drove his toe in. His fingers were almost insensible, yet he could feel the skin catch and stick, freezing against the cold metal. Sharp hard bits of frozen snow dug into his bent knee and he winced, shifting it; but in his bitterness of mind, the pain, like the pain of his bare aching hands, pleased him. He wished in anger that they hurt worse, that he could give

81

himself, the stupid ape, something to remember. "Come on, come on," he thought; for the anger was asinine too; you didn't get anywhere that way.

Past him up the road came the round-faced young Englishman sliding along quickly and easily. Reaching a low place beyond, he sidestepped up onto the deep snow. He kicked his heels about, gave himself a mighty shove with both poles and shot away down the steep slope into the hollow behind. At a hundred feet, going fast, he swerved right, and then left dodging a clump of small pines. With a snow burst like a small shell exploding he executed a neat Christiania turn and stood still, facing back up the hill. Francis straightened up painfully, getting his numb hands into his gloves.

"Gosh!" said Walter. He looked over his shoulder at Francis. "How does he do that?"

"It's a matter of practice," Francis said.

"Show me how."

"I couldn't do it," Francis said. "I'll show you another kind of turn. But not today." He pulled his sticks from the near-by snow pile. "Head over that way," he said, gesturing to the dip, flooded with dazzling sunlight, where the road along the crest of the col went off west. "That will do to start on. All right?"

"Sure," Walter said. "It's a cinch." He pushed out vigorously, sliding ahead until he reached the imperceptible edge of the slope. The acceleration, once begun, threw him off balance.

"Bend your knees!" Francis called, rousing himself. "Bend forward! If you let your feet get ahead of you—" Before he could say it, Walter displayed it in a spasm of acrobatics, flinging his arms wildly. One pole, whose thong was broken, left his hand, spun over and over through the air and landed a surprising distance down the slope. Walter went in a heap, his skis angling every way, and instantly covered himself from head to foot with snow.

Francis pushed off and overtook him. "Hurt yourself?" he asked.

His falling feeling of apprehension was really, he recognized, as much for himself as for Walter. He did not feel equal to it—to alarms and concerns, to saying or doing sensible, decisive things. He saw then that Walter was not hurt. Floundering, Walter began to laugh. "But how do I get up?" he asked.

"Get your skis straight," Francis said. "That's right. Now, catch hold." He pulled him to his feet, still prepared to see Walter stagger or fall when he put weight on his leg; but Walter, looking back at his tracks with admiration, said, "Say, all the way to here!"

"Now, wait a minute," Francis said. "I'll get that other pole." Turning to look for it, he saw that the round-faced English youth, sidestepping his way back up the hill, had already come on the pole. He stopped, looked to see whose it was, swung an arm down and pulled it out of the snow.

"Much obliged," Francis called. He turned his points that way and glided carefully down. The English youth had started climbing again. Rosy, breathing hard, he held the handle out to Francis. "First day?" he said.

"Yes," said Francis stiffly. "Thanks."

He took the pole, ready to return, for he neither wanted, nor wanted the Britisher to have the faintest reason for thinking he wanted, to strike up an acquaintanceship. It took him a moment to head around and before he could move off the English youth said, "Been up here before?"

"No," said Francis.

"Better slope over beyond there."

"Thanks," Francis felt obliged to repeat. "I don't want anything too fast for him."

"No." The round face turned up to where Walter, high above them, stood against the bright blue sky brushing off snow. "Crocked leg?" he asked. His voice had that note of schoolboy solemnity, of doing that duty of manly compunction that England expects every man, and particularly every boy of the upper middle class, to do when he is confronted with the dumbness of dogs and horses; and, by extension, with the plight of a handicapped human being.

"Infantile paralysis," Francis said.

"Plucky kid!" He looked back at Francis and said warmly, "Let me show you this place."

Francis hesitated. The round face, ruddy with the labor of climbing, softened by the spectacle of pluck, had the expression natural to it, the open look of ingenuous friendliness. The small brown eyes, narrowed in a squint against the sunlit snow, shone with good nature—the physical good nature of a person who likes food and gets all he wants of it; the mental good nature of person, sturdy and well-fed, whose idea of fun is so simple and wholesome that he can have it anywhere. Francis would not have expected to be cheered, and in a sense he was not cheered. Relieved or grateful, he simply seemed to find, in the forbidding circle of the world, one point not definitely hostile, not requiring any new resistance or defiance.

"Thanks," Francis said, aware that he had now said it three times. "If it isn't too far—"

"Oh, it's not far. Just over there. What's his name?"

Francis hesitated again. He saw the cordial intention to make friends with Walter, and certainly he could not see any harm in it. Yet having often watched, a little scornful, a little impressed, the characteristic start of wariness, the slight cool withdrawal of rich people—or at least of the few with whom he had been intimate—when someone they knew nothing about attempted what seemed to Francis perfectly natural and spontaneous advances, he was not certain that Mrs. Cunningham would approve if he made Walter some new friends this way. He did not want her to think him unsophisticated, and in the fraction of a second given him to decide, Francis tried to be judicious. He told himself that there was nothing about Walter or Mrs. Cunningham that advertised wealth on a scale likely to allure strangers with ulterior motives—even granting that Francis could be wrong about the friendly eye and adequate manner, and wrong about the accent and inflection, which sounded to Francis indistinguishable from that rarefied bleat, the mark he had been told, of Balliol, and so of all that in England was highest and best; but which might not seem so indistinguishable to an Englishman.

"His name is Walter," Francis said. "He'll have to take it pretty easy. If he gets too excited, he has asthma attacks."

3

THE STATION lamps were lit. Those great snow fields hung luminous in the dusk above the town. The wind had died in fragile silence and a few stars, a few infinitesimal points of light, were white yet brilliant in the darkening zenith of the pure cold sky. Francis, hardly knowing why, told himself that it was a remarkable moment. Years from now he might remember it; he would remember the last light on the snow, the white mountains, the indescribably fine motionless silence of the high air into which they stepped as they left the stuffy electric-lighted restaurant in a hotel otherwise closed for the season, and walked down the short street to the station.

The comfort of hot tea in his stomach soothed Francis. He liked the tiredness of his muscles and the tight warmth over his cheeks and forehead where the wind and glare had reddened the skin. Slow and quiescent, his thought went its way. He thought of Lorna in Paris without undue distress for he had no active plans and hope did not trouble him. Sadly he thought that it might be as though she were dead; as though she had been dead ever since he left Paris. By now the mind accepted it; pain wore itself down. Death seemed all right, the necessary thing; perhaps, the very thing—a thought fairly familiar in poetry; but he had not, by merely reading it, grasped it clearly—that made youth and beauty mean what they meant; and there might be worse things than death—less peaceful. *Unarm, Eros*—grandiloquent, he seemed to feel that beautiful,

86

mortal quiet—*the long day's task is done, and we must sleep.* . . . "Ah, well!" he said to himself. "Ah, well!"

With no warning sound of a locomotive, the Montreux train, as quiet as his thought, came rapidly around the bend against the dim high snow banks, its windows lighted. They got in and Francis sat in pensive silence until the train began to move. Walter roused him then. "Where is this Grindelwald, anyway?" he asked.

"I don't know," Francis said. "Somewhere above Interlaken, I think."

"Is that far?"

"Quite a distance. It would probably take all day."

Mrs. Cunningham had brought out her knitting, but she soon found the light not satisfactory. She rested her hands in her lap. Smiling, she said suddenly to Francis, "Don't you think Toby's a nice name for him?"

"Yes," said Francis, smiling back surprised; for, first hearing it, Toby Troop had seemed to him almost too good to be true.

"Tom's the best skier," Walter said.

"The better of two," Francis told him.

"What is this school of theirs?" said Mrs. Cunningham. "I don't seem to know it."

"Wellington? Oh, it's a public school. I think it's quite a good one."

"Isn't it a strange time for them to be having a vacation?"

"Oh, I think they're out," Francis said.

"Graduated?"

"I think Troop is. From something one of them said, I expect Best was superannuated, if they do that at Wellington."

"What is it?" demanded Walter.

"Well, if you don't get through by the time you're a certain age, they turn you out anyway. They do at Harrow, I know."

"You mean you don't have to pass anything?"

"I think not."

"That's where I'd better go," Walter said. "No more work for poor uncle—"

"Darling!" Mrs. Cunningham said, "you mustn't say that! Of course you can pass."

Walter shifted his shoulders against the seat back. "Of course I can't," he murmured. He smiled feebly.

"Darling!" said Mrs. Cunningham. She looked at him with pained reproof and Walter pushed himself down farther in the corner. "Well," he said, ostentatiously reasonable, "we don't know that I can until I do, do we? We don't know I can even get in. Maybe I'm too dumb."

"Now you're being silly, dear," Mrs. Cunningham said. "Please sit up."

"That shows I'm dumb, being silly, doesn't it?" Walter sat up. He put his arm through Francis's, and rested his head against Francis's shoulder, transferring the question to him. "Doesn't it, Frank?" he said. "Doesn't it?"

"Now, Walter!" his mother said quite sharply.

"You're not dumb," said Francis. "You just do your work and we'll get you in all right." He spoke calmly, confidently, with what, he immediately told himself, derisive, was a note of manly cheer. Since manly cheer was not his real attitude toward the matter, he felt, though every word he said was true, deceitful. Walter was not dumb. If you just kept at him, Walter couldn't help knowing what he needed to. Mere tiresome repetition

88

would din knowledge into Walter's head. He would know how to go about solving the inane cryptograms of certain short Latin sentences; he would remember that the product of the means was equal to the product of the extremes. He would be able to spell apparatus, say whether a clause was restrictive or non-restrictive, and write a few fairly coherent paragraphs about my favorite sport—accomplishments, after all, not to be laughed at. There was a point on the dolorous way of learning when arithmetical ratio and proportion might confound the mind as utterly as the quantum theory. Francis supposed that the fatuity of confounding a mind to so little ultimate purpose was what made him feel deceitful when he heartily recommended study to Walter and cheered him with the promise of success.

From the phantasmagoria of Francis's own experience—sound of voices and the meager smell of chalk in once boringly well-known classrooms; exact colors and shapes of textbooks not seen for years; the tick of the study hall clock in progress through hours much longer and slower than the hour of today (yet not so long and slow that Francis couldn't conveniently idle them away and have half, or even none, of his work done when the bell rang); the occasional late lights under which, while most of the school slept, he tried with vain violence to make himself learn in haste what he had neglected at leisure—there emerged in the end the uncomfortable, apposite picture of that wide worn bulletin board in the main building hall. It was pinned thick the last day of term with typed slips, every few hours a batch of new ones, as master after master finished marking his examinations.

PLANE GEOMETRY IV (*Mr. Blackman's Section*) . . .

Stomach lifting toward his mouth, on how many of those successive little doomsdays had Francis crowded in to learn his fate. *Post II, 95, Upjohn, 92*—in fearful haste his eye went down the column, to bring up, perhaps, with a ringing shock on *Ellery, 60,* thank God! He was by, all right, safe among the saved. Or, at least, sometimes he was by. It had been *Ellery, 50,* or *45,* often enough (*Be not deceived, God is not mocked*—at least, not every time) for him to know, better than the almost emetic spasm of relief, the slow queasy leaden feeling that he could bring home with him; under the excitements of the school going down, and the joy of release, waiting right there on the eventual question and the obligatory answer. It was no good answering untruthfully for the marks would be along from the school office in a few days, sometimes re-enforced by one of those letters in which the Headmaster made it known that he had personally seen the enclosed report and felt that the gravity of the situation ought not to escape Francis's father.

What expressions of grief and disappointment! What reproaches, curt and disgusted, or sad and gentle! What serious talks and suggestions to think things over pretty carefully! The gravity of the situation was duly not allowed to escape; but that was hardly the half of it. There remained those other considerations. Think how proud and happy the mother of a boy like Post II must be! Wouldn't he, for her sake— Didn't he want her to be proud of him— Everyone said that if he only wanted to, he could— Francis groaned, in an evoked memory so real that he could almost feel himself, with alarm, appalled at his wickedness, swallowing down the fantastic shocking yell, the horrible honest answer that struggled toward his lips—*I don't care! What do I care about Post II? Let me alone, why can't you?*

"What I needed," Francis thought, "was a damned good licking, and never mind who was proud of what." But of course that was now, when a few long-ago-beatings would seem well exchanged for the advantage and convenience of having at his command habits of discipline and application that would make work of all kinds no trouble at all. Offered the choice ten years ago he doubted if he would have reckoned the sufferings of this present time not worthy to be compared with the glory which shall be revealed. He might not have cared to insure the future at the immediate expense of his backside. Soundly thrashed, he might, far from turning industrious and tractable, have sought solace all the oftener in the moody comforts of reading in study periods and the nervous release of being idle and impudent.

The implied contradiction—pity for the child consigned to such a piddling yet effective hell, and contempt for the little whiner—would not resolve itself. Francis felt both. He thought it was a shame that Walter had to go through with it, if he did have to; and if he did have to, whose fault would it be but Walter's? Francis said aloud, "And if you just go on doing your work after you're in, you'll never have any trouble."

Walter's look was patient. He looked resigned to having Francis inflicted on him; and if they had been alone this polite boredom might have moved Francis to some imprudent remark, an exasperated hint that he was by no means sure that it wasn't all bunk, too; but Mrs. Cunningham looked at him kindly. Francis saw her gratitude, and even, apparently, her admiration for his vigorous sayings and hearty good sense. Francis let it go. It was only to himself that his mind, sardonic, added: "And when you're dead you'll never have any trouble, either."

✦

By the clock surmounting the grill above the reception desk it was quarter past seven. Mrs. Cunningham said, "Oh, how late it is!"

Though personally she moved without a trace of ostentation, Walter, Francis, and Maggie, making in effect a train or suite, turned her entrance and her progress toward the elevators into something of an event. All members of the staff within sight straightened up, bowed, smiled, made little gestures or movements indicating alertness or readiness to serve. The proprietor, a frowning stout man of military carriage, posted at a point which he often unobtrusively occupied when there was much coming or going, touched his mustache. He made a dignified inclination of his torso. He said, "Madame!"—not only with the deference due any guest who had extensive and expensive accommodations, but also with an unmistakable note of genuine respectful dislike. He must know by now that Mrs. Cunningham felt no uncertainty about what money ought to buy, nor any embarrassment in seeing that it bought it. Probably, though paying plenty, she was paying not a Swiss franc more than what she received was worth. Mrs. Cunningham acknowledged his greeting with a gracious nod. She continued, "Are you starved, Francis? I know we're going to be down late."

Francis smiled and shook his head.

"And not even anything nice for tea. Would you like not to dress? Only you'll both want baths, won't you; so that wouldn't help any. Well, we'll try to be ready by quarter past eight."

From the reception desk the typist with the little pinched face who worked in the inside office called quietly, "Monsieur!"

Francis turned. She had her hands full of mail, and from the mass she detached an envelope. "Voilà, Monsieur!" She gave him a fatigued, mechanical smile.

The square blue envelope lay a moment on the counter where it had dropped while Francis, his knees weak, looked at it. Recovering the use of his hands, he picked it up and said with difficulty, "Merci bien, Mademoiselle."

Facing about, he found that no time had elapsed. Mrs. Cunningham was still not quite to the elevator; Walter, hanging on Maggie's arm, was still in the act of glancing over to see what the girl had wanted Francis for. Francis pocketed the letter. The gate slid shut. The elevator stirred and rose.

Snapping the light on in his room, Francis put the blue envelope on the table. His mind seemed strung to a pitch, ringing and reverberating with a deep tremble of agitation. It was hard to think and he could not repress the continual little quiver of his hands. Opening the wardrobe, he took his dinner coat off its hanger and laid it on the bed. Opening a bureau drawer to get a shirt, he paused, noticing that he still had his overcoat on. He took it off and hung it up. He took off his tweed jacket and hung it on the back of a chair. He pulled his sweater off. Going back to the coat, he got a cigarette from the pocket, went to the

93

table and tore the end from the envelope. In the pen tray lay a box, much worn and almost empty, of Italian wax matches which must have come forgotten in some pocket from Florence. Fumbling with the elastic that kept the lid closed, he extracted a match and lit it. Breathing smoke deeply, he tried to draw the enclosed sheet from the envelope, but the tissue paper lining caught it, so he ripped the envelope down the center. *Darling*—he saw the word numbly, more as if he heard it spoken than as if he were reading it—*I never regretted anything*—

Francis laid it down. He balanced the burning cigarette on the edge of the pen tray and took his shirt off. Picking up the letter again, he saw that the blind was not drawn so he went and pulled it down. Standing by the window he read—*I never doubted anything. Why should you think that? Because I write so badly? I do. I know it. You couldn't imagine what that's like, trying to say something and then you can't, and so you don't write at all. You see, I am a very stupid person. Are you sure you know that?*

Francis moved away from the window. He put the letter down and finished undressing. He slipped on his bathrobe, put the letter in a pocket, picked up the cigarette, and went down to the bath. With the water on, he sat on the edge of the tub and read: *Paris has been horrible, a hell of rain. Do you remember Amiens? Like that, only much worse. And so cold. I wired this morning to ask Aunt Mabel to ask us to Cap d'Ail a week earlier because Gwen says she doesn't care, she is going to buy a fur coat if*—

The sentence broke off. Francis reached toward the water in the tub. It scalded his knuckles and, whipping away, shaking the hand, he turned cold water on and held

94

his stinging fingers under it a moment. Half an inch down the page was written the word *Later,* twice underlined. The flat decorative script went on: *Just before lunch Aunt Mabel wired back we could come any time we wanted. Some people who were going to Africa had to leave. Gwen went right over to see her beau and she actually came back with a two-lits on the blue train tomorrow—*

Mechanically, Francis turned the page back, looking for the date. It was yesterday, he found. *Everything is supposed to be booked weeks ahead to Ventimiglia, but the head of his department has some sort of drag with the P.L.M. My dear, we'll just have to make Mrs. C. come down. I think we can, because you remember she did say something about Menton. This afternoon I dashed around to see Helen—*

Francis shut off the cold water and stood up. He could not see anywhere to throw the cigarette, so he continued to hold it, shifting his fingers gingerly on the hot end. *Mademoiselle almost ate her alive, poor child, because she caught us speaking English in the salon and that is a horrible crime. Helen's going to write her mother that she would like to go down for Christmas. So all you have to do now is tell Mrs. C. that you don't think Montreux is at all good for Walter. There is a nice hotel up the point, called the Eden—*

Unable to hold the cigarette any longer, Francis crushed it out on the window ledge. *My dear, I would be so blissfully happy if you would only come. So you must, mustn't you? Gwen sends her love. She says to tell you that Brentano's has copies of your book. They were English ones. Isn't this a stupid letter, but I am unsteady with joy about going south; and I love you—*

The searching, hardly to be borne heat of the water enveloped Francis. In a plenitude of comfort, he breathed deeper, closing his eyes, feeling his muscles, gratefully warmed, relaxed. It might be twenty minutes to eight, he supposed; so at this instant Lorna and Gwen would be in a taxi bound for the station. The idea caused him a quick, unexpected pang. Thinking of them gone from the hotel on the Rue Jacob, he had a sense of dismay—as though, ten minutes ago, it would have been still possible to go back to Paris, walk down past S. Germain des Prés, turn the corner and find Lorna where he had left her. Now, he thought, now, it wouldn't do any good. There was nothing to go back to.

Sunk in the stone quais of the Gare de Lyon waited the sleek line of long buff-topped blue cars. Francis could hear the bump of luggage, the click of compartment doors opened and closed. Lights gleamed on the sheet steel enameled to look like marquetry; lights blazed in the little washrooms. Down the corridor passed a muffled sonorous voice calling the first service. The cars moved; the high quais went by. That was really the end, the end of Paris; the end of the summer. It gave him a second pang to know that Lorna would be jubilant—probably too happy to eat as she and Gwen faced each other across a table and saw, beyond the black glass, the suburban lights moving faster, growing fewer. Francis could see her sitting there, her face flushed, her fingers locked together, radiant in the glow of the small table lamps, while Gwen with practical calm ordered for herself and Lorna, and calmly, with appetite, ate what she had ordered.

Time passed. Hour after hour, down through the heart of France, the brass bound locomotive, the long shining train drove through the night. Francis could see that, too —the high signal lights coming up, the endless starlit rails. The cars shook gently, jarred on their heavy springs, while in the dark compartment Lorna lay asleep, half on her breast, her neat narrow hip outlined by the thin blanket, her knees bent, her dark hair in disorder against the pillow. From time to time she would stir as some alteration in the ceaseless noise brought her with a sigh close to consciousness.

Back in his room Francis found that it was eight o'clock. He did not think the Cunninghams would be ready at quarter past eight, but they might be ready at half past, and if he hoped to get down and have a drink first, he needed to hurry. He was hastily working studs through the stubborn starched buttonholes of his shirt when Walter's unmistakable limping step sounded in the hall. "Hell!" he said. "Come in!" He attached a collar and took up his tie.

Walter let himself around the door and closed it. Turning his head, Francis saw, surprised, that he had on a bath robe. Walter cleared his throat. "Look, Frank," he said, "we won't be down to dinner."

"Feel all right, don't you?" Francis asked. Maggie's warning jumped to his mind; but, naturally, if Walter didn't feel all right, it would be Maggie who came to tell him.

"Oh, sure," said Walter. He swung the heavy tasseled cord of his bathrobe in a circle. "But, well, Rose died, that is. Maggie started to take her out, and she kind of keeled over—"

"You mean just now?" Francis asked. He spoke with concern, as though the point were very important, in an

97

effort to arouse his mind from its far-off preoccupation, to find something sympathetic and suitable to say. "Has the vet seen her?"

Walter shook his head. "I guess mother doesn't want him," he said. "Rose is dead, all right." He paused. "I guess she thinks he might want to take Rose away and do something to her—you know, cut her up." Francis admired the perception—or was it childishness, bored by explanations and qualifications, not yet much confused by reason? —with which Walter got at unexpressed feelings and things not said. "Very likely," he nodded. "Wait. I'll be along."

Francis thought slowly, the fact bearing in on him, "Poor Rose, poor dog—" Though his mind was still remote, the words set up a stir of probably superfluous pity for the dependent, useless old animal, to whom neither illness nor age nor death could be presented as intelligible, reasonable things; who got stiff, grew blind, until she had no pleasures left outside eating and being warm. She might expect to be allowed to keep those, but her implacable tormentors came around again in a year or so; she could not eat; weak and sick, she still tried to totter through her daily round; so they knocked her down suddenly, poured into her an ultimate, absolute cold; and that was the end of Rose.

"Say, pretty neat!" said Walter.

"What is?"

Walter made a gesture. "Tying the tie. Don't you even have to look in the glass?"

"Yes," said Francis, looking in the glass. He straightened the tie a little. "All right," he said. He slipped into his coat and tucked a handkerchief in the breast pocket.

Maggie was moving about carrying a laundry bag, as though she had forgotten what she planned to do with it, or where she had put Walter's shirts. Her gray hair was loosened, escaping from its ordinary complicated tight pinning-up. Her spectacles were awry on her reddish nose. She made a snuffling sound before she spoke. "Mrs. Cunningham is lying down, Mr. Ellery," she said. She took a handkerchief out of the turned up sleeve of the sweater she still had on and blew her nose. Near the connecting door, which stood ajar, she said, "It's Mr. Ellery, M'am."

Francis looked at what he first took to be a pile of bath towels, part of the half-collected laundry, on the sofa. He saw then that it was Rose, with one towel over her and one towel under her. The towel on top did not quite cover the worn pads of her hind paws.

From the room beyond Mrs. Cunningham said, "Oh, Francis. Do go down and have your dinner. Something's being sent up for Walter and Maggie."

The melancholy distress of her tone abashed Francis. His own unimpaired appetite seemed to him callous. He said, "I'm so sorry about Rose, Mrs. Cunningham. Isn't there something I can do?"

"Well, Francis, have dinner. You must be awfully hungry." With an affectation of composure she said, "I don't know why I should feel so upset. I really brought Rose over because I knew she wouldn't live long. I didn't want her to die alone. I wish I hadn't left her alone this afternoon. It seems a little sentimental, doesn't it?"

"I don't think so," Francis said. "One gets attached to a dog."

"We had her so many years," Mrs. Cunningham said in

a wretched voice. "We got her for Helen, when Helen was a baby."

In the sad atmosphere Walter was ill at ease. He avoided looking at Francis. He sat down and then he got up again. He lifted a crystal bottle of lavender-colored smelling salts from the table, drew the stopper, and cautiously sniffed at it. Francis wondered if it had been brought out to try on Rose. "Sure, she was older than I am," Walter murmured, plainly impressed by the idea.

"Let that be, Walter," Maggie said, taking the bottle away from him. "It's your mother's."

"Whose did I think it was?" asked Walter.

Mrs. Cunningham said, "I don't know that Helen ever cared much about her. She was really my husband's. He was very fond of her." Francis thought of the photographed face, warm with private pleasure or affection; the ridiculous yet dignified droop of the mustache; the sedate stoop to pat Rose's lean white head, while the man gazed down and the devoted bitch gazed up, both well-content. Mrs. Cunningham's voice continued, much troubled, "I don't know quite what to do about—I can't bear to just ask them to come and take her away. Don't you think she could be buried somewhere?"

"Yes," said Francis. "Leave it to me. I'll—"

"I wish she could be put in a box, or something. I mean—"

"Of course," Francis said. "I'll find one." He looked toward the sofa, measuring Rose's concealed form with his eye.

"Oh, Francis, I'd feel so much better if you would! I don't really trust any of these people. But not now. I want you to go and have dinner first."

"I could eat, myself," Walter observed.

"Darling, it will soon be up."

Maggie had moved over to the sofa. She must have noticed that Rose's feet showed, and shaking her head she gave the towel a little tug and covered them. From the floor she picked up the no-longer-required leather lead and began to coil it.

4

AND, of course, another means of decent disposal might be to weight Rose with stones, and take her out and drop her in the lake—*and we commit her body to the deep in sure and certain hope* . . . Francis checked himself, ashamed to idle here over his coffee, making fun of the thing, while Mrs. Cunningham was trusting him to take care of it. He tossed his napkin on the table, nodded to his waiter, and walked out of the dining room to go over to the office.

In the caisse, the proprietor's nephew was counting money. "You look rich," Francis said. He was on friendly terms with the nephew and had several times drunk a glass of beer with him in the evening after the office had been turned over to the concierge.

"Not writing tonight?" the nephew said. He stroked back his thick black hair, stacked together a pile of German ten-mark notes, and tucked them in an envelope. Francis explained about the death of Rose. "I've got to find a place to bury her," he said. "Do you think your uncle would mind if we found a place in the garden?"

"I don't know," the nephew said. He lifted his shoulder a little, tipped his head back toward the closed door of the inner office. "Fait du pétard," he whispered. "Pan! Pan! I wouldn't dare ask him tonight. Soon he's going to the drilling."

"Well, you let me ask him," Francis said. "I've got to do something about it right away."

"Better not," said the nephew, screwing his mouth up. He inclined his head slightly the other way, and Francis noticed that the typist was still working. She pored over some papers, from time to time touching down keys on an adding machine. "He sacked her," the nephew murmured.

"Do you think he's going to sack me?" Francis asked somewhat drily.

"Well, come in," the nephew said. "I'll see."

He went and opened the door to the left, admitting Francis. Then he went over to the door behind and tapped on it. The typist, lifting her tired homely face, showed that she had been crying. "—soir, Monsieur," she said very faintly.

Trying to phrase some friendly remark to make to her —he would have had trouble thinking of one in English; in French he had more trouble—Francis did not hear what the nephew said, but his effort was interrupted by the proprietor's voice in response, a loud snort of annoyance: "Eh, bien! Quoi!"

Through the open door Francis could see him sitting at a desk, his cropped head against the sepia still waters of a large framed photograph of the castle of Chillon. He was wearing a gray-green uniform with stars on the collar tabs. Looking up, he saw Francis looking at him, and he frowned. Then he barked out—in the corner of his eye

Francis could see the typist wince at the sound—"I am very busy, Monsieur. I have an engagement shortly."

Francis stepped to the door. "I'm sorry to have to bother you," he said. "Mrs. Cunningham wanted me to make an inquiry."

Mrs. Cunningham's name had an effect. "Well, what is it?" the proprietor asked, still frowning.

The nephew had drawn aside to let Francis in. His uncle said to him, "Get back and finish! I am late enough already!" He turned to Francis again. "Well, Monsieur?"

There was no particular reason why the proprietor should get up; but on the other hand, Francis saw no reason why he shouldn't. He might be a reserve colonel of infantry; but he was also a hotel proprietor. Francis stared at him a moment to convey his surprise. Then he said, "Mrs. Cunningham's dog has died. Perhaps your nephew told you. She must be buried. Mrs. Cunningham has had her a good many years, and you'll understand how—"

At the word "dog" the proprietor stiffened. "No," he said. "No. I do not understand. My nephew said nothing." His hard light-colored eyes fixed themselves on Francis with a menacing glint. His blond mustache bristled. "What does Madame wish? I cannot spare any more time—" As he looked at Francis the expression of the eyes, the lines of the full face, changed again—a sudden unmasking, a partly voluntary uncovering of more than annoyance or impatience. It was hate.

Neutral for an instant, Francis regarded this disclosure with surprised interest, asking himself what experiences with Americans, or perhaps only with English-speaking people, or perhaps only with hotel patrons, had made the

103

proprietor feel like that; but his disinterested curiosity, a writer's instinctive inquisitiveness, did not engage Francis long. He felt then an emotion of his own rising to answer —the damned cocky little Swiss in his ridiculous uniform! Who did he think he was?

Francis's indignation enlarged itself. It swelled, as he asked himself the question, to a blaze of contempt for the whole monkey house of Europe and Europe's mostly undersized, jabbering, mostly not quite clean inhabitants. In this view, all was lumped together, a year's accumulation of passing annoyances and small disgusts—the shoddy posturing bombast of the new Italy (Francis had not forgotten those sallow blackshirts boarding, at Turin, the train when he came down from Paris with his mother. One of them looked at the book Francis was reading to see if it needed to be confiscated. So they thought they were soldiers, did they? They ought to study their disgraceful history!); La Belle France with its savage avarice and all-pervasive smell of urine; the belching, blockheaded Germans—why should anyone have any patience with any of them? The only demonstrable good reason for their existing was to satisfy the curiosity or serve the convenience of traveling Americans. Francis said, "Perhaps you don't understand because I haven't finished telling you."

"Well? Well?" the proprietor said. He pouted. He made a noise like a pig.

"What we need," Francis said, "is a piece of ground about a yard square. It ought not to be hard to find. Perhaps somewhere in the garden—"

"That is impossible! I have no place to bury dogs. It is unheard of!"

A growing brightness expanded at the back of Francis's skull. Against the heat and light, his conscious thought crossed the foreground in a sort of silhouette. "If you have no place to bury dogs, I advise you to look for one," Francis said. "Mrs. Cunningham wishes the dog to be buried. Now. This evening. Is that clear?"

The proprietor's heavy-seated posture seemed to get heavier. The impatient perked-up tenseness left him. He subsided, paralyzed. From collar to hair roots a flood of dull red suffused his face; his lips shook; his eyes protruded. The resulting appearance of dazed idiocy gave Francis pleasure. Violently pleased, he said, more peremptory, as though he had no time to spare either: "Well, can't you inquire? Call up! Send someone out! Mrs. Cunningham is waiting."

Probably, in the noise of his own breathing, the proprietor did not hear him. Finally, working his lips in and out he managed to say in a thick, husky voice: "You—you tell me—" he hit at his bulky chest, tight under the tunic—"me to look for places to bury dogs?"

It was an object lesson in anger, and seeing before his eyes how anger looked, Francis made an intense effort. "Mrs. Cunningham needs help," he said, forcing mildness and reason into his tone. "I'm doing what I can. I expect you to do what you can."

Francis paused. The sound of battle must be carrying some distance, he realized, for the nephew had reappeared, standing uncertainly in the door. His uncle paid no attention to him; perhaps did not even see him. "You expect—" he cried, choking. He made an effort to stand up. Francis could see the polished black boots drawn in, the fat knees bunch under the straining gray-green cloth. The proprietor's trembling, grabbling hands tried to clutch the chair arms. His voice mounted in a paroxysm of stammering: "You—you—what are you? A boy. A boy. You come to me with dogs—"

The popping eyes, the face now really as red as blood, shocked Francis. He thought, aghast, "Good God, is he going to have a stroke?" He turned, frightened, to the nephew, and said: "I'm sorry. I'm extremely sorry. Is he all right? Is—" Yet, though Francis was sorry, and in the precipitant reversal of feeling, his pleasure and his anger were both gone, he did not like backing down. He said, "He can't shout at me—"

The matter, he saw, was probably being made worse, not better. Francis turned and went past the nephew, out through the office. The typist was sitting terrified, her clenched fist pressed against her mouth, and Francis tried to smile reassuringly at her. He went through the door, crossed the lobby—the concierge too, he saw, had heard something—and walked upstairs.

There were two double pairs of stairs, so a minute or more must have passed while Francis climbed them, but he was not conscious of the interval. Instantly he stood in the upper hall. At the pit of his stomach a sick feeling of exhausted anger made it difficult to get hold of his thoughts; and even his feelings, so many of them at once, were without impelling force. He did not know what to do. In one sense, he was angry still; but it was a low, futile sort of anger—the remediless anger that might fill you when you missed a train, or dropped a watch and broke the crystal. He felt tired, with a slight stiffness or soreness from the afternoon's skiing. He felt baffled and exasperated, wishing he could just forget about the whole business.

This wish was vain; for already he had begun to repeat to himself, searching for the exact words, things that the proprietor had said, and things that he had answered; things that might be said in defense or explanation. But defensive explanation was aside from the point. What exactly had been said, and why, did not matter. If he had involved Mrs. Cunningham—and how could he have failed to involve her?—he had behaved like an ass. He asked her to leave it to him; and she left it to him; and he made of it a stupid occasion to quarrel. You could not get around that!

The apprehension, the self-disgust, the melancholy wish that he had done differently, brought back that uncomfortable vivid moment when, talking about Walter and his work, Francis had remembered those trips down from school, and how his heart had sunk to know so well that the news he brought was inexcusable, that doing so badly was his own grievous fault. Facing the awkwardness of having to report to Mrs. Cunningham that he had done worse than nothing for her, Francis resolved to postpone it. He might go out and talk to the man at the tobacco shop up the terrace; or perhaps the fellow who rented the bicycles could suggest something. He turned, but at the same instant he heard an elevator door clash closed downstairs. At once he had the plausible presentiment that this matter was by no means concluded; that the proprietor, in fury, was going to take it to Mrs. Cunningham. An instinct of ordinary precaution made Francis move quickly. He went down the hall and knocked on the door.

Walter called for him to come in. Walter was twisted

up in an easy chair, legs hanging over one arm, his head against the other, his Caesar propped open against his knees. "We fixed it," he said, rolling his eyes up at Francis. "Martin's going to do it. The waiter. He lives in Villeneuve."

Mrs. Cunningham came from the room beyond. She smiled sadly, but with composure. "Oh, I hope you didn't hurry, Francis," she said. "The waiter took Rose. Martin, that nice one. His mother has a place under some pines where she buries her cats when they die. He's taking Rose home tonight and he's going to put her in a box. We can go up tomorrow and one of his brothers will bury her. Maggie and I will go. You and Walter won't have to upset your morning."

"Well, I'm glad," Francis said. He hesitated, steadying his voice, listening for the rising elevator. "Because I wasn't much of a help. In fact, I expect I put my foot in it." He looked at the palm of his hand and smiled slightly; for he meant to make it a sort of rueful joke, as though he regretted it, but, God help him, he could have done no other.

"The proprietor," he said, "appeared to think that the idea of burying Rose in the garden was insulting. He wasn't very pleasant. I'm afraid I spoke sharply to him."

He looked at Mrs. Cunningham, retaining his rueful expression. If she were to respond, "How stupid of you!" as she so justly might, a rueful expression was what he would need. He would say: "Yes, it was, wasn't it?" meek and deprecatory. The humiliation of not being free to make an ass of himself was something he might as well swallow—that, he realized, was the elevator; and he was in for it. He could hear the quick military tread in the hall.

The sound, if Mrs. Cunningham noticed it, of course meant nothing to her. "Oh, Francis," she said. "I'm so sorry. He's really a very disagreeable man. Was he rude to you? Sit down. Tell me about it."

The relief Francis felt was precarious. It waited on the tramp of boots, almost here now, and probably bringing with them something good for a high look and a proud heart; yet it was relief so great that Francis could breathe again. "I'm the one who's sorry," he said. "I got rather angry. He has a way of speaking—"

On the door came the hard rap.

"Entrez!" called Walter, twisting his head to look.

The door opened briskly. The proprietor wheeled about and almost closed it. He clicked his heels together and bowed. His face had lost its solid apoplectic red; it was still swollen or congested, but the color had ebbed to patches and mottlings. "Madame," he said. He cleared his throat. "I have something that I regret I must see you about."

Mrs. Cunningham looked from his uniform to his face. "It is not entirely convenient for me to see you now," she said. "In the morning would be better."

The cool, even tones were what Francis had expected; but, to his astonishment, they did not have the expected effect. He had never succeeded in it himself, nor seen anyone succeed in it, but Francis half credited the fiction that it was possible, by a dignity of presence (which was certainly Mrs. Cunningham's) or some other mysterious virtue of innate superiority, to abash any impertinent person and, no matter what he had to say or how angry he was, with a word, to silence him. By no means silenced, the proprietor said truculently: "No, Madame. It would not be better."

Mrs. Cunningham gazed at him with utter astonishment. "What did you say?" she asked.

"I said that it would not be better. No, Madame."

Mrs. Cunningham stood speechless, and Francis, angered into defending what he would have said could never need a defense, cut in: "Don't speak that way to Mrs. Cunningham!"

Mrs. Cunningham extended an arm toward Francis and touched his sleeve. The proprietor paid no attention. He went on, "I wish to say to you that I will not be insulted!" Now he did glare at Francis. He gestured toward him with a shaking hand. "He breaks into my private office. He orders me about—"

The insanity of his procedure, supposing the proprietor had any idea of getting redress, of getting Francis into trouble, was manifest. Francis looked at him with unconcerned contempt. "Your nephew asked me to come in," he said.

"I do not speak to you!" cried the proprietor. "Be still, if you please!"

"You are speaking to me," Mrs. Cunningham said. "What is it that you are trying to say?"

"Yes. I am speaking to you, Madame. Good. I am saying to you that you must—"

"Why, really!" Mrs. Cunningham spoke with a sort of gasp. Though breathless, her voice nevertheless had a firmer sound. She must at last be beginning to believe her ears. "I think you forget yourself."

The proprietor, regardless, said, "I do not forget my-self, Madame. I—"

"No, no," Mrs. Cunningham said decidedly. "That will be enough. You are very rude. Go and make out my bill. I shall want it by eight o'clock tomorrow morning. Good evening."

"Yes, Madame," said the proprietor. More than merely preparing for this eventuality, the proprietor showed that he had intentionally provoked it. He visibly savored the costly moment. The excitement of permitting himself in insolence made him shake. "That will be very well, Madame," he said. "I will not have him in my hotel."

"Maggie!" Mrs. Cunningham said.

Maggie had, at some point, appeared silently. Her gaze, full of indignation, rested on the proprietor. She tightened her lips and went and opened the door.

"That will be all," Mrs. Cunningham said.

"Yes, Madame," said the proprietor. "That is all. Good evening."

He marched triumphantly out the door, and Maggie closed it after him so fast that Francis, surprised at the old girl's spirit, guessed she wouldn't have minded if it had caught up with him before he got clear.

"Whee!" said Walter. He laughed. "Desperate Ambrose!" he said. "Where'll we go? Let's go—"

"You go and finish your work, darling."

"Well, why don't we go to Grindelwald?"

"Now, darling, get up. I want you to go to your room and get through. It's long after nine o'clock."

"Ah, heck!" said Walter, getting up. He directed an exaggerated wink at Francis. "Grindelwald," he said.

Maggie said, "Wouldn't I better start some packing, Mrs. Cunningham?"

"Yes. Please do, Maggie. I'll come in a moment." She turned to Francis. "I think we'll move to that hotel by the kursaal. I don't believe they can be very full. That would do for a day or so. Will you see about it, Francis? You know what we need. I hate to ask you to go out, but I don't feel that I want to use the telephone."

"Of course," Francis said. It had been in his mind to say, when they were alone, that he was sorry for having caused all this trouble; but the matter-of-factness of Mrs. Cunningham's tone made him feel that he would surprise her by reopening a subject already closed. If she had appeared a trifle less formidable than he had expected in the face of impertinence, she now showed herself more formidable—not with a grand manner, but with an absoluteness above debate or argument, above explanation or excuse, in her habit of not putting up with what did not suit her. The proprietor had offended; the proprietor, as far as he concerned her, was no more.

Francis remained silent, ready to be dismissed; but Mrs. Cunningham said suddenly, "What would you think of Grindelwald?"

Taken by surprise, Francis answered, "I don't know, really."

The excitements that had crowded his mind, the regrets and fears, still obscured for a moment the importance of the question. With alarm he realized then that it was important. At noon Mrs. Cunningham had no particular reason for leaving Montreux; but now, nine hours later, the decision to move to another hotel, her melancholy over Rose, and Walter's successful afternoon, might make her just about ready to leave. Francis had not a moment to spare if he meant to take a hand in forming her plans for her. "It would depend on Walter," he said slowly.

Trying, uneasy with haste, to scheme intelligently, Francis did not know where to begin. That letter of Helen's to her mother had probably been mailed. It would be indeed a remarkable coincidence if Francis were, to-night, to suggest the substance of a plan that her daughter would be proposing, no doubt with some mention of Lorna, from Paris tomorrow or the next day.

Mrs. Cunningham misunderstood his hesitation. "Is the skiing going to be too hard?" she asked. She spoke directly and simply, looking at him as though he were the one to decide, as though she were ready to believe that his expert eye might have noted more than he had yet had occasion to tell her.

Helen's impending letter prevented a mention of Cap d'Ail; it did not prevent him from insinuating a disadvantage to Walter in Grindelwald. If Francis could not press the plan he wanted, he ought at least to hold up or block any plan that he did not want. He ought to answer regretfully, yes. After all, Grindelwald was not Les Avants. Runs like the one down from Kleine Scheidegg, which Best, with rather vainglorious understatements, had described to Francis, could only be attempted by a skier of some seasons' experience. Francis didn't doubt that it would be too much for him, and if it were too much for him, how could Walter hope—the important yes, thus half justified, and more than half, by Mrs. Cunningham's air of trusting consultation, invited, would not come. Francis waited a moment. If yes were more than he could say, hadn't he the dexterity to say something that would at least imply it, something that might make Mrs. Cunningham rule out Grindelwald herself?

But Mrs. Cunningham was waiting, too. Francis said, "No. It's not too hard. He was all right this afternoon." His mind, rocked by the unlooked-for, treacherous blow to the scheme it had been frantically framing for him, stood off with anger and anguish. Francis said, "But what about this asthma of his?"

"I wish we knew," Mrs. Cunningham said. "It's completely mystifying. He had an attack, not a very bad one, in Paris, during that awful week in October. It might have been the damp. But he has spent whole summers at the seashore without any."

Did Francis expect opportunity to go on knocking forever? He frowned and said, "Maybe altitude has something to do with it. At sea level—" The painfully acquired elements of the art of not making a fool of yourself, remembered in time, shut him up. He finished vaguely: "Perhaps he'd be better off somewhere milder. It might be good for him to get some tennis."

"That's true," Mrs. Cunningham said thoughtfully. "Some friends of ours are at Taormina. They think it would be very good for him there."

This danger could be easily handled, and Francis's hope of being adroit recovered tentatively. "I've heard it's lovely," he said. "But, of course, it's a long way from Paris."

"Yes, it is," Mrs. Cunningham said. "That's one advantage Grindelwald has. Helen could easily come for Christmas."

If he had only dared to mention it, here was a natural opening to bring up a coast, a milder climate, no farther from Paris than Grindelwald. Francis shrank with anxiety. Maybe if he said Menton, or even Rapallo—

Mrs. Cunningham said, "I liked those English boys. It was so nice of them to bother about Walter."

"Yes," said Francis. To cover his inner nervousness he smiled. "They were very decent." He had an idea then. "The truth is, that's one thing I can't help wondering about, as far as Grindelwald is concerned." Mothers being mothers, Mrs. Cunningham might easily find it probable that Troop and Best in Grindelwald would continue to have lots of time for Walter. "I don't think Walter ought to stop work," he observed. "We have a good deal to do. I just wonder how well Grindelwald would mix with study." But that air of arch, honest doubt! That ripe pedagogical concern! Francis stopped, ashamed.

"I know that," Mrs. Cunningham said. She looked at Francis with one of her sudden charming smiles. She said, "Walter hasn't been very well prepared—" She glanced toward the door of Walter's room to assure herself that it was closed. "After all, he's only twelve. I don't know that I really expect him to pass those examinations this year. I don't want you to feel that you're responsible for that. I know it worries you." She paused.

"I've wanted to tell you how happy I've been about this arrangement," she said then. "You've been wonderful with Walter, Francis. There's never been anyone he liked so well; or anyone who was so good for him."

"I'm very glad," Francis said. He felt himself coloring. Mrs. Cunningham's more than kind, almost affectionately maternal, candor spoke, as the show of candor always did, to an impulsive candor of his own. He understood that this was not a virtue. He did not—he was this minute demonstrating that he did not—lack the will to be devious; he simply lacked the skill and patience. How nasty, how damned stupid and tiresome all this ineffective plotting was! The resolution to do no more of it stirred in him; yet abruptly, with passionate distress, Francis felt it less a gesture toward decency or good conscience than as a pusillanimous, a contemptible readiness to fail—still another choice of the less difficult, the meaner way.

Immediately he was possessed with the idea of Lorna. The mute entreaties, the expostulations of a yearning outside reason besieged him. He could hardly bear her absence; he could not bear to let a chance of seeing her go like that. He thought suddenly, standing strained and dry, *And for the peace of you I hold such strife. . . .* The brittle, bitter amusement of seeing that so he did, filled him. The extravagant phrasing—as food to life, as showers—he had to laugh. In terrible silence, he did laugh; but the perfervid wish, the pain of sweetness, survived in things too simple to be touched by the scorn that laughed at extravagance or high-falutin expressions—the way she sank down on a chair drawn out for her; the slight discoloration of nicotine, for she smoked too much, on her graceful emaciated fingers; the bruised undercircling of her eyes, periodically marked enough to show its cause—there was no sure limit to the things like those that, tenderly recalled, he did not find any obvious way to mock.

Still smiling, Mrs. Cunningham proceeded, "I know those boys wouldn't have much time for Walter, and I certainly wouldn't want him to be a nuisance. But they seemed so really interested I thought they might go on taking a little interest in him. I mean, he wouldn't be thrown absolutely on his own."

"I'm sure they would," Francis said apprehensively. He saw their irrelevant faces—Troop's, round and amiable; Best's, pink and white, perhaps conceited; but conceited in a way that would make him do at all costs the kind or decent things he would be admired for doing.

"Francis"—Mrs. Cunningham gave his arm a light, earnest touch—"wouldn't you like to go down to Florence and spend the holidays with your mother? I know you would. And this hasn't been very much fun for you. I'd like you to have a change. Would you go down over Christmas and New Year's? I want to pay your expenses. This is the tenth, isn't it? Suppose we go to Grindelwald at the end of the week. You go down the twenty-third and come back sometime after the first. Would you like that?"

Francis looked at her. The sympathetic generosity of her gaze made him feel like a child. With a sort of despair, he said, "How kind you are."

Three

FRIDAY was a long day. Of course, it had been understood for several days that they were leaving for Grindelwald Friday; but Francis put off writing Lorna until Thursday night. He wrote that Mrs. Cunningham had unfortunately other plans; and how he felt about that; and how he felt about life; and how he felt about Lorna. The task was painful; but he had the writer's fond faith in the power of words; and by the time he had combined the best parts of two drafts in a third and final version two o'clock was past. He went to bed tired, and, if not happy, resigned. In the morning his letter seemed less good, but it was already posted. Francis shrank to think how sad and brave he had sounded; and, anyway, what it boiled down to was that he wasn't a free agent (a fault not easily forgiven in love), and therefore was contenting himself with the hope that absence made the heart grow fonder. The hope was too silly to stand examination by daylight.

Meeting Francis's mood halfway, the whole Oberland was under clouds; and at four o'clock in the afternoon a light drizzle had just ceased falling on Interlaken. The open gravel platforms of the Bahnhof Ost were soaked. Mist hid the mountains. The surrounding fields stretched away damp and silent.

They walked across to the Hotel du Lac by the narrow, canalized cold waters of the Aare between lines of miserable pollarded trees. Walter was tired. Maggie's general attitude, while not exactly disapproving, was that of hoping for the best—as though going to Grindelwald, wherever that might be, were a natural calamity not to be averted, since it was Mrs. Cunningham's wish; but in facing it Maggie meant to exercise foresight so that as little harm as possible would come to Walter from the rash project of encouraging him to slide down mountains. Feeling the dead weight of her glum entourage, Mrs. Cunningham showed traces of exasperation. She spoke sharply to Walter who had begun absent-mindedly to pick his nose while they waited for tea. With impatience she disposed of Maggie's notion that Walter ought to eat a nice egg. The moderate delay caused her to send Francis to find the maître de hotel, or manager, or whoever was in charge.

The train up the valley to Grindelwald did not leave until after dark. Somewhat heartened by the tea, Francis made an effort to keep Walter interested in a game of chess played inconveniently on a small folding pocket board whose men were slips of red and white celluloid and whose squares were slits in the leather. The train, which was cold, seemed to make no progress. They waited a long time above a brilliantly lighted hydroelectric plant. They waited even longer under the massive timbered shed of an avalanche gallery while the windows froze over.

Walter had been restlessly playing to lose the chess game; and in the end he succeeded. Relieved, he scraped clear a small space on the windowpane. They had stopped again and Walter was apparently able to see a station sign.

"Burglauenen," he said. "Is that near? How much farther is it? Say, it's snowing."

Since no one could tell him how much farther it was he subsided and started to draw pictures with his fingernail in the white frosting. Eventually the train moved, began with infinite deliberation a jerking rack-and-pinion climb. After three quarters of an hour they reached Grindelwald.

The vast barn-like bulk of the hotel, seen through the falling snow, rose above them as high as a cliff, with few lights. In the ill-lit lounge, a large glass-enclosed court beside the entrance, there were two people. One was a young woman, obviously English, with pale shining hair, brows arched in a permanent aspect of astonishment above blank wide-open eyes and the characteristic disdainful or ostentatiously fastidious lift of the upper lip. She wore an unbecoming green evening dress with stockings of the wrong shade on her well-formed but too long legs. She was drinking a cocktail and smoking a cigarette in a holder. Not far from her sat a pursey, choleric-looking elderly man, obviously English too, who was still wearing his knickerbocker suit with boots and extra socks. For some surely remarkable reason he was reading a book.

Upstairs the long dark halls were empty. As they passed down them—the heavy tread of the porters with the luggage, Walter's limp, the murmur of the assistant manager's voice as he walked apologetically beside Mrs. Cunningham—they moved echoing through a profound silence that must show most of the building was empty. The lights turned on in the big warm rooms were low and feeble; but nothing could be done about this because some auxiliary system was supplying the electricity. The regular system would be working tomorrow. To the assistant manager, who was explaining, Mrs. Cunningham petulantly said, "This is very inconvenient—"

She left it unfinished, realizing suddenly that she was too tired to care, and wishing only to be bothered no more about it. She said to Francis, "You'd better go with him and see your room. Be sure you're comfortable. At least it is warm enough. I didn't expect it to be." She sat down, and with an heroic effort, smiled. "Poor Francis!" she said. "Hasn't it been a dreadful day! We won't go down to dinner. I don't think we'd better try to have lessons tomorrow. We'll just get up when we feel like it. Good night. Perhaps it won't look so dismal in the morning."

Alone in his room at the end of the hall Francis looked at his luggage. He brooded a moment on the pleasures of a bath but to get dressed, he would have to unpack. "Why, this is hell, nor am I out of it," he thought at random. He washed his hands at the basin. He snapped the light off and went downstairs to the bar. This was empty, except for the man behind it who was drawn close to the low light reading a German newspaper. He made Francis a martini. "Pretty quiet," Francis said.

"Yes, sir. We will not have many people until next week." He went back and took up his paper.

The martini, painfully cold, tasted of varnish. "Let me have another," Francis said, though the effect of the first had been not to warm or cheer him, but to start above his eyes the faint throbbing of a headache. *How comes it then that thou art out of hell?* His mind mechanically returned the senseless lines. *Why, this is hell, nor am I—* "Ah!" he said, with a cold quaking, a drawing-tight of his stomach, he remembered sitting in the bar at the hotel in Milan drinking martinis. He saw Miss Robertson's big solemn

121

face and sturdy legs. He could hear her saying, "You mustn't ask me. You mustn't—" Francis could hardly swallow what was left in the glass. "God damn you!" he said to himself. He stood up and took out a billfold.

The dining room was empty, too; but beyond, in a large dim room that opened from it, there seemed to be a number of people. Francis could not immediately understand what they were doing; but the woman in the green dress, he realized, must be a sort of hostess connected with the hotel staff. She moved about with brisk artificial sprightliness, directing or instigating whatever it was. Several times, informal applause rose. While he ate, Francis could catch glimpses of the applauders, some dressed, some not. From one of these visible groups a girl of fourteen or fifteen, wearing the sort of frock a child would wear to dancing class, stood up and went forward out of his sight. Loud, and in a childish way firm and clear, with elaborate expressiveness, Francis heard her voice: "O what can ail thee, knight-at-arms . . ."

Astounded, Francis realized that the people in there were listening to recitations by their own children and those of their fellow-guests. He sat still, nursing his head by taking care not to move it abruptly, and lifted his eyes from time to time, looking past the open glass doors. The woman in the background, smiling a thin-lipped but loving smile, must be the young performer's mother. She had the strong features of a refined horse. Her hair was piled in great loose wads all over her head; and, as far as Francis could see, she had dressed herself for dinner by pulling around her an ample sheet of puce-colored silk, pinned at various points to cover her undergarments or otherwise spare her modesty. She was surrounded by additional

122

children and two grown-up girls. A marked similarity in
the line of nose and eyebrow made it plain that the man
beyond these girls was their father.

Unlike his wife, he was elegant, though in a manly
way—narrow-headed, spare, and tall. His high forehead,
his direct look, and the clean military cut of his graying
hair gave him the integer-vitae-scelerisque-purus air that
so becomes a person past his youth, and that, perhaps, can
only come to those who have lived a life of gentility, made
materially easy by money, but rigorously bounded on the
public side by the decent duties of respectability, and on
the private side by the ascetic exercise of cleaving to a
conscientious wife, pure, you might feel certain, in
thought, word, and deed.

Francis drank his coffee. These little studies of the
people in the other room depressed him more than ever.
It dispirited him, it added to his loneliness, to consider
the long English occupation of Switzerland implicit in
the artless scene—a hundred years of university mountain
climbers; of deans in mufti inspecting the wonderful
works of God; of lovers of Alpine flowers wandering
lonely as a cloud; of middle-aged walkers, out in stout
boots for their constitutional, ascending (2¼ hrs. guide
unnecessary) to this or that magnificent *VIEW. The holi-
daying families, aloofly jostling each other, bringing their
tea, ordering bottled water, discreetly ascertaining the
whereabouts of the w.c., had—while they preserved its
"foreignness" just as game was preserved at home—made
the country theirs.

Watching the ingenuous, indeed, the boring and stuffy,
means by which this home from home was set up, Francis
felt excluded from them, the only human beings in sight.

They would normally have a deep-rooted dislike or resentment of Americans; but, just as bad, Francis was excluded by his own instinct or unconscious opinion. Speaking to him, Englishmen were almost always kind enough to conceal their abhorrence of him or of America; but how could Francis conceal from himself his feeling—his real feeling, ineradicably established in childhood, and no matter how he tried to correct it by reason or observation, still his—that England, in planting the American colonies, had served her purpose; that her blood and language, her literature and laws, were all in the hands of the rightful heirs? While one might feel a perfunctory gratitude for the long-ago gift, there were limits; and England, by her continuing pretensions, made herself tiresome and ridiculous. Not really unfriendly, but for this reason faintly impatient with the presuming English, what could Francis find to say to that vapid high-minded woman, to those grown-up gawkish girls—since Romney painted Lady Hamilton, had they, Francis wondered, had in England a girl anyone would particularly want? Behind the man's distinguished but fatuously stiff front there might lie interesting things; but where Francis's prejudice ended, the Englishman's began, and he would not be likely to share his interests with any callow young American, whose mere presence at an hotel where one had stopped for years was an example of the pushing transatlantic cheek that made all colonials so hard to bear.

Francis shrugged and prepared to leave. He found then that, seeing, he had not been unseen; and that he was right about English kindness. At least, the woman in the green dress was ready, in her official capacity, to include him. She must have had an eye on him and noticed that he was finishing his dinner. Taking advantage of the recitation's end, she sallied suddenly through the doors with plain purpose.

"Oh, God!" thought Francis, unable to move. Her intention of speaking to him could not be mistaken and he knew that the very dreariness of her proposal, the intensity with which the prospect bored him, would work, not to make him refuse her, but to prick him with compunction for her; and, reluctantly, with bad grace, he would do what she wanted.

But, thus half-resigned, he found himself delivered. A voice cried, "Oh, Miss Poulter! Miss Poulter!" The little reciter in her party dress darted in pursuit, probably not willing to stop showing off so soon. "Miss Poulter, could we—"

The woman in green turned, and Francis's compunction did not go to the quixotic point of missing such a chance. Furtively he sprang to his feet and was out of the room in an instant, and in an instant more, safe in the lift.

The hasty escape had set his head throbbing. Francis walked down the hall to his room screwing his eyes up against the distracting low ache. He kept yawning while, with chilly fingers, he got things out of his bags. Partly unpacked, he sat down on the edge of the bed, trying to make up his mind about having a bath. He did not feel like it so soon after dinner, and the difficulties of looking up a bathroom, of waiting while the water ran, seemed enormous and exhausting. On the other hand, going to bed without taking a bath, not having a bath after traveling all day, seemed a dirty idea. Francis sat in wretched indecision, pondering as desperately as though he had to choose between his money and his life. He held his head.

But in the Eighteenth Century, surely the age of the most civilized human beings who ever lived, people rarely bathed. Instead, they powdered themselves with—the name of the perfumed powder used to mask the odor of sweat eluded him. Francis pressed his head harder—empasma! They employed an empasma.

"Oh, God!" said Francis. "Oh, God—"

He got undressed and put on his pajamas, and went and opened the ventilating device at the window. A scurry of snow, dimly illuminated, drove past the double panes. He put the light out and crawled into bed, shivering against the cold sheets, pressing his aching head into the pillows. He tried to think of nothing; but in his mind formed slowly the picture of an extravagantly tropical shore—the palms, the gardens to the water with marble balustrades and corniced pillars through which showed a sea of cobalt, of a poster-blue not of this world. Quiet surf creamed white where, far off, beyond the Mexique bay, the rocky headlands pushed into the ocean, while Francis surveyed the beautiful coast, calm and remote, as though from a great height. The mythical, the golden afternoon lay over it in enchanted stillness, a marvelous mild radiance. Cool, fitful airs stirred beneath the myrtles and olives where in the shade my love lies dreaming, her beauty beaming—

The picture dissolved and Francis found himself thinking of a girl he had known when he was at college, of walking with her happily in the sunny haze of a bright autumn afternoon through the colored woods beyond Wellesley. With pain he thought, "I could have had her—"

The pain was not for lost enjoyment; but for the recol-

lection of the person walking with her; the dolt, too ingenuous to make his own opportunities, too timid to take
the ones she gave him, who besieged her so many months;
the jackass, with his affectations and posturings—the silly
things he said; the awful, inexperienced things he did!

"Oh, God—" Francis murmured again; but he was
drowsy, only indistinctly aware of his cold feet and his
painful head; and suddenly he slept.

✦

At Montreux most visitors come for the whole winter;
and, with several months to pass, they settle into a careful
monotonous routine. The damp lake's edge, where an
occasional rose blooms in December, is thought to have a
salubrious climate. It attracts semi-invalids whose com-
plaints are not too serious or too incapacitating, or who
suffer from the general indisposition of old age. At any
rate, Montreux's dank thin sunniness is a not inappropriate
setting for invalids. Because they hope, if they do what
the doctor ordered, to put off dying or being reduced to
the last resort of spas and sanatoria, much of their attention centers on the close scrutiny of themselves.

Their symptoms and natural functions absorb them, and
the resulting ups and downs of hope and fear give inward
excitement enough, and more than enough, to lives apparently so humdrum. They go for short slow walks, looking
at the lake, but listening to their fluctuating heart beats.
Some of them take a glass of wine for its medicinal prop-
erties with their meals, and some of them simply take

medicine. They borrow novels from the English library and try to read them while they wonder what that pain during the night meant. Unwilling, worried scatologists, they find books in a chamber pot, sermons in bowel movements—something to ponder when, for consolation or distraction, they sit enjoying a little Offenbach at a kursaal concert; or, in Sunday best, wait in their pews at Saint John's or Christ Church for morning prayer to commence. (O all ye Beasts and Cattle, bless ye the Lord. . . .)

Grindelwald is a different world.

The late dim-lit depressing arrival obscured it for the moment but the difference came to Francis at once, as soon as his eyes opened the next morning. Perhaps people laughing as they went downstairs or the mere animated rise of voices going by in the hall—things never heard at hotels in Montreux—reached Francis when the valet de chambre came in; perhaps from outdoors the noise of sleigh bells, a hearty shout, or the sound of someone whistling had nearly awakened him a moment before. The room was full of the lucid reflected glow of a clear cold day and Francis, even while half-asleep, could feel his heaviness of mind gone as completely as last night's headache; and, in its stead, a light joyful anticipation, as though he were a child and this were Christmas morning.

The tea was hot and good. Francis drank it sitting up in bed and ate his rolls. He got out of bed then, lit a cigarette and, moving to the window, beheld abruptly the gigantic mass of the piled-up mountains.

"My God!" he said, incredulous.

Closing the valley to the south, the solid wall of the Eiger, the immense Mettenberg, the Wetterhorn's vast elevated granite shoulder, stood over Grindelwald in a splendor of morning sunlight, in great bare precipices, in immeasurable sweeping scarps of snow. Far up there, across those exposed sky-high snow fields a tremendous wind must be blowing, for every minute or two puffs arose like a flutter of white flags, drew out, thinned to sparkling smoke and were gone against the deep icy blue. Staring, standing motionless, Francis's heart beat harder with a quick exquisite festivity. It mounted, shining and immortal, in a world immortal and shining, too. Putting on his dressing gown, he went, exultant, along to the bathroom.

Downstairs everything looked cheerful. In the lounge, those expanses of glass that served last night to let in the dark and to show the blind whirl of snow, let in now a blaze of sunlight. The high, ample corridors, then obscure and empty, now seemed bright and cheerful. With a burst of chatter, a group of people came out the dining room doors together and separated in purposeful haste to prepare for some expedition. A couple of young women, plain but pleasant in colored sweaters, their fur coats bulging over their arms, left the elevator and went by Francis with a whiff of carnations. They were followed presently by the father of that family Francis had watched during dinner last night. He looked less forbidding. He lounged along, smiling and agreeable in good tweeds, smoking a pipe from which a pleasant fragrance drifted after him.

Francis had paused, standing aside while he watched. He felt contentedly idle, and in any event, he could do nothing until the Cunninghams got down; but the possibility of Troop and Best appearing among the passers-by occurred to him. He would not want them to think that he had been standing around with the idea of not missing them. He crossed the hall and went down the double steps into the lounge, took up a two-days-old copy of the Paris *Herald* and seated himself in a concealed corner. The stale news was not interesting; but he kept the paper open because it gave him an occupied air, if anyone happened to look in. From time to time voices arose beyond the hall pillars.

Loud and hearty, someone said: "Good kit, that, Mrs.—"

"Oh. Thanks so much, Admiral! I—"

What on earth admirals were doing around here Francis could not imagine, but he pricked his ears up. The subject of his new book had led him to read a good deal of naval history and it would have interested him to talk to somebody who had been through an actual engagement —Jutland, perhaps. Not that there would be much resemblance between the *Huascar's* affair in 1879 and Jutland; and not that any eyewitness except yourself ever noticed the right things—but on the battle cruisers they must have known, like Admiral Grau, that they were for it; and though Beatty's celebrated remark told you something, what men with less chance of being recorded for posterity thought and said might be worth hearing.

More people passed.

"But, good Lord, man, in that case . . ."

". . . the blasted limit!"

The speakers were gone and the sound of the door, revolved for them, arose.

A new voice said with emphasis and satisfaction, ". . . and that takes doing, let me tell you!"

Nobody denied it.

Coming up, someone said good morning, and two people answered together. There was a pause and the door went around. One of the answering voices then said clearly: "Who the devil was that?" A woman responded, "No idea." The door went around again with a stir of fresh air and the sound of horses stamping in the snow and shaking their bells.

"Morning, Miss Poulter."

"Good morning, Admiral. Curling today?"

"When those fellows have the snow off. Good kit, that. Most becoming—"

Looking past his paper Francis saw that the naval dispenser of compliments was the old boy who had been reading in the lounge last night. Though he was of the age—well past sixty—common in Montreux, he did not therefore spend all his time knowing his end or the number of his days. His ruddy, irascible face softened as it followed Miss Poulter, who was clad completely in white —a skating skirt, tights, and a brief braid-covered detachable cloak like a dolman, as though she were the daughter of an hussar regiment, or possibly of a circus. To the admiral the effect was evidently piquant. He looked her up and down with relish, enjoying her show of long legs. "The old goat!" thought Francis, smiling; for the stout, frank display, the forthright, damn-your-eyes adultery going on in his heart was cheerful to see.

Through the glass, beyond the dazzling banks of snow, Miss Poulter came in sight again, passing down the drive and across to the rinks. In summer these were tennis courts, but they had been flooded and several men were now working with big pushers and shovels, still clearing snow from the far end. The posts supporting the back-stops had been topped with gonfalons of colored bunting, lifting and flapping in the wind in a long gay line before the scattered façades of the open platz, and, on the high side, the short spire and snowburdened roof of the English church.

"Hello," said Walter. He propped himself on the arm of the chair and bent his head down to look where Francis was looking. Miss Poulter had appeared on the swept surface of the ice with a skinny black-clad man—probably a professional instructor; though it was apparent that Miss Poulter did not need instruction. The good kit was no doubt one of a number supplied her for advertising purposes by some dress-making firm.

"Who are they?" said Walter. "Say, did you see the notice about the hockey team?"

"No," said Francis.

"It's over there. They're going to have one. I saw Tom and Toby down. Why don't you—"

"Nobody asked me," said Francis. "Besides, I haven't played since I left school. I doubt if I'd be good enough."

"Nobody has to ask you. You just write your name on the list. I'll write it for you, shall I?"

"You'll do nothing of the sort," Francis said.

"Ah, come on! Please, Frank."

"What is this, anyway?" said Francis; but he knew. With proprietary enthusiasm, Walter, as soon as he saw the notice, put Francis mentally on the team, had him perform in dashing and applause-commanding ways; and envisioned, as a result, all kinds of triumphs in which, since Francis represented the emotional equivalent of our side, our team, they could share and share alike.

Sense of self-interest, even if its exact nature was not clear to him, made Walter apologetic. He said defensively: "Well, I know you played hockey. You said so. You—"

"We'll see," Francis said, fending it off.

"You did, didn't you?" Walter insisted, with what was either anxiety or suspicion.

"I did," said Francis shortly.

During those first days with Walter he knew that he had let drop plenty of off-hand remarks from which a bright boy would hardly fail to deduce (and possibly even exaggerate) Francis's decent acquaintance with manly sports. Francis was abashed; both to think that he had done it, and to think that Walter, with one of his ingenuous, unexpected flashes of penetration—a thing Francis never thought of then: the study of Walter was instructive—might have sized-up silently the effort to impress him. "I'll play," Francis said, "if we have time and they need someone. And listen. Go easy on this Toby and Tom stuff. We've hardly met them, and we can't do the kind of skiing they want to do. I think maybe Troop won't mind giving you some pointers sometime; but don't ask him to."

"Gosh, I wasn't going to," said Walter. "I just saw their names. Why don't we find out about some skis?"

"Is your mother down yet?"

"Oh, she's in the office. They're trying to get Paris for her."

"Anything wrong?"

Walter shrugged. "Helen sent her a telegram about somebody going to Geneva or something. Heck."

"Now what?"

"She'll probably be coming tomorrow or the next day. We'll probably have to take her skiing."

"Why not?"

"Oh, it won't be any fun." He swayed back and forth on the chair arm. "She's too bossy."

"You're not very polite," said Francis, feeling that a rebuke should be administered, but not knowing just what, since Walter was very likely right, in the sense that holidays with Helen meant that, to his mother's and Maggie's solicitude, Helen's would be added.

"I know her," said Walter. "She wasn't coming until next week, but she's just sick of Paris. She wanted to go somewhere—I forget. She wrote mother. It's where Lorna Higham is. Do you know?"

Francis had forgotten that letter of Helen's. It dropped from his mind, since he had known before it came that it would be to no purpose; but of course it had duly come and Mrs. Cunningham had duly read it. He paused, considering what he wanted to say. He said then: "I think it's Cap d'Ail. It's near Monte Carlo. It's very pleasant, I'm told."

✦

Francis wished he knew what was in Helen's letter; but to get it out of Walter, supposing Walter knew, he would have to show an interest, by continuing the subject, that might strike Walter as odd. Trying to imagine what Helen would be likely to write was difficult, for Francis had seen little of her. That afternoon when he came to tea with Lorna she had been there; but she was unobtrusive—a tidy, quiet girl with hair somewhat lighter than Walter's. She wore it in a sedate way, smooth, with knots over her ears, and it gave her a quaint grown-up air at variance with her evident shyness. She sat with lowered eyes, speaking when she was spoken to, not looking at anyone—because, you might think, she feared that if she did she would find someone looking at her.

In the lighted dusk of the hotel sitting room, made more comfortable by the outside gloom of an October afternoon in Paris when it was, naturally, raining, Francis had found little time for anything but his own thoughts. Mrs. Cunningham had talked, asking pleasantly about his mother, keeping away from the real point, which was whether, if she stayed in Europe, Walter could be trusted to Francis. From her standpoint the matter was delicate, and her delicacy was so perfect as to be a little disconcerting. While this was new to Francis, Mrs. Cunningham had been all through it often before. Her kindness and consideration—she wanted to put him at ease, both for his sake, and for the sake of seeing more than his best behavior—showed practice.

Thinking back, Francis now understood her position better. To find in Paris someone like Francis, who would be all right on a half dozen counts, probably seemed a stroke of luck to Mrs. Cunningham; but she was practical, and wary for that very reason. If the arrangement were made, and then proved unsatisfactory, there would be complications. She might have to explain, for instance, to Francis's mother, which would be awkward. She could not let herself be hurried, and until she had reached a decision it was more convenient, in case the decision were no, to proceed as though he and Lorna had just dropped in to tea.

This really suited Francis very well. To show himself

to advantage, to try to please not because he liked to be liked, but because he wanted a job, was (wasn't it?) unthinkable. He did not mind pretending that he was not doing it. He wished that he could not see Mrs. Cunningham's purpose as she led the conversation here and there. Surely politeness made him answer her—though with what humiliating self-consciousness!—more or less as she wished to be answered. Meanwhile Walter fidgeted; and poor old Rose lay on her side dozing and illustrating her pleasant dreams with faint eager whimpers and minute motions of running; and Helen looked down, diffident with an older sister's friend, and spoke shyly to Lorna; and Lorna was marvelous.

Lorna sat against the worn dark yellow brocade of an empire settee, brass-mounted with stars and bees. The arms were swan-necked. It had been one of the moments when she seemed to Francis distractingly charming and he was delighted with her—with the color of her eyes, with the infinitely appealing hollow-cheeked face and wide but beautiful mouth, with the dull shine of silk on her crossed legs, the supple use of her fine slender-boned hands in putting a tea cup down or lighting a cigarette— but he had to give his attention to Mrs. Cunningham. He held himself ready to meet at any moment Mrs. Cunningham's eye, readiness or unreadiness to do which, he was fairly sure, Mrs. Cunningham would regard as one of the tests of virtue.

In confused discomfort, Francis tried to keep his wits about him—not knowing what impression he was making; wanting the job because he needed the money; detesting the necessity; thinking how pleasant Mrs. Cunningham was, and what a bore with her questions. One half his mind hoped that his answers suited her. The other half entertained outrageous impulses to say that he had no interest in school requirements, no time for twelve-year-old brats, and no qualifications for the job since he had never learned any of his own lessons outside a few subjects he happened to like. As for his character, he had what might as well be called a marked taste for wine and women, he was self-seeking and self-centered, and she must be crazy if she didn't see that his only motive in taking such a position was to get his keep and a little spare cash while he finished the book he was writing.

When Mrs. Cunningham finally came to indicate that enough ground had been covered for today, the relief of his freedom to leave, of being about to have Lorna to himself, filled Francis with affectionate gratitude to everyone. He said that he would like very much to try some tennis with Walter tomorrow, and noted an address on the Rue des Belles Feuilles. Through this arrangement Helen, who had jumped up prematurely, stood straight and stiff. She wore a grayish-brown skirt and a thin, closely knit, pull-over sweater, also brownish. About her round, still childish, neck was a string of smooth dark beads like beans. Nothing made her conspicuous, unless it was a trick she had of doubling her right arm behind her back and clutching tensely her left elbow. Mrs. Cunningham disapproved of the pose, either for its juvenile awkwardness, or for the unmaidenly way in which it brought out the breasts. Still talking to Francis, Mrs. Cunningham tapped the arm to make Helen stop. Helen let her elbow go, blushed, shook hands with Lorna, and offered her hand then to Francis. Francis took it and said good-by. It was the only conversation he had had with her, and he did not see her again.

2

FRANCIS wiped the undersides of his skis clean and stood them against the wall. "Got it?" he said to Walter, who sat on the bench by the door bent double while he worked at the harness straps.

"Sure," said Walter. He freed his other foot, moving his bad leg stiffly and began to scrape the thick cakes of snow from the wool socks doubled down over his boot tops. "I'll bet we beat them by a mile," he said, peering up sideways.

"Now, don't get cocky," Francis said. "We started first, and this way is a good deal shorter."

"Well, even so—say, you've got a swell tan! Have I?"

"Good enough," said Francis. "It was the glare up at Alpiglen yesterday. Does it bother your eyes?" The painted door beside him opened and a man with a napkin in his hand put a bald head out, blinking at the trampled snow of the road.

"Mittegessen?" Francis said.

"Ja, mein herr—" He began at once to reel off what must be the menu. "What's he say?" demanded Walter. "I haven't the faintest idea," Francis said. He held his hand up. "Jemand hier der englisch spricht?"

"Nein, mein herr."

"In a minute!" Francis said. "We're waiting for some others."

"Ja, ja." The door closed.

"That's all the good German A ever did me," Francis said. "I can read it a little, but—"

"Never mind," Walter said. "If we meet any Romans you can always talk Latin to them."

"That will do from you!" said Francis, amused, but embarrassed too by the "never mind," that seemed to touch unerringly the ruffled pride that would wish, in smiling ease, to speak fluent German while Walter and everyone else looked on with respect and admiration; and perhaps touched too the self-consciousness that (through fear of causing smiles, or of failing to be instantly intelligible) made him hesitate over the little he did know. "All I could understand was something about an ox," he said. "Or maybe it wasn't."

"Maybe it's boeuf-à-la-mode. Ugh! Or just veal. I'll bet it's veal. Or horse. Toby said he thought that stuff the other night was horse. You had it. Remember? Say, what's the difference between an ox and a bull anyway? Are they the same?"

"It's the same animal," Francis said.

"Well, isn't there any difference?"

"The difference is that oxen have certain glands removed. It tends to make them fatter and heavier. Are you cold? We'd better go in if you are."

"I want to see them come down. It's not cold. It's swell in the sun." Walter leaned back against the white wall, closed his eyes and smiled.

On Francis, too, the radiance fell. It lay keen and hot across his face; hot, not on the skin which tingled pleasantly to the freezing air, but under it, permeating the web of muscles (were there thirty of them?), warming the maxillae until the curving bone glowed with comfort, absorbing sun. The shining air had a quality like the clearness of cold water, refreshing you at every breath.

Francis looked at Walter, whose eyes were still closed, his faintly smiling face turned up. Expressed in the smile, Francis saw suddenly, was all the pleasure, inexpressible in words, of being alive. For the moment Walter was completely happy—and happy in a way, Francis would almost have said, and to a degree that he might never reach again. The trouble with this affecting thought, in theory so sound, was that in practice Francis did not find it true. In the rare shining air, lit by the golden snow, sheltered by the warm wall, Francis though taught by experience how to worry, and by the elaboration of ideas and desires, how to be discontented at a moment's notice, was nevertheless completely happy, too—as happy as he had ever been in his life, as happy as he would ever hope to be.

Francis had been looking up the steep rise to the fringes of the pine wood. Abruptly, over the crest, down onto this dazzling expanse, flicked the crouched dark figure of a skier coming like the wind. His poles angled up behind him; the lengthening line of his track streaked a clean shadow on the hanging slope. "Wake up!" Francis said to Walter. "There's Best."

Walter jerked himself erect, lifting a mitten to shield his eyes. "Golly, look at him!" he said. He began to laugh.

Two other figures had appeared by the high edge of the pines. Screwing his eyes up, staring off under his hand, Walter laughed again. "Helen took a spill," he said. "Gosh, she's terrible!" He waved his arm vigorously.

Best, bare-headed, wearing dark goggles, his jacket tied

about his waist, his shirt open on the loose folds of a scarf in his school colors about his neck, slued with a flurry of spangled snow dust into the road above and headed down toward them.

✦

—turned up Sunday, Francis wrote. *Mrs. C. asked at tea how you were and she said you were fine, she saw you just before you went south. I felt like yelling yes, yes, go on; but I said not a word and she immediately dropped it for the dreary topic of herself and her travels—mostly time-tables and how she got from Geneva to Interlaken. Somebody was with her as far as Geneva, for I gather her Mademoiselles regarded such a trip by an unescorted seventeen-year-old girl as little short of épouventable; and maybe Helen herself was not unimpressed by the potential perils and dangers of this night in a wagon-lit—enlivened, no doubt, by visions of suave and sinister Frenchmen with spade beards and boutonnières of the Legion of Honor making improper advances.*

Francis held his pen. "Anything for a laugh!" he said. He went on: *Actually I doubt if such thoughts crossed her mind, for she is a level-headed little thing under her bashfulness. Our Britishers have been fairly attentive and Troop at least gives signs of being much smitten. We've been skiing with them twice, and she was around this afternoon for some time while I futilely tried to show a fantastic hockey team we are getting up which end of the stick you are supposed to hold—we're scheduled to have a game with a hotel up the road tomorrow. Troop, who was al-*

ways falling down, would limp over and sit beside her to recover, very jolly and admiring; but I noticed that her reserve is great enough to keep matters at the Miss Cunningham stage. I think the hitch here may be that it is Best, whose looks are distinguished in the conventional young-blonde-god manner, that takes her fancy, if fancy she is not too shy to have; and he, alas, is aloof—bored and rather hostile to us all, as well he might be, I suppose, since Troop came with him, not with us—

Francis broke off. Then he laid his pen down, took the sheet and ripped it back and forth until he held a handful of fragments. He shot them into the wastepaper basket and drew out a fresh sheet. *The mountains, he wrote, go on being unspeakably grand—nobody could ever imagine anything like the Wetterhorn in the morning—but man is as vile as usual, and I am sick of these damned winter sports. Helen had arrived. Wretched child, she is oblivious to her good fortune in, hardly two weeks ago, having seen and talked to you. Wednesday I'm leaving for Florence to spend Christmas. These dreary festivals! I hope you don't have too merry a time, and as for the new year, to hell with it. Many more months like these last will be the death of me. I must do something about it and so must you. You might begin by writing to Florence that you love me madly . . .*

He sealed the envelope and addressed it—*Villa Apollon, Cap d'Ail, Alpes Maritimes, France.* "Suppose," he said to himself, "I simply went down there Wednesday?"

He sat quiet a moment, thinking of it with attention— probably there was some fairly short way to get over to Turin, to Genoa, and up the coast—as though good clear planning might make it feasible. But what nonsense! By the time he arrived he wouldn't have a cent, nor the slenderest hope of getting a cent. Still, the fact was, he could do it; he was physically able to do it since he had money enough to pay for the tickets. If he went straight to a hotel and registered he could probably count on his clothes and luggage to give him a week at least before anybody began worrying about whether he could pay the bill—anybody except Francis himself. He would worry plenty.

The mere imagining of his plight made him shrink now —shrink not only from the inevitable, appalling show-down in which it would have to end, but also from the few days of grace he could expect, for he would not have even an ordinary amount of money to tide him over those—like that so-called "beau" of Gwen's in Paris; an intense, hollow-eyed youth living on some miserable salary in French francs (for wasn't his bank giving him, free, experience in the foreign service, and opportunity?), tied to long and dreary hours, who, if he bought Gwen a drink, paid for it with his meals next week. This surely was real devotion, a classic, heroic passion that you might think a girl would be moved by. Gwen was moved, all right; she was almost distracted. "But I hardly know him!" she said with a sort of despair. "I met him once at a dance, and he was on the boat last spring. He can't afford to take me to dinner again. I know he can't. My God, what shall I do? I think he's sweet, but—"

Yes, but, but, but!

Francis stood up. He took off the dressing gown in which he had been sitting, straightened his waistcoat and put his coat on. Downstairs he dropped his letter in the box and went along to the bar. Miss Poulter, gowned in

143

a color that must be the one meant by the term "electric blue," sat on a stool talking to the barkeep. "Hallo, there!" she said cordially.

"Good evening," said Francis.

"Are you going out?"

"Not that I know of. I have some work to do."

"My dear man, you have indeed! Everyone under ninety seems to have gone on some razzle up the road. You can't possibly let me down. The orchestra's come and we're supposed to be having dancing."

"How about Troop and Best?"

"Oh, they went. They were in here toping until a few minutes ago."

In the mirror between the fancy bottles and pyramids of glasses Francis saw his face. The snow glare had burnt his skin to a red-brown tone deep enough to make it hard to tell whether or not he had flushed. The barkeep set a cocktail glass in front of him and filled it.

He said, "Thanks, Karl," and took a swallow. Drily and carefully, with detachment, for he did not mean to give Miss Poulter an inkling of anything so absurd, so humiliatingly absurd, as the chagrin he felt to know that, though Troop and Best had been on the rinks with him most of the afternoon, he had not learned anything about this "razzle" to which everyone else under ninety had gone, he said, "I'm afraid I will have to let you down. I have some work I've really got to do." He smiled indulgently. "I am a drudge by nature," he said. "My youth is behind me."

Francis drank the rest of the drink, nodded to her, and to the barkeep to indicate that he should write it down, and went out as though in haste. It was fifteen minutes before the Cunninghams appeared.

✦

Helen's peach-colored dress must have been her best last spring in New York. Something new, made in Paris, had doubtless superseded it; and, rescued by Maggie with exclamations of admiration from the crush of packed clothes, hung now upstairs ready for Christmas or New Year's Eve; but the peach taffeta, simple and good, looked like a party still. Helen herself had a gently flushed, beautifully washed look. Her smooth hair had been brushed until it shone and was arranged with a neatness in which Maggie or her mother must have had a hand. Almost indistinguishable, a scent of rose-geranium surrounded her. She wore a little string of suitably small real pearls. She was all dressed up, and since the chances were she had taken special pains because of Troop and Best, it seemed too bad. Mrs. Cunningham paused a moment at the desk to speak to the clerk, and Francis said, "What a charming dress."

"Thanks," said Helen and added, "it's awfully old." She colored then and literally bit her lip, commemorating awkwardly the fact that once again she had remembered too late that grown-up women do not deprecate compliments, they just acknowledge them gracefully. She moved ahead with Walter, and Francis went into the dining room after them with Mrs. Cunningham.

Mrs. Cunningham, seated, gave Helen an affectionate

critical glance. Satisfied with Helen's appearance, she looked at Walter, and at once said pleasantly, "People will think you haven't any handkerchief, darling."

Walter squirmed a little and investigated his breast pocket, producing a folded corner of linen. "That's better," she said. She looked, Francis thought, highly personable herself, as much a credit to her children as they were to her. The headwaiter stood at her side and she smiled, gracious and agreeable, accepting a menu card. From a chain about her neck hung a collapsible lorgnette in thin white gold and she brought it up, opening it. "Francis, you must be famished after all that hockey," she said. "Do eat a great deal. I think we might have some wine. You choose it. Walter, dearest, look at the menu. You mustn't keep everyone waiting."

"Gosh!" said Walter. "Gray pearls of Volga. I want some of that."

"All they mean is caviar," said Francis.

Mrs. Cunningham said, "Do you suppose the chef is a poet? No, dear, you don't want any. It doesn't agree with you."

"O.K.," said Walter. To Francis he said, "Say, what does S period, A period, G period, mean?"

"Walter!"

"I'll have potage and poule aux what's-it."

"Very well."

"What does it mean, Frank?"

"I don't know. Where did you see it?"

"Maggie writes it on her letters and then puts the stamp over it."

"Oh," said Francis, laughing, "that means Saint Anthony

146

Guide. It's an old Catholic, or maybe Irish, custom. So the letter won't get lost."

Mrs. Cunningham gave up the menu, folded her glasses together and let them fall. "Francis," she said, "I think you're really remarkable. How do you know things like that?"

Francis smiled, not displeased, for by a natural sweetness of address Mrs. Cunningham did make it seem rather remarkable. Walter was craning his neck to look at the table in the corner where Troop and Best ate. "Where is everybody tonight?" he said. "Toby and Tom aren't there."

"I think they went out," Francis said.

Swaying over toward Helen, Walter raised his hand and whispered loudly behind it, "Tough luck!"

"Oh, you keep still!" said Helen, though with good enough temper.

"What did you say, dear?"

"Oh, he's being silly again."

"Walter, please don't sprawl on the table." Turning to Francis she observed (when gentlefolk meet, and the compliments have been exchanged, conversation on general topics of intelligent interest follows as a matter of course); "I was just looking at the paper. Did you see that the German cabinet had resigned? Do you think anything serious is going to happen?"

"It's hard to tell," Francis said; but to answer so poorly was to shirk his social duty and put Mrs. Cunningham to the trouble of selecting another topic. "It's interesting about the Scheidemann business," he said.

"Who's he?" said Walter.

147

"He's the fellow who said in the Reichstag that Gessler and the Monarchists were secretly arming."

Helen volunteered abruptly, "Mademoiselle says there's going to be another war." She then subsided, abashed.

"Maybe she's right," Francis said. He looked from Helen to Walter to Mrs. Cunningham and they made together a pleasant sight, grouped in innocent calmness, and he was struck—he would have liked to write about it, if only he could grasp the dramatic inner meaning that lies in the simultaneous occurrence of diverse things—by the picture of them sitting here in the Alpine night in a flood of light and warmth contained by the shell of the hotel. While good and expensive food was put before them, while a waiter held in a napkin the bottle of Moselle Francis had ordered and twisted a corkscrew, while they waited quietly for the wine and for more food, they looked down from this high mountain on all the kingdoms of the world in a moment of time, and spoke of what they saw, or thought they saw.

Francis went on speaking about Germany, mentioning the names of men he had never seen and knew nothing about, repeating what he more or less correctly remembered reading in some newspaper; surveying Germany from the mountain as it lay out like a map in his mind, the million lights of Berlin in an incandescent vast pattern leagues to the north. The glibly-mentioned Scheidemann, whoever he was, whatever he was trying to do, would be there somewhere—Francis tried to think of him as he must have looked when he finished speaking and the jumble of voices in pain and fury roared traitor, traitor. Francis would have joined any such roar, it seemed to him—at least he would unless, impelled by some awful necessity of conscience or ambition or self-expression, he had been the one to rise and speak, he had been the one roared at.

His eye went out, over Prussia, over the Vistula, over Tannenberg and the snowbound Masurian lakes. Far to the south stretched the incredible, still-feudal fiefs of the Polish counts; far to the east glowed Moscow; all one in the unity of the winter night of Europe, a unity of nightmare in distances, in mountains and rivers, in millions of men and millions of buildings—huts, palaces, fortifications, hospitals; in the intricate web of circumstance, of local condition, of complicated history, of incomprehensible language, of resulting ideas and efforts that Francis would never know enough about to understand.

Where, for instance, was Trotzky tonight? Francis tried to think of him, too; of the tailor's body like a dwarf in its Cossack's greatcoat, of the hope and fear, the love and hate, behind the screwed-up Jewish comedian's face, brooding (in ever deadlier personal peril as, his great services forgotten, enemies in his party worked to pull him down) on the havocs and ecstasies of the Soviet apocalypse—the Byzantine treachery, the torture chambers, the spies in the wall, the concealed revolvers, the monster parades, the waving red flags, the broken furniture and the frozen plumbing. Like scenes from Gulliver's Travels, all day and all night a double column serried past the mummy of Lenin; and in the factories the moron mechanics sang as they ruined the new machines; and in the fields the peasants like Nebuchadnezzar ate grass; and in crowded halls a thousand commissars shouted speeches; and in a thousand frowzy committee rooms the illiterate architects of the future scratched for lice and made mistakes in arithmetic as they tinkered with their millenium. Meanwhile the wine was poured for Mrs. Cunningham and Helen and Francis, and a half a glass for Walter; and down the long bright room came Miss Poulter in her electric blue gown.

Walter and Francis stood up while she paused by Mrs. Cunningham and said to them, "Oh, please don't move. Mrs. Cunningham, we're having a little dance this evening. I hope you'll all come in . . ."

✦

Helen was amiable by nature, and she had been taught to dance well; but once out on the floor, which was far from crowded, she was half-paralyzed. She held her body as though she loathed it and wished she had left it upstairs. When the obligation to speak arose, she spoke with a difficulty that made plain her fear that she was about to say something stupid. She was afraid, too, that Francis danced with her only because he had to; and this fear was so plausible that she must next be afraid that he might think she didn't realize it, and that she was such a fool that she actually imagined dancing with her was fun. Since he thought her a fool and a bore, he certainly didn't have to dance with her. She hadn't asked him to. She didn't really want to dance.

At this point her natural amiability, functioning as common sense, would probably point out to her that he couldn't help it; and that it was her mother's fault for bringing them in here. This was unfair, too; since her mother only wanted her to have a good time; and if, instead, she was

having a simply ghastly time, why, that was her own
fault; for being her hateful self, and not like other girls
who always knew what to say and who danced with grace
and ease so extraordinary that nobody could fail to enjoy
dancing with them.

The struggle to control and conceal these feelings made
them obvious to Francis and easy to follow. He regarded
Helen with compunction (another thing she might fear he
would regard her with); but helping her was uphill work.
He asked about Paris and the school.

"Well, we do a lot of things, I suppose," she said. "I
mean, we're always having classes and things."

"Do you like it?"

"Yes. I like it."

"Are any of the girls amusing?"

She gave him a guarded glance. Either it had never
occurred to her that she was qualified to decide such a
point, or her apprehensive mind, feeling acutely her own
failure to be amusing, wildly wondered if he intended the
question sarcastically.

"There's a Mexican girl," she said with a sort of anguish. "She doesn't speak very good English."

"I thought you weren't allowed to speak English."

"Well, we're not." Helen let her eyes go off toward the
orchestra to see how much longer they were going to continue this interminable music. "But in the—well, everybody does when Mademoiselle isn't around."

"What happens if you get caught?"

"Well, you have to stop. I suppose we're there to learn
French, so—" She gave a shamefaced little shrug. She
missed a step and touched his foot with her slipper. "Oh,
sorry," she said painfully. Her desperate eyes went toward

the orchestra again, but she stopped herself, ashamed of her bad behavior. To make amends, she began a question; but Francis, not expecting such a thing, had begun one, too. They both stopped and she flushed deeply. "Sorry," said Francis, laughing. "What did you say?"

She swallowed, made an effort, and answered, "Nothing. I was just going to ask if you'd heard anything from Lorna."

"Not for some time," Francis said, reminded that Helen was, or had been, a fellow conspirator of his. It gave him a shock, for you could as easily think of Helen, bashful and artless, simple and single-hearted, cast as Lady Macbeth and demanding the daggers. Being incapable of conspiracy, Helen would have little taste for it, and he might as well ignore the (naturally) unsuccessful business and let her, if she would, suppose that Lorna had not told him of it.

"Oh. I thought you might have," Helen said.

Some fresh wave of awkwardness came over her—Francis recognized it by the now-familiar increase of tension under his hand on her firmly formed back. To puzzle out what exactly she meant seemed useless, since there was so good a chance that she meant nothing at all; but her awkwardness could be explained by supposing that she suspected Francis and Lorna of being in love; and this fussed her, for she probably did not like love. Love, too, was a form of conspiracy, its pretty first stage of presents and kisses no more than means to an end. What this end was her mother would not have failed to impart fully and clearly, in the nicest possible way. However, few parents, or none, could keep in countenance through a full explanation without harping on the sacredness and beauty of the arrangement; and an adolescent girl was more likely to come away intimidated than reassured. The sacredness and beauty would not be very clear without the solicitations of strong feeling. If she knew nothing of these solicitations, they were not readily imaginable. If she had discovered their nature by herself, subsequent remorse and self-reproach were sure to have made them distressing and repellant. In either event she would try to think of "all that" as little as might be; and in either event it was natural to view her sympathetically.

To make a diversion, Francis murmured: "Don't miss the Admiral."

At once he wondered if his diversion, picked at random, the first that occurred to him, had been fortunate. The Admiral, swelling with exertion, his eyes glinting in a foxy triumph of appetite over senescence, trotted rapidly in and out of the moving dancers, hugging Miss Poulter in time to the music; and, viewed squeamishly, the spectacle had its disgusting side. However, Helen, if squeamish, was not so squeamish as that. Magically, the stout bouncing old man must have restored for her a comfortable school-girl's-eye view of life. She gazed past Francis's shoulder a moment and giggled. Trailing out, falling to pieces with much pounding of his drums by the tall sunken-cheeked drummer the music came to a halt. A dreary silence, broken by the sound of someone clapping and the scuff of feet as the dozen, mostly middle-aged, couples turned to leave the floor, descended.

Released, Helen stood an instant with the school-girl's repressed grin still lighting her face. She colored then, returning to her painful age. "Thanks very much," she said, precipitate and husky in renewed self-consciousness. She moved quickly to get back to her mother.

Mrs. Cunningham said, "You look very nice on the floor, dearest." Sitting just behind, in the second of the two rows of folding chairs arranged around the walls, Maggie had appeared; and putting aside her knitting, she shook out a shawl. "You'll be catching cold," she said to Helen.

"I don't need it," Helen protested; but she let Maggie settle the folds of silk over her shoulders. "How lovely," Francis said, looking at the intricate burst of big embroidered flowers.

"You know, it used to be my mother's," Mrs. Cunningham said. "I was so pleased when they started wearing them again. Though I don't believe it ever was worn; I'm sure mother thought it was too loud. A friend of hers, who was a missionary, brought it back from China. I always thought it a rather odd thing for a missionary to pick out."

"Was he the guy who wanted to marry her?" asked Walter.

"Well, darling, I don't know that he really did. And I don't know how you know anything about it."

"You were telling Edith when she said Helen could have it. I know. He's a bishop."

"Well, darling, he was a bishop. He died several years ago. His wanting to marry her was an old family joke your Great-aunt Clara used to tease her about."

"Then there was all that lovely lace—from the Philippine Islands, I think," said Maggie. She half stood up and shifted the shawl a little on Helen's shoulders.

"Oh, please don't, Maggie," said Helen. "It's all right!"

"It was all falling down, dear," Maggie said, settling back again.

"Francis," said Mrs. Cunningham, "I think it would be an act of charity if you would go and dance with poor Miss Poulter. She was having a very hard time with her elderly admirer. Why don't you."

"She's the queen of the village green," said Walter.

"What a silly thing to say, darling. Do go, Francis, before the music starts or she'll be caught again."

Francis arose and crossed the floor to Miss Poulter who was standing down by the pine trimmed bower which housed the orchestra, talking to the leader.

"Will I not!" she said to Francis. "Would you like a waltz? Everyone else would." Her hand dropped on his arm, holding it, and she spoke to the orchestra leader in German. Switching about, he faced his musicians, struck two sharp taps, and out of the bower, with a ponderously gay rocking-horse swing, the Blue Danube began to gush.

✦

Miss Poulter, moving into Francis's embrace, proved to be peculiarly made. Her head rose to within an inch or two of his; but her neck was long enough to make her shoulders lower than you expected. On the contrary, her arms in proportion to her height were shorter than you would expect. Under the blue gown a kind of tight garment encased her and gave her high stomach a flat board-like front, from beneath which her long well-muscled thighs moved with vigor and precision. She smelt of clean sweat and some borated dusting powder with orris root in it.

Though nimble and light on her feet, Miss Poulter did not let herself be led easily, and Francis found that she required firm handling. This she resisted for a moment or two, covering her stubbornness in going her own way by a real or affected absorption in the review of her social charges. Then abruptly she gave in, let her boarded-up stomach come against Francis, tightened her fingers a moment on his left hand and said, "I was awfully angry at you before dinner."

This could only refer to his flight from the bar. To explain that, if he had been rude, he had been rude in revenge, because he was offended; and that he had been offended because a couple of kids neglected to ask him (he couldn't and wouldn't have accepted) to go out with them, would not please her and would be painful to Francis. He feigned great surprise. "You appall me," he said.

"Why did you say you had to work?"

"Because I did have to. And I still do."

"Why don't you chuck it? I'm going out to skate later. There's a marvelous moon. Why don't you come?"

"It would be too embarrassing," said Francis. "I've seen you skate. I'm not quite in your class."

"What rot! I saw you playing hockey this afternoon and you're frightfully good. You made our Public School men look a bit silly, didn't you?"

Francis thought with interest, "So that's how it is!" The acid emphasis, the not-altogether-convincing tone of amused disdain, could mean only one thing. Making her way through the intricacies of the English social system,

Miss Poulter, like the Ephraimites, came down to Jordan hoping to get over; but the Public School men, having heard her say one or more of a hundred well-established shibboleths, killed her with a look; and she would just have to make the best of the limbo where the lower classes were lost. Francis dared say she was now, wounded and angry, making the best of it. "Speaking of ice," Francis said, "would you mind if I asked an idle question?"

"I don't see why. Should I?"

"How did you learn to skate like that? I didn't know ice had been introduced into England yet."

"Oh, we have ice. Quite often. However, I didn't learn in England." Her upper lip lifted a little in her fastidious expression. "As a matter of fact, I was at school in Switzerland when I was a kiddy. My people were in the Diplomatic Service."

Best or Troop, Francis reflected, would probably know that they were like hell. At any rate, you could take it as proved that Miss Poulter had a natural wish to represent herself as a person of quality; and the vanity of so wishing could hardly be more apparent. Her present circumstances, she meant him to know, were misleading; appearances were deceptive. Francis found himself growing uncomfortable, for there had assuredly been times in the past (and he did not know but what they continued into the present) when it had seemed desirable to him to make such a point on his own behalf. The hard fact was, circumstances rarely misled, and appearances were always full of truth. Neither he nor Miss Poulter, by credible or incredible claims on a more impressive background, would change the fact that people of worldly consequence are not obliged to earn their living as professional hostesses at a hotel, nor as private tutors. People who are poor, while they may be estimable and virtuous, confess in the fact of poverty an incapacity for mastering their environment; and what excuse or justification their incapacity may have interests only themselves.

Miss Poulter, with disconcerting aptness, said, "You're a writer, aren't you?"

"At the moment I am mostly a tutor," Francis answered, fresh from his lesson.

"I think the little lame lad is sweet. Is he nice?"

"Yes, he is," Francis said, feeling that in some ways it was an understatement. Walter's patience in his affliction, good temper, and politeness cost him, being expressions of a disposition, no special effort and so perhaps deserved no special credit from the moral standpoint; but they were none the less ornaments to character.

"Is that his sister? I think she's frightfully attractive. Shy, isn't she?"

"Is she?" said Francis, repelled by a tone intent and predacious that seemed to pick over the Cunninghams rapidly with an eye eager for any little things it might be useful to know.

"Yes," said Miss Poulter. "But she rather fancies you."

Flabbergasted—the suggestion was put forward with such positiveness; annoyed—was she felicitating him as one freebooter to another on solid advantages bound to result from his shrewd imposition on a school-girl?—Francis began tartly: "As a matter of fact—" The habit of speaking first and thinking afterward had nearly made him say that if Helen fancied anyone she fancied the Best boy. He bit his lip and said, "You're mistaken, I think."

"My dear man, she never takes her eyes off you!"

"I must see about that," Francis said coldly. He pivoted Miss Poulter around and looked over toward the Cunninghams. Helen was talking to Walter, obviously in an argument. The effect of the beautiful flowered shawl was demure, like a dressed-up child. Though she sat with the straightness of good training, the argument made her wriggle with belligerence; and it would have been no great surprise if, finding herself scored on, she began to poke and pull Walter. "She seems to have lost interest," Francis said sarcastically.

"Are you offended?" Miss Poulter asked. In order to look at him, she backed off, becoming hard to lead again.

"Not in the least," said Francis. He tightened his arm brusquely, forcing her toward him. "Come back here!" he said with irritation, for she resisted him. "I'm running this."

"You *are* offended!" Miss Poulter said. She squeezed his hand. "Don't be." Docilely she moved close against him. Past his ear she murmured: "Of course you know we're the cynosure of all eyes."

"I should hope so," Francis said shortly. "Don't you like it?"

Miss Poulter was silent an instant. "What would you think if I said yes?" she asked finally.

"Say it and I'll see," said Francis, baffled by the change in her voice.

"Can't you tell I do?" she said, speaking in a whisper. "Much too much." She squeezed his hand again. "Come skating, won't you?"

Francis almost let go of her. "Why, the simple bitch!" he thought. "Does she imagine—" The music sank rollicking into silence, and he did let her go, trying to compose his features. The sense of outrage had made him flush; but Miss Poulter scanned his face with a knowing, soft-eyed look that plainly credited his color to the emotional effects of his coy little courtship by friction, and to excitement over her hint of more, and more complete, satisfactions possibly to come later. "About eleven-thirty," she said, dismissing him as she turned to go up to the orchestra.

"Why, the simple bitch!" Francis repeated to himself. He was incapable of speaking; but Miss Poulter seemed not to have expected any response. He moved across the floor to the Cunninghams suffering surges of mortification. The low and vulgar intent she must have seen in his measures to get her close enough to be led, the insulting assumption that he had no better taste than to be attracted to her, kept him hot with anger; yet, at the same time, he could not close his ears entirely to the still small voice, like that of conscience in its punctual awakening and calm persistence (and in the incidental complacency of being right, not unlike that of conscience), which heeded his indignation very little and whispered: *You know, you could lay her if you wanted to. . . .*

Mrs. Cunningham welcomed him with a smile. "Francis, you waltz beautifully," she said.

Francis regarded her, surprised; for, though pleasing, the compliment discomposed him. It was one thing to dance well; it was another to be beautiful about it. He said lamely: "She's really very good." It sounded, to his chagrin, much like one of Helen's rejoinders, and to cover it up he added, "Have you seen her skate? She's marvelous."

"You know," Mrs. Cunningham said, "I think I saw

her skating last night—very late. She seemed to be by herself. Where do you suppose she comes from? Do you think, from an agency, or something of that kind?"

"The cat brought her in," said Walter.

"Walter, I think you'll have to go upstairs in just a moment."

"Aw, heck, what did I do?"

"You're too fresh," said Helen.

"I don't want to have to speak to you about it again, Walter."

"I was only joking."

"Well, darling, it wasn't very funny. We'll stay for one more dance."

Helen, Francis felt sure, would much prefer not to dance again; but he saw that he would have to ask her. To his surprise, she got up with alacrity, not easy, but much easier than she had been before; and easier in some ways than Francis, who was not unaware when Miss Poulter, over the shoulder of a new partner who was too short for her, looked at him and Helen (very likely to see what licentious exercises he was practicing now). In annoyance he turned sharply away, making Helen miss a step.

"My fault," he said.

"No, it wasn't," said Helen. "I didn't follow." Though apologetic, she spoke without confusion; and Francis, with a start, dismayed at his own denseness, saw why. Mrs. Cunningham had noticed Helen's discomfort during the first dance and taken the simple steps to relieve it. She told Helen that she looked well on the floor. She sent Francis to dance with Miss Poulter so that he would not just sit there patiently waiting for duty to call again. When Francis returned, nominally she told him, but actually she told Helen, that he, too, danced well. And there it was. Helen, without knowing why, found herself composed, and even, from her own point of view, bold. "You're leaving Wednesday, aren't you?" she said.

Francis said that he was.

Since that had been all right, Helen drew a breath and went on recklessly, "Does it take more than a day to get to Florence from here?"

"I'll have to stay over night at Milan," Francis said. Recollection of the last occasion of his staying over at Milan made him wince; but he could not help seeing that Helen was growing nervous. Her phenomenal feat of initiative had surprised her as much as it surprised Francis, and she was elated; but if she did not get any help, all Mrs. Cunningham's deft work would be undone. "When are you going back to Paris?" Francis asked quickly.

"After New Year's, I think," she said. "I suppose, when mother leaves."

Taken aback, for Mrs. Cunningham, though certainly she did not have to give him advance notice, had not mentioned leaving, Francis waited a moment. To ask when her mother was going, and where, would be to let Helen know that nothing had been said to him, and he was reluctant to do that. He said: "I think it's fine here for Walter. But we have a lot of work to get through."

"I don't think it's very good for him," Helen said. She blushed, nearly stammering over so positive a contradiction; but the female prerogative to warn, to comfort and command supported her and she pressed on with severity. "He had some asthma the night before last. Maggie and mother think it was something he ate. I think it's too much excitement." Her attention was attracted, and she said, vindicated, "I guess Maggie's going to take him up now. Yes. She is. It's about time! It must be ten o'clock."

Turning his head to look for Mrs. Cunningham, Francis's eye came first on Miss Poulter. As she moved across the floor it could be seen from this angle that the shaved armpit disclosed by her lifted right arm could stand shaving again. Walter and Maggie were on their way to the door down the side, and Mrs. Cunningham sat alone, Helen's bright shawl hanging over the back of the chair beside her. Francis met her glance, and Mrs. Cunningham smiled and shook her head, reading his question.

Helen was preparing (you could feel the resolution rise in her) to make another remark, which would probably be something more about Walter, and so would get them even farther from the subject. Francis saw that he had better give up the credit of omniscience. He said: "Did your mother say where she thought of going?"

"Oh," said Helen. "Well, I thought probably you knew. I don't think she's told Walter. I think she's going to the Riviera. I thought maybe you'd heard from Lorna. I know she wrote Lorna's aunt about a hotel near there."

"I see," said Francis. He spoke weakly, conscious of the loudness of the music. He moved numbly, hardly knowing what to think, what to make of it, what it meant.

"That might be good for Walter," he said. The remark sounded strained and false to him, since, if it were good for anyone, he was the one for whom it was good, for whom it was wildly desirable. Either because his mind, trained to have no serious thought of seeing Lorna, refused to credit the simple statement; or because this way of hearing it, blurted out incidentally in a trivial conversation, somehow spoiled it, the thing Francis had so much wished for did not bring much satisfaction.

Still numb, his heart still beating heavily with shock, Francis was thinking then of Miss Poulter—the muscled legs, the flattened abdomen, the raised bare right arm. With slow incredulous recoil he knew, because now she wouldn't, that five minutes ago it had been as good as certain that when eleven-thirty came Miss Poulter would have found him waiting for her in the bar.

Four

THE DOORS, decorated with criss-crossed greens bound by red ribbons, closed behind them and Francis came with his mother from the windy vestibule onto the Lung'Arno. Above the joined wings of the near-by Corsini palace, the sky, darkened by moving storm clouds and late afternoon, was one of those invented by Gustave Doré to emphasize important Biblical calamities. A colorless light filled the empty quay. Up toward the fine flattened spans of the Trinità bridge, cold little waves about the same color as the stone wrinkled the river. His mother took his arm and Francis said to her, "Do you really want to walk? It must be almost a mile."

"I think so," she answered. "Doctor Giglioli said I ought to walk more. If I feel tired there are usually cabs down by the Grand Hotel. You didn't have a very good time, did you."

"No," said Francis. He felt the glum repletion that may be expected to follow a holiday dinner with several wines begun in the early afternoon.

"Still, I think it was kind of them to ask us."

"No doubt," said Francis. "Mrs. Jasper thought so, all right. This damned business of being poor!"

His mother said, "Sometimes I wish you didn't remind me so much of your Grandfather Ellery. That was his complaint, too. He always felt that he was entitled to live on a certain scale; and so he did, long after there was really no money left. For years before your father died, he was always paying the debts."

"Oh, Lord!" said Francis, exasperated both by the arbitrary non sequitur, and by the justness of the resentment that had provoked her to it. She responded not to his words, but to a complaining tone; and Francis could hardly doubt that she was right. It was the tone of the selfish and conceited old man, the spoiled sexagenarian baby, who considered the part of a gentleman of leisure done when he had called attention to any straitening of his circumstances; who sulked majestically at criticism of his debts, since they were no fault of his—he hadn't chosen to incur them, and it was a humiliation to him that he owed any man a penny. What he did owe, he owed because the world at large had stopped, without right or reason, making him proper provision. When the world came to its senses and recognized that he, not it, was the one entitled to judge his financial requirements he would set everything in order and meet every obligation fully and promptly. His creditors knew his name and knew him; and they had his word. What more did they want?

This senseless presumption, and the stupid irresponsibility, the (to give it its right name) dishonesty, on which the presumption rested, were not agreeable to think about; and, angrier, Francis said, "Am I supposed to like it when a couple of overstuffed old imbeciles like your Jaspers can go around being kind to us? Lord God, that dining room! Those stamped leather curtains. Those beautiful, beautiful oak carvings! Those gold inscriptions! All from Dante. Did you hear Parker"—he let his voice mimic Mrs. Jasper's addressing her husband—"tell how he came to pick them out? Fiorian Fiorenza; and how about the seven muses pointing Parker, pot-belly and all, to the Bear?"

"I think it was a great deal pleasanter than having Christmas dinner at the hotel. I suppose poor Parker is a little dull. I remember that everyone was surprised when Carrie married him."

"Surprised?" said Francis. "I would have thought they were made for each other. Dullness with transport eyes the lively dunce!"

"Well, darling, let's drop it. They were friends of mine many years ago, and they've been kindness itself to me this winter. I wish you'd be able to talk a little more; you seemed so sullen; but I know it was hard for you." They came to the corner by the opening of the little Piazza Ponte Carraia and crossed over. "Faith Robertson's mother lives there," she said. "I've had tea with her once or twice. Did I write you? She told me that Faith said you were so nice to her, going to Milan."

"Did she?" said Francis.

"She said you had dinner with her. You never wrote me that. She's such a plain girl, I suppose men don't bother with her much. It shows you can be pleasant when you want to. I never understand why you don't want to."

"I don't understand either," Francis said. "So let's drop that, too."

"Francis, another thing I never understand is why you are so rude to me. I don't like it."

"Sorry," Francis said. He walked in silence, feeling that it would not have hurt him to make a better apology (it was certainly not her fault that he had found her comment uncomfortable), yet unable to make it; just as, though recognizing them, he was helpless against the complicated,

167

mostly misbecoming impulses that made him (the term was not too strong) rude to her. He heartily hoped, understanding why so well himself, that she never did understand. He could not excuse and he would not care to avow the plain fact that anger filled him when she courageously made the efforts she must make if, being ill and alone, she were to support her circumstances at all. He was ashamed to think that far from admiring as he should the patience she must show if she were to be liked by the after all agreeable and kindly people on whom she depended for any sort of society or companionship, he detested her patience as a humiliation in itself, a wound to pride reaching through her to him.

"Far enough?" he asked, trying by solicitude to show himself that he had some virtuous principles. He paused at the corner of the Piazza Manin, looking at the disturbed sky as though a weighty concern for her immediate well-being could count as a point in his favor. By the cramped front of Ognissanti were two cabs. "I think we'd better take one of those," he said. "It may rain in a minute, and I don't want you to get wet."

His mother said, "No, I'm not tired. It's a little shorter, I always think, to go over and up the Via Montebello." They walked on, and she added, for they were suddenly sheltered from the bitter river wind, "That's better. We should have done that before."

"Are you cold?" he said alertly. The effort of penitence was becoming successful, and he was really feeling the anxiety he wanted to feel.

"No. I'm very warmly dressed." She took his arm again and said, "You haven't told me much about Grindelwald."

"There's nothing to tell. Walter's in heaven. It almost

seems a shame to take him away. But on the other hand, I suppose we wouldn't get much work done. He'll have all this week."

"What kind of a girl is Helen?"

"Harmless."

"Do you like her?"

"Yes."

"She's going back to Paris, isn't she?"

"Yes, as far as I know."

"Did you see a great deal of her?"

"Well, she was there. Why?"

"I wondered. You'll be seeing Lorna Higham when you go to the Riviera, won't you?"

"I imagine so. Mrs. Cunningham's planning to stay at a hotel at Cap d'Ail. She knows Lorna's aunt. I don't think very well."

"I suppose Lorna's going to be with her aunt for some time?"

"I really don't know."

"It would be rather a blow to you if she left as soon as you got there, wouldn't it?"

"I would be sorry. Why do you ask?"

"Well, darling, I thought you seemed rather fond of her in Paris."

"I like her," Francis said uncomfortably.

"I thought she was a pretty girl."

Preferring to take this as a comment needing no answer, Francis made none.

His mother said, "If you don't want to talk about her, I won't make you. You like her better than Helen, don't you?"

"Good God!" said Francis. "Why should I like Helen?"

"You said you liked her."

"What is this?" asked Francis. "A plot?" He laughed.

"What do you mean, dear?"

"It's a long story," Francis said. He laughed again, asserting, against his embarrassment, a great ease or good humor. "An English girl, a sort of hostess at the hotel, took it on herself to insist that Helen had a sentimental interest in me. It just isn't so; and I don't feel any in her, either."

"Don't be cross, dear. When we get back I have something rather amusing to tell you."

"I'm not cross. What is the amusing thing?"

"Wait. I'll feel more like telling you when I've had some tea."

They passed behind the Garabaldi monument in the gathering dusk and turned up the Via Solferino. A single weak light burned in the entrance hall of the hotel. Beyond, where a little sun parlor opened in summer on the garden, Francis saw the dark shape of a man huddled in an overcoat, sitting in one of the wicker chairs. Slumped down, he seemed to have been asleep, but their steps on the bare tiles roused him. He stirred, his face turning toward them. With enormous difficulty he got to his feet and stood not quite straight. He gave Francis's mother a shaky, infirm bow.

"Who in God's name is that?" Francis murmured.

"Sh!" said his mother. The man had begun to move out purposefully, looking up to see where they were and down to see where he was walking. Rising and falling in the poor light, his face, incredibly old and sick, was like the face of death. Francis's mother said: "I'm very glad to see you up again, Mr. Woodward. I hope you're feeling much better."

"Thank you," said the old man. "I feel pretty well. I wanted to wish you a merry Christmas, Mrs. Ellery. This is your son, I suppose." He swung his wasted face toward Francis and advanced a hand, bony and loose-skinned; and though dry, slippery to the touch and cold. Francis let it go and said, "How do you do, sir."

"Merry Christmas to you too," said the old man, beginning to move away. "I just sat down to rest a moment," he said, still moving. "I find I tire easily. Good night. Good night." Slowly and cautiously he went on into the darkness along the hall.

"Look into the dining room and see if you can find Victor, darling. I suppose you aren't hungry, but he might as well bring up some tea. Poor Mr. Woodward! I feel so sorry for him. I must tell you about him."

When Francis, following her upstairs a few moments later, reached her room she had taken her coat and hat off. "Light the fire," she said to him. "It's an extravagance. They really keep the house quite warm, but it's more cheerful. Faith Robertson's mother told me it was simply freezing where she is. I think Faith is in town, by the way."

Stooping over the grate Francis struck a match. "What about this Woodward man?"

"Oh," said his mother, arrested, "he's been very ill. His wife died a year or so ago. They'd been living here for a long time. I don't think he has anywhere else to go. He's so old and he has very little money—" Though distressed, as anyone would have to be, she spoke with animation, unconsciously laying to herself the grand solatium of the idea of people lonelier and worse off, much older than she was, and yet still living, or still not dead.

Francis said, "I know. Montreux was full of them."

"I thought he might interest you. He used to be an editor of some quite good magazine. The *Century*, perhaps. He was the friend of a lot of people—George William Curtis, and Frank L. Stockton, and Brander Matthews . . ."

"Lord!" said Francis.

"I know you don't think much of them as writers; but they were quite distinguished once. Before he was ill he asked me to lend him one of your books. He said he thought it was a very fine piece of work."

"What else could he say?" asked Francis. "Mother, I wish you wouldn't do that."

"Do what?" she said rather sharply.

"Well, force my damned books on people. No one's interested in them."

"He was very much interested."

"Does it seem likely?" said Francis. "In the first place I don't write books for friends of Brander Matthews. In the second place—"

"You sound so silly and self-conscious, Francis. I never mentioned you to him. Miss Wilson told him that you were a writer. He asked me if—yes! Avanti! Oh, thank you, Victor. I think we could have it here."

In the increasing light of the fire Francis stood silent while the tea things were disposed. When the door had closed his mother said, "Sit down and have some tea. We won't say any more about it. Though I wish you wouldn't act always as if you thought I were a complete fool. I'm really not, you know. Naturally I'm interested in your work."

"I don't think you're a fool. It's just that the books aren't good, and the less people see of them, the better." He sat down wearily, recognizing that (while he meant what he said and it was true) his real feeling was that what he wrote was his own. He did not want work of his pressed with maternal pride on other people, who, bored and perhaps privately derisive, would skip through it, tchick-tchicking with the satisfaction of superiority over faults that Francis was already aware of.

"Well, darling, I don't think they're bad. But of course you're going to do better. How do you like your new book?"

"That's lousy too."

"Oh, darling!"

"Well, I don't know. At this rate I'll never get it done anyway and maybe that would be just as well." He spoke sincerely, for like most writers, he had begun to write before he had the judgment to see the almost hopeless difficulties; and by the time he was old enough for judgment to begin to develop, it was too late, he liked to write. He drank some tea and said, "You were going to tell me something amusing."

"Yes. I was." She paused and the firelight on her face and carefully arranged gray hair seemed to flicker a little as she overcame a quiver of indecision. She said: "I had a letter from Mrs. Cunningham. Really a very nice letter."

"When was this?"

"Well, yesterday. I didn't know whether to speak to you about it or not."

Francis frowned. The hesitation, indicating some difficulty, surprised and disquieted him. His relationship with Mrs. Cunningham had become settled and easy, and he was confident of her liking for him; while her candor, as of one discerning person to another, gave him pleasant assurance of a good understanding with her. "Has she decided she'd like to get rid of me?" he asked. "I can't say I'd blame her."

"Oh, no. I don't think so. Why wouldn't you blame her?"

"I don't think I'm entirely fitted for the position."

"Well, darling, she speaks very highly of you. I think she's more than satisfied that way. She said that Walter was devoted to you; and that you'd been most helpful to her. She seemed really touched by what you did when her dog died at Montreux."

"What I did was have a stupid row with the manager. That's why we left."

"What kind of a row?"

"Oh, he didn't want to bury the dog. Never mind that. What else did she say?"

"She said a number of nice things. About you and Walter. She said you told him so nicely about the difference between a bull and an ox."

"So I did," said Francis, laughing. "He must have told her. Perhaps he didn't believe me. Let me see this letter."

"Well, darling, I didn't keep it. I'll answer it some time soon. But I knew that if I kept it, I would be so provoked every time I looked at it—"

"You couldn't have minded hearing of my delicacy about the bull." Planned as a bit of raillery to cover his confusion while he cast about, trying to imagine the thing she might mind hearing of, it was a failure; but his mother, though she had heard him say something, could not have heard just what.

"No," she said slowly. "You remember I asked you about Helen."

Francis frowned again. "Perfectly," he said.

"Well, she wrote that Helen had arrived, and that you'd been together a good deal, and that she was rather concerned about it."

Francis sat stunned. "How extraordinary of her!" he said finally, flushing.

"Well, you see. I was a little put-out too."

"What were her exact words?"

"She said quite frankly that anything like that would upset her very much."

"Upset her?" said Francis. "And what about me? Why, she must be crazy!" He spoke spitefully, striking back in chagrin; for at a touch, the whole comfortable edifice in which he had been living seemed to go down, and he was left stultified. "God damn her to hell!" he said to himself. "Does she think I'd want to marry her stupid brat! Why—"

But these venomous outbursts were no help; and in fact hurt him, since he could not miss the splenetic, hitting-the-air silliness of shouting, even if it were true, that you did not want what you had been told you could not have. He put out a hand, took up his teacup as steadily as he could and drank the cold slop remaining in it.

"Francis," said his mother, "don't be upset. I think it's possible that, whether you knew it or not, Helen was a little taken with—"

"What nonsense! Helen was fooling around with a couple of English kids. You would think that!"

"Now, please! You must not lose your temper, dearest. Mrs. Cunningham had, or thought she had, some reason for writing me about it. Either she thought that Helen was getting a little interested, or—"

"Or what?"

"Well, Francis, you won't like this, but you have a silly, cynical way of talking sometimes. She knows you haven't any money, and you always say that money's the only thing that matters. I suppose you only do it to shock people; but if Mrs. Cunningham were to hear you say something like that she might reasonably be a little worried."

Francis tightened his mouth. "And so," he said, "you wish I'd stop saying things like that so people like Mrs. Cunningham won't be a little worried."

"Yes, since you ask, I wish you would stop." They looked at each other eye to eye; and Francis saw that he might be like his Grandfather Ellery in some respects; but in some others he was not unlike her. She said: "It always has a very sophomoric sound."

"Thank you," said Francis bitterly. His ebbing anger was no longer high enough to support a quarrel in which, to his great and conscious discredit, he snapped at her because he could not reach anyone else. "Well," he went on, "I don't know whether I ought to go back or not." He said it sulkily, less as a serious question than as an experimental attitude to try on himself and see how it looked.

"I know how you feel," his mother said. She paused; and by an easy transference of thought Francis realized that she was putting from her mind the consideration, necessarily first, that not going back would mean among other problems, a financial one, unless he could get something else to do; and what could you get to do in Florence?

Tempted for a moment to point out that money was making its customary prompt appearance as the thing that mattered—would he go back for any reason but money? Would she want him to go back, leaving her alone here, for any other reason?—Francis opened his mouth; but he closed it again, for the truth was a mean and senseless sort of triumph, and, anyway, it was too true. She said, "I don't know that it's as serious as that. I wish I had saved the letter. So much of it was really very nice. Perhaps I oughtn't to have told you about Helen. I was so put-out; but I really did think you might be amused."

"Of course you should have told me," Francis said. His irritation feebly revived. "Why else did she write it to you? She felt my ambition must be checked. Naturally I would like to tell her to go to hell; but—" But how could he? He thought, aghast at the tyranny of impulse, of Cap d'Ail for the first time; and, frightened, he let go any last notions of intransigence. "—but I won't," he said. "It doesn't seem feasible."

"Francis," she said, laying a hand on his arm, "you don't have too bad a time. I can tell by your letters. I don't think any of us is ever entirely suited in this world. I think you're very fortunate, really."

"Yes, I am," Francis said, for the word, satisfying his unconscious want, telling him that he was enviable and a little out of the run of common men, aroused him from despondency. The virtue of the vice of pride was the impossibility of self-pity; and Francis's mind, when it went to work on its private picture of himself, to please him was obliged to show him always fortunate—with uncanny luck, attaining successes he had not stooped to deserve; in his failures, still fortunate, since reflection was never at loss

177

to see ways in which the outcome might have been much worse. Gathering confidence, he took a little heart.

His mother said, "You're really very young, you know. You have everything before you. In a few years you'll feel differently about all this."

"Don't worry," Francis said, restless, "I'll live."

"Yes. Well, I think it's nice that you're going to the Riviera. And I'm glad you're going to see Lorna."

To avoid answering, Francis said, "What are you doing about supper? I don't want any. I think I'll go out and walk for a while."

"Oh. Isn't it raining?"

"Not yet." He got up.

"Well, darling, if you really want to. Don't go out by the Fortezza. Several people have been robbed there."

"A hot lot they'd get off me," Francis said. "If I see anyone who looks rich I'll probably try a little robbery myself. If it rains, I'll be back soon enough."

He put on his coat, and went downstairs and out into the dark street. The air was raw with dampness and the dampness was aromatic with a blended odor, both revolting and agreeable, of sewer sludge, of rancid oil and cooking tomatoes, of crumbling mortar, and of what seemed an exhalation from church vaults sooted by incense smoke and the grease of burnt candles. Francis buttoned up his coat and walked.

A half an hour later he was in the Via Strozzi, passing through the great two-story arch into the piazza. Cold and smoky, the cafe had only a few people in it. A quiet domino game with several spectators was going on in one corner. By himself among the empty tables sat a uniformed militiaman, his tunic belted tight over his fat little torso, the gold fasces pinned to the collar of his black shirt. His eyes fixed on Francis with the important, truculent air of one who watches for suspicious characters.

Francis returned the stare disdainfully—as though he gave a damn for a lot of absurd wops dressed up to frighten other wops!—but not too disdainfully. In Florence the Sicurezza never bothered much with passports, and Francis did not have a *Soggiorno degli Stranieri* receipt. One of these little rats, if he wanted to make Francis trouble, could probably get him a night in jail while the technicality was adjusted. The exchange of stares, continuing a second or two, began to make Francis uneasy, for the last thing he really wanted was trouble; and yet he could not bring himself to look away first, trouble or none.

Curiosity, probably never anything but idle, satisfied, the man did look down first. Spread on the table in front of him were the diapered backs of a pack of tarot cards arranged, as for a peculiar kind of solitaire, in rows under several of the trumps-major turned face up. Francis could see the striking, crude-colored images: the moon, the wiseman, the fool, the wheel of fortune, the card of judgment, the hanged man. Passing by, he seated himself against the wall not far off. After a while a waiter, who had been loitering, biting his nails, beneath the figure of King Gambrinus, came over. Some time later he brought Francis a glass of beer and writing materials.

✦

The beer tasted both thick—as if a good deal of dirt had been dissolved in it; and thin—as if the keg were regularly watered. Francis had forgotten this unpleasant peculiarity of Italian beer. "Siren tears," he said to himself, "Distill'd from limbecks foul as hell within . . ."

He began again: "What potions have I drunk of Siren tears,"—seriously this time; for the iambics, falling in their double alignment of sound and meaning, amused his mind by that prestidigitation that kept everything—words and sentences, the metrical feet and the alternate rhymes, all dancing in the air together, and for a moment at least made other thoughts unnecessary.

Once, with the wish to be a poet, and if possible an Elizabethan one, Francis had learned—a laborious course of instruction—the sonnets by heart; but that was four or five years ago, and much of what he had learned fell into disuse when, with pleasing simultaneousness, his own poetry, and poetry in general began to dissatisfy him, and to seem too trivial for serious attention. Now he could not think of the third line. The pattern broke up and he let it go. The blackshirt, he realized, was not playing solitaire. Shuffling and shifting his cards, he was getting ready to see what they said—inviting fate, with furtive and awful absurdity, for a sign.

Francis shrugged. He lifted the pen that had been brought with the ink pot and looked at the sheets of flimsy lined paper on the blotter before him; but he did not dip the pen in ink. As though he too required a sign, and he too were asking reassurance, he waited. His idea had been to write a note to Lorna, and so by a subterfuge to escape himself, for the person who wrote Lorna was naturally a character in fiction—not always the hero, but at least the protagonist of a continued story, the product of the important arts of selection and elimination.

To write, Francis had first to become this person; not as an act of deceit, but like a monologuist clapping on a cocked hat or turning up a collar to suggest an appearance that helped the part. Tonight the change would not come. Instead of that other, lively and sardonic, witty, worldly wise, and adventurous Francis Ellery like to the lark at break of day arising, he remained the glum one, who sat with half a glass of stale beer in a dreary café—he let his eyes go around, past the domino players; past the adenoidal waiter who was scratching himself in a way that seemed to indicate that he had piles; past the blackshirt fussing with his cards, and all the empty tables, to a range of wall mirrors framed in tarnished gilt where he found himself several times repeated in diminishing scale. His forehead was still brown, burnt by the sun on the Swiss snows; and he remembered, astonished, that he was not much more than twenty-four hours in Florence. Tuesday night he had been in the Alps having dinner with the Cunninghams.

At the thought of that dinner on his last evening, Francis quailed. Mrs. Cunningham, who could not have appeared more gracious, had already written her letter; and, everything else aside, Francis was crestfallen to know how effectively, as far as any acumen of his went, her fears had been dissembled. He could not think without a qualm of how he must have looked, sitting there unsuspecting, prattling away, much of the time with the direct intention of interesting and amusing Helen—a piece of helpfulness he had resolved on following that night when they first had dancing, and one he thought Mrs. Cunningham would approve of and appreciate. In fact, all the while Mrs. Cunningham, though she sat imperturbable, patiently putting up with his fatuous intermeddling, must have been saying to herself that it would not be long now; that, dinner over, Francis could be dismissed to pack; and in the morning he would be gone hours before they were up.

To swallow the mortifying truth, Francis was obliged first to laugh, to show himself certain absurd things in his situation or his notions about it. Given his choice, he would perhaps have preferred Mrs. Cunningham to mistake him for a sinister and dangerous schemer, weaving, resourceful and unprincipled, his subtle web; and that was good for a laugh, because she never could have made that mistake. There was only one fool there, and Francis was it. He was dangerous not because of his resource, but because, as Solomon so justly observed, the instruction of a fool is folly; and Mrs. Cunningham had Helen to think of.

Without reaching, except in some strictly legal sense, the age of discretion, Helen had grown to the age of consent; and Mrs. Cunningham, alert, too wise to command, began to plan or arrange. If not necessarily best, mother indubitably knew better, for she could think, while Helen merely felt or thought she felt. "Poor kid!" Francis said with compunction. He seemed to himself an age, practically a generation, older than Helen, and beyond the touch of those special feelings, in the sense that they might distort his judgment; yet, open to them, in the sense that he could still take her part against the adult world, and be warmed by the compliment of a possible secret and innocent regard. The delicacy of this sentiment was so blameless that Francis no longer felt embarrassment in supposing that Helen might have found him attractive. Instead he began to feel superior to the distrust Mrs. Cunningham's treatment of him showed. If she had simply been frank, he thought, how much anxiety she might have spared herself!

He sat rolling a cigarette around between his fingers while, now in a solemn mood, he reminded himself of those extra and unnecessary distresses that the human mind adds to the regular distresses of living. He must admit to adding one when, full of the rancor of his hurt pride, he said of Mrs. Cunningham, God damn her. Helen added one (for they came in all sorts and sizes) when turning her mind on herself, she saw everything wrong. Mrs. Cunningham added one when she let herself in a crisis of nerves suppose that Francis—sweet Francis, kind Francis, true Francis, valiant Francis—needed to be schemed against.

Francis drank his beer.

Beyond the arcade, falling rain swept the piazza, and he would have to see about getting a cab. He signaled to the waiter and counted out money for him. Passing the blackshirt's table, Francis was in time to see the man sit back, holding in his hand, crowned with dirty broken fingernails, the last card. Then, with a fine gesture, he turned it over. It was the Queen of Cups. Clasping it in both hands, he stared with an immobility that might be either joy or consternation. Francis silently wished him luck; for why hate the little rat? What had he ever done to Francis?

The cornices streamed water. Dimly lighted from all sides, Victor Emmanuel II sat his pawing charger, his pedestal pointing him up the storm. By the curb waited a

183

cab hitched to a drenched, drooping horse. As Francis looked at it, its driver started from the shelter of the arcade, gesticulating.

Francis called his address out, and got in. In the musty dark he sat silent, listening to the rain on the roof while the horse, beaten to a trot, went splashing through the muddy puddles. Francis felt old, charitable, and only slightly sad.

Five

THE ROOM was shadowed, but the large window framed a section of steep hillside. Pocked masses of rock rose from mounds of jagged debris, some of it gray, some of it brown, and much broken up by patches of vegetation. Cliffs showed through clumps of trees and the sweeps of stone rubble were overgrown with shrubs. Afternoon sunlight fell full on the hill and this light was reflected down into the room.

Sitting on the edge of the bed Francis held the telephone, looking at the deep pink façade of a house whose square cube was set about with umbrella pines halfway up the hill. Lower, on the road behind, Francis could see the windows of a couple of shabby little detached stores. He had just been cut off, and from time to time he said, "Allo!" Eventually a voice broke out in French. "Ecoutez, s'il vous plaît," he said, exasperated, "Je—" The voice was silenced with a crack. "Allo!" said Francis again.

English suddenly filtered through the receiver. "Isn't this annoying! You're Francis, then." There was a pause and Francis realized that the speaker must be Miss Imbrie herself. "Yes," he said. "I'm so sorry to bother you—"

"I'm bothered to distraction," the voice replied. "But not by you. Are you alone?"

"Yes, I am."

"Well, come to dinner, do. I couldn't ask the Cunninghams. I don't know that we'll have any dinner. The truth is, I'm in the act of firing the cook. Do you speak French very well?"

"Abominably," said Francis. Looking at the high-up pink house, he began to smile, pleased by the nasal, humorous voice. He had not known what Lorna's aunt was going to be like. "But often people find me intelligible," he said. "Can I help you?"

"Would you really like to? I always thought I spoke French myself; but I can't understand the monster. I warn you, it's the most formidable—"

"How do I get there?"

"Where are you? At the hotel? I can't send the car up. The girls and Eric went to Nice in it. Well, it's really not far. You go right down through the hotel gardens. There's a footbridge across the railway by the station that lands you on the road. Turn left—no, right, downhill around two rather long bends, down to the point. It has a long white wall. Rather pretentious looking, with lions. They look like dogs. There's a gum tree in a kind of well. I may have it all done before you get here. She keeps saying she'll take me to a party. Would you have any idea what that means?"

"Well, yes," said Francis, "I think so. It's probably just talk. She may think she's going to sue you." He hesitated, asking himself if he would not be well-advised to mind his own business, for the agreeable feeling of rushing to the rescue was dampened a little by a question of how effective he would be in a good rousing domestic altercation in French with fine points of law on the side.

"Oh, do come down at once!" she said. "Ought I to

186

telephone for a lawyer? I know one. A nasty little man who got me the lease here."

"You might tell her you're going to."

"What would be a rather stern way of saying that?"

"I'd just say," said Francis, scowling in concentration, "Alors, faut en finir! Je fais—er—appeler un avocat—no, avoué, un avoué."

"What a comfort you are! Do come. She'd probably listen to a man. She frightens me to death."

"I'm on my way." Francis put down the telephone and paused a moment, for he was just off the Genoa train, his bags not even opened. He looked at himself in the mirror, straightened his necktie, and catching up his hat trotted downstairs, out through the long lofty hall onto the terrace where a few people reclined in the shade of striped umbrellas, reading; or in the sun asleep, or blinking out at the sea which extended under them burnished and metallic to a high horizon haze. All of them were well wrapped, for though the sun was fairly warm, the persistent breeze was cold.

Francis headed down the wide walk edged with low iron hoops through the thickets of the garden, now in sloping curves, now in little flights of steps. Across the railway he found a narrow macadam road between successive garden walls and hedges of sickly looking geranium. It ran a long way to the right and then, obviously wasting ten minutes of his time, a long way back to the left. Beyond a second curve he could see the water much closer through an iron gate overhung by a couple of casuarinas trailing down stringy foliage toward him. A hundred yards ahead was what must be the gum tree, in a railed cement pit cut out of the sidewalk. The white wall had begun, running on a slant before a house of whitened stone with a heavy tiled roof of bright green. Sure enough, at the break in the wall were two lions sitting on their haunches supporting blank shields. A flight of stone steps went down, crossing an areaway, to a door whose little porch rested on twin caryatids. The door was plate glass behind an intricate bronze grill. Centered in a stone rose, one of a carved garland of flowers with which the architect had averted the threat of a plain stone casing, was a bell button.

Francis pushed it and stood looking at the door. Lorna had gone through it scores of times and he felt a stir of emotion to be standing here, able to touch the handle her hand had closed on, standing on the threshold her neatly shod, though not in fact very small, feet had often crossed. Behind the grill and the curtained glass a dim shape moved and the door swung heavily in. "Miss Imbrie?" he said, which was silly, since he saw at once that she could be no one else.

"It is, indeed," she said. She was rather tall, with a mobile, splay mouth and bobbed brown hair thickly threaded with gray. She was wearing a blouse with a great frilled jabot, over a short black shirt. "Are you admiring our grand luxe?" she said. "Come in, and I'll show you more. Francis—I shall have to call you that; it's Francis this and Francis that around here all the time—your plan worked like a charm. She's gone! Look in there. Isn't that absurd?"

She nodded toward a sort of atrium surrounded by a railed stone balcony opening on the second floor and topped by a skylight. In the floor was set a circular fish pond, ten or twelve feet across. On a stone in the center crouched the metal figure, life-sized, of an extraordinarily nude woman who was tilting from an amphora a thin jet of water to splash in the pool. "That's Mrs. Sweeney," said Miss Imbrie. "Yes, she left. When I said it to her, she grew pale. I think she thought I was crazy. I've telephoned an English woman in Monte who runs a kind of agency. She says she'll have somebody for·me tomorrow. It's very awkward, though. I have a chauffeur called Raymond, and I think she was his mistress, so I suppose he'll leave. Oh, dear! Come into the kitchen. I'm trying to see if she's poisoned everything. You know, I liked your last book very much. Do you mind being told that?"

"I love being told that," Francis said.

Cocking her head at an alabaster clock on the drawing room mantel, Miss Imbrie answered, "Why, it's after four. I don't think we can have any tea. I'm sure the fire's out. Wouldn't you rather have a drink? The girls said they'd be back by five; but of course they won't. Did you ever see a gold piano before? This place used to belong to a Greek, but he borrowed money on it, and lost it all at the Casino. Poor man, how happy he must have been here! I think the dining room's rather nice, looking out over the water that way. The thing you see down there is a swimming pool, but it has a special pump to bring up salt water. Raymond thought it didn't work well enough, so he took it apart, and now it doesn't work at all. The water's so low that if you ever got in you'd never get out. I was really just as pleased. Gwen went swimming Christmas and we had to put her to bed afterward. Will you drink whiskey and soda?" She caught up a bottle of Scotch in the pantry and carried it with her.

Francis followed her into the kitchen. "I don't know

what we were to have for dinner," she said, standing still. "I used to tell that camel what I wanted, but we almost never got anything but what she wanted. Do you cook, too? I've yet to find a man who didn't think he did. You don't know Eric, do you? Fortunately he's a very good cook, so we'll probably get something when the time comes. I know he won't let himself starve."

Since Francis had been about to say that he could make muffins, he was forced to smile. His pleasure in Miss Imbrie was great; but he began to feel a little uneasy, too. It was hard to see how anyone else ever got a word in edgewise; and entertaining responses are useless when the remarks they respond to are lost under several further remarks before you can open your mouth. Miss Imbrie extended a hand over various parts of the long range. "Cold," she said. "I'm sure she did it deliberately. Nobody can start it but Raymond, so heaven knows when we'll have dinner."

"Well, now, I think I could start it," Francis said.

"Oh, could you?"

"I don't see why not." Francis advanced and began lifting lids and looking in doors.

"Well, do fix yourself a drink first. Look, here's some Perrier water."

Downstairs in a cold whitewashed room Francis found some tidy French bundles of kindling and briquets of coal wrapped in paper. Carrying them up, he heard Miss Imbrie, who had begun with unexpected efficiency to put things in order, whistling the Indian merchant's song from *Sadko*. As his step approached, she lifted her voice and sang: "Les diamants chez nous sont innombrables . . ." She said, "Isn't that lovely? Eric says it must have been the Greek's slogan. Every time he passes the gold piano he sits down and plays it. Oh, Lord, there's the tele- phone!"

She darted out; and Francis set about shaking down the ashes. He had filled an empty coal scuttle with them and laid his fire before she returned. "That was Eric," she said while he washed his hands. "He thought they might stay and have dinner some place near Nice. I told him they would do no such thing, that he had dinner to get here."

Francis lit the fire, opened the draft, and stood up. "Would you mind telling me who Eric is?" he said.

"Oh, he's Eric McKellar. He's a sort of cousin of mine, poor lamb." She looked at Francis with interest. Francis leaned on the edge of the table and took a sip of whiskey. "He lives in England. Like Henry James, rather." She paused, still looking at Francis. "He's fifty-four years old," she said suddenly.

Francis set down his glass, aware that he had colored, for the supervening thought that had made her say it was easy to guess. "Thank you very much," he said with con- scious composure. "I sometimes wish I were."

Miss Imbrie gave him a smile. "There," she said. "Would you mind if I washed these dishes? There are so many of them. I was going to be strong-minded and leave them, but I find I can't. I think the hot water ought to be all right. It comes from a sort of furnace Raymond takes care of. I haven't seen Martha Cunningham for years. How is she? When is she coming?"

"Sometime tomorrow, I think," Francis said.

"She used to be amazingly beautiful."

"Well, she still is really."

"How tragic about the child!"

"Yes," Francis said. He took a dish towel from the rack.

"Oh, you don't want to do that!" she said.

"Yes, I do," Francis said.

"You're a very amiable young man," Miss Imbrie said. "I think they'll be along pretty soon. I told them you were here."

✦

At quarter to five Miss Imbrie said, "Doesn't it get dark early! Something to do with the sun, I suppose." She held up her dripping hands. "Will you snap that light on?" In the resulting yellow glare Francis could see that her eyes, like Lorna's, were actually dark blue, not brown.

The kitchen grew warm from the fire in the range. Distantly the alabaster clock struck five. Miss Imbrie did not stop talking for any length of time, and Francis was interested in what she said, both because it was often amusing, and because out of it he was forming an idea of the life, animated, busy, and purposeless, of the Villa Apollon; yet he was growing inattentive. At last Miss Imbrie emptied her dishpan and set to work scrubbing the sink.

It was now half past five, but by a great effort Francis did not ask her how long it took to come from Nice. "Shall I put these away?" he said.

"They go in the pantry," she answered. "You—"

Francis had already started to stack the plates with care, but the third one he picked up slipped in his hand. On the floor it smashed to fragments. "I'm frightfully sorry," he said, crouching to get the pieces together.

Miss Imbrie, drying her hands, said, "Oh, break all you like." She began to laugh, hung up the towel, and reaching down, gave his shoulder a pat. "Let it be," she said. "You go in and put some lights on. They'll be here any minute. And have another drink. That will—"

In the pantry an electric bell rang.

"Get up," she said, tapping his shoulder again. "That's the front door. Open it. But please don't fall in the fish pond."

Francis got up. The sharp sound of the bell seemed to stay on, ringing through him while he felt something not readily distinguishable from anguish. He was swallowing down agitation, and it made the heart sick—not in the peevish way of hope deferred, but sick through and through with one of those suspenses that come at the end. He thought suddenly of that man in the café at Florence Christmas night, the card with the Queen of Cups on it turned up. There it was, and now he knew.

In distress, because he must look comic—fit to fall in the fish pond—Francis could only say, "All right. I'll try not to." His voice shook, and his hands, which also shook, he pushed, to conceal them, into his pockets, turning to go through the pantry.

"Light by the door!" said Miss Imbrie.

Francis got the door open and felt down the wall. A half a dozen crystal brackets sprang up glittering and he walked ahead. The barely supportable beating of his heart filled his chest so he could not get his breath in. Beyond the columned arch at the end of the drawing room he groped in the darkness, but he could find no switch.

"Hell!" he said, standing still, for this was ridiculous, and he forced air into his lungs and held it there hard.

193

The bell rang again, and so he walked down toward the oblong of dimmed light broken by the shadow of the grill and the shadows of people behind it. He depressed the heavy door handle and stood back while the glass swung in and cold air poured on his face. Above, on the street, he saw the flood of headlights and the shining car. In front of him they stood together, darker than the light stone steps.

"Well, welcome, stranger!" said Gwen.

"Francis!" said Lorna. Both her gloved hands found one of his and closed together on it convulsively.

Francis said, "I can't seem to find any light here."

"Right here," said Gwen. She moved, and a bronze lamp suddenly poured down a glow on them.

"Francis!" said Lorna again, releasing his hand. Francis looked at her nervelessly, seeing with a new spasm of the heart the faint hollows of her cheeks and her lips twisted tight in a smile.

"You don't know Eric, do you?" Gwen said. "Mr. McKellar, Mr. Ellery." Francis took the hand held out to him. "The kitchen!" said Gwen. "I saw the light! She isn't trying to cook, is she? For God's sake, let's stop her, Eric." She grasped Mr. McKellar by the sleeve of his overcoat, tugging him after her through the dark atrium.

The door closed with a solid click. Lorna let her hands drop. Hanging open on a plaid frock, she wore a straight dark blue coat with a couple of gardenias pinned to the lapel. "Oh," she said, almost recoiling. "Raymond will—"

"To hell with Raymond," said Francis. Her slight, thin body came against him, her arms went up around his neck. "Ah, darling . . ." she said.

194

Francis could feel her lips move under his, and at the same time, the cold petals of the gardenias, lifted with the lapel, touching his cheek. Her hat slipped back and fell on the floor, releasing her dark hair in disorder. "Sorry," he murmured. The latch sounded, and he let her go. He stooped and snatched up her hat. The man in chauffeur's uniform, several boxes under one arm, came around the door, touched his cap, and passed them.

"Lipstick," Lorna said. Her eyelashes were shining wet. She pulled a folded handkerchief from her sleeve, waited while the man went through the door at the back, and applied it with hard unsteady strokes to Francis's mouth. "All right," she said. Her voice broke into laughter, but the tears in her eyelashes overflowed, running down her face. She took the hat out of his hand. "I'll have to go upstairs," she said. She went by him, running on the shallow steps.

"Lorna, darling," Gwen called.

Francis walked into the drawing room. "She went upstairs," he said.

Pulling her hat off, Gwen came through the room toward him. "Greetings," she said. "How are you?" She shrugged out of a coat of splotched calfskin, and Francis caught it.

"Thanks," she said. Her fresh-colored round face, while not unfriendly, had a cast of annoyance. She surveyed Francis with critical reserve, inspecting him for some sign that he acknowledged her service in removing herself and Mr. McKellar. She was grimly ready to despise his complacence if he showed it, and his ingratitude if he didn't.

"Have a good time in Switzerland?" she asked.

"No," said Francis.

"Poor you!" she said. She took the coat from him and went upstairs.

✦

Fixing something to eat took so long that it was almost ten by the time they finished dinner. On the dining room table stood a high silver candelabrum with six lighted candles in its branches. There were two cheeses, several plates of biscuits, coffee cups, a gold inlaid port decanter and glasses to match it, a bottle of crème de cacao, some of which Miss Imbrie drank with cream, and a bottle of brandy, some of which Francis drank, though he did it circumspectly. Before dinner—Lorna was upstairs some time; then (it happened as soon as she came down) Lorna and Miss Imbrie and Raymond held one of those interminable conferences with proposals and counterproposals, ending finally in Raymond departing for St. Laurent to fetch an aunt of his who would assuredly wash the dishes, but might or might not accept a permanent position; and then, to keep Mr. McKellar company, they all sat around the kitchen watching the cooking—Francis, in the impatience of living through all these delays, all this confusion and chatter, had taken more cocktails than he meant to.

The dining room, large and airy—a little too airy for the cold night—was filled with shadows rising to the high white coffered ceiling and moving on the white curtains drawn in folds to cover the terrace doors. In this chilly serenity Francis sat dejected, his head swimming slightly, his heart sunk. Mr. McKellar's principal dish had been a sort of stew of sweetbreads with cream and mushrooms and wine. It was delicious. Its savor excited the mouth, and Francis's stomach, flushed by the repeated doses of cold gin and vermouth, was hollow with hunger; but between the two his tense throat seemed to rebel, choking him with agitation. He had to swallow by main force.

Mr. McKellar had begun to talk as soon as a full audience was gathered in the kitchen; and, though that must have been hours ago, he really had not stopped a moment. He talked while he cooked, he talked while the table was laid and the food brought in, he even managed to talk while he ate; or at least, he managed not to let go of the conversation, by starting a sentence, suspending it while he took a mouthful, and finishing it as soon as his mouth was empty. He did not eat much, so he was through before anyone else. He pushed his plate away, poured himself a glass of port; and, like a river spreading out broad and full after a short passage of rapids, he talked on, raising and lowering his glass to admire the light through it.

Even Miss Imbrie was silenced. From the head of the table Mr. McKellar simply held forth, the candlelight bright on his large rugged features and mop of wiry gray hair worn just long enough to tuck behind his ears. His skin was weathered like a farmer's, with deep down-drawn lines about the mouth and a fine puckering of wrinkles at the corners of his eyes, which were big and dark brown beneath dense brows. It seemed that during the afternoon they had discovered an ostrich farm out the Route du Var.

Mr. McKellar told about it. "Unspeakably splendid creatures!" he said. "They have such pride, such assur-

ance! All plum'd like estridges that wing the wind!"
Starting, Francis thought: *I saw young Harry with his
beaver on* . . . but the gratification of guessing that he,
probably alone there, knew the quotation, was faint. His
knowledgeableness could not be turned to any advantage,
and Mr. McKellar was already off, impassioned, on a new
tangent. With peans and apostrophes he contrasted the
state of creatures living as nature meant them to, and of
man, living as a foul and flagitious civilization dictated.
Spoken by Mr. McKellar, the English language died in
extremity, was solemnly buried, and rose again having put
on incorruption. It became more English, not in the imita-
tive sense of resembling an Englishman's speech—until
Mr. McKellar took up his residence there such an accent
could hardly ever have been heard in England—but absolutely, in the sense of resembling a Platonic ideal, with
"a's" so nobly broad and feats of synaeresis so extraordinary that the most supercilious don would have to go
down, and Mr. McKellar bore the palm alone. If it did
not abash, this way of speaking was likely to irritate people
hearing it for the first time.

Francis had felt the irritation. He had even expressed
it, by listening with exaggerated politeness while he extended a conscious confident forbearance to this astonishing
old freak. Presently, out of patience, he dropped an ironic
remark or two, meaning to demolish him. They sank without a ripple, and Francis began to swell with secret indignation.

That was long ago. Like irritation, like forbearance,
like irony, indignation had been swallowed up in despair.
Mr. McKellar was murdering time. The moving finger
wrote and Mr. McKellar quoted D. H. Lawrence. Fran-

cis tightened his hands together and found them damp
with sweat. He fixed on his face a smile intended to show
reflective amusement; but Mr. McKellar gave a synopsis
of one of E. M. Forster's works. He did not show the
least sign of stopping and getting the hell out and taking
Gwen and Miss Imbrie with him. Meanwhile, across the
elaborate still-life of cups and glasses, the cut cheeses, the
assembled bottles, Lorna leaned on her elbows, her chin
on her hands. Her face looked warm, drowsily flushed,
for she too had drunk a number of cocktails and they were
making her sleepy.

"Well, children," Miss Imbrie said at last. "Let's move.
Are you through, Gwen?"

"Completely," said Gwen.

"How right she is to contemn abstract discussion," Mr.
McKellar said, standing up. "All young people are materi-
alists! What good is it if you can't eat it? Well, be quick.
Gather therefor the rose whilst yet is prime! Gather your
self-indulgence while you may. When you're young it
doesn't show; but when you get to be thirty you will find
that you face a choice. After that it does show. You must
decide what you want to be when you're fifty."

"Suppose I want to be dead?" said Gwen, going into
the drawing room.

"Nonsense, nonsense!" said Mr. McKellar. His great
shadow aped him on the wall as he swallowed the last of
his port. "No one wants to be dead. Ah, the conceit of
youth! If you can't be ever young and fair you have the
confounded cheek to think you won't play. You will.
You'll insist on playing. It will be like trying to get Lorna
home from the casino when she knows that next time it
just has to be pair et rouge. You don't arise from the table

gracefully. No one does. Lucretius was an ass. What does he say? Well, now I have forgotten."

"Cur non ut plenus vitae conviva recedis," Francis said distinctly—almost viciously, for he felt entitled to one triumph and what a wretched one this was! "Aequo animoque capis securam, stulte, quietem."

"Bravo!" Mr. McKellar said, startled. He swept a bow to Francis. "I acknowledge my master! Plenus, indeed! You can always use a little more."

"She wouldn't leave because she was winning," Gwen said. "Tomorrow we'll go and win again."

"Just because you lost all your plaques!" Lorna said.

"Hold your tongues, sauceboxes!" Mr. McKellar assumed a ferocious mock scowl. Sirrahs, impudent saucy dear boxes! Propped up in bed in his nightgown, Jonathan Swift wrote—the unwieldy elephant to make them mirth —to Ireland to his young women, little dears both, tasking them to love poor Presto. Mr. McKellar was having a wonderful time. He bent his rugged profile on Gwen and said: "Tomorrow we're all going to Grasse; yes, so we are. Ellery and I will discourse on the Latin poets while you buy vile perfumes, grossly overpriced."

"Oh, let's!" said Lorna.

"Faith, and now we'll have music," Mr. McKellar said. He stalked to the gold piano and seated himself before it, sweeping his hands left and right across the keyboard.

"No, wait," said Gwen. "I must get my— Oh, Lorna, darling! Your dress! We must show Aunt Mabel. Come up and put it on at once!"

"I won't," said Lorna. "It's a fright. It has roses as big as your face. It's black taffeta."

To Miss Imbrie Gwen said with enthusiasm, "It has

two huge silver roses on what might as well be called the thigh. Such fun! We went into Rouff's, and—"

"Be gone!" said Mr. McKellar. "Get what you're going to get. You can describe the fascinating circumstances any time. I am about to execute 'The Twelve Days of Christmas.'" He began to play.

"No, wait, wait!" cried Gwen.

"Francis," Miss Imbrie said, "would you light that fire? It seems awfully cold."

✦

Time passed. The alabaster clock struck eleven. The fire under the broken and irregular marble curves of the rococo mantel burned lower. Mr. McKellar remained at the piano. Songs, mostly old English, occurred to him, and he sang them with humor or sentiment. He extemporized, he played Schumann; he did excerpts from *Iolanthe*, constituting himself, most amusingly, a whole company of players. Miss Imbrie and Gwen were both sewing; Miss Imbrie, embroidering initials on the pocket of a blouse; Gwen, who sewed very well, replacing an ostrich feather hem on a frock of pale pink chiffon. Busy, they spoke infrequently.

"There!" said Gwen, biting off her thread. "The damn thing's done. Shall I try it on?"

"Yes," said Lorna.

"No," said Gwen. "You wouldn't try yours on. I'll have to wear it Thursday anyway." She stroked the hem. "You know, I thought they killed the ostriches, like egrets. But they don't. The man said they didn't, this afternoon. Isn't that nice?"

"Francis," said Miss Imbrie, "you'll go to this, won't you? You must. I'll tell Johnny we're bringing you. It's a dance some people near Menton are giving."

Lorna said, "Well, I wondered if I'd have to ask him myself." She too had spoken infrequently, lighting cigarettes and crushing out the ends marked with lipstick in a silver ash tray shaped like a scallop shell. Relaxed, her feet doubled up under her on the sofa, she now looked pale and tired, the skin dark under her eyes, the hollows in her cheeks more marked. She smiled at Francis, but the effect was wan.

"I don't know about taking Ellery," Mr. McKellar objected over his shoulder. "I have to have an exclusive supply of polka partners. I must start giving you lessons, both of you." He played a polka.

"You don't have to give me lessons," Lorna said. She pressed her knuckles to her lips. "I learned about a thousand years ago at dancing class. Eric, stop! It gives me a headache. You can't mean to say that people did that when you were young for pleasure. Play something soothing."

She did have a headache, Francis realized. He was filled with bitterness, as though it were somehow Mr. McKellar's fault. Thanks to this superannuated buffoon, it would soon be midnight. Lorna ought to be in bed and he ought to leave.

The superannuated buffoon, shifting his hands gently down the keyboard, caught on a tune. He began to sing: "There is a lady sweet and kind." He swayed his head, scattering a cascade of clear notes. "Was never face so pleased my mind . . ." Reduplicating the chords without

202

hurry, he said: "Soothing, very soothing." He sighed, burlesquing regret or renunciation. "When I was young," he said.

The remark, delivered in Mr. McKellar's ordinary orotund manner, produced no impression on Francis for a moment. Then something in the words, "when I was young" made him look up. Mr. McKellar, jesting at scars, spoke lightly, but not lightly enough; and Francis saw, exultant, the secret wound. Invited once too often, at the eleventh hour Mr. McKellar got something for his pains in overriding Francis all evening, for his Age-of-Queen-Anne baby talk, for his learned lust for life, for his rugged, gallant glances that did not miss Lorna's legs doubled up on the sofa, or Gwen's small but well-defined breasts as she laid aside the chiffon frock.

Easy and slow, the notes moved on. The air unfolded. "I did but see her passing by, and yet—" Mr. McKellar's aloof accent hovered. Probably imagining that his chagrin had been secret, he put it down. To show his ease he decorated his performance with tones of tender wisdom. He reproached the inhumanity and imperception of youth. He extracted consolation from the thought of the things he understood that youth did not understand. In words and music he showed himself nonchalantly relishing the rarer spirit of the Seventeenth Century, with its innocent lusts, its passions profound but blameless, its perfect poetry. Deep and soft, he concluded ". . . I love her till I die."

Francis stood up contemptuously. "I must go," he said.

"Oh, don't go," said Miss Imbrie. "We sit here and yawn until all hours. It's the custom."

To hear her describe in calm terms his wasted evening stung Francis back to an awareness of his own hurts, not, after all cured by the pleasure of seeing Mr. McKellar hurt, too. "I must," he said bitterly.

"Well, you'll go to Grasse tomorrow, won't you? We'll stop and pick you up."

Irresolute, wanting to go, but seeing an indignity in going as Mr. McKellar's guest on Mr. McKellar's excursion, he said, "I don't know when the Cunninghams are coming. When would we get back?"

"Not late," Mr. McKellar said. He faced about and gazed at Francis cordially.

"Well, I really don't know. Perhaps I could give you a ring in the morning." Did he imagine that by punishing himself he could punish Mr. McKellar? Francis said, "I'd love to go. They probably won't be here until tomorrow night."

"Good. We'll try to leave about nine."

Miss Imbrie said, "Oh, you haven't any coat! It will be freezing!"

"I'll be all right. It was so nice of you to take me in."

"Come any time," Miss Imbrie said.

Lorna sat up. "Can you get out?" she said.

"Yes," said Francis. Disconsolately he blamed her too— for being so tired, for having a headache, for so surrounding herself with people. The agitation of yearning—she was offering in spite of everything to come to the door with him—shook him; but he thought: "If she wanted to, she would without asking. If she doesn't want to—" And could he blame her, if she recoiled, as he recoiled, from the intolerable advertisement to Miss Imbrie and Mr. McKellar and Gwen that he could not leave without fondling her for a while in the partial privacy of the hall? "Good night," he said. "Good night."

Out of the room, he took his hat from the table, faltering in the hope that she might still come; repenting the lost chance, ready now not to give a damn what they thought. The awful evening grew too heavy for him. His anguish of disappointment that, after so long, it should have fallen out like this reduced the pride that required her to want to come. He set his teeth together, full of resolution too late for tonight, too early for tomorrow. The door jarred shut behind him and blindly he climbed the dark steps to the street.

He stopped then. Twenty yards to his right stood a lighted gas lamp, and stock-still, he gaped at it. Past the lighted panes of glass, like a thick veil, snow was falling. The damp pavement was beginning to whiten. Fine snow whirled and spun, dusting off the fronds of a palm raised above the garden wall.

Francis took a step and then another. With a crack like a dam breaking, floods of rage poured into him. He tasted salt in his mouth, he felt blood at his eyes in the torrential passion, small enough to make him kill, great enough to make him cry. The snow drove hard across his cheek, around his neck, a hundred times unkinder than man's ingratitude. Invulnerable, unanswerable, it derided him, careless of what he thought or what he did, executing its aimless joke on him, on the January flowers, on the whitening palms.

Francis got his breath in. He was shaking with cold, and turning up his collar he began to walk fast along the blank walls, up the endless empty street. From the bridge across the railroad he could see the colored signal lamps dim in the murk. On the sloping walks of the hotel gardens there was snow enough for him to leave clear black

205

tracks behind him. A whistling, moaning blizzard swept down the terrace of the hotel, obscuring the line of palms in wooden tubs. He stamped up the steps and jerked open the big door. Into the still air with him whirled a flurry of snowflakes.

A chasseur in blue jacket and brass buttons started up, advancing on Francis with eager solicitude, a brush in his hand. From the recesses of the vestaire another appeared, also with a brush, and possessed himself of Francis's snow-covered hat, exclaiming, uttering apologies, extending commiserations.

In proper dignity the concierge left this menial work to others. "Telegram, Monsieur," he said. He put his hand up to the rack above his desk, produced the folded green sheet, and bore it grandly across the floor.

Francis took it. "That will do, thanks," he said to the brushers. A man in a striped apron had now appeared discreetly, and as Francis moved, he whisked out a mop and began to wipe up the tassellated paving. Francis unfolded the sheet. It was from Genoa at noon. *Arrive 19:09 please meet Cunningham.*

Francis stared a moment. The printed letters looked remote, the words inscrutable, the 19:09 senseless. A sort of meaning began to force its way toward his consciousness. He said uncertainly, "The fourth. That's Monday. Today, then."

"Yes, Monsieur. Directly after you departed."

"Mrs. Cunningham is here?" he said, incredulous.

"Yes, Monsieur. They are arrived. Several hours ago. Madame inquired for you. If you would come up, if you returned before ten." They both looked at the clock, which

showed quarter to twelve, and the concierge's eyes came
back to him.

"I see," said Francis, annoyed by something in the look
that seemed to show that the concierge also thought he
ought to have been here. "Well, that's too bad," he said
lightly. "I wish I'd known. I'd better be called at eight."

"Bien entendu, Monsieur. Bon soir, Monsieur."

Folding the telegram blank absently into smaller
squares, Francis stood silent while the elevator went up.
"That was not so good," he said to himself.

The thought came to him that, whatever else he did,
he would not go to Grasse tomorrow; but he put it by in
infinite weariness, thinking that soon, thank God, he
would be asleep.

2

THE SNOW was gone. The morning was very fine. Into the
blue sea, Cap Ferrat, a lighter grayer blue, extended far
off against the west. The cloudless sky was a third blue,
tender and pure, a dome of light above the stony mountains. Coming a hundred miles over the Gulf of Genoa,
the wind brought a moist feel and smell of spring. Everything shone with melted snow water. Water rippled
sparkling down the paved walks into the breezy semi-
tropical thickets of the garden.

Before Francis did anything else, he had to let them
know at the villa that he could not go to Grasse. Harassed,
afraid of calling too early, yet pressed to get it done before
he presented himself (and he must not be late) to Mrs.
Cunningham, Francis had picked up and set down the

telephone several times while he was shaving and dressing. Probably he ought to ask to speak to Mr. McKellar, since it was Mr. McKellar's party, but he shrank from the idea. When he thought of the lofty expression on that rugged, intelligent face, and of his own furtive rudeness, his sulky silences, and the way he had gone off in what was doubtless seen to be a huff, leaving, you might guess, Mr. McKellar to exchange glances with Miss Imbre, it put Francis out of countenance.

At quarter to nine he could not make his mind up. At ten minutes of nine, mind made up or not, he would have to call; and he did. Miss Imbrie answered the phone herself. "Oh, Francis!" she said. "You're all right, then? I suppose you must be. We thought we'd have to send the dogs out for you."

Francis said that he was all right, but that Mrs. Cunningham had arrived, and so—

"Well, Eric thought we'd better not go to Grasse," Miss Imbrie said. "It's quite high up and the roads may not be good. Well, do tell Mrs. Cunningham I shall come to call—" Francis held the telephone tight, relaxing with relief, for she spoke in a friendly way. After he had listened a reasonable time (it was five minutes to nine) he said, "Could I speak to Lorna a moment?"

"Oh, I don't think she's awake," Miss Imbrie said cheerfully. "Call later, won't you? Oh, she is awake—" Her voice faded, and she cried faintly, "Angel child! You'll catch your death of cold on those damned tiles! Take these. And put this around you. And here. It's Francis. I'll get you some coffee." He heard the telephone passed over and Lorna said, "Hello."

"Oh, God!" said Francis. "I woke you up?"

208

"It's all right. I'm only half awake."

"Is Miss Imbrie there?"

"She's getting me some coffee."

"And you have no slippers on?"

"I have hers on."

"Lorna."

"Yes."

"Ah, what am I going to do about you? Will I ever see you alone?"

"If you want to."

"What does that mean?"

"Nothing. I don't know. I haven't had any coffee. Why don't you come down later?"

"I can't. Mrs. Cunningham is here. Would you mind saying that you loved me?"

"I'm so cold."

"Then say it quickly."

"Gwen's making fun of me."

"Tell her I'll knock her block off," Francis said. Since it takes two to talk of love, he felt disconsolate and foolish; but the picture of Lorna stupid with sleep, shivering in pajamas, brought with it a deep ringing of nerves. "You're sweet," he said. "Good-by."

It was nine o'clock. In the high corridor Francis walked quickly looking for the number of Mrs. Cunningham's sitting room door—303, 307, 309, 3B. Francis had this first meeting all worked out. Christmas night he had shown himself why he ought not to be angry, and why Mrs. Cunningham's letter was more to be pitied than censured. During the next few days in Florence he kept pitying at odd moments, her unnecessary anxiety; but soon his wounded feelings were near enough whole again for Mrs.

Cunningham's plight to seem somewhat less pathetic. He began to show himself that her concern, though groundless, was reasonable—more to be respected than pitied. He did not blame her in the least for her vigilance. Authors were two for a nickel (by the contemptuous appraisal he took himself down a peg, of course; but, then, he took down the celebrated and successful several pegs and the exercise was not unpleasant); and though by some miracle your choice fell on a good author, art was long, the egotism inseparable from it tiring, and meanwhile everyone knew that two could and would live at least as cheaply and meanly as one. Mrs. Cunningham ought not to let Helen risk her happiness and welfare that way.

Nevertheless, Francis had his self-respect to think of. To forgive Mrs. Cunningham for worrying was one thing. To forget that in her worry she had let herself believe him capable of starting something like that was another thing. Francis decided that he would view his situation more strictly. He would be less familiar. He would think of himself as an employee; agreeable and efficient, but reserved; attentive to Mrs. Cunningham's interests and wishes, not because he had a friendly regard for her, but because he was conscientious. It seemed reasonable to hope that she would feel the difference. Without having presumed to reproach her, Francis would artfully bring her to reproach herself, and to be sorry that she had misjudged him.

To this end Francis had thought carefully of what to say and what to do. More than that, Mrs. Cunningham's part, too, was tentatively arranged for her, since Francis was prepared to meet various openings or attitudes with rehearsed exchanges in which he had taken pains to give her good lines, even if his own were, by and large, better. Unfortunately he had not prepared one to be begun by him with an apology for failing to do some of those duties whose perfect performance was to make her sorry. The conscientious employee had got off on the wrong foot. He was an expense to Mrs. Cunningham the minute he reached the hotel; and they were both agreed that she was not paying him to amuse himself; and he was afraid that they both would agree that he had no business to go away and stay away on the irresponsible assumption that she could not need him.

Standing at the door, Francis tried to summon up his forces, to gather head as far as conscious effort could do it, against the unreasonable feeling that everything was going wrong. He showed himself that this was not the case. His own impatience and ineptitude had made his position a little uncomfortable, a few trifles went wrong; but here he was with a kind of magic ease at Cap d'Ail. By no other exertion than wishing for what a month ago seemed the impossible, he was here; and that was the main point. That was the main point, all right; yet from the corner of his eye Francis kept scrutinizing the happy fact. He held himself above superstition, but he had not failed to observe that, as one thing follows another in life, patterns, often repeated, are formed. Viewed with detachment, a number of these patterns seem to be jokes. Francis stood apprehensive, with a kind of pricking of the thumbs, wondering if it were not just possible that he had seen all this before; and if, though still inchoate, the pattern of a joke everybody knows might not be emerging. It begins with a man wishing; and then the man gets his wish; and then (you could die laughing) he wishes he hadn't got it. Francis raised his hand and rapped on the paneled door. The room glowed with sunlight. Whistling *Valencia* slowly and shrilly, Walter slouched in a chair, scowling at a jig-saw puzzle, half completed in the cover of a large white hat box in his lap. "Say, hello!" he said, breaking off his music. "Say, Frank, Tom and Toby and I went pretty near up to Salzegg. Gosh, you should have been there! It's much better—" He got up impulsively, let the box cover slip, and sent a hundred pieces of the puzzle rolling over the rug.

"Walter," said Mrs. Cunningham, "how careless you are!" Pen in hand, she sat at the writing desk, pressing flat a folder of travelers' checks to be countersigned. She wore a suit of brown knitted silk that Francis had not seen before, and a Victorian gold bar with large topazes and small pearls on her breast. She looked very handsome. She said, "How are you, Francis?" Turning, she gave him her hand and smiled, while her voice, easy and pleasant, bore down on the "are," making her sound anxious to know.

Francis said, "I'm so frightfully sorry about—"

Walter was on the floor, sheepishly picking up his puzzle; and, stepping back, Francis bent to help him. Busily he picked up piece after piece, enlarging his apologies because he could not seem to stop. He accused himself with abandon.

Mrs. Cunningham took it in good part. When she came to answer, she did not say that his absence didn't matter; she simply told him, as though he would be (and he was) relieved to hear it, that she had been put to no serious inconvenience. She told him she had been afraid that he might not get her telegram because she wasn't certain when he was to arrive.

Francis then told her about Miss Imbrie and Miss Imbrie's cook—really an emergency. Nothing less would have tempted him to leave his post. All the pieces of the puzzle had been collected, so Francis straightened up.

"They were getting dinner themselves, so I stayed to help," he said, a little lamely, for the state of emergency that explained his going did not seem quite to cover his staying until eleven o'clock. Mrs. Cunningham asked how Miss Imbrie was, and how the girls were. She paused; and added, "Helen was so pleased when Lorna came to see her in Paris."

The simple remark, or perhaps the minute pause that preceded it, threw Francis into confusion again. Taken at face value, the meaning was that Mrs. Cunningham, reminded of Lorna, was reminded that in Paris Lorna had taken the trouble to be pleasant to Helen, and Mrs. Cunningham thought that was a nice thing for Lorna to do. If, as Francis's strained alertness immediately suggested, more than that was meant, and Mrs. Cunningham had said it to see just how he would react to a mention of Helen, it was important that he respond easily; since he was, first, innocent, and second, unresentful. But Mrs. Cunningham might mean (conscious, or would-be, ironists see irony everywhere. They have their reward) that she knew all about Lorna's reasons for bothering with Helen; and that she thought Francis ought to realize that if he were in Cap d'Ail now, it was not because of such attempted management.

"They seem very well," Francis said promptly, for he could keep his composure and prevent a change of color best when he was talking. In the nick of time, he caught himself, and undoubtedly he did color. He had almost told her, logically enough, that he had just been talking to Miss Imbrie, and Miss Imbrie had asked him to say that they would come to call.

But why had he just been talking to Miss Imbrie? If Mrs. Cunningham felt surprise to find him gone away Monday afternoon without waiting to hear from her, what would she feel to learn that he intended (another emergency, perhaps) to be away all day Tuesday, too, when he knew that she was virtually certain to arrive sometime? Francis had seen this danger well in advance. The danger he did not see until the last moment was one arising when, prudently practicing to deceive, he suppressed the projected trip to Grasse. He had been about to invite Mrs. Cunningham to wonder why he telephoned so early in the morning unless the villa were so much on his mind that everything else must wait. With a mental movement analogous to wiping his forehead, he dodged again. "Miss Imbrie asked me last night to say she was coming to call," he said.

This time it was too late. It would have to stand, complete with its exemplary blunder, its fine specimen of that folly that answers questions before they are asked. Did he have to say last night? He did not. He had not even sense enough to imply his falsehoods instead of telling them. Such trivial involvements, taken in their stride by intelligent liars and disposed of with easy precision, rattled Francis to distraction. He jumped from the frying pan into the fire and back again. In a frenzy of snap-judgments, of stop-gap answers, of quick unthinking, Francis covered a break here, snipped off a loose end there; but he had never yet failed to find himself, when the dust settled, left holding, sick with exertion, a masterpiece of botchery, fit only to be thrown away before somebody caught him with it and recognized him for what he looked like—willing to deceive, but incapable of deceit. It was Francis's unalterable conviction that honesty is the best policy.

Mrs. Cunningham made a conventional remark expressing pleasure at Miss Imbrie's suggestion—Francis did not hear just what; for he was intent on getting out of his mess the shortest way. He waited a painful instant or two and then said brightly to Walter, "Well, how do you feel? Pretty well rested?"

"Ah, heck!" said Walter. He smiled guiltily. He writhed with reluctance.

Francis looked at Mrs. Cunningham to let her see that though duty had pushed him to waste no more time, he now checked duty to defer to her wishes. "I really think," he said, frowning, "that if it's convenient for you, we'd better—"

"Aw, heck!" said Walter.

"Yes, I think so," Mrs. Cunningham said. "Now, darling, let's not have any of that. You mustn't make it hard for Francis."

"You've been given quite a break," Francis said, kindly but firm. "And we have a lot of work to do. Are your books unpacked?" He spoke with unfeigned zeal, for the bad moment was over; and with unfeigned zeal he (though in a different and humbler spirit than he had planned) introduced at last the conscientious employee.

"Heck. Maggie's got them," said Walter. "Hey, Maggie!"

"Now, Walter, go and get them yourself. Maggie has—"

The connecting door opened and Maggie brought the pile of books in.

"Good morning," Francis said.

"How do you do, Mr. Ellery," said Maggie. "Good morning." Her tone was civil and obliging; but Francis heard it with a start. Maggie, he had observed before, was one to think her own thoughts; and last night she must have thought them when no Francis appeared; and now she was probably thinking a few of them. His sense of regenerated conscientiousness was impaired, for Maggie might be considered something of an expert on conscientious employees—or at least, Maggie would know one when she saw one.

3

It was not exactly a matter of getting permission to go to the dance Thursday night. Walter's lessons ordinarily took up the forenoon, and the afternoon went into Walter's exercise or amusement. They had tea about five and dinner about eight. When dinner was over Mrs. Cunningham said good night and took Walter upstairs. Francis did not see them again until nine o'clock the next morning. Usually—Mrs. Cunningham might suppose, always—Francis went upstairs too and worked on his manuscript until midnight; but Mrs. Cunningham had no way of knowing what he did and she never asked.

Just the same, Francis felt obligated to let her know that he was to be out Thursday night, and probably out late. To say nothing was impossible. Mrs. Cunningham would think it so odd of him—or so rude of him; and he himself would think it was so furtive of him. There was not even a remote chance of her having an objection; so, as a matter of form, what could be simpler than asking if she had any?

All Tuesday morning he was busy reviewing Walter's work. Walter had forgotten a good deal; and, in natural loathing of the things to be remembered, practiced an effective obstructionism by asking for longer and fuller explanations. By noon they were both worn out. Francis meant to speak of the dance at luncheon and get it over with, but no good opportunity presented itself, and he did not feel like making one, so he let it slide. On second thought, speaking of it at luncheon might be a little precipitate. It might seem to Mrs. Cunningham a kind of going-on-from-where-he-left-off, and an indication that Walter's lessons had interrupted his thoughts very little. Some simple opportunity would probably come before the afternoon was over.

After luncheon they went to Monte Carlo to get tennis rackets, and Walter wanted to see the Casino. This took a long while, and though Francis was watchful for good openings, none that suited him appeared. He thought that a good time would be when they had tea. They had tea on the partly sheltered terrace of the Café de Paris, but it did not prove a good time, for Walter could not keep quiet. The Casino had knocked his eye out. Though he had been coached into taking some creditable first steps in the fine art of learning what not to admire, he derogated with a bang. The elegant columns and colored marbles in the floor enchanted him. The crystal and red plush ravished his soul. Plainly he felt a holy joy, like that of Lord Byron surveying the noble remnants of the Parthenon, or Walter Pater noticing that the Gioconda's eyelids were a little weary. He lingered, peeping in at the empty theater; he kept taking out his admission card and looking at it; he loitered down the Salle de Jeu staring shyly at the tables half-filled with careful afternoon gamblers, rolling his eyes to the fake Persian vaults and trappings. With guilty glances—for it was clear that his mother and Francis did not share his enthusiasm—he measured the chances of delaying their departure.

Finally dragged away, Walter began to rouse himself, to come down to earth from the realms of romance as conceived by M. Blanc and splendor as constructed by M. Garnier. He reached a pitch of pleasure and hilarity. By biting small pieces out of a brioche he tried to transform it into a bust. He put a little butter in his chocolate. Reproved by his mother, he ducked down as though to hide his head under the table. At last abashed by her expression, he succeeded in sobering somewhat, and plied Francis with questions about roulette, about the Prince of Monaco, about how many people committed suicide. Mrs. Cunningham was both displeased and concerned, and Francis felt that it would not be tactful to introduce the subject of the dance. Perhaps it would be better, anyway, to postpone the whole business until tomorrow.

Wednesday Francis did not see Mrs. Cunningham until noon. It developed then that Miss Imbrie and Lorna and Gwen had come up about eleven, while Walter's lessons were going on, and had sat for half an hour with Mrs. Cunningham in the garden. Here was an opportunity of the most convenient kind; but Francis could not take it.

He was tongue-tied. That they should have come and
gone without his knowing stirred in him a sense of injury
—of that unwarrantable injury he regularly did himself
by tameness and submission. How intolerable to waste
mornings upstairs with Walter and schoolbooks! Who
gave a good God-damn whether Walter ever learned
anything? This whole preposterous farce—what was he
doing here, anyway, studying Mrs. Cunningham to see
how she felt, worrying about whether he could do this or
that? Pettishly, Francis let himself imagine scenes of
repudiation and declarations of independence. "Mrs. Cunningham," he might say, "this really won't do. I'm not cut
out for this. In many ways it has been very pleasant; but
it takes too much of my time. I think, if you can possibly
make some other arrangement, I must ask you to do
it. . . ."

But since Francis spoke nothing aloud, Mrs. Cunningham went on with her luncheon, observing that she
thought Lorna looked much better, that she had really
been concerned about her in Paris—she looked so tired.
It occurred to Francis that a mention of the dance might
have been made during the visit, and that Mrs. Cunningham, knowing of it, might be expecting him to speak, was
even inviting him to. In that event, Francis told himself,
she could go right on expecting; for the idea renewed his
sense of injury and aggravated his indignation. If she
were waiting to see him do what she knew he was going
to have to do, why, let her wait. She needn't worry; he
would ask her; but he would ask her when he got ready,
and she mustn't suppose that he felt any anxiety or much
interest. Viewed this way, it was a minor triumph for him
when Mrs. Cunningham changed the subject, and said that

she had some shopping to do, and that she and Maggie would go to Nice after luncheon.

The afternoon went slowly. They had planned to play tennis after Walter had his nap; but at two o'clock the King of Sweden, an aged, animated beanpole of a man with frail-looking long legs encased in narrow cylinders of white duck, turned up from somewhere to use the hotel tennis courts. To start another game while this was going on would be lese majesty in its modern meaning—a special sort of bad taste, a vulgar bumptiousness that saw in a simple and democratic monarch's loss of all practical powers a chance to treat him just like anybody else. The royal game was therefore the only one. As a further mark of deference it appeared proper for everyone to restrain his curiosity and to stay at a distance, so that the old man might play in peace.

Walter, coming down in flannels at half past two, was excited and interested by an actual king out on the courts hitting a ball around; but he was sensitive to the element of fantasy, almost of farce. From the glassed-in porch at the northeast end of the hotel, Walter gazed, shaking his head and grinning, at the distant tall figure. Walter's instinctive sense of values was nice. The King did not lack dignity, even when he ran or skipped; but it was dignity of the mild sort that would have suited a distinguished but senile preacher, or the president-emeritus of a rich university. The royal entourage of three or four ordinary people who had descended with the King from a large but ordinary automobile, left Walter unsatisfied. Whispers, hushed in good behavior, to look, that was the King of Sweden, struck him as funny. Maybe Julius Caesar or Napoleon would be along in a minute. He grew bored and restive. He murmured: "Hey, come on, King! Let's go!"

After an hour the King went, and Francis and Walter were able to have a short game. They had tea alone. Mrs. Cunningham got back a little after seven and sent word to Francis that she and Walter would not be down for dinner. Francis ate by himself, debating whether or not to call the villa. Calling must amount to asking them to ask him down, and he did not like it; but after dinner he did call. The man, Raymond, told him that they had all gone out to dine. Francis went upstairs, put on a bathrobe, and tried to get some writing done.

Thursday morning Mrs. Cunningham was there when he came for Walter's lessons, but she was merely waiting to say good morning to him, and Walter was ready to work, so it did not seem just the moment to mention the dance. However, he really would have to say something at luncheon. Finishing work at half past twelve, he stayed a moment to see if Mrs. Cunningham were upstairs and would come in. It was Maggie who came in. "Mr. Ellery," she said, "Mrs. Cunningham has had to go out. Some friends came unexpectedly—"

"Who are they?" said Walter.

"Well, a Mr. and Mrs. Peters. I don't think you'd remember them. They were friends of your father's."

"Gosh, are they here?" said Walter. "They're awful."

"Pipe down," said Francis.

"She'll be back before tea, Mrs. Cunningham said to tell you."

"Well, what are we going to do?" said Walter.

"What do we usually do?" said Francis. "We'll have

lunch, and you'll lie down, and then we'll have some tennis."

"I thought you said we might go to La— What was it?"

"La Turbie," said Francis, "but we'll have to speak to your mother. Perhaps we can go tomorrow."

"Promise?" said Walter.

"How can I promise until I know what your mother's plans are?" Francis asked reasonably.

✦

Beyond Beaulieu, above the headlands of Cap Ferrat, the sun was getting down. The extended shadow of the hotel covered the tennis courts. Francis kept an eye on the door, but he could not watch it all the time, so he missed seeing Mrs. Cunningham drive in. He had been delaying the end of the second set by taking five games and then letting Walter begin to win; for he wanted to be still playing, but able to finish quickly. Mrs. Cunningham would be fairly sure to come down to the court, and since they would have to wash before tea, he would have a chance, when Walter had been sent up, to get a moment alone with her. He had the eighth game at deuce when she did appear. She settled on the bench under a striped canvas tilt at the courtside to watch. Walter, his hair blowing forward across his forehead, yelled passionately, but much winded: "We have to finish! We have to finish!"

Anyone could see that Walter was tired, so without wasting more time Francis tossed the red ball over his head. It mounted against the late sunlight on the rock masses of the Tête du Chien, he eyed it carefully, dropped his racket back and drove it hard to the inside corner of the service court. Walter, too far over, had to let it go. "Good!" he panted. "Nice one!" but he hugged his racket in disappointment.

"Ad in," said Francis, hardening his heart. He held a hand up and the fat little ragamuffin of a ball boy bounced him two more.

"Say, set point!" said Walter. He changed courts with agility, acting out for his mother's benefit the importance of the moment. Francis fed him an easy one, and then put back Walter's return where he could not fail to get it. Pulling in the new return, Francis lobbed it to land well to Walter's left where Walter was weak. With a dramatic frenzy of effort, Walter tied himself up and backhanded into the net. "Ah, gee!" he said. The ball came coasting slowly back to him and he stopped it with his foot.

"What's wrong with your backhand is that you don't hold your racket right," Francis said, coming around the net. Taking Walter's damp hand, he loosened the fingers, shifted them on the handle, and pressed them closed again. "Like that," he said. "You'll get it. Come on. Put a sweater on. It's cold." They came off the court toward Mrs. Cunningham.

"Say, how about some lemonade?" Walter said to her. "Gosh, I'm thirsty."

Mrs. Cunningham said, "All right, dear." She looked toward the enclosed end of the porch above. "We'll have tea there. I don't think they like people in the lounge in flannels. Maggie would probably like to come down. Will you tell her? And wash a little, darling. You look very warm."

Francis slipped on his jacket, turned a scarf about his neck, and tucked the ends in. The persistent cold wind, blowing off the water, went through the wizened orange trees. Mrs. Cunningham was getting her things together silently, and Francis, waiting to take some of them, felt panic, for this was his moment to speak, he absolutely must; and yet he heard himself saying, "It's really quite cool, isn't it?"

"Yes," Mrs. Cunningham said. "It isn't as warm here as I hoped. I've noticed that it gets very cold about sunset."

In another moment they would reach the steps and go onto the glassed-in porch. Walter must be already upstairs; perhaps, his washing no more than a lick and a promise, already hurrying Maggie along to the elevator. Was he, Francis asked himself, or was he not, going to say at once, this instant: *Mrs. Cunningham, I've been meaning to ask you* . . .

Hushed but insistent, someone said behind him, "Hè. Tiens, Monsieur. Hè!" The ball boy, running with the box of balls, had overtaken him, and Francis stopped in confusion, shifting the rackets under his other arm, and groping in his jacket pocket for some franc pieces. "Fort bien," he said automatically, "à demain."

But how did he know what Mrs. Cunningham had in mind for tomorrow? Taking the box, Francis nearly dropped it. He flushed and said to her, "Sorry. Had you other plans? He's always hanging around anyway."

"Well, Francis—" Mrs. Cunningham said. She appeared to hesitate. "I know it's hard for you when we

don't keep to a regular schedule. You see, I didn't interrupt you this morning." She smiled and then looked seriously at him. "But tomorrow I do want these people—
they're very old friends of ours—to see Walter. They're
at Monte Carlo, but they may be leaving soon. I thought
we'd go over there to luncheon. If we left by twelve it
would be time enough, so most of the morning wouldn't
be disturbed. What do you think?"

"I think—" said Francis, and drew a breath. The note
of consultation, the confident question, doing him if not
the honor, at least the justice, of assuming his responsibility and real concern, seemed to bring them back in an
instant to where they had been at Montreux. The difficulties he had labored under during the three days past resolved themselves, for they were difficulties of relationship
or attitude, and could exist only if, feeling himself dis-
trusted, he returned the distrust.

"I think," he repeated, smiling, "that it certainly
wouldn't do any harm. I don't think it's good for Walter
to feel that too much is going on around him. But going
out to luncheon one day couldn't very well amount to too
much. Speaking of that," he added—a little stiltedly, but
without losing composure, "some people in Menton are
giving a dance tonight. Miss Imbrie asked me if I'd care
to go; but it occurs to me that when I'm making Walter
toe the mark, it might be better if I didn't—"

"Oh, Francis," said Mrs. Cunningham. "I don't see
that. You have Walter on your hands all day. There's no
reason why you shouldn't go if you want to."

"Well," said Francis, nervous with delight, "I thought
I'd wait a day or so and see how things shaped up." His
sense of virtue was strong and pleasant—a little too strong,

considering that the things he had waited to see shape up were mostly elements of self-interest. He said deprecatingly, "As a matter of fact, I did rather want to go."

"Then do go!" Mrs. Cunningham said. Her charm of manner was never greater. "I'd really like you to."

Six

THE CHILL, noticed by Mrs. Cunningham, that fell at sunset was generally succeeded by a return of warmer air. You felt it about seven o'clock; and it continued through the evening. Moreover, Francis was warmed by his own high spirits; and he was sure that he would need no overcoat for the trip to Menton. He did not bring one downstairs, where he waited, with time to kill after Mrs. Cunningham and Walter went up, for the car to come.

Waiting, Francis thought of having a drink; but he remembered Monday night, and he thought it likely that Miss Imbrie might have observed that at supper he was not quite sober. It seemed better not to turn up now smelling of liquor; and in too fine fettle to want a drink anyway, he went instead into the empty billiard room. He took down a cue and set himself to knocking the balls around; missing easy ones; to his astonishment, accomplishing occasional shots much too hard for him.

While he moved about the table Francis hummed, and then under his breath he sang, and then he stopped and laughed; for he was singing: *Now the Queen of seasons bright, with the day of splendor* . . . and he saw, a little fussed by the unconscious mind's irremissible naïveté, the hymn's connection. At school, ranked years ago in chapel, they used to feel good to that tune, when the triumphant gladness of Our Lord's resurrection was given a compelling fillip by the thought of the impending Easter recess. Raising the strain at the top of their lungs, several hundred off-key singers in common celebration raised the roof. Francis was not sure that he liked these often-discovered proofs that, too young to have a say in the process, he had been marked for life; but, glancing to see that no one was near enough to hear him, he soon went on singing. Across the radiant green woolen broadcloth the running balls struck and broke apart like magic. Several times he laid his cue down and walked out on the terrace to test the temperature. Though not warm, the night seemed to him delightfully soft and mild. The truth was that neither of the two overcoats he had with him was entirely suitable for formal evening wear.

At half past nine the car came, and Francis went out to it. He was not halfway down the lighted steps when Miss Imbrie got the window beside her open a crack and called, "You can't go that way, Francis! It may turn very cold!"

"I'm quite hardy," Francis said, smiling.

In Florence the local bloods, the often-not-spurious Russian princes, the sporty Italians, cousins and cadets of noble houses whose grand cinquecento names embellished the evening, achieved (whether because they were inured to the climate; whether because they had not the price of an overcoat) an effect indubitably dashing and continental when they arrived, even on bitter nights, bearing in their left hands a pair of folded gloves, a dress scarf of black or white silk, and a soft black felt hat. Francis lifted his left hand, showing Miss Imbrie these objects. He laughed and turned his face up to the stars above the mountains. "I don't think it's going to snow again."

"Well, then you'll have to come in here."

"Not at all," said Francis, realizing that to avoid crowding it had been planned to seat him in front with Raymond. Raymond stood waiting for the final word; and Francis stepped past him, opened the front door, and got in. "Perfectly all right," he said through the pushed-back glass.

Out of the depths Mr. McKellar said, "I might offer to change places with you, Ellery, were I but now the lord of such hot youth as when brave Gaunt—but I'm not. I prefer to be lapped in women and luxury." At patriarchal ease, one elegant thin leg thrown over the other, his patent leather slipper winking in the light, Mr. McKellar occupied the back seat with Lorna and Miss Imbrie. An opera cloak shrouded his shoulders. He was bare-headed, but he held his collapsed hat in his white-gloved hands. Francis guessed that he was costumed with precious care exactly as he used to be a generation ago in his polka-dancing prime.

Francis laughed again, for everything, even Mr. McKellar, appeared agreeable to him. Wonderful old ass! "Please don't worry about me," he said. Impatiently he was preparing to look at Lorna. She was folded in a wrap of dully shimmering gold cloth with a scarf bound over her head. Her lips opened in the shadow and she said, "Hello."

"Hello," said Francis.

He could hardly speak the word. His heart enclosed her. Without the use of hands, his heart cupped up her face and held it. Her bound head, her shadowed eyes, her

229

smiling, twisted lips, possessed, as much as his mind, his pumping blood—not by beauty, for the instant was one of those when he noted (and admitted; for what did he care? What difference did it make?) that her face, at other times so enchanting, could seem plain, even ugly. He looked at her face, and hunger, the wild imperative wish, consumed him. He wanted her; and not merely in terms of coverture and access. He wanted all that, and he looked at her body, distracted because he could not even touch it; but in his mind he saw the sexual connection as a step, means to a vital emotional end. It was the entering wedge to be pushed home until, sooner or later rendered by pleasure beside herself, she let all go, convulsively gave up to him the something more, he did not know what, that, over and above her body, have from her he must.

He thought he must. In that longing, while it lasted, there was no choice; and in that helplessness, Francis saw with surprise (it was naturally not the first time; but he often forgot or made fun of it) that all the self-devotion and all the obscenity of love in literature or in court records was comprehensible. He understood. Men who could not stop their longing did crazy things. Through ardent temperament, or extreme constancy of mind, or, perhaps usually, through a thick-headedness that formed few thoughts and so did not easily replace one with another, some wretches, remarkable for their grossness or their delicacy, loved their women night and day. Frantic all the time, what would you stop at? She could despise or cheat you and that would be all right. She could be a nun or a motion picture actress and you would be fool enough to love her. She could be married to Simone de' Bardi; she could be a dirty old worn-out tart; she could be dead;

while you, *lacrimans*—the word was sniveling, Francis remembered; and he recoiled—*exclusus amator*, groveled through the hopeless days or years, still loving, still locked out. Shaken, Francis thought: "To hell with that!"

He turned his head. On the strapontin in front of Miss Imbrie, Gwen, her hair bound up, too, faced him. She was close to the window and Francis found that he need not have worried about that drink he didn't have, for the scent of brandy hung pleasantly on her breath. "You smell like a barroom," he said, still trying to steady himself. "I wish I'd been along."

" 'Twas a balmy summer evening and a goodly crowd was there," said Gwen. She stuck her tongue out at him. "Now would you just as soon close that glass and freeze by yourself?"

Francis smiled and closed the glass. His shocking thoughts had become suddenly silly, a neurotic's-eye-view of what was in practice not like that; a parade of images about as life-like as the procession of the passions in the *Faerie Queene*—Gluttony on a swine in vine leaves, Lechery on a goat with a burning heart in his hand. He thought at random that Gwen probably lived a happy life, unfanciful, orderly, humorous without the tension of great attempts at wit; progressing gravely and intelligently from a neat happy child, to a neat amiable young woman, to the neat comfortable marriage whose reasonable affections would operate to make her the mother of more neat happy children.

The cold air blew in on Francis. He put his hat on and began to dig for a cigarette case that was in one of his waistcoat pockets, glancing about to see where they were. Up through the dark, past bits of wall and infrequent houses, past overhung olive trees, the headlights lifted steadily along the rising paving stones and the white retaining ramps of the long traverses.

"Grande Corniche?" he said to Raymond.

"En chemin. Yes, sir," Raymond said. "Regardez à droit—down."

Francis turned. Over the moving door frame, over the near parapet edge paralleling it, the tremendous void fell away. A lacework of lights was stretched out, hanging from the mountain, sunk in crumpled folds about the bays and crooked headlands of the coast below. Linked by festoons of gold points, the towns beyond Cap Ferrat showed like far-off rakings of embers. On the night above Monte Carlo glowed a hazed radiance, a pleasure-dome of light. Francis swung back his hand and rapped on the glass behind him. "Look down!" he said, pointing. "Look down there." He was shivering a little, but more from festivity or excitement than from cold.

"This way is the quicker," Raymond observed. "We go to Roquebrune and down a little. The other way, we go to Menton and far around and up a lot." He nodded his head with that peculiar Gallic satisfaction, that perpetual soyons-sérieux, by which foreigners and even other Frenchmen are persuaded that the evidence of their senses is in error, and that to live in France is to live by reason. Francis wondered where Raymond had learned his English.

2

"Lord Bardo," said Mr. McKellar, "allow me to present Mr. Ellery."

Having heard his host named only once, several days ago, and then as Johnny, Francis could not wholly suppress his surprise and interest. He was not in the habit of being presented to British peers; but he composed himself and inclined his head with the polite reserved look copied by close observation from the bearing of those who seemed to show to best advantage when meeting, along with Francis and a good many other people, a bishop, a senator, or the president of the university.

As in some of those encounters, Francis's first sensation was of being let down. If he acknowledged a duty of politeness to defer to his civil or social superiors, they surely owed it to him, or at any rate to themselves, to look as though they ought to be deferred to. Lord Bardo was not as tall as Francis. Spare, small, somewhere between forty and sixty, he had a shrewd pointed face, not much hair, and a pleasant leathery tone of skin. His manner was that of a shy man who wishes people would leave him alone, yet realizes that they mean no harm, and so shrinks from offending them by suggesting it. When Mr. McKellar caught him, he stopped, stood harassed, making ingratiating grimaces, but glancing aside with twitches of consternation that seemed to say that all this—the massive fantasy on a Pompeian villa surrounding him; the movement of guests down the cross-vistas, one terminated by a long linen-draped table set with punch bowls and clusters of bottles, the other by a band obviously French playing behind a breastwork of flowers *I want to go where you go* . . . had nothing in particular to do with him and he was a stranger here himself.

Disregarding, or not noticing Francis's bishop technique, he thrust out a hand shortly, looked up to a point just past Francis's shoulder and said, "Of course, of course. How-do-do. Glad you could come."

Hastily Francis took the hand, hoping he had not been convicted of some notable gaucherie by his failure to realize that Lord Bardo would expect to shake hands. Mr. McKellar, however, seeing somebody he knew, had turned away with a flourish to speak to him. Lord Bardo stood at obvious loss. He looked covertly past Francis again. He cleared his throat and said suddenly, "Here for long?"

"I've just come up from Florence," Francis said; and realized then that, for no reason he could think of, he had mistaken the question.

"Florence, eh?" said Lord Bardo. He brooded a moment on the remarkable circumstance. "Know a number of Americans there. D'you know the Robertsons?"

"I'm afraid not," Francis said.

"Girl's a singer. Good one. Sang for my wife once."

"Oh," said Francis. "Well, yes. I didn't—Mrs. Robertson's a friend of my mother's. I don't know them very well."

"Let me introduce you to a charming young lady," Lord Bardo said in answer. He gave Francis's arm a quick, directing tap.

"Thanks awfully," said Francis, "but I'm waiting for Miss Imbrie to come down."

234

"Just as you like," Lord Bardo said. "Make yourself at home." He nodded, his manner more harassed than ever, and went away, skirting the loiterers at the foot of the great stairs, and slipped along the red wall painted in classic rectangles with griffins, baskets with thyrsi, and branches of herbs.

"Johnny," said Mr. McKellar, swinging about, "I—"

"He got away," said Francis.

"Interesting fellow, Johnny," Mr. McKellar said, perceiving that it was true. "Lady Bardo's an American. Old friend of Mabel's. Bardo's the celebrated yachtsman and ichthyologist."

Francis smiled at him, but Mr. McKellar did not appear to see anything funny in the twin occupations; and Francis guessed he was right; there wasn't. Down the noble staircase Miss Imbrie and Gwen and Lorna were coming at last with a number of other women. "That's Lady Bardo, talking to Mabel," Mr. McKellar said. "Delightful person. You must meet her."

Francis looked up at a stocky, hearty woman in old rose satin under row after row of short crystal bead fringes. On her head grew amazing fluffed-out, towy hair that looked like (though doubtless it was not) the result of a bad accident with some dye or restorative. Her expression was lively and intelligent. She might very well be, as Mr. McKellar said, a delightful person; just as Miss Imbrie was excellent company, esteemed by all who knew her; but, descending the pseudo-Roman stairs in step together, dressed with the idea of looking pretty, nodding together with affectionate animation, chattering away, the cruel touch of caricature was on them. They were old.

Francis marked it and was given pause. He had the writer's laboriously cultivated, unnatural habit of mind and eye. Like the froward and odious child, overpraised in the fairy tale, this habit of eye sees, along with most other people, that the emperor hasn't any clothes on. There is then no holding this habit of mind. It has to tell everyone.

Past the adipose, coarsely rounded flesh of Lady Bardo's bare arm Francis saw Lorna's arms and shoulders, slight and white against the bodice of the black dress. Lorna's freshly painted lips were a vivid sullen red. Her face, perhaps partly because of the lipstick and the black taffeta, looked pale and tense; but that was nothing. The line of her cheek and chin, not unlike Miss Imbrie's, and close enough to compare with it, was delicate and charming. For skin, Miss Imbrie had a sort of tough tegument, well scrubbed, suitably rouged, well powdered; but who would want to touch it? Lorna moved with a limber unconscious ease just behind the older women, the joints of whose thighs were certainly no longer like jewels. On Lorna's thigh, close to the dipping waistline, those two big silver rosettes that she and Gwen had exclaimed over shifted and fell.

To meet them, Francis and Mr. McKellar advanced onto the central paving circled by Ionic columns, walking across a mosaic of a mighty wheel of fortune with numerals and signs of the zodiac. Other people had come up, some just arriving, some leaving the dance floor, to speak to their hostess.

Hanging back, Francis moved near Lorna. "Here," she said. Putting out her hand, she slid a gold compact into

his coat pocket. Standing closer in the press, she let her
hand fall, held his a moment.

"—and Mr. Ellery," Miss Imbrie said, waving an arm
toward him. Francis bowed to Lady Bardo. Somebody
stepped in front of him, and groping quickly, he caught
Lorna's hand again. "Run along, children," Miss Imbrie
said.

✦

"But I don't care to meet anyone else," Francis said.
"I don't want to dance with anyone else. If I do, I'll
dance with Mr. McKellar. I've met him."

Lorna choked with laughter. Swaying back against his
arm, she turned her distorted face up. "You're such a
fool!" she said. "Do you know something? Ever since you
left Paris, I— oh, I'm so glad you're here. We're going to
have fun, aren't we. But, look, darling. Quick. Someone's
coming to cut in. He's an artist named Goodwin Kirkland,
from California. His sister's a friend of mine, and I—"

"You have more damn friends," said Francis. He felt
a moment's pang, his sense of possession affronted, the
inconvenience of his situation emphasized, for he knew no
one here, and the way his days were arranged made it unlikely that he would come to know anyone. The high
spirit of his happiness faltered; and, spiteful and reasonable, his mind invited him to go on, to look at the fact
that he was in a poor position if he hoped to keep Lorna
for himself; and then to look at several more facts like it.
What did he mean, "keep Lorna for himself"? Did he
think he was going to marry her? That was certainly in-

237

teresting. What would he use for money? Did he, perhaps, think he was going to have her without marrying her? That might present a few difficulties, too. Then, what was he doing? What did he have the half-wittedness to feel so good about?

Francis did not know. The questions were unanswerable. He looked at them steadily, and he could not offer a suggestion nor indicate any possible plan; and this stubborn muteness which would not rise to insults, nor offer objections, nor answer arguments became suddenly his best defense. The vindictive mind, in its turn, seemed to falter. A kind of silence fell, prolonging itself; and Francis, still not answering, simply thinking, thought: *I don't know and I don't care.* He looked at Lorna and found her just lifting her eyes to look at him—all of it could hardly have lasted a second, for she was looking to see what he meant. He took a breath and holding her eyes he said, "Well, don't get gay with any California artists, or I'll break your neck."

The effort of deliberate compulsion to hold her gaze was unnecessary, he discovered, for she did not try to look away. "All right," she said. "I won't. But I'm not. I—"

"I believe you," Francis said.

The expected hand touched his elbow. Before this, Francis had observed that on the Pacific coast a new race was being bred, or at any rate, a marked mutation, larger, handsomer, and not much stupider than the pre-existing Eastern types. Francis, with his shoes off, lacked nearly half an inch of being six feet tall. The evolving Californians were always three or even four inches more than six feet. Francis glanced at this specimen, this grinning lumbering cub, with tolerant approval—Napoleon pinching his guardsman's cheek. He relinquished Lorna and turned away.

Crossing the hall to go along and get himself a drink he met Miss Imbrie face to face. With presence of mind, he said, "Will you dance with me?"

"You are very kind," Miss Imbrie said, "but, no, thank you, I won't. I am not much of a dancer, and you can dismiss me from your mind. We have a couple of tables of bridge in the library, and I shall stay until I lose all my money. Then I shall probably go home at a reasonable hour."

"How long does this affair last?" Francis asked.

"Indefinitely. Till morning, I suppose."

Francis had turned to walk along the passage with her, and she continued, "I shall slip away when the time comes. It has nothing to do with the rest of you."

Whatever happened, whenever it was over, Francis remembered that he would have Walter's lessons at nine o'clock. "Do you think I could go down with you?" he said.

"Oh, you don't want to do that."

"I don't want to. But, alas—"

"Well, I shall be in here. If you're really serious I'll try to let you know." Through the tall open door Francis could see walls of books behind glass and wire grills so lofty that the top shelves were accessible only from the rungs of a mahogany ladder. In the corner a bust of Edward Gibbon stood on a pedestal. A huge varnished terrestrial globe stood beside a desk covered with silver-framed photographs. One of them signed, with several lines, was of the King of Italy. There were also two bridge tables, a couple of champagne buckets, and a half dozen people standing laughing together. A woman who was talking to Lady Bardo wore the only diamond stomacher Francis had ever actually seen. Turning on the threshold, Miss Imbrie said, "Stay and have a good time. I would if I were you."

Her look was one of liking. The grave lift of her eyes and the humorous line of her long mouth offered nothing so definite and solid as advice, which she would neither presume nor trouble to give; but, for a whim, she seemed to be intending a hint based on some casual hunch, that he was free to take or leave.

"Very likely I will," said Francis, smiling. Of course there was nothing Miss Imbrie could, or for that matter, would, do for him; but from her expression he had the pleasure of being able to guess that she found him not bad at all, and that, strictly aloof, amused, even ironic, she would at least not hinder any proper or reasonable designs he might have on her niece. Asking her to dance had been a good idea; and, pleased with her and feeling better about himself, Francis found his way to the buffet where a footman served him with brandy and soda.

He stood aside, holding the glass and watching the crowd, listening to the music beat up to the caissoned Roman vault beyond the hall. Though not much good to dance to, it was that French music, hilarious to hear, whose master-tune is called le jazz or le fox-trot. The drums and horns, no matter what they are supposed to be playing, abandon it after the first bars, and furiously strike up something that might or might not be the *Sambre et Meuse*, while the strings and piano set faintly against it

American tunes of last year. Swallowing his drink, Francis put down the glass and went with decision to cut back on Lorna.

✦

At half past twelve supper was served in a sort of conservatory, a large room with a glass roof that seemed to be Lord Bardo's aquarium. The walls were lined with lighted tanks full of swimming fish, some unremarkable except perhaps to an ichthyologist, some extraordinary and highly colored. The effect, for there was no direct light, was the disconcerting but beautiful one of thirty tables at the bottom of the sea. They were arranged around a piscina, lit from beneath the water. Aquatic plants and immense lily pads grew in it, and there was nothing to keep an inattentive person from falling in. Francis wondered how soon someone would—if not a guest, then perhaps a footman serving, or the young man who had detached himself from the orchestra and, strolling around with a concertina, entertained them with songs.

By half past one, nobody had fallen in. It was in fact apparent that the party was fairly serious. The Prefect of the Department was present, the officials of the municipality of Menton in what must be a body, and a number of important-looking Monégasques, almost all wearing the ribbon of the Order of Saint Charles. Francis had seen very few of them dancing, but they had been sitting around all evening on the edges, patronizing the buffet and greeting each other with dignity and satisfaction. They remained now with their cigars, their decorations, and their dressed-up wives in the submarine glow below the fish tanks. Though the orchestra was playing again, the singer with the concertina remained, too. So did Francis and Gwen.

The young man from California, who seemed to be known as Goody to his friends, had sat down to supper with them. He brought along a girl named Emily, who was married, though not to him. She was large and well-made, with dark reddish hair and the rounded, somewhat pasty features and heavy eyelids that often go with such hair. Her voice sounded as if she had laryngitis. At the sound, most men would prick up their ears; and at sight of her, to most men various impure or improper thoughts, whether welcome or unwelcome, would occur. It was plain that she was not sober, and also plain that she either was, or would soon be a confirmed alcoholic, for she showed the characteristic stuporous amiability that comes from adding a great deal of fresh alcohol to a system more or less permanently saturated with it. Tomorrow morning or afternoon she would wake up with no idea or only the haziest, of where she had spent the evening. From certain small indications—a swelling of his face when he looked at her, and an unconscious shifting in his chair—the Californian left little doubt that he was nowadays the man she frequently found in her bed when she did wake up.

He—this Kirkland—though drinking plenty was not at all drunk. Heated by an inadvertent thought or glance, he would forget himself, look popeyed an instant at Emily, and move his big frame in the guilelessly indecent squirm. Then he would recover, be ingenuously worried about what Emily might take it into her head to say or do next. He was friendly to Francis, polite to Gwen and

Lorna, and in a manly, frank, western way respectful to Mr. McKellar and to Miss Imbrie who had joined them soon after they sat down.

Kirkland must be rich; he was assuredly simple, for this seductively rounded slob Emily obviously looked exotic and exciting to him— the kind of passionate and tragic fatal woman found drunk in France in one or two recent novels. What his art was like Francis couldn't guess; but he had the diffidence sometimes seen in a big man brought up as an athlete—it seemed that he had rowed a year or two ago in one of the great University of California crews —who discovers or thinks he discovers (and it is almost always too late) that his real interests are intellectual or artistic. He sat around humbly regretting the sane and wholesome way he had wasted his youth.

All this amused and interested Francis, and he was not offended by Kirkland's show of regard for him as a genuine author; but he could easily have done without him and his girl; and he did not like it when, the orchestra having begun to play again, and some man having come up to dance with Emily—she arose in a kind of sagging trance, just not slumping against him—Kirkland asked Lorna to dance. Mr. McKellar said, "Well, Mabel, shall we tread a measure?"

"Part of one, perhaps," Miss Imbrie said, and they arose, too.

Subduing his annoyance, which he had no right to feel— this was only the second time Kirkland had danced with Lorna—Francis said to Gwen, "I guess I'm stuck with you."

"And how!" Gwen said. He made to rise, but she clapped a hand on his wrist. "Sit still!" she said in a loud whisper. "Give a girl a break! If you must know, I've just got my shoes off. Oh, why did I buy those damned things! They looked so sweet. I'll probably have to go home barefoot. All right, laugh. I wish you had them on. Give me a cigarette."

Francis gave her one. "Look," he said, "just as a matter of curiosity, who is this pie-eyed Emily, and why?"

"Her name is Hartpence," Gwen said. "Mrs. Hartpence. She goes around with Goody. There's a very big important scandal about her. D'you think she's good-looking? I don't. Though I will say her clothes are gorgeous."

"Goody!" said Francis. "It's true, then. Do you have to call him that?"

"Oh, do I?" said Gwen. She rolled her eyes. "That could be my man. Beautiful blond beast." She drank some champagne. "Oh, my poor feet! Do you think anyone would mind if I went and sat with them in the pool?"

"I think everyone would mind," Francis said. "That's the Chief of Police, right over there. He—"

"Oh, he's going to sing again!" Gwen cried. She clapped her hands hard and the man with the concertina inclined his head toward her.

"Sh!" said Francis. "Do you want to wake up in Buenos Aires? I'll have to take that glass away from you."

"I wish you would. Think how my head is going to ache tomorrow! No, please, please! I want it."

"Reason subdues the appetites, as usual—" Francis began.

"No, I want to listen! I want to learn the words!" She clenched her hands and shook them in front of her. "Oh, he sings so fast!" She seized Francis's arm. "What was it after that? What was that?"

"Modesty," Francis said, "forbids—"

"Oh, I'll bet you didn't get it either! What did she have—petons?"

"Feet," said Francis. "You know, like yours. Itsy-bitsy ones. Then, well, she had also tout petits tétons, que—"

"Tétons?"

"Let it suffice," Francis said, "that most women do have them. In moments, I suppose more or less intimate, he says he was in the habit of—well, que je tâtais à tâtons. Didn't they teach you any French at college? It's the language of art, diplomacy, and the passions."

"What's this about passions?" Mr. McKellar said. He let himself grandly down in the next chair. "I have been deserted," he said. "Tell me about passions."

"They are a closed book to me," Francis said. "I was just trying to spare Gwen's modesty while still giving her some idea of what he's singing."

"My dear Ellery," said Mr. McKellar. He shook his head. "Have you yet to learn that women know no modesty? Well, I can't pretend that I found it out any quicker. You presume to imagine that you can spare Gwen's modesty? Never believe it. Of course, it's you that makes her blush—"

"On the contrary," said Francis, who did not feel in the mood for an oration, "she practically made me blush."

"In a word, in a word!" said Mr. McKellar, and Francis saw that he was going to get the oration anyway. "Being male, you suffer from false modesty, and of course there is no other kind. You make her blush. If she likes you, she knows enough about men to know that she will have to blush to oblige you. If she doesn't like you, she blushes because a blush serves to bring up your own fatuous notions about modesty, and so may keep you from being a nuisance. At heart Gwen never blushed in her life. Do not confuse it with chastity. Chastity is innocent of affectation. Hamlet says to Ophelia: 'Lady, shall I lie in your lap?' She answers: 'No, my lord.' He says: 'I mean, my head in your lap.' She says: 'Ay, my lord.' 'Do you think,' says he, 'I meant country matters?' She says: 'I think nothing, my lord.' How exquisitely right! Like Gwen's, her chastity is as clear as day."

"I am as modest as anything," Gwen said. "And if you have to talk about chastity, would you just as soon not talk about mine? It makes me feel like one of those articles on should a bride confess, or that last lecture in freshman hygiene."

"My dear child," said Mr. McKellar, "I apologize!" Fondly, he patted her hand. "I was carried away on the high tide of allocution. When I meet a young man of wit and sense, like Ellery, I feel a great obligation to hand on my hard-won store of wisdom and experience. From my faltering hand, may he catch the torch—"

That was right, Francis realized. Mr. McKellar had been a little carried away; and not altogether by allocution or any other intellectual disturbance. Francis drank the rest of the champagne in his glass. His mind, which seemed gradually to have taken on the same gold tone as the wine, moved distinct and lucid. Poor old man, he thought, for in his genial comprehension or understanding a mellow mild pity, without disgust at others or distress to himself, ruffled the moment's smiling surface. Mr. McKellar ought to pay more attention to Lucretius. *Con-*

viva recedis . . . Here Mr. McKellar sat at the table, the litter of the supper on it, half the people gone, and bent his cavernous eyes on Gwen. "Now, come and dance with me," he said.

"Eric, I can't," Gwen said. "My damned pink slippers are killing me." She wailed. "There. They're on," she said to Francis. "But it's no use. I won't be able to endure it. Do you know, I'm going to have to go home with Aunt Mabel."

"Well, maybe we ought all to cut along," Francis said. "The truth is, I've got to be on the job tomorrow morning."

"Nonsense, nonsense!" cried Mr. McKellar. "Let her go down and get more slippers and come back. Any girl worth her salt danced out six pairs an evening in the good old days."

It was, Francis told himself, as though the Ancient Mariner, instead of detaining pleasure-seekers for an edifying homily, were, at sound of the loud bassoon, to cut a caper; and far from preferring a walk to the kirk, made tracks for the merry din where he only hoped they wouldn't go home until morning. Francis hesitated.

"More champagne!" said Gwen.

"You little drunkard!" said Francis. He pulled the bottle out of the pail and poured her some. Abstracted, he was still hesitating, trying to weigh his own desires, so he poured himself some. He did not want to stay up all night, especially with no chance of outstaying Mr. McKellar, and certainly no chance here of getting Lorna to himself. The thought held him up; as though something in all this, going contrary to his experience, did not make sense; and then he recognized it. Did he really suppose Lorna so lacking in resource that, if she wanted him to get her alone, she would not easily arrange it? Turning the stem of the glass slowly around in his fingers, watching the fine bubbles come up, he began to think how little Lorna here was like Lorna as she had been in Paris.

For one thing, she did not sound the same; indeed, she said almost nothing—what, after all, could she say, since he himself (if not because of Mr. McKellar or Miss Imbrie or Gwen; then because of the racket of dance music or the expectation that someone would cut in on him) had certainly said little. "I've got to do something about this," he thought suddenly. "All this damned nonsense—" One thing he could do was let Gwen and Miss Imbrie go, wait an hour or so for them to get to bed and asleep, dodge Mr. McKellar, and see if Raymond, who would probably be sent back for them, wouldn't in consideration of a hundred francs run them down and go back again for Mr. McKellar. Mr. McKellar might not like it, but Francis had had enough of Mr. McKellar anyway. "Well," he said aloud, "I know better; but I've never done it yet."

"Bravo!" said Mr. McKellar. "Youth at the helm and pleasure at the prow!"

✦

At half past two Miss Imbrie and Gwen left, but not without putting a hitch in Francis's plan. He came out to the portico with Mr. McKellar to see them off, and Miss Imbrie said: "Eric, I believe I'll let Raymond go to bed.

Telephone to that place in Monte Carlo and get them to send for you when you want to go, will you? I know they're open all night."

Re-entering the great hall with Mr. McKellar, Francis saw that he would have to discover where this place in Monte Carlo was, and do some telephoning of his own. Kirkland would be very likely to know. Francis found him having a drink by the buffet.

"Well, old boy," he said to Francis rather boisterously. "How is it?" He clapped him with warmth on the shoulder.

Francis did not know just when they had got to be such good friends; but it was after all complimentary, and if Kirkland liked him as much as that, Francis in return found the circumstance a reason for liking Kirkland. He took a drink too, and asked him if he had any idea where this place in Monte Carlo was.

"Why, hell!" Kirkland said. He began to feel in his pockets. He produced some keys. "Got a car outside there," he said. "Take the damn thing, why don't you? Red Renault. The chasseur will get it for you."

"Thanks a lot," Francis said, evading this happy-go-lucky generosity, "but I want to go home. I hear there's some place in—" God alone knew what it would cost him, and he wondered if Kirkland wouldn't be just as ready to lend him, instead of a car, five hundred francs, which would be enough to put him on the safe side.

Kirkland still held out the keys. "No, look, Francis," he said. "Take it. I wish you would. Emily's got a car up here. She's putting some of us up."

"No, honestly," Francis said. "I don't have a permit de conduire."

249

"You don't need one. Nobody ever bothers you. If they do, mine's in the side pocket. Take it. I don't want to leave it here. Where are you staying? Cap d'Ail? I'm near Eze. Run the girls up for a cocktail tomorrow afternoon—they know where it is—and I'll drive you back. How's that?"

"I—" began Francis, for this was insane. He couldn't possibly go to Eze tomorrow afternoon—unless, of course, having the car he used it first to take Walter up to show him the Ligurian trophy at La Turbie—after all, an educational thing to do. Lorna and Gwen might go along, too. Afterward they could run over to Eze and deliver the car. Walter would be enchanted.

"All right," Francis said. "Much obliged. I'll take care of it." He slid the keys into his waistcoat pocket.

3

SLOWLY, with caution, Francis turned the Renault up the long cypress avenue. He knew how the gear shift worked, for he had driven one a few times in Brittany the summer before; but this was probably a later model, and the clutch action was different—or he was nervous, for he had trouble getting it out of neutral. He had given the chasseur ten francs for acting as though the infernal, embarrassing screeches he evoked were perfectly natural and due to the wickedness of the machine and not to Francis. In the dark he said to Lorna, "If this were my car, I'm damned if I'd let myself drive it." But that might alarm her, and he added, "I've got it now. It was just a battle of wills. It is as gentle as a lamb." He glanced aside, saw far below the wink of the pharos on the Menton breakwater. "Left," he said. "That's right. We'll pick up the Corniche at Roquebrune. Raymond gave me a lecture on geography coming up. Are you going to be warm enough?"

"I'm all right. You ought to have a coat."

"Over here I would have died long ago, if exposure could kill me. Though as a matter of fact, this is about the same latitude as Portland, Maine; and I don't think they go driving there on January nights in open cars."

"Is it?" said Lorna.

"Look here," said Francis, "do you feel cold?"

"I'm all right. I think we should have told Eric."

"Your friend Goody will tell him when he needs to know. I simply didn't dare tell him. He'd probably come along. You aren't seriously worried about that, are you? He's old enough to go home by himself—" He made a turn and said, "Now this ought to be Roquebrune. It is. Sens Unique. It would be. We'll try through here. Do you suppose everyone is dead? Look, see that? The iron balconies. Isn't that charming?"

He was shivering a little. January night in the latitude of Portland, Maine, was right! "Ah," he said, "there's the Corniche. That's pretty good, if I do say so." Bending his head, he brushed her cold cheek with his lips.

"You don't have to do that," she said.

"Did you say," said Francis, letting the car slow down, "that I didn't have to do that?"

"Yes."

"Would you just as soon tell me what you mean?"

"It seems perfectly clear. You don't have to. And I wish you wouldn't."

Francis cast his eyes around. Up came a neat sign,

Défense de Stationer. "To hell with them!" he said. "No, wait."

The curve of an observation point bent out in the star-light and he turned the car sharp, jerked it up with the headlights shafting over the parapet into space. Cutting the engine and the lights, he took her angrily in his arms.

"No, please," said Lorna. "I want to go home. No, Francis. I don't want you to."

"What is this nonsense?" said Francis. Angrier still, he kissed her with indignation, repeatedly and hard.

"You're hurting me," she said between her teeth.

"You must have been reading a book," Francis said. "I'm not hurting you."

"Oh, Francis. Please. It's so stupid. What's the good of kissing me?"

"None," said Francis shortly, letting her go. "If you feel that way."

"It isn't the way I feel. That doesn't matter. I won't tell you about that. It would just be so much easier if you'd—"

"If I'd what?"

"If you'd let me alone, drop it. I would like to know one thing. Why did you go to so damned much trouble with me? Was it for fun?"

Speechless, Francis searched for cigarettes. When he found them, he lit one, held it out to her, and lit another. "Now, let's get this straight," he said slowly. "What's to be let alone? What was so damned much trouble? What was fun?"

He paused, his effort to be reasonable wilting a little in the face of the phrase, "just for fun." He knew what that was. That was something from the fantastic female world of the emotions, with its usually low romantic taste, its unpredictable fancies, its folklore of pursuit and marriage by capture, its cherished fairy tales of Cinderella, of Beauty and the Beast. The never-quite-adult habit of a woman's thought—no doubt Lorna actually believed that, just for fun, just for a practical joke on a trusting little girl, men went to so damned much trouble—checked him. She ought to have been exempt from nonsense. The wonderfully clear intelligent cast of her blue eyes ought to have meant a clearness of sight that recognized the world as it was, not—*The hours I spent with thee, dear heart, are as a string of pearls to me*—as it was sung. "It's a hard thing to phrase," he said. "It's so ridiculous. But are you trying to tell me that I am tired of you, or something like that? That"—he couldn't resist the temptation—"I forgot to remember?"

Instantly Francis regretted it, penitent, even frightened; for the cheap strains of that music might be taken with reason as a mortal insult. He did not know, unless it was the injury of an obscure insult offered him, how he had been driven to say it. Francis opened his mouth to cry out that he never meant that; but she said first, with what would have to be described as a little laugh, "That's about it, I guess."

"So you think that's about it." He sat appalled, looking at her. He looked at the beautiful hollow face, the gold wrap and the tied scarf. For a moment there seemed to be nothing he could say. Trembling a little, he felt the sharp cold of the air. Then slowly he said: "It's not true." For it was not. Ah, she could have it her way, on her terms! "You will have to tell me why you thought it was."

"What is there to tell?" she said. "When I wrote you

from Paris, the day you went to Italy—you see, it was very serious to me. I didn't want—I'm trying to say, I suppose, that I'm a kind of coward. I don't want to be hurt. If I hadn't thought that—" She stopped. "What's the use?"

"If you hadn't thought that what?" said Francis, putting the cigarette to his lips. By holding his arms close against him he felt the cold less.

"I don't know. Paris was marvelous. It was the happiest time I ever had in my life." She drew a breath. "I suppose nothing would ever be like that again. You see, it meant more to me—well, I decided long ago I wasn't going to care about anyone. It's not worth it."

"I see," said Francis. He looked at his cigarette end with a kind of anguish. The remark, so silly, so fatuous even, cut him with terrible tenderness, a sort of quick killing of any scorn or derision. It must be love, for how would mere liking ever survive the blow of getting to know these things a person really thought?

She said, "I loved your letters. They were so sweet and funny. I was in heaven when I knew you really were coming down. I suppose I expected something. Well—"

"I see," repeated Francis. Reaching out, he took her hand. "Sweet and funny." A contraction of pain or nervousness nearly made him laugh. "And when I got here I was only funny," he said.

"Yes," she said steadily. "The other kind of funny. You were so funny Monday night. And then I didn't see you for days. When you got into the car tonight you gave me a kind of stare, and then you began to laugh and tease Gwen."

"Do you know what I was thinking then?" said Francis. "Do you know why I—"

"No, I want to tell you. When we came downstairs I thought perhaps I was being silly. And when we danced, you said that about Goody. You see, I haven't any sense. I didn't know how it was done. You'd dance with me now and then, and laugh and go away—"

"When somebody cuts in, what else can you do?" said Francis. "Knock him down? If you want to know, I damn near did knock down that spick—"

"And then at supper," she said, "you did nothing but talk to Gwen. And stayed there with her afterwards—"

"Good God!" said Francis. "I thought you liked Gwen."

"I adore her."

"So I supposed," he said. "And the only reason I paid her any attention was because she was your friend." The way he heard himself saying it, in tones of self-justification, of having an explanation for everything, was futile and depressing—not sweet and funny. It wasn't even fair to Gwen. Attending Gwen was no chore. If it came to being sweet and funny (or was he just paying back the vexation of being told that he had changed for the worse?) Lorna could not be called, since he had been at Cap d'Ail, very sweet and funny herself. Gwen had been ten times as entertaining, if you wanted entertainment. Only he didn't love Gwen, and that very fact— "I can believe that you don't know how it's done," Francis said. "I can only tell you it isn't that way. You can't have been jilted very often. I can only tell you that I am serious, that this is serious. You don't know how serious. You must learn about that—"

But he did think the matter could be explained in a short lecture, that she would learn by precept? One more asseveration, and the girl is mine? He put an arm around her and she made no resistance. He kissed her, and she rested passive a moment, as though measuring her own reaction. She drew a breath then, returned the kiss with a quick firm air of stopping him, of giving him what he wanted as a matter of policy to forestall any possible use of force. "We'd better go home," she said.

"Not yet," said Francis. "I don't think I can leave it like this." His tone was disspirited. Despite his anxiety, he was tremulous with cold, and tired.

"It's late. It must be five o'clock."

"I don't care what time it is."

Meant to show masterful ardor, it was plainly so poor an imitation that she shook her head. "Please," she said. "I get to a certain stage where things don't seem real to me." She spoke with nervous weariness. "It isn't I any more. I might say something I'd be sorry for. So let's go home."

"All right," Francis said.

He did not know whether he was making a mistake or not. She could be, herself, mistaken. She might only think that she wanted to be taken home and left alone. To his past faults of failing to amuse her, of leaving her last fall in Paris, of not seeing her since Monday night, he might be adding now the inexpiable one of doing nothing, of letting her have her way.

"All right," he repeated. Though this generally understood danger filled him with still more anxiety, no answering resolve arose to meet it. What he felt, looking at her dim face, was not desire but an extreme painful dejection; and he was so cold that he could not think carefully about it. He jabbed the switch on. The awakened engine roared up, and he craned back over his shoulder. A solitary pair of headlights was coming up fast so he waited in silence to let them go by.

Near La Turbie he picked the wrong turn, for they came presently into steep vacant streets and faced an octroi sign: *Principauté de Monaco*. "God damn it to hell!" Francis said. He swung right, but the next curve began to turn him up hill, and he went right again. The cobblestones dropped off as steep as the roof of a house, and he slammed his brakes on, got into low, and crawled down with a great racket between echoing close-packed house fronts. What they reached seemed to be a sort of high viaduct. Below at a distance he could see the pattern of occasional lights around the mass of the castle beyond La Condamine, so at least he wasn't too far west yet.

"I know where we are," Lorna said. "Just keep going. You'll see a church in a minute. Yes, down there."

But she was wrong, for they ran into a sort of park. "I'm sorry," she said. "I shouldn't interfere. I just thought that looked like—"

"Well, this is the tram line," Francis said. "It runs behind the hotel sooner or later. You were pretty nearly right. There's the corner."

The exchange of listless, formal sentences echoed in his head. He put out a hand and laid it on her leg. "It's all right," he said. "You'll be in bed in a minute." He took his hand back quickly, afraid that she would mistake the touch's meaning.

They went down past the long curved garden walls. "There you are," he said at last. He saw the street lamp that he remembered as the one he had seen snow falling past Monday night. A light shone in the elaborate door and he halted the car. "Key?" he said.

She felt in her evening bag and gave it to him. Stepping out on the curb, Francis saw that it was starting to get light; the darkness was dimmer; the heavy roof of the house was darker than the sky. "It's morning," he said. He slid the key into the lock and turned it.

"I'm sorry about tonight," Lorna said. "Francis."

"Yes." He looked at her in the obscurity of the overhanging entry, and then he kissed her. The lipsticked lips were cold; but she smiled, tightening them with pain or tiredness. "Good night," she said. "Ah, darling, don't let me be that way."

Seven

IT WAS half past six when Francis got to bed. He was
called at eight o'clock; but to his surprise he did not
feel particularly sleepy. He was no sooner awake
than his thoughts were animated with a nervous cheerful-
ness. The temporary possession of Kirkland's car enlivened
his mind with plans and schemes. He had left it in the
drive, and when he had dressed he went down with a certain importance to speak to the concierge. "I brought that
Renault in last night," he said. "I'll give you the keys if
you want to have it moved somewhere else. I won't be
using it until this afternoon."

Punctually at nine o'clock he knocked on the door of
Mrs. Cunningham's sitting room with that active sense, a
little distorted by fatigue, of successfully managing many
arrangements.

"Wild party?" said Walter.

"Not very," Francis said.

"Good morning, Francis," Mrs. Cunningham said. "Did
you have a nice time?"

"Very pleasant," Francis said. "But as a result I am
stuck with a car. It belongs to a California fellow who
was going home with some other people. He asked me if
I'd take it for him. It's rather awkward because I can't
get rid of it until this afternoon late. I drove"—he found
that he did not want to say simply Lorna, so he said

—"the girls down, and I had to bring it up here. Though as a matter of fact, I thought it might be handy. If you hadn't any other plans, I thought I might run Walter up to La Turbie this afternoon. He ought to see the monument. We could go over to Eze then, where this fellow lives. He'd drive us back and drop us."

"Who is he?" said Mrs. Cunningham.

"Well, actually, I have no idea," Francis said. "He's a friend of Miss Imbrie's. I hardly knew what to say when he asked me if I'd take the car. It's down in the drive, and—"

"Let's see it!" said Walter.

"No," Francis said. "We have some work to do now."

"Well, Francis, if you're sure it's quite safe. Aren't you afraid something will happen to it?"

"Well, no, I'm really not," Francis said. "I drove one like it a good deal last summer. I think it's just possible that it's safer with me than it is with him." He smiled to show that any sound of self-esteem his remark might have was not serious, but that she need feel no uneasiness about Walter.

"Hurray!" said Walter.

"You wouldn't be very late, would you?"

"Oh, no. I explained to him. The girls were going up there to tea, and I said we'd run them up, but we'd have to come down." He felt at ease, and spoke easily, but Francis could not help experiencing a moment's hesitation, since he had now, in effect, uncovered his hand; and the various harmless half-truths, or evasions of choice, that he had used in proposing the expedition might, some or all, be plain to her.

"Well, I think that would be all right," Mrs. Cunningham said. "As it happens, Mr. and Mrs. Peters are coming to dinner here, instead of our going there to luncheon. I wouldn't want Walter to be late." With discomfort Francis saw that, at least in a small way, he had put his foot in it; for the matter of the Peters had slipped his mind altogether, and Mrs. Cunningham must naturally see that it had. She said, "When were you picking up the girls?"

"I thought, when we started," Francis said, no longer easy. That had been very stupid of him; and there was no possible way to repair it now. "It won't hurt them to go to La Turbie," he said as casually as he could, "and that would save time."

"Yes. Walter should have his nap, I think. That would give you time to go down and pick them up." She paused thoughtfully; and Francis wondered, with some alarm, if she were going to observe, surely with asperity, that, since he was in this situation with the car that wasn't his, and had engaged himself the way he had described, it might be simpler if he didn't take Walter. However, she said, "All right, darling," to Walter, gathered up some letters, and went from the room.

✦

At the shop door hung a wire rack of picture post cards. Glancing at them, Francis lifted one out and gave it to Walter. It was divided vertically. One half showed the Ligurian trophy in conjectured restoration, a vast polygonal pile, tier on tier of columns and bas-reliefs, friezes

261

and moldings, and on the top platform, the crowning colossal statue of Augustus. The other half contained the lines of the inscription pieced out from the discovered fragments and Pliny's text. "There you are," he said.

Walter looked at it. Then he looked across the road to the battered part of a tower rising on the sunny dilapidated mound of broken brick and stone, with an enclosure around it and the roofs of mean houses closing up one side. "Gosh!" he said. He held it out politely to Lorna. "It's Latin," he said.

"So I see," said Lorna. "Can you read it?"

"Gosh, no," Walter said sheepishly.

"Oh, yes, you could," said Francis. "It begins with the titles of the Emperor; and then the list of the conquered tribes. One or two of them are old friends of yours—well, we'll let you off this time."

Walter returned it to the rack hastily. To Lorna he said, "Did you have to learn Latin?"

"As a matter of fact, I did," Lorna said. "I even used to act in Latin plays at college. So did Gwen."

"You mean a real play? I'll bet it sounded crazy."

"It did at that," said Gwen. "How young we were then!" They were walking on, and she added, "How young I'd be still if I hadn't clothed myself from head to foot with the apparent idea that we were bound for Baffin Bay. I don't mind saying it is hot."

Below the escaping tendrils of sandy hair a delicate sweat shone on her forehead. "It seems to me," Francis said, "that every time I meet you you are complaining about what you have on. I've read somewhere that the poor workman quarrels with his tools."

"Oh, you have, have you? How would you like to have

your shins kicked?" She slid a hand inside her jacket experimentally. "Oh, dear," she said. "I can't take it off."

"Why not?" said Francis. "You seem to have an adequate undercovering."

"Because," she said, "it was impressed on me as a child that nice girls do not sweat. I do. I am. Look at Lorna. There is how a nice girl ought to look."

Francis looked at Lorna. She was walking slowly ahead with Walter, who limped along pursuing the incredible but interesting subject of the Latin plays. "You mean nobody says anything except in Latin?" he asked. Lorna wore white, a white silk jumper and pleated skirt with a white coat over her shoulders. It was something she must have got with the notion that it was really warm here. For the moment, in the full afternoon sun, it made her look as it was meant to, wonderfully fresh and cool.

"Come on," said Francis, realizing that he was again, no matter how casually or indifferently, laughing and teasing Gwen. "We'll give you a good airing." They approached the car.

"In Switzerland," Walter was saying, "they have soldiers who go on skis."

"And they speak Latin," Francis said, compelled to laugh by the process of association that made Walter return for one fantastic circumstance another one.

"Ah," said Walter, "they speak French. Or German." He began to giggle. "You ought to hear Frank speak German," he observed.

"Yes, you ought to," Francis said. "You let Lorna sit in front with me. She'll have to show me how we go. Tell Gwen about coming down from Alpiglen. She feels warm, and she's one of the best female skiers in Europe."

"Say, are you?" cried Walter.

"I am not," Gwen said. "I couldn't ski a foot."

"I'll bet you could," Walter said encouragingly. "Gosh, you know Helen, my sister? She could even ski. It's easy. We met these English fellows—"

Francis smiled, feeling his heavy eyelids stick a little. The sunlight lay in a haze over the mountain slopes. In Monte Carlo below the glistening blocks of the big hotels, the clear white shape of the Casino with its towers, the patches of park, the wide but short asphalt strips of palm-lined boulevards, though small in perspective, looked closer; and he saw that the majestic sweep of lights last night was only an illusion.

Francis stood an instant, staring, bemused. His muscles, with no rest to speak of for thirty-two or -three hours, took what they could now by making him postpone slightly every movement. Vague sad thoughts of this coast, covered, below the then resplendent trophy, with villas two thousand years ago, much as it was covered now, weighed down his mind. He felt about two thousand years old himself.

Gwen said to Walter, "You and Goody must get together. He knows a place back of Nice somewhere where they have skiing."

"Is it far?" said Walter. "Is it—"

Close to Lorna as he opened the door for her, Francis murmured: "You look enchanting." Surprised, for he had not planned to say it, he saw that she was surprised, too. An instant tinge of color showed on her cheekbones. "My dear," she said, "thank you."

Simultaneously their eyes made a move to see whether his remark had reached Walter or Gwen; but it had not, and so they both laughed. "Why couldn't we go there?" said Walter. "Gosh, I wish we—could I ask him?"

"I don't see why not," Gwen said.

Francis started the car.

"He's sweet, isn't he?" Lorna said under the mounting sound of the motor. "Don't you think his mother would let him?"

✦

The damp dark stone stairs came down into a big low vaulted room, perhaps a couple of cellars made into one. There was a cavernous overhung fireplace with the embers of a fire in one part of it. On the whitewashed stone hung paintings of various sizes, probably by Kirkland, in cheap wood frames. A great scarlet cope was spread out on one wall. To Lorna, Francis murmured, "They must have shot a bishop last week and skinned him."

She did not hear.

Kirkland introduced a man named Frost, who by his speech was a southerner, and who seemed to be living there, too. Francis guessed that Frost was another artist and that they rented the farmhouse together.

Whatever had happened since three o'clock this morning, Kirkland was a good deal the worse for. His blunt strong frank face was puffed and tumid, his blue eyes bloodshot; but he seemed to remember that he and Francis were old friends. He kept cordially taking him by the arm, and through him including the girls and Walter in haphazard introductions to people already there. "Mrs. Farr," he said to a fat woman, "Miss Higham. You and

Gwen know each other, don't you? And Mr. Ellery. And
Mr.—er—Cunningham—" Dazed, but plainly delighted
by this description, Walter was very polite. "Justin
Gourbeyre," Kirkland said with the conscious accenting of
syllables that showed the names were supposed to be
important, well-known ones, "and Fred Armingeat—"

As far as Francis went, the names meant nothing, and
the immediately observable fact was that they were a
couple of French fairies. Kirkland closed his hand on
Francis's arm again and said, "You've met Emily—Mrs.
Hartpence."

"Yes," said Francis.

She smiled at him in a friendly, abandoned way. Finding it, as usual, hard to dislike anyone who smiled at him,
Francis moved off, resisting, too, the irritating difficulty,
really, the impossibility of looking at Mrs. Hartpence for
more than a moment without thoughts of her undressed
or in bed. "Some drinks are coming," Kirkland said.

Mrs. Farr cried out, "Now, Goody, I want my tea.
Young Mr. Cunningham must come and sit by me, and
we'll have tea like civilized human beings." Her voice
was shrill and her ruddled cheeks repellent; but Walter
was gratified. He limped over and sat down with shy
covert glances around him. Mrs. Farr said something to
him and he turned civilly and answered, blushing a little,
but composed.

At the end of the room, doors stood open on a terrace
under a pergola supporting the branches of an enormous
bare grape vine. The worn stone blocks of the paving were
littered with many old leaves. An empty stone conduit ran
along to an open cistern half full of stagnant water. You
could look right across at Eze, the compact round of walls

and roofs crowning the little summit lit with sunset against the distant low hills and long narrow harbor of Villefranche in diaphanous shadow a few miles away and a thousand feet below. "Look at that," Francis said to Lorna.

She stepped out the door with him and they stood near the parapet. In the air was a faint smell of smoke and a faint keen chill, like the end of a fine October day. Closing his hand over hers, Francis said at last, "You don't want to stay very long, do you? Walter and I will have to get down. It's quarter to five."

He stopped. Tightening his fingers on her hand, he said, "At quarter to five this morning we were having a discussion up on the hill, you may remember There hasn't been a chance to say anything to you about that. What I am going to say now is this. I don't want to hear any more nonsense." He spoke pre-emptorily, out of a numbness of fatigue that simplified everything by leaving him no patience nor energy to waste on doubts or alternatives. "I am going to take care of you. I have not decided exactly how; but never mind that. I am. And you are to be a good girl, and behave yourself, and not make a lot of difficulties. Do you understand?"

"Yes," she said, looking at Eze.

"Yes, what?" said Francis.

She switched her head sharply, looking at him. She began to laugh. "Yes, please," she said. Her eyes glinted with an abrupt crowding-up of tears. Twisting in his, her hand turned over, clutching his fingers. "Ah, Francis! Nobody was ever so sweet to—"

"Now, now!" Francis said. "Come along." His tiredness gave him the sensation of being partly disembodied, in buoyant tranquillity, in clear, happy light-headedness. "I must keep an eye on Walter. God knows what he's making of that obscene tramp Emily, and that pair of tapettes in the corner. And more important, what he'll tell his mother."

Inside several big candles had been lighted and there was a new log flaming on the embers. Thin disturbed veils of cigarette smoke floated toward the arched ceiling. Mrs. Farr, Francis saw, had been successful in getting her tea; and Walter, still very polite, nursed a hot cup. The taller of the two fairies was telling Gwen something in French. Kirkland was nowhere around, but the Frost man came up at once. "Now, Lorna," he said, "what you need is a great many martinis right away." The fairies, Francis decided, must be friends of his. "Mr. Ellery, what will you have? There's brandy, Scotch—"

"Is Goody around somewhere?" Francis said. "I'm afraid we'll have to go pretty soon, thanks."

"Oh, but do have a drink. As a matter of fact, Goody ran Fred Armingeat down to their place to get a bottle of absinth. Emily wanted some. I'm sure he won't be long."

Francis found it on the tip of his tongue to say, though as a joke only, for he felt remote, beyond annoyance: "Aren't you jealous?" He managed not to. Turning to a refectory table under the big candles, Frost poured out a cocktail and gave it to Lorna. "Darling," said Gwen, "Monsieur Gourbeyre says that—"

"I'll have some Scotch, if I may," said Francis.

✦

At quarter of six Kirkland had not returned. To get down to the hotel would probably take less than half an hour, so if they left at six, it would be time enough. If they left much later than six— Francis said to Lorna, "If he doesn't show up pretty soon, I'm going to be in a jam. Mrs. Cunningham is having people to dinner." Frost was passing, and Francis said to him, "You don't know when Goody's getting back, do you?"

"Why, I'm sure he said he'd be back. I'll ask Emily again." Mrs. Hartpence was leaning against the wall by the scarlet cope, holding a glass and looking up at a thick-set dark man who stared with absorption down the front of her dress as he talked. When Frost spoke to her she shrugged, closed her eyes a moment, and said clearly, "I don't know where the son of a bitch is!"

Walter, eating a cookie, started; for it was unlikely that he had ever heard a lady use the expression before. To Lorna, Francis said, "I wish Mrs. Hartpence would be a little less forthright. With one thing and another, Walter is getting an earful. For all I know, that aged harridan is telling him dirty stories. I'd better see, I guess." He stood up and went over there; but Mrs. Farr proved to be telling Walter, to his vast interest, about the training of dogs, Saint Bernards and Great Pyrenees, that were company mascots in some of the Chasseurs d'Alpine regiments. They were making a great hit with each other. As soon as Walter saw him, he said, "Frank, I found out where it is. Mrs. Farr knows."

Mrs. Farr showed Francis a haggard smile. "He wants to go to Peira Cava," she said. "I know Goody's been up. It's a petite station de sports d'hiver—" Her accent was very French. "One of the Chasseur regiments has a big barracks there. I was just telling him about their wonderful dogs."

"Well, that's very kind of Mrs. Farr," Francis said to Walter. "We'll have to see what your mother thinks—" Though the Scotch he had drunk proved, as far as exhilarating him went, about as effective as so much water, and it was impossible to doubt that he was cold sober, Francis found slight embarrassing difficulties in enunciation. Exhaustion alone or alcohol alone would not do it; but against both of them together, the effort to speak clearly was trying. "We must run along in a moment," he said. "The trouble is that Mr. Kirkland isn't here. He was going to drive us down. I think I'd better see if I can telephone." He went back to Lorna, and Frost, who stood talking to her. "Emily doesn't seem to know," Frost said to him. "I—"

"So I heard," Francis said. "You don't happen to have a telephone, do you?"

"I'm afraid we don't. It's really quite primitive." He laughed. "I'm awfully sorry."

"Well, damn it all," said Francis ungraciously, "I don't know what to do. I've got to get down by half past six."

"Oh, well it's only five or ten minutes of. I'm sure he'll be back. It doesn't take any time to get to Cap d'Ail."

"What is all the trouble?" said Mrs. Hartpence. She wandered up with her glass in her hand. By now she had drunk enough to be approaching what must be normal for her. "You want to get down? It's really too bad of Goody. They probably met some people. Take my car."

"Oh, God!" said Francis. "I mean, that's awfully good of you; but I can't take any more cars. I've just brought

Goody's back." He sounded so ridiculous, the next thing to hysterical, that he had to laugh.

"There, there," Mrs. Hartpence said. Probably she supposed he was a little drunk. "Of course you can. If you just turned it loose it would come home by itself. Anyway, Pink can drive you down. Can't you, Pinckney darling?"

"Well, yes, I could," Frost said. "If you really must go."

"I hate to upset everything," Francis said. "But I have to get Walter home. I'd appreciate it very much if you'd come down with me and bring the car back."

Mrs. Hartpence regarded her glass a moment. With a casual underhand flip she shied it into the fireplace where it smashed loudly on the stone. Heads turned, and Walter, who had jumped, gaped at her. "Think nothing of it," she said. "I'll drive you down. And, Pink, just tell Goody he can go—" She apparently noticed Walter gaping, and stopped. "Come along," she said, and presented her back to them crossing the room.

To Frost, Francis said, staggered, "Well, I don't know. Can she drive?"

"Probably," said Frost. "But tell her you'll drive. Everybody does. She's very tiresome. I'm awfully sorry about all this. I hope you will come up again. It isn't this way all the time."

In the dark court Mrs. Hartpence had the engine started in an Italian car. Francis walked up and said firmly, "I'll drive." Without comment, Mrs. Hartpence slid herself over on the front seat. In the light of an iron lantern, Lorna gave him a smile. "All right, Walter?" Gwen said.

Francis made a gingerly experiment with the problem of what gear shift this was going to be. For once at least, it worked right. The car moved and swung slowly out the arch. "Good!" said Francis. He turned to smile at Mrs. Hartpence, feeling that after all she was being a great help. The clock on the long glittering dashboard said quarter past six, which was all right. "This is awfully kind of you," he started to say; but Mrs. Hartpence, slumped down in a light-colored camel's-hair coat, was weeping. Her bruised-looking mouth worked in spasmodic twitches. The tears squeezed out her swollen eyes. With difficulty she said again: "Think nothing of it." Francis felt along the board until he found the light switch and snapped it out. "Thanks," she said.

In back, Walter said, "I found out where. It's Peira something. We're going to see if—"

Francis drove in silence. There must be a short cut straight down, but he did not want to risk looking for it, and if he went up to the Grande Corniche, he knew now where the Cap d'Ail road cut in toward La Turbie. Once he reached that he would have no trouble.

In the darkness Mrs. Hartpence continued to cry, shaking slowly with a succession of weak quiet sobs. Perhaps ten minutes had passed when the smooth fast flight of the car broke on a jolt, immediately succeeded by more and harder jolts. Startled, Francis threw out his clutch and got his brakes on. "Oh, what's that?" said Mrs. Hartpence faintly.

For any intelligence to convey itself into Francis's head took several seconds. The car came to a halt then, and he said, "Well, that's what's called a flat tire."

✦

There were two spare wheels locked one on the other behind, but neither of them had enough air in it to support the car. Francis did not find this out until, having groveled underneath, got the jack placed and raised, and the flat tire exchanged for the first spare, he let the jack down, and the new tire getting the car's weight on it, immediately flattened to the rim.

Francis, on his knees, with the loose handle of the jack in his hand, looked at it. The car was equipped, a piece of good fortune with which he had tried to tell himself he ought to be satisfied, for how would he like working in the dark, or by lighted matches, or a briquet flame?—with a spotlight, really a small searchlight, mounted on a nickeled post on the running board. In this glare, moistening his lips, which tasted of grease, he regarded the folded side of the heavy shoe. He trembled with anger. He shook in the demented fury with which the sentient mind encounters the cogent It-is, so much like hate or malice, of insentient things. With the jack handle in his hand he would have liked to beat the collapsed tire to death.

"Ah, gee!" cried Walter. "Say," he said to Mrs. Hartpence, "you haven't got any air in it!" The sound of his own indignant voice committing what he had been assured was the mortal sin of impoliteness to a lady, scared him, and he amended it. "I guess they forgot to test it at the garage."

"Oh, God, how ghastly," said Mrs. Hartpence. She had been obliged to get out when he removed the tools and she leaned against the low stone wall, her tear-stained face lit by the glare, a cigarette between her lips. "How really awful!"

Francis could not bring himself to speak to her. It was

just what you would expect in a car kept by a drunken moron. He could feel the weary slugging of his heart. The sweat ran down his chest and back. "Oh, Francis!" Lorna said. "I'm so sorry. Isn't there something we can do?"

"No, thanks," Francis said. "We'll try the other."

Getting up, he went and lifted it with difficulty from its position. Walter had taken the hub wrench and was attempting to apply it. "Wait," said Francis. "It isn't on the jack. And better let me do it. First, let's see what we have here."

Holding the wheel as high as he could, he let it drop on its tread. It bounced; but the casing was heavy, so that really told him nothing. "Hang on," he said. "Who's got a hairpin?"

Lorna lifted a hand to her head and held one out to him. It was a fortunate idea, for when he had depressed the valve, the contained air showed so little pressure that this, too, would certainly have collapsed.

Francis got up again.

"Has someone a cigarette?" he asked. He held up his blackened hands to show that he could not get at his own.

"Here," said Lorna. Sliding one from her case, she put it between his lips.

"And here," said Gwen. She sheltered a flame for him.

Bending his head forward, Francis got the cigarette lit. "How gratifying!" he said. "Men must work and women must weep—" He laughed; but he was a little giddy and he shook his head to clear it. "Well, now I'll have to see if I can't get some help. There was a driveway into a place back there. It looked fairly fancy, so they'd probably have a telephone. I'm afraid there's nothing for it but to settle down and wait."

The clock on the dashboard said ten minutes of seven. He looked at his watch, and that said five minutes of. "I guess I'll go with you," Walter said.

"Better not," said Francis, "I—" He had nearly said "—will have to keep moving." With the unsteady sense of catching it on the fly, he said, "I don't want to leave the girls alone here."

It was hard to believe that Walter could accept the idea that he was going to protect them; but seemingly he could and did. "O.K.," he said seriously. "That's right."

Francis found himself shaken by a light high silent hilarity, touched by Walter's tone, touched too by his own patience and good temper. Clearly, he surpassed himself. He stood off with astonishment and looked at himself with wonder.

The heavens were brilliant with clear stars, and the cold wind was pleasant on his face. Francis threw the cigarette away and walked faster, looking for a light.

✦

"Francis," Mrs. Cunningham said, "I have been frantic with worry." She was quite white. "How could you not let me know?"

"Ah, mother," said Walter, "it wasn't our fault. Frank had to walk about a hundred miles—" He had managed to get several smears of grease on his face, and one arm of his overcoat was covered with dust.

"Maggie," said Mrs. Cunningham. Francis had not noticed Maggie before. Mrs. Cunningham had come out of the lounge dressed for dinner, and Francis could see the people she had left, these Peters, a stout important-looking old man and a soft stout woman, attempting politely to maintain some small-talk with each other over the empty cocktail glasses on the stand before them while Mrs. Cunningham—Martha—handled this awkward misadventure in her own way. Maggie must have come down and been sitting inconspicuously in the passage, frantic too, no doubt. Mrs. Cunningham said, "Take Walter upstairs, please."

"Mrs. Cunningham," Francis said, "I'm frightfully sorry. I really did all I could. I finally found a place where I could get a car. They didn't have a telephone, and since we could get home in fifteen minutes, it seemed a waste of time to stop anywhere."

"Oh, Francis," she said. "Why did you do it? You must have known when you left this place that—it's quarter past eight."

Francis shook his head. "We left at six o'clock," he said. "We had this flat tire, and there was no air in the spares—"

"Francis, I can't talk to you about it. My guests are here and I can't keep them waiting for dinner. I think you'd better go to bed. Did you get any sleep last night?"

"Oh, yes," Francis said, "I—"

"Well, we really will have to talk about it in the morning. I'm sorry to say it now, but you know I feel quite free to terminate this arrangement whenever it doesn't seem to be serving its purpose."

"Of course," said Francis.

"Well, go along now." Perhaps she found his appearance pitiable, for she said equably enough, "Good night."

"Good night," said Francis. "I'm really very sorry."

In his room he put the light on and began to pull off

276

his clothes. His hands, and in the mirror he saw, his face, were very dirty. Stripped to his undershirt, he ran a basin full of hot water and began to lather his cheeks and neck. He would have to get a bath; but if he wanted anything to eat, he'd better arrange for it to be sent up before eight-thirty. With the dirt off, he discovered that he had skinned the knuckles of one hand. Feeling in his toilet case, he found a small bottle of iodine and painted them.

The exquisite sharp stinging made him wince, and clasping his wrist, he sat down on the bed. After a moment he got up, put on his bathrobe, and stood looking at the telephone. It did not seem worth the trouble. Wrapping the bathrobe around him, Francis snapped the light out, went and lay down on the bed. No special thought came to him, but he seemed to see, against the darkness, bloated and disfigured, Mrs. Hartpence's foolish face shining with her alcoholic tears.

"The unspeakable bitch!" he pronounced, and immediately he was asleep.

2

HIDING the hillside, a dense white mist hung in the still air. On the calm, subdued morning a few sounds—the clatter and low grind of a hidden tram; the soft bang and bump of movement somewhere down the hall—made the essential silence seem greater. It closed in sad and heavy like the damp gray air. Shaving by electric light, Francis paused from time to time, his heart failing him, looking himself in the eye with a settled anxiety, but no settled resolve.

He could go back to Florence, and there were reasons why he ought to. He could really work on his book, get it done—maybe in a couple of months. He made an effort to see himself industriously writing away all day and most of the night (like Balzac), to feel in anticipation the power-ful satisfactions that a writer can count on occasionally feel-ing; but in fact Francis had already done enough writing to know that the writer feels most of the time something quite different, something no humane man would want his worst enemy to feel. To be in that hell-hole Florence, without money of his own, without any hope—

He unfolded a clean shirt and pulled it on. He would go to Paris. It was not impossible to pick up a job on one of the English-language papers, for their staffs were al-ways changing; and on one he knew a man who had been at school with him (where they had not liked each other particularly; but after all, that was long ago, and during the summer Francis had run into him once or twice, and they had got on well enough). He did not say the chance was any less than desperate; but, if not desperate, what were his circumstances?

And if as desperate as that, why be so moderate?

Francis's heart began to beat more heavily. If he threw out so much of caution and commonsense, why try to keep any of it? He stood still with a necktie in his hand. Why not marry Lorna and take her to Paris?

Francis tied the necktie carefully. Why not? Why not? He would go down to the villa and, conveniently finding Lorna alone, say: "Hurry up. Get some things together. We have an engagement at the Mairie; and then we are going to Paris. Now, don't argue. Hurry—" Partly fright at what, if he did this, he would find that he had done;

partly the trembling of the senses that jumped past successive pictures to one of her in the dark in his arms, the agitation Francis felt grew so great that he began to walk up and down. At that instant, shocking him as if he had been shot, the telephone rang.

Snatching at it, Francis knocked it over. "Allo!" he said.

"Mr. Ellery"—it was Maggie—"Mrs. Cunningham went down to the office. She will be in the writing room in a few minutes, and she wants will you please go down there before you come up here?"

"Yes," said Francis. "I will."

He set the telephone down. From a hanger in the wardrobe he took a coat and put it on. With Maggie's words, he had felt for an instant the queasiness that used to come when, fairly often, word solemnly conveyed reached him to report to the Headmaster's study at once; but this was absurd, for he was no longer a schoolboy. The flight to Paris, he saw, now that the terrible and exciting story he had been telling himself was interrupted, was just as much a survival—one of those well-circumstanced dramas, passionately envisioned but never played, that, while he expected the dreadful summons or while he went to answer it, he used to make up for himself. Francis went downstairs through the empty lounge to the door of the writing room.

In the gloom of the mist outside Mrs. Cunningham sat at the far end writing a note. She held her pen an instant and said, though without smiling, "Good morning, Francis. Come and sit down. Excuse me just a moment." She wrote another line, blotted and folded the sheet. Putting it in an envelope, she said, "Francis, I really don't know what to do." She looked around her. "I don't think we'll be dis-

279

turbed here. Walter told me about the accident. I can see that it wasn't your fault, and that once it had happened, you couldn't have done anything except what you did do. There's nothing more to be said about that. What I must speak to you about is your whole attitude."

Though there was not yet anything to say, the indictment, larger and more general than Francis had expected (and, in discouraging truth, not new to him. Through the years, how many people had found themselves as time went on, less and less pleased with Francis; and so, sooner or later, had felt, often for Francis's own good, that they must speak to him about his whole attitude!), made it hard to keep still. Francis shifted a little in his chair and Mrs. Cunningham continued: "It isn't responsible enough, Francis. You see, above everything else, I must feel your definite responsibility."

"I don't know what to say," Francis said. "I had hoped you did feel that."

"Francis, I think you mean to be responsible. But it is so much a matter of judgment. I must depend upon your judgment so much. I think you are impulsive; and sometimes I think you look at things from your own standpoint a little too much. I don't think you have the habit of looking at things from other possible standpoints—from mine, for instance. Unless you can put yourself in the place of the person to whom you feel responsible, I don't think you can be very successful in satisfying that person. I have to have someone who can do it. On one or two occasions before this I have been a little worried—" She broke off.

Since the phrase brought instantly to mind that letter to his mother, Francis could not help flushing. In defense, he reminded himself that he was not always alone in lacking judgment. Mrs. Cunningham herself was not right every time, so he need not, at least in his own mind, take this lying down. He said, "I wish that on those occasions you had told me. I wish you would tell me now."

"Well, Francis," she said, "I don't think it's fair to bring up, long after they happened, things that weren't after all of enough consequence for me to speak of them at the time."

"If you don't mind my saying so," Francis said with as much of a smile as he could manage, "I think that letting me wonder is—well, hard on me." Automatically he had taken out a package of cigarettes; but, noticing it, he put them away again.

Mrs. Cunningham noticed, too. "Yes, do smoke, if you want, Francis," she said. "Perhaps you're right. As an instance, I had in mind that trouble at Montreux when the hotel proprietor was so unpleasant about Rose. I could see that it was partly because you were upset, because, I suppose, you saw that I was upset. Which touched me very much, Francis. But at the same time I felt—and unless I was greatly mistaken, you really felt yourself, didn't you? —that it could have been handled differently."

"I did," said Francis. "I lost my temper."

"Francis, you have excellent judgment in many ways. I think you handle Walter extraordinarily well." Her fear of not being fair was speaking again; and Francis listened, disquieted. When she said it would not be fair of her to rake up what was past, he had not understood what she meant. His own instinct was to dismiss the past because discussing the past was futile. Mrs. Cunningham did not care to discuss it because she must be afraid of its cumulative effect. A heady tide of resentment mounted in her as, woman-like, she thought back over the carefully kept account of displeasures felt or wrongs done her.

The remarkable thing, Francis told himself, was that, notwithstanding, she recognized and valued fairness, and applied a concept, wholly unreal and alien to most women, to check that mounting indignation. Her voice had sharpened at the mention of Montreux; there was a tremor in it when she put, very carefully and mildly, the question to him. When he answered yes, it must have needed self-restraint to proceed directly to points in his favor. Francis did not doubt that she stated them by an act of will, against her impulse; and now that she had made herself be just, she would be free to go on with more and more bitter things she must say on the subject of responsibility. It was like the Second Commandment. The passionate and jealous god of her maternal love spake these words: Francis must not make unto himself any graven image. He was here to watch out for Walter.

After the briefest pause, what Mrs. Cunningham said was: "You know, I had a note from Lorna this morning."

Astonished, Francis said, "Did you?"

"Yes, I did," said Mrs. Cunningham. "Francis, did you ask her to write it?"

Francis could feel a stiffness, an involuntary tightening, tingling a little at the nostrils, spread over his cheeks. "Now, for God's sake!" he begged himself. He touched his tongue to the inside of his lips, and looked an instant at his cigarette. "Mrs. Cunningham," he said, "I don't know anything about this note—" Could Lorna, knowing that Mrs. Cunningham might be annoyed, have taken it on herself to try to excuse him? She surely could not!

"Anything," Francis said, "that I wanted told you or explained to you, I would tell you or explain to you." He looked across the ringing air. "You seem to be under some misapprehension about me; and so I—"

"Francis!" said Mrs. Cunningham. "Now, really—"

"Yes. I'm sorry," Francis said. He held his breath a moment. "Would you mind telling me what the note said?"

"She wrote, very nicely, suggesting that a party might be got up tomorrow, when Walter wouldn't have any lessons, to go to a place in the mountains where they have skiing."

"Yes," said Francis. "I know of the place. Some people at Eze yesterday knew about it. I told Walter that we would have to find out more about it, and see what you thought. If any plans were made, nobody told me about them. I didn't know that Lorna felt any interest in it. She and Gwen must have decided after they got home last night that it would be fun for Walter."

"Well, Francis, do you see what I thought?"

"Not entirely," Francis said. "I don't see how you could think that I would make plans without consulting you."

"Well, Francis, I think you have sometimes made plans first and consulted me afterwards. I came to Cap d'Ail for several reasons, but one really was that I hoped it would be pleasant for you. I really had thought of going to Taormina. I thought it would be nice for you to see some friends. Perhaps I ought to examine my own judgment—" She smiled for the first time. "One thing I didn't think of was that they would have friends, and that you would naturally meet them, and that it might be quite hard for you, when they were running around all the time, to be so tied down. Much harder, perhaps, than if you were somewhere else."

"Yes, I see," said Francis.

Though not, maybe, in the exact way she wanted, it seemed to him that he could put himself in her place well enough. The honesty of mind that made her, without any pause to consider, say "for several reasons" impressed him. It was not merely a form of speech. Moreover, if the decision to bring him down here, instead of to Taormina, to let him see a few, as she said, "friends" was also part of the fantastic strategy to protect Helen, she had not denied it. Her regard for truth was not (like many people's; like his own?) regard for the benefit or credit of a reputation for being truthful, but for the thing itself. Whatever happened, she would not tell a lie; and, abashed, Francis wished that, whatever happened, he would not.

Mrs. Cunningham said, "I told you that I wanted you to go to the dance Thursday. And I did. Perhaps I didn't really consider that it was likely to last all night, and that even if you wanted to—which would be a good deal to expect—it would be inconvenient for you to leave before the others. At any rate, it did last all night, and it was fairly plain that you weren't in any condition to take Walter's lessons yesterday morning. Then there was the matter of this man's car. I didn't like that, Francis."

"I didn't like it much myself—" Francis began. But didn't he? If truth interested him, hadn't he, yesterday morning, liked it very well?

"You see," Mrs. Cunningham said, "I don't know whether you were conscious of it or not; but it looked so much as though, by telling yourself that you would use it to take Walter driving, you had arranged to more or less continue the party."

"No," said Francis, "I didn't plan that. It all came out of trying to get away a little early. I was going to see if I could get a taxi or something. He insisted that I take it."

"That, of course, is different. But you see there had already been that slip-up Monday night when we arrived. And then, the first time you had an opportunity to go out with your friends again—it upset me very much. I was upset this morning, when Lorna's note came up. I thought that you had arranged that, too."

And justly, Francis reflected. This time he hadn't; but how about other schemes, other times, when he had! He said, "I knew nothing about it. I had nothing to do with it."

Mrs. Cunningham looked at him intently. "Francis," she said, "when you told me a little while ago that I seemed to be under some misapprehension about you, I think you were right. I'm very sorry."

But suppose Lorna had, by some chance, mentioned the plan to him? Would a plan to spend Sunday with her have seemed to him a good idea or not? Francis found himself unable to say anything.

Mrs. Cunningham said, "I'll be glad to have Walter go tomorrow. I think the skiing is good for him. It helps him to feel that he can get around like anyone else. When it doesn't interfere with his work, I'd like him to go off with other people as much as possible—really, to get away from me and Maggie."

Taking the envelope that held the note she had written,

she tore it up. "You see what it is that I must be sure of, Francis. That I can count on you, that nothing else is more on your mind than Walter is. I simply have to know that when he's with you, I needn't worry."

"You can know that," Francis said.

Eight

"GEE, what do you want?" said Walter. He was half-way down the steps. "They're coming. That's the car."

"Put these in your overcoat pocket," Maggie said. "It's some dry socks, so if your feet get wet. You have your other sweater, and your extra scarf—"

"I know, I know," Walter said. "Gosh, I'll be all right."

"I'll see that he changes," Francis said.

"Yes, he oughtn't to drive back when it may be cold with his feet damp. Mr. Ellery, I hope you'll make him take his shoes off and let you feel. Sometimes he doesn't realize—"

"I will," Francis said.

Out now in the sun, Maggie said, "My, isn't it a beautiful day! It seems very warm. I think he'll be warm enough." Lifting a hand, she shaded her eyes to look at the car coming up the drive. "He oughtn't to have veal for luncheon, Mr. Ellery. Some nice chicken, perhaps—"

"Oh, Maggie!" Walter cried.

"Now, Walter, you know what happened—"

The good that Mrs. Cunningham might see in releasing Walter from his bondage to women would not be so apparent to Maggie. She came down the steps hesitantly, rubbing her hands, drawing back to efface herself, peering forward to find out where they were going to put Walter. "Hello, Maggie," Lorna said.

"Good morning, Miss Higham." Maggie came down another step. The little confidence she had in Francis, or in men, was clear, for to Lorna she said appealingly, "Walter has all his things if he's just made to put them on, if he needs them."

Lorna said, "Don't you worry, Maggie. I'll remind him."

"We'll take care of him," Kirkland said. "You hop in here with me, Walter. We'll put Francis with the girls."

"And away we go," said Gwen. "Oh, my," she said, looking at Walter's skiing trousers. "If I had a pair of those I might even try it myself."

"Say, aren't you going to?"

"You just want to have a good laugh," Gwen said. "Lorna has a motion picture camera. We'll take pictures of you."

"All set?" said Kirkland. The car began to move.

"Walter!" Maggie cried. "Put your gloves on!"

"Sure, sure," Walter said, but he was out of Maggie's reach now, so he made no move to. "Say, it's pretty hot!" he said to Kirkland. "I hope it isn't melting up there. I hope it's good and high." From his pocket he pulled a small can. "If it's sticky, you have to have a lot of wax," he said. "I thought I'd better bring some along. Is the snow deep?"

"Couple of feet," Kirkland said. "It's way up."

"How long does it take? About when will we get there?"

"Well, we go to Nice; and it's about two hours from there."

"Gosh," said Walter, "I hope we don't have a flat tire or anything. We had one Friday night with Mrs. Hartpence's car. Frank and I tried to fix it. Gee, it took two hours. Did she tell you?"

"As a matter of fact, I haven't seen her," Kirkland said.

Raising his eyebrows, Francis looked at Lorna. She shrugged and shook her head. "And damned good riddance!" Francis murmured.

Gwen gave a snort. "This story only goes to show," she said, "that there ain't no good in men."

"I'll be the judge of that," Francis said, keeping his voice low. "What happened?"

"If I knew, I wouldn't tell you." Behind the more or less friendly gibing tone, Gwen's voice rang with indignation as though Mrs. Hartpence were her best friend, as though Gwen hadn't been happy to disparage her Thursday night; and Francis gaped.

"Yes, you!" Gwen said. She screwed her face up comically. When she was younger she must have been in the habit of playing the clown to cover these seizures of strong feeling, coming with no warning, and on so little provocation that she shrank from letting anyone see what the provoking trifle was. In this case Francis could see that when he said good riddance she read into it some smug maleness. She looked at him; and if cats thought, a cat might look at a dog that way—the gross, clumsy, noisy animal; despised, but feared, too; disdained because you could so easily make a fool of it (in a pinch, a cat could, if spitting and arching the back failed, run up a tree, which no dog could do), yet deferred to (for if no tree were handy and the angry dog caught you in the open, he would finish you).

"How disagreeable you are!" Francis said. "I didn't do a thing." But he was glad to turn to Lorna. She, paying no attention to the exchange, was listening to what she could hear of the conversation in the front seat. Putting a hand on Francis's arm, she pressed it for his attention. "That's the beginning of a beautiful friendship," she said, nodding toward it.

Walter was saying: "—it's a pretty fast run, believe me. They have some wands in for you on the long fall; but, gosh, if you miss one, you could kill yourself. We had Helen, my sister, along, so we couldn't make such good time—"

"He does all right," Francis said. "You'd be surprised."

"Did Helen go on all this?"

"She did while I was there. The Britishers gave her a big time."

"And how about you?"

Francis could feel himself flinch. Helen had proved to be no joke, or if a joke, a painful one, a joke on him, and he didn't want to hear any banter about that. What disturbed him more was that Lorna could lightly make the remark. At best, taken as a conventional bit of coquetry, he did not like it, because it was not like her. At worst— he did not know how to put it; but what he felt for her was something he would not care to joke about; not—the galled jade duly winced; but still, it was not—a fatuitous game he played with every female he met, and so must regard lightly, and so would not mind her regarding lightly. He said, "Oh, they were mad about me. They gave me a big time, too."

Lorna laughed. "Fool!" she said. "Darling, let's have a lovely day!"

The shadow of her hat brim was on her face. The artificial but pure red tint of her lips stood out from the white skin. Her eyes in this light were the deepest imaginable blue. Oddly moved by the decorative effect, Francis almost said: "You look like the French flag"; but he bit his lip, no longer believing (and wishing he never had believed) that such original humors, such gay capricious turns of thought, by their spontaneity and whimsical suddenness set him apart from commonplace people and in general did him proud. "Why not?" he said. "Why not?"

✦

In the streets of Nice there was a vacant Sunday morning calm, and they went through quickly; but outside, toward La Trinité-Victor, they kept meeting or overtaking cartloads of people dressed up in black to go to Mass. This held them back, and as the rocky, windy valley bottom extended, Francis saw that Kirkland was mistaken about his couple of hours. At half past eleven they got to Lucéram, but the real climb was only beginning. They stopped in the frosty sunlight of the mean steep square while a waiter from the hole-in-the-wall café brought chocolate for Walter and coffee with rum in it for the rest of them.

Kirkland, leaving his engine turning over, got out and raised the hood to look at it, so Walter got out, too. He walked up and down on the cobbles impatiently, knowing that it was getting late, but too consciously polite to complain. "It's all right, isn't it?" he said to Kirkland.

"Just changing the carburetor adjustment a little. It's a pretty hard pull from here."

"How far?"

"Oh, twelve or thirteen miles."

"And I wouldn't mind arriving," said Gwen, giving Francis her empty glass. "Emancipating myself as well as I can from what Eric calls false modesty, I feel sure they do not have one here, and I would be glad to see a ladies' room."

Up the slow successive hairpin curves of the military road they came presently to the snow—melting patches in the shadows, then a thin crust over the frozen ground, then snow deep and unbroken through the hanging pine groves. It was one o'clock before, leveling off, coming slowly through the hazed shadows and vertical shafts of sunshine, past sledges loaded with logs and big horses breathing steam, they reached the first houses, the flimsy chalets in the woods: *Mon Rêve, Mon Repose* . . . They drove along the great weathered wall of the barracks, past the arch of the gate and drew up in a line of cars and several busses across the road from the small hotel.

"Thank God!" said Gwen, stepping out on the packed snow. "Come along, darling."

"You know," Francis said to Kirkland, "I think I'd better see if I can get a call through to Cap d'Ail. It's a little longer than I thought. I think I'd better tell Walter's mother we may be a little late."

"Say, tell her we just got here!" said Walter.

"Good idea," Kirkland said. "I'll see if we can scare up some food."

The hotel was unpretentious and cheap. The cramped hall, paneled in varnished pitch-pine, and the public rooms opening out of it, were crowded—officers from the barracks with their visiting families; French excursionists from Nice in inexpensive, not-smart sports clothes. At the desk Francis asked for a telephone.

"Occupé, Monsieur. Prière d'attendre."

"How about a small drink?" said Kirkland.

"Well, maybe I'd better find out where we get skis," Walter said.

"Well, maybe you'd better wash first," Francis said. "We'll have lunch right away."

However, on inquiry, it proved that the dining room was full, and they would have to wait with the people who were already waiting. Persuaded that the French would do anything for money, Francis showed the maître d'hotel, a lourish unprofessional youth in a threadbare dinner coat, fifty francs. With a spasm of obligingness the maître d'hotel discovered the possibility of serving them in the family dining room. He went himself and brought them vermouth and cassis.

"Once Walter finds out where the skis are, there'll be no holding him," Francis said. "Look, Goody, order any damned thing, except no veal for Walter, and let's start getting the girls fed. I'll have another try at the telephone." Lorna and Gwen came downstairs. "We're going to eat in back," Francis said to them, "more or less secretly, because there are a lot of people ahead of us." Touching toward her the glass in his hand, Lorna bent her head and took a swallow from it. "Preserve thy body and soul," Francis said, "unto—"

"You shock me!" Gwen said. "And why can't we have some of our own?"

"You may," said Francis. "Order me anything. I'm try-

ing to call Mrs. Cunningham." He could see most of the
waiting people looking at them. Whether because some
understood English, and they had heard enough to know
that in spite of justice and reason the Americans were
going to be served first; whether because the short army
officers bridled to see Kirkland, who, if big in America,
in France was a giant, holding the center of the floor,
eclipsing their virility and bewitching their women, the
looks were all cold and irritable.

Francis went back to the caisse. This time the man let
him through. The telephone was in a little room behind
and Francis sat on the edge of a table waiting for his call
to get through. Smudging the rim of his glass, Lorna had
left a trace of lipstick, and the perfume was distinct from
the aromatic smell of the vermouth. "The blood of Our
Lord Jesus Christ," he thought again, though the wit, if
any, in that comment had been obscure, and showed a
silly taste, surely not his, "which was shed for thee. Preserve thy body—" The fine wording made him think of
the Anglican doctors, the Seventeenth Century nest of
singing divines, serene in chaos—George Herbert tuning
his viol to set, as a pastime, an anthem to his dear Jesus;
Robert Sanderson facing in patience the Covenanters who
tore his prayer book. Today, Francis told himself, men
were not half the men they had been. "Allo," he said.
"Allo, allo . . ." But there was no response. On the
table lay a mussed, some days old copy of the *Eclaireur de
Nice* and he started to read a column describing a process
for the amelioration of the oils of olive of the middle
grades. After fifteen minutes Mrs. Cunningham answered.

Francis said, "No, everything's fine. Walter's having a
grand time. But it took longer than we expected. We

haven't had lunch yet. I was afraid we might be a little late getting down."

She said, "Oh, well, Francis, I won't worry if you're late. Don't try to get here for dinner, if it's too hard. I'm going out with the Peters. We thought we'd go to the evening service at the English Church in Monte Carlo, and get something to eat afterwards. I'll be in very early. By nine, I should think. You won't be later than that, will you?"

"Oh, I don't believe so," Francis said. "We ought to be down by eight."

"Is it nice there?"

"The hotel is dreadful," Francis said, "but it's marvelous and clear, and there's lots of snow, and wonderful pine woods. It looks like the top of the world."

"How lovely! Have a good time, all of you— Oh. Yes, I will, Maggie. Maggie's afraid Walter will forget the socks in his overcoat pocket. Remind him, won't you."

"I will."

"And if anything should delay you, you'll try to let me know, won't you."

"I will. And I'll try to see that nothing does." To Francis's left was a window, and looking out at the soiled sunny snow of the road he saw a car appear, swing slowly, and head in to park across the way. It was an Italian car, like Mrs. Hartpence's. "Good-by," he answered, smiling, put the receiver down, and stood up.

"Hell!" said Francis then; for the car was not merely like Mrs. Hartpence's, it was hers; and she was getting out of it.

✦

The family dining room was small, with a round table. It had a bright south window half filled with potted plants. On the vilely papered walls hung religious pictures —the Sacred Heart frilled with flames; Saint Vincent de Paul surrounded by the poor. It was warm, and smelt, unless you liked the smell, unpleasantly of anisette.

"Get her?" said Walter. His mouth was full, and he was eating furiously.

"Yes," said Francis. "Now, take it easy! We have lots of time."

He sat down and the maître d'hotel entered by the other door from the kitchen and put before him a plate thinly arranged with a soggy collection of hors d'œuvres. "Thanks," said Francis.

He did not know what to say about Mrs. Hartpence. If he had left the telephone a minute sooner, he would not have seen her; so perhaps it would be simplest to pretend that he hadn't, to mind his own business and say nothing. On the other hand, though Kirkland might have known she was coming, Francis did not think he did. Kirkland, it seemed, was trying to shake her; and she was resisting the attempt; and God knew what tipsy or hysterical scene was in preparation. Not to warn him was a betrayal of those decent principles of male solidarity, so important if any peace or trust were to exist in a society overrun by women—in short, a dirty trick on Francis's part. Francis said, "By the way, Emily Hartpence's car just came in."

"That so?" said Kirkland casually, but he acknowledged the important tip-off by adding at once, "Who's she with?"

"I didn't see anyone."

"Oh," said Kirkland. Forewarned, he was forearming. On his face appeared the progress of his thought, and he was sick and tired of Emily. A woman—Emily herself, Gwen, any woman—might see it in affecting terms (*she was in love, and he she lov'd prov'd mad, and did forsake her* . . .); but what Kirkland saw was that she he loved had swindled him. He had taken her with the understanding that she was romantic and desirable. She had as good as promised him ineffable pleasures in private and the admiring envy of all his friends in public; but what did she give him? In private she was a disgusting maudlin nuisance; in public she made a fool of him. The bitch had misrepresented herself. Of course, it was mostly his own fault for not seeing that she was a bitch. Kirkland admitted that; and if she would decently accept the fact that the game was up, and go about her business, he wouldn't wish her any hard luck. But, by God, if she were going to—

Kirkland said, "Well, maybe I—" He pushed back his plate, arose, crumpled his napkin and dropped it on the table. Not finishing the remark, he went out the door and closed it after him.

Walter, who had watched with interest, said, "Hot dog!"

He ought to be reproved; but if Francis were to ask him censoriously what he meant by that senseless exclamation, the chances were good that Walter would further embarrass matters by defending his meaning, after all made amply clear by his voice. The connection between Mr. Kirkland and Mrs. Hartpence he had easily identified as a sentimental one, and he knew what that always meant. Suddenly abandoning everything that they said or implied to Walter or the world about their dignity and reasonableness, adults, seized by love, went into a sort of vaudeville act, side-splitting at first, but much too long; holding hands, kissing, bandying pet names; until, for no ascertainable reason beyond their own silliness, they fell to fighting and yelling, and the women at least to crying.

Walter surveyed these antics cynically sometimes hiding a smile behind his hand, sometimes risking a guarded jeer. It did not seem feasible to say to him: "Don't laugh. Mrs. Hartpence is a fool and drinks too much; but she is probably in great pain. Mr. Kirkland's behavior is not to his credit; but he is in a jam, and you will be lucky if you get to be his age without ever finding yourself in one like it. . . ." And anyway, though perhaps not a bad speech, it was aside from the point. All Walter maintained was that love looked funny; and who could deny that from the first infatuated ogles and formal beatings-about-the-bush to the last ridiculous position and brief pleasure, it did, it did? Walter hardly knew the half of it! On consideration, Francis decided that this was not the moment for reproof. He said, "How about the skis?"

"Gee, they're terrible, mostly!" Walter said, ready enough to return to the world of common sense. "I found some pretty good pairs for us. But I don't know about Mr. Kirkland. It's pretty hard to find him any."

"Why is it pretty hard?" Lorna said brightly. Francis glanced at her with gratitude.

"Oh," said Walter, "you see, he's so tall. He'd need awfully long ones. The way you tell is, you stand them up, and if you reach your hand over your head, you ought to just touch the tip—"

Francis looked over to Gwen. "I wouldn't tell you, even if I knew," he said. "How do you feel? Better?"

"I believe you think you're smart," Gwen said. "Here. Have some wine. It's ghastly."

✦

What to do about a woman, your mistress, who would not take her dismissal, and who was rich, so that you weren't able to free yourself by the simple expedient of leaving her stranded somewhere (or if you could not quite do that, of buying her off), Francis did not know; but two general plans of action suggested themselves.

The first, and undoubtedly the better, for it was the method almost invariably used by men experienced in getting and in getting rid of women, was to be resolute, to persevere. A number of insults and indignities had failed; but, never say die! Insults could be made more open, indignities more brutal; and both could be better aimed, at tenderer points of pride (there were always a few) and the more cherished fragments (no one could lose them all and live) of self-respect. A lucky hit, one stroke dealt with no squeamishness, might pull it off; and it ought not to take long.

However, not everybody was capable of simple directness and the other method, whose outstanding disadvantage was the practical certainty that it wouldn't work, was to reason, to explain that you could not love her so much, were it not for the fact that you loved honor more—in short, to make her see that it was no good; but in a way that spared her and gave yourself the treat of trying to act like a gentleman. This must take longer—anything from an hour to a hundred years—and, when twenty minutes passed without Kirkland coming back, it seemed probable that this was the method that he was using. Francis felt a certain relief.

Walter, finished long ago, had been restlessly entertaining Lorna with more of his exploits at Grindelwald; but as soon as he saw that Francis, who had started so much later, was through, too, he said, "Well, I guess I'd better go down and see that nobody took those skis."

"All right," Francis said. "Run along. But don't start off until we get there. If you see the maître d'hotel, he's probably in the dining room, you might ask him to bring me a bill."

When he was gone, Lorna said, "This is my party." She reached for her pocketbook under her coat on the chair behind her.

Francis said, "Mrs. Cunningham gave me very particular instructions to do what I could to pay our way. I think she felt that since you had arranged the transportation—"

"Gwen did it," said Lorna. "And arranged is the word. It was the next thing to blackmail. After we got home Friday night, Goody called up. So sorry and all that. So Gwen invited us to drive up here in his car."

"I did not!" said Gwen. "I told him Raymond was going to drive us up, and—"

"Darling, I was only fooling," Lorna said reproachfully.

"I know you were," said Gwen. "Don't mind me. I am a great one for knowing what everybody ought to do, and for not seeing why they can't behave themselves; and when they don't, I get a little bit cantankerous. Now, I must either shut up, or start what I believe is called back-biting.

Let's go and see Walter ski. I expect Goody can find us, if he wants to."

A waiter had come in with the bill. Taking it, Francis glanced down the line of figures, not really expecting an overcharge, since the maître d'hotel was fifty francs ahead to start with; but it was there, all right, a little matter of twenty-three francs. "Voyons, voyons!" he said indignantly. "Cent dixhuit et onze—" But it was not likely to be the waiter's work. "I'm damned if I'll let them get away with it!" He said, "If you'll excuse me, I'll just carry the battle out to the caisse."

"Well, we might as well see where Walter is." Gwen dropped the end of her cigarette in her coffee cup and stood up. "Come, darling. Put your galoshes on, and we'll go for a nice long tramp in the woods."

Through a labyrinth of little passages Francis reached the front hall. The rush was over. The people waiting had all been admitted to the dining room. In the caisse was one of those formidable, high-bosomed French women, on a few million of whom the economy of France appears to pivot. Francis supposed that she was the wife of the proprietor, the mother of the maître d'hotel, and the calculating author of the slight slip in arithmetic.

Peremptorily she took the bill, shooting at Francis a look of suspicion and contempt. Swift and efficient, she added it, and then added it again. Pulling a pencil out of her pile of glossy black-dyed hair, she corrected a figure or two. "Voila!" she said, triumphantly solving his stupid difficulty for him.

Francis thanked her and paid. The larcenous old gorgon delighted him, and, gathering up his change, he turned away smiling. He found himself looking into the shabby lounge at Mrs. Hartpence, who sat alone in the early afternoon shadows with a half-empty glass of brandy and soda on a stand beside her.

"Oh, hello," she said.

"Hello," said Francis, recoiling.

He lifted his hand in embarrassment, meaning to give her a casual wave and get out of here. She sat slumped down, one knee over the other, her wool skirt rucked up a little, so that a person standing where Francis stood could see, above the tight stocking top, against the light colored silk of a slip, much of her bare thigh. Francis shifted his eyes, outraged by his incontinent stir of interest; but before he could move, she said, "Going skiing?"

"Yes," said Francis, acutely uncomfortable. "I was just straightening up a little misunderstanding about the bill." He gave a laugh that sounded foolish to him. "I'm looking for Walter. I'll have to—"

"Goody went down with him to see about some skis."

"Oh," said Francis. Hearing her say Goody, it was impossible to shut out of the mind Kirkland's relation to her. Francis held his eyes rigidly on her face; but certain thoughts, though always spurned away, kept coming back; and not alone. As the saints, beseeching women to be virtuous, knew to their trial; as the fastidious often find to their disgust; the knowledge of a woman's looseness persists, through every revulsion of hate or anger, through every chaste resolve, in steadfastly promising (just in case you happen to change your mind) that what men have done, man can do. Francis said with another laugh, "Well, we'll all break our necks, probably."

"May I come along?"

302

"Why—" Francis began in consternation; for how could you answer no? "Well, of course; but I don't know where we're going, exactly. This is more or less Goody's show."

"Are Lorna and Gwen going?"

"They're not skiing. I think they thought they'd watch awhile. I expect it's rather dull unless you—"

"Well, maybe I could go with them."

"Yes," said Francis in confusion. "Why not? I don't really know what they're planning to—"

"Oh, go to hell!" said Mrs. Hartpence. Dropping her face forward, she brought her hands up shakily, pressed them over her eyes and broke into sobs.

It was not Francis's fault if Kirkland made Mrs. Hartpence unhappy. It was not his fault if, putting him in an impossible position by a request she had no right to make, his answers failed to satisfy her. She had no right to have hysterics in public—there were people in the dining room beyond; there was that loutish maître d'hotel snooping around; there was the superb extortionist in the caisse; and some or all of them would soon hear, stare, ask themselves what Francis had done to her.

"Look, Emily," Francis said. "You must stop that! Please. I'm so sorry—"

But she was not going to stop. The crowding tears wet her hands; in spasms of anguish her shoulders heaved and jerked; the inconsolable sobs grew deeper. In what was practically an anguish of his own, Francis said: "Look. Wait here a minute. I'll get one of the girls to come up and—"

Downstairs, outside an open door ending the passage in which skis were stored, Walter and Kirkland, their skis already on, stood waiting while Lorna, holding her camera, moving to keep the sun behind her, frowned, shielding the finder and trying to get them in focus. Gwen stood in the door. Francis approached her from behind and tapped her shoulder. "Come in here," he said. "I have a little job for you. It's Mrs. Hartpence. We'll have to do something about her."

"What's wrong?"

"She's up in the lounge bawling. She caught me when I came back from getting the bill fixed. I cannot cope with it."

"I don't know that I can, either."

"Well, you come right up and try. Get her out of there and make her wash her face or something. You must know what to do. What do females generally do to each other?"

"What happened? What did she say?"

"She didn't say anything. She asked if she could come along with you and Lorna, and I said yes. What else could I say? Then she began to cry. I don't know what went on with Kirkland. I suppose he just told her to go home, and then walked out—"

"I could kill him!" said Gwen. "Come on. Where is she?"

✦

When Francis came downstairs again, Lorna was waiting alone at the end of the deserted passage. She set her hands on her hips, tilted her head to one side, and with an exasperation not entirely humorous, said, "Where have you been? Walter and Goody started off, and Gwen has disappeared somewhere—"

Francis glanced behind him, touched up her chin, and, though she tried with the same half-humorous exasperation to draw her head back, kissed her. "None of that!" he said. "We have our hands full. It's this damned Emily. Gwen is up giving her a sister's care. You know. Still for all slips of hers, one of Eve's family. It's pretty as a picture."

"Oh, Lord!" said Lorna. She slipped the strap of the camera case off her shoulder and held it out to him. "Take this. I'd better go up."

"I don't see why," said Francis.

"I can't leave Gwen to—"

"Well, damn your friend Kirkland to hell! He has the most ineffable brass! You know, it's a gift, this leaving somebody else to pick up the pieces. I wish you'd tell me sometime what you see in him."

"Francis, I told you that I knew his sister. She wrote him that we were down here, and so he looked us up. Now, will you please stop, every chance you get, implying—"

"You know I didn't mean to imply anything; though if he isn't a friend of yours, what is he?"

"Oh, Francis! Why will you go on and on—"

"I'm sorry," Francis said. "I'm simply fed up with these bums and their hell-raising. They're all part of the same bunch of stupid drunks that lies around Paris pretending to be artists or writers or the lost generation—good God, I mean!"

"Francis, will you please go and ski? They went over

305

to some hill somewhere below the barracks. We'll come down later."

"Well, all I mean is—"

"Will you please not say any more about what you mean or don't mean? It doesn't matter—"

"On the contrary," said Francis, "it—"

"Francis, this isn't a joke. Will you—"

"Now, listen," Francis said. "What I mean does matter. What I mean is that Kirkland is a cheap bastard; and she is a vulgar slob; and I don't want you mixed up with any of it."

"You needn't worry about me."

"Damn it, I worry myself sick about you!" He took her by the arms.

"Francis, if you do not let me go—" She was white with anger, and her angry face, which he had never seen before, was like the face of every angry woman, spiteful and furious. Confronted with it, a man's right instinct was to beat the little hell-cat until pain and fear brought back her senses (and, at the same time, brought back his; because her fright or injuries would rearouse tender feelings); but nowadays this was seldom done, and Francis let her go. Jerking away, she turned and went upstairs.

Since she had left her camera with him, and he could not put it down anywhere, nor ski if he carried it with him, Francis, who did not feel much like skiing anyway, went out the door, climbed the packed snow of the path and walked along the road past the barracks gates to look for this hill. It was not by any means the first time that, angry or resentful, he had, for little reason and that not good, said what it was stupid to say and done what it was foolish to do; so he understood very well that there was no remedy for the resulting dismay, except to try to stop thinking about it.

2

THE HILL where they skied proved to be no more than a sharp short fall in an open glade in the pine woods, a quarter of a mile along the road. Thirty or forty people were coasting down it or climbing up it, shouting cheerfully in the sun; but it would not be Walter's idea of skiing at all; and, in fact, Francis found him standing by himself watching a squad of young soldiers, probably now conscripts, in a line on skis being shown by a tough fat sergeant how to stand up.

Seeing Francis, Walter said, "Gee, it's not so hot. Aren't you going to try it?"

"I thought I'd see what it was like. Where's Mr. Kirkland?"

"He's down at the bottom. He's having a terrible time. His skis aren't any good." Considering the disappointment Walter must be feeling, it seemed to Francis that he was bearing up very well. He leaned, subdued, on his poles and nodded toward the sergeant and his squad. "Gosh, you ought to hear him swear at them!" he said. "They're terrible. Where is everyone? Lorna said she was going to come and take some more pictures."

"Mrs. Hartpence wasn't feeling well," Francis said. "They're staying a minute to see about her."

"Oh. Well, I guess I'll go and sit down awhile."

"What's the trouble?" Francis said, rousing himself sharply.

"Oh, nothing. I was kind of winded. It feels a little tight in my chest." He tapped his breastbone with his mittened hand.

"You mean, like asthma?"

"No, you don't get that in the afternoon. You only get that at night, usually. It will go away in a minute, I guess."

Francis pulled off his jacket and laid it on the snow. "Sit on that," he said. It seemed to him that Walter was perceptibly paler. Walter stood a moment looking at Francis's jacket; and then he said slowly, "Well, maybe I'd better go back to the hotel for a while."

Because Walter must know how unlike him it was to suggest such a thing, his tone was defensive. The expression in his eyes was withdrawn, turned intently on the sensations in his chest. It was plain to Francis that, just as adversity is said to make a man a philosopher, ailments like Walter's could serve to make you a rudimentary but sound psychologist. Walter did not let himself become frightened, for he must have discovered that a little fright sometimes turned what was only a threat into the thing itself. Furthermore, if he did not want to be frightened, he must not frighten other people; because frightened people around him, by their aghast expressions and their panicky movements, could infect him with their fright.

The thing to do then was at all costs to remain calm; to look at Walter's peculiar leaden pallor without surprise, to treat the whole thing as a trivial mishap—something to be attended to; but to be attended to merely as a matter of everyday prudence, like a cut finger or a bump on the head. "Think you'd better take your skis off?" Francis said.

"Yes. Would you do it? I don't want to bend down." From the nice balance of definite urgency against simulated unconcern, Francis judged that Walter's sensations, while no worse, were no better, either; and that this must be unusual; that Walter, keeping a tight grip on himself, tightened it to meet the insidious suggestions of a deeper fear—not the fear that this was the same old terrifying thing coming back, but the fear that it wasn't.

"All right," Francis said. "Step out. I think you started too soon after lunch. I think it's indigestion. Do you feel sick?"

Walter shook his head. "I think it feels better," he said. "It will go away, I think, if I sit down awhile."

"Well, we'll get you back to the hotel."

This was all very well, Francis reminded himself; but if Walter were going to have an attack, Francis had no idea of what ought to be done. He must find out at once. "If you feel that way, what does Maggie do for you?" he asked casually.

"Oh, she has a kind of vapor lamp she likes to try. Sometimes I smoke one of those cigarettes. I have some. If it gets bad, there's some stuff they give me. They inject it—" He gave a sort of yawn, and Francis could see that unplanned act must be a suggestive symptom, for the expression of anxiety in his eyes increased. "Better take it easy," said Francis, picking up the skis.

"Hey!" said Kirkland.

His shadow sloped across the snow before them. He came to an ungainly stop by driving in the point of one pole and running, like a Roman on his sword, against it. "Uh!" he said as it hit him in the ribs, and laughed. He was flushed and warm; his eyes sparkled like a child's. Skiing was new to him, but he was fitted for any kind of sport, and with the confidence of a person who knows he will get the hang of it, and in high spirits and for fun, he threw in a few buffooneries—the comic technique of the float, the boathouse, and the training table.

Francis, whose mind had been set against him almost with malignancy for the damage he did, was unwillingly disarmed. Far from being vicious, or in the meaning of the word when it applies to a man, brutal, Kirkland was full of genial impulses. If he were selfish, the selfishness was a boy's, coming not from calculation but from urgent appetites; a sort of exuberant grabbing of what he wanted; a sort of truancy or skipping-out on what was tiresome or hard, in no case deterred by the stick-in-the-mud reflection of what would happen if everybody did that.

Francis said, "I think Walter'd better rest awhile. I think he ate too fast and got out too soon." He did not know whether it was a help to Walter to have this theory insisted on or not. Walter looked at Kirkland with a faint, sheepish smile. "Gosh, go ahead and ski," he said. "I'll be back—" He yawned again; and clearly he didn't like it at all. The anxiety in his eyes went a little further along the contested line; and though he stopped somewhat short of the point where it would get out of hand, he turned, and began to walk, not too fast and not too slow, toward the road.

"Is he all right?" Kirkland whispered.

"I wish I knew," Francis said, unable to be cold and distant. "I'm afraid he isn't. I'll get him back and see—"

"Go on," said Kirkland. "I'll be along as soon as I can get these things off my feet."

Francis opened his mouth to say that this would not be necessary; but he recognized it as a silly last impulse of his anger or indignation. He might say, don't bother; but he didn't mean to save Kirkland trouble; he meant to tell him (speaking of childishness!) to go on, to do something else for Francis to despise, to show how right Francis was to think of him with contempt. Francis nodded, and overtook Walter. "How is it?" he said.

"Gee, don't worry," Walter said. He spoke with an effort, as much to himself as to Francis. He limped along doggedly, but he glanced frequently ahead to see how far it was now.

"Take it easy," said Francis, as lightly as he could. He was thinking that Walter would probably weigh sixty-five or seventy pounds, and he could not help measuring the distance himself.

From the staff projecting over the gate arch of the barracks, the hanging tricolor stirred, bloused, lifted up and down softly. The sun on the weathered old wall was soft and mellow, splashed here and there by water from icicles melting at the high eaves. Back and forth across the shadowed entrance the sentries passed each other, pivoted at the end of the beat, advanced and repassed. Francis observed the scarlet collar tabs and hunting-horn insignia. Upright, their bayonets, polished like silver, flashed on the turn. The pale shifting shadow of the flag lifted and fell away; and from the great court within arose the succinct but softly struck roll of one or more military drums, broken off soon, and then begun again, as though in practice, or at the direction of an instructor.

311

The afternoon was so fine, clear and peaceful, bright with sun, bright with snow, that Francis began to take a kind of reassurance from it. It was not the setting in which anything serious (he resisted a closer defining of his doubt) could happen. Walter's face was definitely less pale. He seemed, in fact, to be gaining a good color.

Kirkland caught up with them, and they reached the hotel together, standing the skis up at the door. Inside safely, Francis looked at Walter with relief. "How about some water?" he said. "I'll get you a bottle of Evian. Do you think you ought to lie down?"

"I don't know," Walter said. He stood perfectly still; and then, turning abruptly, he let himself sink on a bench. "I—" He broke off. His hands came up and he pressed his crossed wrists to his chest. "Frank!" he said. "Look. I'd better go somewhere. I—"

"Goody!" Francis said. "Tell that hag we've got to have a room. Right away—can you walk?" he said to Walter.

Walter could not answer. "I mustn't lie down," he managed to whisper. That good color was flushing his face crimson in the shadow. "Can't breathe—"

"Walter!" said Francis. He dropped on the bench. "Can you stand? Do you want to be picked up?"

"Here!" said Kirkland. "Give him to me." He encircled Walter's shoulders with his big arm, bent and slid the other under Walter's knees and lifted him with no difficulty. "Upstairs," he said to Francis, nodding toward the back.

Halfway up Francis could see the spread, sateen-covered rump of the woman from the caisse bobbing ahead in haste. "Goody," he said, "I'll have to telephone. I'll have to put a call in. I'll have to get Maggie. His mother was going out. We'll have to find out what to do. Ask Madame if there's a doctor anywhere. They must have one at the barracks—"

"Go on. Go ahead," Kirkland said. "We'll take care of him." He was steady and calm. His voice was unruffled, firm and reassuring. "All right, old timer?" he said to Walter. "We'll get you fixed in a minute." That lack of imagination, making him at other times such a dolt, now made him invaluable. There was no way through to his nerves. He knew only what he saw, and he saw only what was put in front of him. For never tasting death but once, it was as good as valiancy—it was really better, because what might happen to other people it feared no more than what might happen to itself.

A waiter, the one who had brought the bill, popped in, stood gazing around in surprise, his hands hanging; and Francis, distracted (if he stayed here, he could not know what was happening upstairs; if he went upstairs, he could not put in a call) saw a way to handle it. He said to the waiter, "Ring up the Eden Hotel at Cap d'Ail. Ask for the manager. Let me know at once when you get him. I'll be upstairs." Francis stared at him, astounded, for the waiter's face relaxed in an uneasy deprecatory smile. Not moving, he began to shake his head.

"Hurry up!" Francis cried in agitation. "Don't stand there! What's the matter with you—" With a jar, he saw then what the matter was. "Pardon!" he said, "Allors, vite, vite—" but he had to stop, not able to complete the mental shift that would let him think in French. No words came.

"Francis!" said Lorna. "What happened?"

She stood three feet away, her hands clasped together.

"I don't know what to do," Francis said. "I must telephone. It will take forever to get a connection. He had an asthma attack or something like it. Maggie knows what to do—"

"Go up," she said. "I'll get it for you."

"No. I'll have to talk to her myself. I—"

"You can't talk to her until she's on the line. Go on." Moving up, she pushed his shoulder. "Here," she said, catching the strap of the camera case, "you aren't going to need that."

In a room just beyond the head of the stairs Kirkland had put Walter on the bed. "Better lie down, old boy," he was saying.

"No, don't," said Francis. "The trouble is he can't breathe. He has to keep his head up. Get some pillows behind him." To the woman, he said, "We need more pillows, Madame—encore des oreillers."

She cried, "Tiens, tiens!" snapping her fingers in the face of a little old man wearing a black apron. There was also a chambermaid, who stood fascinated, both her reddened hands, as she heard the wheezing struggle of Walter's breathing, brought up to squeeze her own throat.

"We'll have to get a doctor," Francis said. "Lorna's downstairs putting through the call for me. Look, Walter," he said, grasping his arm, "would one of those cigarettes be any good? Do you want to try one? Can you manage it? Try in his coat pocket, Goody."

Walter's face looked choked up, half asphyxiated. Francis had seen him working hard—climbing a slope on skis, peddling a bicycle along a rising path—but long before he

314

reached such a state as this Francis would have made him stop and rest. Under Francis's hand, the muscles in Walter's arm knotted tight, for the work of breathing—*easy as breathing,* Francis thought with horror—seemed to involve his whole body. He made his utmost effort and, wheezing and whistling, forced in a little of the desperately awaited air. After he got it in, he had then to get it out. Merely to watch was exhausting; you asked yourself how long that could be kept up, how many such struggles a moderate—really, with the harm done by paralysis, an impaired—physique like Walter's could be good for.

He was not the only one asking that question. In Walter's dusky flushed face the pupils of his eyes, starting wide, were almost black. Wild and mute, they were full of terror, for the struggle, if horrifying to watch and hear, must stab the frenziedly engaged heart with unspeakable fear. Locked up there to fight it out single-handed, Walter could look from the nightmare and see people, and they could see him; but he could not reach them, and they could not reach him to help him. Kirkland pushed a small box into Francis's free hand. "Where is Madame?" said Francis. "We must get a doctor—"

"She's gone to do it. Here. Steady on! Give me that." Kirkland took back the box and picked a cigarette from it. Holding up a match he snapped his fingernail over the head, shielded the flame, and lit the cigarette. Taking a puff, he grimaced at the taste. "Now, let's see. Walter?" He brought it down to Walter's lips. "Want to try? Atta boy!"

"Monsieur," said the waiter in the door, "en bas, s'il vous plaît."

"Yes," said Francis, his eyes fixed on Walter. Walter was willing to try; but though he could close his lips and fill his mouth with smoke, he could not breathe it in any better than he could breathe in air. Francis turned and ran downstairs.

"All right, here he is," said Lorna.

Someone had fetched a chair for her and she sat on the edge of it, her legs twisted together, the toe of her left foot doubled behind her right ankle. Clapping her hand over the mouthpiece, she held it out to him. "It's Maggie," she said. "But Mrs. Cunningham hasn't left yet. They're sending downstairs to stop her. I said Walter wasn't feeling well and you—is he all right?"

"No," said Francis.

He took the telephone and put his back against the wall. Maggie's voice rang faintly, "Oh, Mr. Ellery! What is it? What—"

From her pocketbook laid with the camera case on the table Lorna slid out a cigarette case. "Shall I go up?" she said. Francis waved a hand at her. "No," he said. "You can't do anything. Stay away. Yes, Maggie. Yes—well, just a moment. Did that woman come down to see about a doctor?"

"They sent someone for the medical officer."

"We're getting one," Francis said into the telephone. "Yes. I understand. He's not to be moved. Oh. Yes, Mrs. Cunningham—" His hand was shaking, and so, he realized, was his voice; and that would never do. "I think we're going to have one in a minute." To Lorna, he said, "Listen! I want to be sure about this! Yes. No morphine unless the doctor thinks it's absolutely necessary. And not

316

more than a quarter grain. That was a quarter, one fourth of one grain. Yes. And ask if he ever tried adrenalin. Yes. I understand. If he never has, he'd better not—"

From her pocketbook Lorna pulled an envelope, unstopped a lipstick, and marked on it the quarter grain of morphine. "Yes," Francis said. "Yes, I will. I will see that it is. Yes." Slowly, he dropped the telephone into its cradle. "She's coming up," he said.

"Here—" said Lorna. She pushed the envelope over to him. "Not more than one quarter grain." She opened the cigarette case and slid that over, too.

"I must go up," Francis said.

"Francis," she said, laying a hand on his sleeve. "It may not be as bad as you think. He's had them before."

"It couldn't be worse," said Francis. "This isn't like the others. He would not be so frightened if—I ought to take that back about Kirkland," he said. "He's a good deal more good than I am." He meant it, but in the still, darkening room, his words had a sorry, stilted sound, as though, much too late in the day, he were trying to call attention to the fact that he was just, and humble, too; yet what was he really but afraid? He took up the envelope and looked at the rude, but clear enough red markings. They ran across the torn flap where, written under them in a round feminine script, was a return address.

Francis read: *F. Robertson Pension Vittoria Via Stella Milano Italia.* The reaction of surprise was to make him feel physically sick. He stared at it, revolted; though certainly Miss Robertson had a perfect right to correspond with her dear old school friend if she wanted to. "I must get back up there," he said.

"Hadn't I better come?"

"There's nothing to be done. Better wait for the doctor."

✦

Of the state in France of medical science Francis was uninformed. If you had to go anywhere, the American Hospital at Neuilly was the only thinkable place. Francis had never been inside a French hospital; but the phrase called up pictures of an Hogarthian pest house or bedlam where the dead lay in their soiled beds because nobody got around to removing them; and the dying, *munies des conforts de notre sainte religion,* but otherwise unrelieved, went on dying (Que voulez-vous? C'est la vie). In harmony with such harrowing squalor would be the doctors: men who could be bought by American advertisers to say that phenol was good for women, and yeast was good for everyone; men like Madame Bovary's husband, or, if you read best sellers, like the physician in *La Garçonne* who had naturally taken the unexampled opportunity of a gynecological examination to have a try at raping the heroine.

Francis wanted a doctor badly enough, any doctor; but with the news that one was coming he enjoyed only an instant of relief. He wondered if one from the army, presumably callous and cynical, with a short way with malingerers and a way not much longer—salvarsan for fifty, calomel for a hundred; and if they weren't better tomorrow, why what the devil!—with the indisputably sick, would not be less use than nothing.

Meanwhile in the room upstairs the afternoon sun fell in a slanting oblong, partly on the floor, partly on the wall. The old man had brought more pillows; and Walter, sitting nearly straight, rested against them stiffly. The sharp thin smoke of burnt belladonna hung on the air; but Walter was breathing with no less difficulty. Instead of being flushed, he was now growing pale again, and a clammy gleam of sweat had appeared on his forehead.

Francis tightened his mouth. The pallor and the sweat hit him with a new impact of shock. It did not shock the eyes; it hit something deeper, maybe the cerebral cortex, a heavy and a shaking blow. The human face should not be gray. It did not sweat for nothing. Francis looked at Walter; and at Kirkland, big, not fat but full-fed and hearty. Kirkland was sober and concerned; but not shaken by any blows. His heavy frame (he must weigh more than two hundred pounds), sagging the edge of the bed as he sat on it, was in calm repose. Francis looked at the sunlight on the floor and wall; and because he could not help it, he admitted the waiting thought. Preposterously, in violation of the ordinary probabilities in defiance of the things you had to trust and must count on—the narrow plain room, the usual midafternoon sunlight, the setting-out from Cap d'Ail on a fine morning in Kirkland's car—there was notwithstanding no law, human or divine, against Walter, in an hour or less, being dead. Walter could get grayer; the ghastly sweat could get colder; and if he could not breathe Walter would not live.

That this was too awful; that nobody dreamed of such a thing; that, if it happened, Francis would have to go out and meet Mrs. Cunningham getting out of a car sometime after nightfall and tell her; were not exactly reasons why not. To or about the course of events you could say what you liked; but events never stopped to argue with you. If Francis wanted to think that it couldn't really be he who would have to do that, Francis could go right on thinking it. If Francis liked, he could continue to show himself how absurd such fancies were—it couldn't happen; it was utterly unheard of; and how unlikely it was that a child born years ago halfway around the world (what was he doing here?); and at noon perfectly well; would (why today, out of the possible thousands of days?) at three or four o'clock die in this bleak but sunfilled bedroom in a cheap hotel in Peira Cava (who ever heard of such a place?). For years Walter's mother and Maggie and innumerable doctors had watched over him; and how could that all go for nothing, leaving him on this last day with no one near but Francis, whom he did not know six months ago, and Kirkland, whom he did not know three days ago, and Kirkland's sluttish mistress—where was she, anyway? Gwen must be doing something with her—and Lorna downstairs, and God knew what kind of French quack or degenerate for a doctor—

But, of course, it all could, maybe it all always did, go for nothing; and if you asked how; why, this was how. It was perfectly simple. One rainy afternoon last fall in Paris Mrs. Cunningham made up her mind about engaging Francis, and after that it was only a matter of time, while they moved closer and closer—from Grindelwald to Cap d'Ail; and Thursday night Francis met Kirkland. It was getting really close now. On Friday, for the first time, someone (Gwen, Francis guessed) dropped the fatal name, Peira Cava. On Saturday Walter talked of nothing else.

320

On Sunday, with a can of ski wax and his extra socks in his pocket, he went there; and—

"All right," Francis said to himself, for with the piling up against him of the odds or omens (*I look'd toward Birnam and anon methought the wood began to move . . .*) the heart resisted, the mind struck back in anger. "All right. Even so. Even so, God damn it, I will do something. I will make this doctor—"

In the silence there was no response, no help, no reassurance; but he expected none; and, though Walter's labored wheezes sounded in his ear, Francis began to breathe with deliberate measure. He heard the slam of the closed door below; and, starting up to step into the hall, Lorna's voice speaking French.

Upstairs came a short man in a captain's uniform. Behind him a sergeant, his oversized beret drooping on his forehead, carried his case.

"Par ici, Monsieur," said Francis.

"Yes, good day," said the captain. "I speak English." His face was oval and brown, with a cropped mustache. He smiled soberly, showing white, even teeth. His eyes, which were alert and intelligent, went to Walter on the bed.

"Ah, just so!" he said.

Kirkland drew back and the captain sat down, taking his place. Silent a moment, he looked at Walter carefully. "You can't inspire, eh?" he said. "Yes, I know. I have had it. It is not pleasant."

With precise movements he stripped off a pair of tight black gloves and laid the back of his hand against Walter's cheek. "How long now?" he said to Francis. "An hour, or more?"

"Yes," said Francis, "I think so." He looked at his watch. "An hour and a half," he said, surprised. The woman from the caisse was close beside him, her monumental features warm with sympathy, but with a natural ghoulish hunger of interest, too. The old man with the apron looked sad and frightened. Lorna had come up. She stood tensely, her hands, terrible and expressive, twisted together, near Kirkland. She had taken her hat off—as though, Francis thought, she lived here; and what a surprise that would be, like finding something beautiful or valuable in a rubbish heap.

"Bon courage, mon petit," the captain said to Walter. "Be tranquil." He put his hand on Walter's stomach. "Very hard," he said. "They strain so hard. Well, we will not lose time." He gestured to the sergeant, who opened and brought up beside him his case. "I will give him a little injection."

"You aren't in the habit of using adrenalin?" Francis said.

"No, Monsieur. Morphine sulphate."

"I see," said Francis. "I must tell you that he won't tolerate more than a quarter grain."

"In that case, we will not give him more than a quarter of a grain." He drew a glass syringe from its case and fitted a needle to it. Looking at Walter attentively, he said, "You will not mind this. It will not be painful. You will be easier very soon." He held up a glass vial and passed the needle through the rubber cap. "Let us see, now. There. The forearm will do. We will not disturb him to take his coat off. Now, we will wipe it with this, and—there! It's in. Did you feel that?"

He laid the syringe aside and with the bit of cotton

322

went on rubbing the lump down. "Soon it will be easier," he said. "You are up here for the skiing, eh? Yes, that's right. Try to breathe. Now, quietly, again. The first time I took skis, you would have laughed. I was not very proficient—" Talking on, he put his things away methodically, closed the case, and motioned to the sergeant to take it.

"There," he said. He dropped a hand over Walter's wrist and clasped it. He said, "I cannot often get out for a run. It requires much practice, skiing. Yes. Breathe in. Slowly, slowly. That was a little bit better, wasn't it? No? Well, soon now it will be."

He was silent for a moment, studying Walter. "Soon it will be a little better," he said again. "Do you speak French? Some, eh? We have a saying: petit à petit, l'oiseau fait son nid. Do you understand that?"

The silence fell again for a moment. Then, Walter's face contorted, and gasping, he said, "It's about a bird."

"Ah!" said the captain. He raised his left hand and gently pinched Walter's cheek. "You see now?"

He held Walter's wrist a moment longer and then he laid it down. "Now, it begins to stop. Yes, that is how the bird builds the nest. There, that was good! It feels good, eh? Soon you will breathe all you want. You can lie down then and take a little sleep. Is that better?"

"Yes, gosh," said Walter. He spoke feebly, wheezing still, but with an ecstasy of relief.

"Yes. We will wait. Soon you will feel a little sleepy. That will be good. I do not think we need so many people here. You see, all your friends have been worried. Now, we have nothing to worry about. One will be enough, I think."

"Yes. I'll stay," Francis said. "His mother is on the way up. We telephoned her."

"That is good. I think he must remain here until tomorrow. It is a piece of work, one like this. We will make him easy and he will fall asleep. If he does not wake up until morning, that will be good." Extending his hand, the captain drew down one of Walter's eyelids. "Yes, we are over the bad part," he said. He patted Walter's cheek. "Your friend will be here; and I will be within reach; but you are not going to have any trouble."

✦

From where he sat Francis could see the cold shadowed mountains, the darkening tone of the nearer mounds of pine tops, and a roof or two covered with a thick crusted layer of snow. On the wall the block of sunshine had moved up, deepening from yellow to dull orange; a winter glow, reflecting less and less light through the room.

Huddled under a blanket, Walter was asleep, his head pushed into the pillow. From time to time he stirred, sighed, or getting his face too far down, snored lightly for a moment. The first time, Francis started up, alarmed; but at the sound, Walter unconsciously moved, breathed easy and even again; and Francis sat down. The sunlight on the wall disappeared and an early dusk filled the room. Over the pine tops and the snowy roofs extended a limitless, frigid, thinly turquoise sky, made infinitely remote by the long perspective of the now obscured mountains.

324

Across it moved shoals of small clouds that were nearly pink.

Francis sat exhausted. One like this, he told himself, was a piece of work, all right. The final great relief took in its way as much out of you as the anguish of doubt—perhaps more, for a certain amount of anguish kept you from reflection. Once it was over, the spent mind was left at loose ends and shifted at random, looking with a discouraged eye at everything.

The possibility that he had not known how he could face, the possibility of having horrible news for Mrs. Cunningham, was gone; but she would still want to know how it happened. Francis did not know himself how it had happened, because whatever he had done afterwards (and though done agitatedly, he could look at it now and see that it had been fairly prompt and sensible) he had not done the one thing he promised her he would do. He had let himself be otherwise engaged, he had not kept an eye on Walter; and in short the whole thing was a mess, and he might as well drop it.

Dropping it with disgust, his disgusted mind wandered its ugly and futile way. He thought of the doctor, whose manner with Walter, whose sympathy and intelligence, had been so different from what Francis wildly expected; and yet (how mean and petty to think of it; how impossible not to notice it) the collar, or neckband, or whatever it was, of the shirt worn under his tunic could be seen inside the uniform collar, and it was greasy with dirt. Recoiling in disgust from human beings, you had to recoil, in another disgust, from your own recoiling; and so it went; and after years of distaste, with little done and nothing not somehow spoiled, you could look forward to the appropri-

325

ate rewarding of patience or effort. You would be old—
like Mr. McKellar, with everything going, so that wit began to labor, elegances grew grotesque or sinister, zest for
life creaked at the joints—nearly a joke. And then, perhaps, you could hope to grow into an outright joke, like
the Admiral at Grindelwald, with everyone secretly laughing; and then (far past a joke, a horror) you might enjoy
the longevity of that old man, what was his name, his
mother's acquaintance, the friend of George William Curtis, in Florence. Mr. Woodward—

There was a tap at the door, and quickly, to prevent a
second louder one that might disturb Walter, Francis
sprang up and opened it. Light shone from below up the
staircase, and though there was no light in the hall, a last
dusk came from the end where through a window you
could see snow and the fading colors of the sky. Lorna
was standing there. She whispered, "How is he?"

Francis drew the door closed. "All right," he said.
"He's sleeping."

"Don't you want to go down and get some tea? I'll sit
with him."

"Not if Emily is there. I have seen enough of her." He
got out a package of cigarettes. "I'm sorry," he said. "I
seem to go on and on, don't I?"

"What—" She stopped. "Francis, I'm sorry I lost my
temper. Let's forget it, shall we?"

Francis looked at her dim face. "Yes, let's," he said.
He lit a cigarette for her, and then he lighted his own.
He filled his lungs with smoke and let his shoulders touch
the wall behind him. She said, "You must be worn out."

"In some ways. You'll be going down tonight, won't
you? There's no reason for you to stay."

"Well, we'll certainly stay until Mrs. Cunningham comes. I think Emily's going pretty soon. There seems to have been a slight rapprochement."

"Isn't that nice," said Francis. "I like everyone to be happy. You wouldn't care to marry me tomorrow and go to Paris, would you?"

Taken by surprise, she gave in the gloom a marked start. "I—" she began, and stopped; though with her lips left parted in some commotion of feeling. For an instant it appeared that she might be nerving herself to say yes. Her lips came together then, contracted in a strained smile, and she shook her head. "No," she said.

"Why not?" said Francis.

"Well—because you don't really want me to, for one thing."

"I will pass that over," Francis said. "I thought I would ask you. I'll probably be leaving Cap d'Ail tomorrow."

"Why?"

"Because Mrs. Cunningham is not going to require my services any longer."

"You mean, because of this? Why, how absurd! How could you help it? You were wonderful."

"The answer to that is, something happened to Walter; and nothing is supposed to happen to him while I am there. It's all in order."

"It's too unreasonable. She couldn't do that!"

"If she can and does, will you come to Paris with me?"

"No." She began to shake her head again.

Francis looked at his cigarette end. "I can't make you," he said. "What, if anything, you could see in me isn't clear. Of course I am trying to take advantage of you. Of course it isn't prudent, and so you are afraid. That's why you keep saying that I don't really want you. I think you'd better come. You see, I think you want to."

"Francis, I don't know," she said. "You could be right. Sometimes with all my heart I—would you do me a favor? I mean, really. It's rather a rotten trick, and I know it; but this has been a hell of a day. I can't think. I just don't know. Ask me tomorrow—I mean, if you still want to." She drew a breath and added: "That's not very fair, is it?"

"If you do it, it must be," Francis said.

"My dear—" She lifted a hand and laid it on his cheek. "Did you mean that; or were you being—"

"I meant it." Taking her wrist, he brought her hand over and kissed the fingers.

"Yes. Do mean it," she said. "I implore you—" She began to laugh. "I sound absurd, don't I. Of course it really isn't fair. I mean, what have I promised you?"

"Nothing," said Francis.

"And you don't mind?"

"I mind. But what can I do?"

"Ah, darling, I wish—"

"So do I," said Francis. He dropped her wrist. "Now, go downstairs like a good girl. I've got to keep an eye on Walter."

"Don't you want some tea?"

"No," he said. "Oddly enough, I don't." He stepped into the dark room, closed the door after him, and sat down on the chair again. In the sky beyond the darker pattern of the window sash the stars were coming out.

3

THE DOOR was open and a light had been put on.

Blinking, Francis saw Maggie, her face pinched with cold, her coat and hat still on. "Oh, poor Francis!" said Mrs. Cunningham.

"I'm afraid I was asleep," Francis said. He stood up with twinges of stiffness. Walter, disturbed, but not quite to the point of waking, moved on the bed.

"I'm sorry," Francis said. "I meant to get downstairs to tell you—" Lights were on in the hall outside, too, and there was a bustle of people coming and going—proof enough that Mrs. Cunningham had arrived. Beyond the door, Madame from the caisse gesticulated, the little old man scurried by, the chambermaid passed and repassed. Thousands at her bidding speed, Francis thought in the dazed levity of uncollected wits, and post o'er land and ocean without rest—

He said, "The doctor thinks he ought to sleep through. He did give him an injection. He seemed quite intelligent, so I just told him about the quarter grain, and let him."

"You were quite right," Mrs. Cunningham said. "I think we'll move him to another room, with two beds, so that Maggie can sleep there. It's being got ready now. Maggie, would you go and see how they're getting on?" Bending over the bed, Mrs. Cunningham put her hand on Walter's forehead. "He's not the least bit feverish," she said. Straightening up, she repeated, "Poor Francis!

I felt dreadfully when I saw you asleep on that hard little chair. I could imagine how exhausted you were."

"I must have been," said Francis, embarrassed. "Though I don't know what I did, really. I don't know how it happened. Walter was all right at luncheon. Out on the hill he began to feel queer—"

"Lorna and Mr. Kirkland told me. Francis, I think you managed it wonderfully. They said you thought of everything. I blame myself very much for not having told you more about it. You see, it comes on at night, usually—"

Francis said, "The truth is, if anyone was wonderful, Walter was. And Kirkland. He got Walter upstairs while—"

"Yes, he seems to be a nice young man. He and the girls are waiting downstairs. They mustn't wait. It will be a very long cold drive for them. Won't you go and tell them? Tell them I'm deeply grateful for everything they've done. It's such a shame that it turned out this way! You haven't had anything to eat, have you?"

"No," said Francis. "I—" Looking at his watch, he discovered that it was eight o'clock.

"Lorna told me you wouldn't have any tea because you didn't want to leave Walter. I'll come down as soon as we have him settled, and we'll see if we can get some supper. I had Maggie pack a few things for you. I imagined we'd have to stay, and I thought you'd be more comfortable. I suppose you can use this room. I'll have them put in here."

"How are you going to move Walter?" Francis said.

"Oh, Maggie and I can do it. It's quite easy. Do go

now and see that they get off. I really feel worried about that long drive in the dark."

"They won't have any trouble," Francis said. "Kirkland's good with a car."

Downstairs in the lounge, Gwen was sitting alone. Seeing Francis, she said, "How's the patient?"

"All right," Francis said. Deserved or undeserved, Mrs. Cunningham's expressed approval had made his spirits lighter. "How's yours?" he said.

"You mean Emily? She went hours ago."

The touchiness in her tone was a great temptation and Francis said, "Yes, I meant Emily. Did you dry those tears? Did she tell you the story of her life?"

"Oh, you!" said Gwen. The jerk of her head showed mixed feelings; grudging amusement, for maybe Emily had done just that, and Gwen must confess the hit; indignation, at his unfeeling phrases. "Men are such pigs!" she said. "I've never, never, seen one yet who gave a damn, a single solitary damn, for anything but himself."

"You must mean Mr. Kirkland," said Francis. "I'm not like that."

"Oh, aren't you?" said Gwen. "You're one of the worst. I suppose it comes from being a writer, too. As if they weren't conceited and selfish enough without that." She made the sound and movement of tasting something nasty. "I could kill them all—sometimes." Reluctantly, she grinned; but you could see that she was not far from meaning it. Men were a great trial; and, often, paraphrasing Posthumus, she probably asked herself: is there no way for women to be, but men must be half-workers? It was not that Gwen disliked men; just, sometimes, she felt like killing them. It was not that they didn't attract her;

they did; and of course the conflict of her feeling came
out of the subconscious—its archetype perhaps in childhood memories of being happy playing some intricate,
orderly game with other little girls; and, at the best moment, having it broken up noisily and stupidly, for no
reason, by horrid boys—all the horrider, since she might
have been wishing that boys would come, admire, and
play nicely, too.

Francis stood looking down at her, entertained by the
explosion; but also a little disturbed; for he began to see
where he came in. Gwen opposed disorder, all kinds of
disorder; and Francis would certainly bear watching. Out
of affection for Lorna, Gwen had been friendly; but now,
still out of affection for Lorna, she listened to the messages
of that extra sense, no doubt telling her that this had
gone too far; that more of the man-made disorder, actual
and impending, lay in what he was doing with Lorna.
Gwen believed in love, all right—but not sentimentality,
which would never be sensible; and not passion, which
upset everything.

Gwen kept her eye on the main point. As well as a girl
who had a right to something called romance (not quite
so frenzied as in Romeo and Juliet, not quite so fatuous
as in a new musical comedy), Lorna was a valuable investment. She was a work of reason and order, the finished
product of invested money, a good deal of it, well spent
to feed and clothe and educate her; of invested time,
twenty odd years of patient shaping by precept and example to fit her with special skills and accomplishments to
keep house and raise children, not any old way, but in the
style to which the sort of man she was meant to meet and
marry would be accustomed. This fortunate man had con-

ditions to fulfill; and one of them—not, to Gwen, mercenary at all, not snobbish at all, just orderly and reasonable—was to lay on the line the cash to take up this investment. Then it would be time enough for him and Lorna to begin worrying about whether it was the nightingale and not the lark.

The thought was sobering, one of those thoughts he tried to put aside, but Francis began lightly: "Now, as writers go, I am a very nice one, and—" He saw Lorna coming through the hall then. He said to her: "Mrs. Cunningham is worried about you. She asked me to see that you got started. She sends her regrets and thanks, and so on—"

Gwen said, "Goody went to get the car." She stood up and crossed over to the door and looked out.

"How is he?" Lorna said.

"All right."

"What did she say?"

"Oh, that," said Francis. "It seems that she got very good reports of me. As far as I know, I am still in her employ. I am afraid it eases your mind."

"All right," Gwen called. "Here he is."

"Francis, it really would have been mad."

"You must get started. You probably won't be home until midnight."

"Well, call me when you get down."

"Yes." He stepped out and stood on the hard snow by the car. Reaching to unlatch the door, Kirkland said, "How's Walter?"

"All right," said Francis. "It's a good thing you were here. I'd have been in a jam—"

"Bunk, old boy. You were the hero of the occasion."

To Gwen he said, "Pile in. Both of you get in front. We can make it. It'll help keep you warm."

In the starlight Francis felt the biting air, and he pushed his hands into his pockets. Encountering something in one of them, he drew it out. "Here," he said to Lorna, "I forgot." He gave her the envelope with the lipstick scribbling on it.

She turned it over. "Oh. Thanks. It isn't anything."

"I didn't know. It felt as though there were a letter in it."

"It's just a note from a girl I know in Milan. She's coming to stay with us next week."

"Is she?" said Francis.

"Yes. She's studying at Milan. She has a marvelous voice."

"I know," said Francis.

"Darling," said Gwen, "get in!"

"Faith Robertson? Do you know her?"

"I have met her."

"Darling, Francis is freezing. Do you want him to get his death of—"

"All right!" Lorna said. She got in and Francis closed the door. "Go inside this minute!"

"Be seeing you," said Kirkland. The car began to move.

"Good-by," Francis said.

✦

The grateful warmth of the lobby enclosed him. Mrs. Cunningham was coming downstairs and mechanically

Francis went to meet her. She smiled and said, "Did they get off all right?"

"Yes."

"Good. I've arranged to have some supper brought up for Maggie. They'll give us something in the dining room whenever we want it. Do you suppose they'd have a possible sherry? I feel as though I'd like some. You'd like a cocktail or something, wouldn't you?"

"Very much," said Francis.

"Poor Francis," said Mrs. Cunningham. "I should think you would. Shall we sit in here?" She led him into the empty lounge.

"If you'll excuse me," Francis said, "I'll get something ordered, and wash. I haven't had time to—"

"Yes. Of course."

After he had found the maître d'hotel, Francis went to the small washroom under the stairs. There was no soap and the towel that hung on the wall had been in use for a week; but Francis did what he could without soap, and stood waving his hands in the air to dry them. He thought how astonished Mrs. Cunningham would be if, when he returned, he were to say to her: "The reason I look so queer is that something has just happened that upset me. You see, I care a great deal about Lorna. I even thought of marrying her and going to Paris tomorrow; but, of course, I'd have trouble supporting her, so I was only going to do that if you fired me—" (At this point, Mrs. Cunningham could hardly fail to think he had lost his senses, so he would have to get on with it quickly.)

"Well," he might say, "that's water over the dam. I seem to be staying on here with you; so that's all right. Or, at least it would be, except that, when I was coming up to join you at Montreux, I happened to try to seduce a girl I didn't like very much at Milan. I was feeling depressed, and we'd had a couple of drinks, and she was there, and you know how it is—" A painful nervous laughter shook him. His hands were still wet, so he took out a handkerchief and finished drying them. "Well, at any rate," he could go on, "she—this girl—knows Lorna. I don't mean that I think she'd say anything about my making a pass at her; but she's coming for a visit next week; and somehow I find the idea of seeing her again a little awkward. In fact, I can't do it. Not with Lorna around. What would you do, if you were I?"

What, indeed? What advice from Mrs. Cunningham to the lovelorn? You could not easily imagine telling Mrs. Cunningham such a story; but you could imagine easily enough what she, what any woman, would say to the problem presented: *It serves you right!* My advice is: it serves you right. Francis opened the door and crossed the lobby. A bottle of sherry, two glasses, and a plate of biscuits had been brought in and set before Mrs. Cunningham. Francis would have preferred something a little stronger; but he had not cared to make a point of the preference.

He sat down; and Mrs. Cunningham sipped her sherry, and he sipped his. She was tired, too, he saw; she, too, had had no tea; she too had had her anxieties; and in spite of his ironic reflections in the washroom, he looked at her with respect; just as, in spite of his distressing quandary, he felt a sort of ease, as though, like her, he had been through a lot and earned a rest. She smiled when he came in; but for several moments she said nothing.

"I have been thinking a little about plans," she said at last. "You remember I've mentioned some friends of ours

336

who are at Taormina. I wonder if it might not be a little warmer there—" She was looking at him, and perhaps she saw some change in his face; for she said, "I wasn't thinking of going at once. Perhaps next month. Of course, I know we mustn't keep moving around. I know it upsets Walter's work. What do you think?"

My advice, Francis thought, is: it serves you right. They put the question to you fair: woul't weep? woul't fight? woul't fast? woul't tear thyself? woul't drink up eisel? And what did you say? You said: I loved her very much, her face was charming. There was something about her I wanted. Maybe it was her soul; maybe it has a coarse name. But, on the whole, no. I will not weep, fight, fast, tear myself, nor drink up eisel.

Francis said, "It would be better for Walter, wouldn't it?"

"Well, it is so hard to tell. I think it might."

Francis faltered; but he was, he remembered, always fortunate. When he wished, the wish came true. When he did not know what on earth to do, Mrs. Cunningham, all unaware, told him; and all unasked, decided to buy him a ticket to Taormina.

Francis said, "It seems to me that if there is any chance at all that it would be better, we ought to go—"

This was the end of Lorna, of course; and for a moment, though so fortunate, Francis was in despair. He hung on the sharp tenterhook of desolation—*Since there's no help, come let us kiss and part*—taking a long vain look back. He said then, "I really think it might be best to leave as soon as possible. Before Walter settles down. This week, if it can be arranged."

Mrs. Cunningham did not, perhaps, expect quite such

337

a full agreement. She gazed at him with mild inquiry. She said, "You wouldn't mind leaving so soon, Francis?"

Francis hardly trusted himself to speak. He tried smiling and shaking his head; but Mrs. Cunningham had asked a kind question, and to answer by signs was impolite. "I would be glad to go," Francis said.

Out of the dining room came the maître de hotel, bustling and important in his hand-me-down dress clothes. He proclaimed: "Madame est servie!" With a clumsy but respectful flourish, he bowed, laying his hand on his heart.

THE END